A Choi<

MW01615253

The Blade Remnant, Book One

D.N. Woodward

© 2021

Edited by Tim Marquitz

Cover art and design by Ryan Schwarz

Created in the United States of America
Worldwide Rights

To my loving wife, Kelsey, who encouraged me to finish, and to my three kids (Josiah, Ruth, and Ethan) who inspired me along the way.

Table of Contents

Chapter 1... 1
Chapter 2... 15
Chapter 3... 29
Chapter 4... 45
Chapter 5... 53
Chapter 6... 61
Chapter 7... 79
Chapter 8... 89
Chapter 9... 101
Chapter 10... 111
Chapter 11... 131
Chapter 12... 139
Chapter 13... 155
Chapter 14... 163
Chapter 15... 173
Chapter 16... 193
Chapter 17... 199
Chapter 18... 213
Chapter 19... 229
Chapter 20... 239
Chapter 21... 253
Chapter 22... 261
Chapter 23... 279
Chapter 24... 289
Chapter 25... 307
Chapter 26... 327
Chapter 27... 337
Chapter 28... 349
Chapter 29... 369
Chapter 30... 381
Chapter 31... 395
Chapter 32... 411
Chapter 33... 423

Chapter 1

The sun burned hot on Leon and the old roping chute, but he didn't flinch as he leaned into the scalding metal. His wrench tugged hard on the rusted nut. It didn't budge. Frustration mounted as sweat dripped down into his eye. Tightening his grip, he dug his heels in and took a deep breath. Just before he gave a second tug, a tremor bubbled up deep within his chest.

Something like a low voltage electric shock pulsed through his core. It spread outward and down the arm still clutching the wrench. His hand clenched and spasmed. The nut held, but the bolt snapped. The spasm's momentum threw him off balance and drove him to the ground, flat onto his back. His mood soured in the sun's heat, and he was slow to roll onto his knees.

Son of a biscuit, that hurt!

Attempting to repair the rusted chute was a downright miserable job for a scorching Texas day in late July. The only gusts of wind came and went with the flicker of a fly as it circled near and drifted off. Its droning buzz mingled with the mournful bellowing of Corriente roping calves from a nearby holding corral to form the perfect melody to complement his growing agitation.

Squatting, he cleaned his jeans as best he could with his leather gloves, then mopped the sweat from his forehead. His best guess was the shock had something to do with a damaged component in his cell phone. Hadn't he read about something like that happening somewhere?

Whatever the cause, the jolt alarmed him, like the kind of alarm that happens when briefly brushing up against a hot wire on the Bull setting. His body still tingled as the sensation slowly faded.

He patted the front pocket of his faded denim button-down. Nothing there. Glancing up, he realized his phone still sat on the shaded edge of the chute. Right where he'd placed it a few minutes earlier.

What the…? No way that little phone had enough juice to light me up like that through all that pipe!

Yet, as he continued to consider a potential culprit, the thin profile of his smartphone was all that came to mind.

The broken bolt lay beside him in the dirt. A solid steel chunk of metal torn in two. Although strong for his size, Leon was not a big man. In fact, at three inches shy of six feet tall, and wire-thin, there was little doubt in his mind this was not a case of him underestimating his own strength. He could only conclude there was some inherent defect in the bolt causing the metal to snap like it did.

The chute repairs would have to wait. He pushed himself to his feet, chuckling at his bad luck. He was filthy to boot.

He ought to have quit the rodeo dream years ago, but that ambition had never really been his to lose. Gus Silberman, his grandfather, on the other hand, had been seeing rodeo notoriety in Leon since the first day he threw a wobbly loop over a skinny calf. Leon didn't especially want to give his grandfather any more reasons for disappointment. Life had served the old man plenty a bitter pill already.

So, instead of hanging up his rope when he no longer felt the itch to compete, the way he'd done with so many of his other pursuits, Leon continued, feeding the old man's aspirations by constantly working the scrawny Corriente calves through the faded blue chute.

Now, though? Now, Leon had reached his limit. He eyeballed the busted latch atop the chute and shrugged once more.

It's past time I put this sucker up for sale online. Should have stopped after that first buckle, back when I was still riding in the black!

Unfortunately, he would now have to put even more work into that dilapidated hunk of metal if he was ever to get any decent money for it from some other kid with lofty parental expectations.

He turned around to collect the reins to his gelding, Duke. Only, when he looked up, no horse lingered within the shady area beneath the hackberry tree branches alongside the arena. Instead,

Duke stood three-quarters of the way down the opposite end, pawing at the sand, acting awfully spooked. He squinted over the horse's sudden display of obstinance.

Leon took a step forward. The gelding laid his ears back and shifted weight ever so slightly. "Come on, Duke, it's okay, boy. What's got you so fired up?"

He took another step. The horse's head jerked up and down. Leon could see the whites of his eyes. A panicky disposition had somehow found purchase in the mind of a normally sane and well broken-in horse.

On his third step forward, the horse turned and bolted...right into the top pipe-rail of the corral. The *clang* reverberated, breaking the quiet stillness of the afternoon heat as the horse stumbled back.

The gate, not ten feet from Duke, was shut but not locked. It slowly creaked open in hinge-squealing suspense as the reverberations of the horse's collision caused it to swing outward. Leon tensed. Duke tensed.

In a voice as tempered and gentle as possible, Leon pleaded, "Easy, Duke. Good boy. Don't..."

He didn't finish. Duke bolted through the open gate and into the cleared pasture beyond. Leon ripped the cap from his head and threw it to the ground. "Son of a biscuit!"

His high-blood roping horse, likely worth a few thousand dollars after two years of painstaking training from Leon, careened through the open pasture in a wild gallop, oblivious to any potential gopher holes or drought cracks that might lay in wait for just such an occasion. Thankfully, he eventually slowed his wild dash to a mildly condescending trot before disappearing over a small rise.

No sense in chasing him back across the pasture in this heat. I'll have to bring him in later.

Leon swallowed the sick feeling in his gut. He had suffered through many heated debates on account of that stubborn horse. Now, those debates were one wrong step away from blowing up in his face. Though to be fair, it wasn't the horse that was the basis of

3

most of the arguments between him and Gus, those debates had more to do with the purpose of the ranch itself, and by extension Leon's role in it. If Leon had it his way, the ranch would derive the bulk of its income from horse breeding and high-end training. Only it wasn't his ranch to run, and its current lifeblood consisted of over two hundred head of commercial Brangus cattle.

Now, thoroughly disgusted at how his day had panned out so far, Leon bent to pick up his dusty cap. As he pulled it down over a well-trimmed mop of curly blond hair, he searched for his dog.

Merle, his trusty old ranch mutt, gave him the stink eye from the nearest corner of the arena.

"What, Merle? You planning to run off, too?"

Merle sneezed and wagged his tail, as if to reassure Leon of his uncompromising loyalty, no matter how ill-placed it might be. He trotted over and gave Leon's hand a lingering sniff.

Leon's crooked grin crept out from the patchy start of a three-day beard. "Nope, you're the lucky knucklehead who's stuck with me. Isn't that what you mean?"

No response. Typical.

Movement in the distance caught Leon's attention. He eyeballed a dust cloud's twisted approach. It clamored through still pines along the edge of the pasture, billowing outward with indiscriminate haste before petering away, forcibly extinguished against the mid-day heat. A moment later, Leon heard the steady roar of an overtaxed engine rumbling above the scraping crunch and creak of a low axle.

Thick brush mostly blocked his view of the gravel road as the vehicle curved north, jostling speedily toward the main house and away from the roping arena where he stood, covered in dust and stink. Yet, he saw the silhouette of an expensive-looking car as it sped by from a handful of openings in the dense vegetation along the wooded pasture's perimeter.

Uninvited visitors were an uncommon, if not rare, occurrence. An uninvited visitor in a car cruising fast enough to require a new pair of shocks was something worth further consideration. Leon couldn't ignore the sinking feeling in his gut. He might be naturally inclined to think the worst of any given situation, but people just didn't brave that old, washed-out ranch road in a car to bring good news.

He decided to head to the house. It wouldn't do for Gus to have to repeat any unsavory news so soon after hearing it himself. Plus, he ought to be there for moral support. Not that Gus would need it, or ask for it, but Leon opted to be there to offer it, regardless.

He stooped down for his wrench and other tools lying near the chute, but Merle barreled into him, knocking him back a step or two.

"What the heck, Merle? We've got a good half-mile hike ahead of us. Stop goofing around."

Leon went to shove Merle out of the way, but he let loose that whining noise all dogs use when you force them to do something they don't want to do.

"You can be a real moody old grump, you know that?"

Merle actually gave him a head-butt as he unsuccessfully tried, once more, to sidestep the animal. As it was, Merle didn't do anything in a petite manner. At over one hundred pounds of bird dog mutt, getting his point across with a head-butt provided a pretty convincing means of saying no without saying much at all.

Leon stumbled back, landing on his hind end for the second time that afternoon. As he rose to give Merle the mother of all bad dog tongue lashings, an all too familiar sound to any Texas rancher rose. It resembled a pair of Mexican maracas strapped to the top of a revved-up tractor engine, minus the tractor engine. Leon struggled quickly to his knees and peeked over Merle's shoulder the same moment a massive rattlesnake reared up and cocked its head back, preparing to strike.

Leon didn't think, he just reacted. His love for the big mutt told him to try to stop what his mind knew couldn't be avoided. He saw a blur of motion as the snake struck. His hand snapped forward to stop it, almost in slow motion. Then the same rippling, shocking sensation ripped through him as before.

In less than the blink of an eye, his hand smacked into the snake's head, which ricocheted back into the chute's piping. The whole incident happened so fast the sounds blended together to make one loud *thh-whack*.

The snake writhed on the ground, completely disoriented. It gradually slithered off, and Leon had no inclination or ability to chase it down.

For one or two heartbeats, he leaned on Merle for support and didn't move a muscle as he allowed his nerves to shift out of sixth gear. Then, taking a few deep breaths, he pulled off his glove and checked his hand for the tell-tale puncture marks he expected to see. Yet he couldn't even find the slightest sign of a venomous nick.

Leon had quick reflexes, there was no doubt about that. Back in high school, when he ran the eight-hundred-meter sprint, his grandfather used to tease him that his fast-twitch muscle skills were wasted on the track team. "Hard off the block and easy on the finish, you oughta stick to sports that last eight seconds or less!"

But this scenario felt different. No explanation actually fit with what had just occurred. After a few moments of quiet consideration, Leon came up emptyhanded. Without a better explanation, he chalked it all up to blind luck and thanked those lucky stars his fingers weren't a split second too late…or too early for that matter.

After taking a moment to savor the thought, Leon returned to the task at hand. Much more cautious, he poked around the dry weeds at the base of the chute, gathering up his tools and placing them where he'd remember to collect them later.

A long hot hike to the house lay before him. At least the pines between the pastures would provide some shade along the way. Loblolly pine trees seemed to sprout in every nook and cranny not used for grazing on *Cool Water Ranch*. Leon and Gus lived out there all on their own, growing grass, feeding cattle, and causing trouble, like all the Silbermans who came before them had done for over a hundred years. Well, maybe the causing trouble part was something Gus just liked to say, but the other descriptions pretty much hit the nail on the head.

Cool Water was located on the south side of the Colorado River, near Smithville, Texas. Most people just called that region the Lost Pines. It was a strip of loblolly pine forest somehow cut off from the larger sister forests of east Texas. Loblollies had the same evergreen look as typical pine trees but with more rounded edges to their profile, less Christmas Tree-esque in shape. No one Leon had ever talked to about the trees knew for certain where all the Lost Pine Loblollies came from or why they stayed but, at some point, those pines sunk deep roots around the area. Even if they no longer fit in with the landscape, they didn't seem to care.

Leon had long since given up wondering why his local forest island proved such an enigma to the natural order of things. He always felt they did a fine job of existing, of thriving even, where they had no business making a home. The fact was, such unavoidable observations often made him feel he had more in common with those towering pines than he did with most folks he knew.

Taking a long look into the wooded path ahead, he ignored all the other thoughts that threatened to further delay his jog to the house. After latching the gate to the corral, he smiled down at Merle, "Well, boy, no use in putting off what's got to be done. If we want to be there for Gus, we had better get going."

Leon took off in a well-practiced stride. Considering his circumstances as he ran, he took comfort in the sole sliver of silver-lining that stood out above all the other shortcomings he had experienced so far that day—at least he wore a comfortable pair of cross trainer shoes and not his heavy work boots. Together, he and Merle took the shortest shortcut back to the house through the woods.

# # #

Five minutes later, Leon stumbled out into the clearing near his house. There, rising out of the forest, stood an off-white, weather-worn, one-story ranch house. Out of breath and ready for a cold drink, he still did a double-take as he caught sight of the black Mercedes S500 with blacked-out windows parked in the gravel circle next to his beat-up white Ford truck.

The front gate was open, and a red-faced Gus Silberman stood tip-toed in cowboy boots on the top step of the porch, his arms in full animation. He spoke slowly and deliberately but gradually gained momentum, enunciating, and punctuating each syllable. His old Stetson hat shook with every word he stressed, until at the crescendo of his speech, he dished out the kind of rip that had that straw hat bouncing like a Mexican jumping bean atop his silvery head. He might have even popped a button on the denim shirt he wore if he didn't stop to take a breath every minute or so.

As Leon neared the yard, Gus continued shouting in an angry Texas drawl. His ire clearly aimed down at a pale-skinned, dark-haired man, standing casually before him in the yard below. The stranger wore a long-sleeved white business shirt, gray tie, polished dress shoes, and checkered slacks, without a crease. Dark aviator glasses hid his eyes as he held out some paperwork in his right hand. Leon hopped the fence and cut across the lawn to get to the action a little quicker.

Gus stuck a gnarly, weathered finger toward the man's face as Leon reached the porch, "...son, you're about as windy as a sack full of farts! If you really think you're here doing me a favor, you don't know horse apples from truffle butter!"

The man's voice had a slight New England accent, causing him to put an edge on every R as he responded "Sir, I understand you're upset, but do try to be reasonable. It's not like you have to sell the whole ranch, just the—"

"Just the part that's been in my family for upwards of two hundred years?

"Listen here, boy, I've banked with the Lost Pines Credit Union for over forty years, and this ain't the way they do business. Why haven't I received a call from Jim Traeger directly?"

The man's response was worded to reconcile, but his tone held an edge, "Mr. Silberman, as I said, Lost Pines is under new management. Jim no longer works for this branch. That's why we felt it prudent to come out here in person, to—"

"Horse-hockey! You just can't wait to git yer money-grubbing hands on my land is more like it! Get off my dad-gum property, I've heard enough!"

The man took a casual step back, a toothy grin showing. "Yes, sir, I understand."

He turned to Leon as if noticing him standing there for the first time. His nose twitched at the combination of sweat and whatever Leon may have inadvertently fallen into earlier, but he extended his hand nonetheless, "Sorry to interrupt your day sport."

Without knowing what else to do, Leon shook it in response. "Mr. Banker, can't say it's nice to meet you based on what little I've heard, but I'll shake your hand."

"Likewise, I'm sure, the name's Joseph Romano."

Leon looked Joseph in the eye and gave him a good tight squeeze before he released his hand. "Leon Waldman."

Joseph turned back to Gus, his smile sweetening into a condescending smirk. "Hired help?"

"Grandson."

"Of course. Well, please, remember Mr. Silberman, you have forty-eight hours to make a decision." He spread his arms wide. "I suggest you take the money. You will be well compensated."

Leon could practically see the steam coming from Gus' ears. When Gus involuntarily slid his right hand down to grasp the hilt of his old bone-handled hunting knife, Leon saw a dangerous look descend over Gus. A look he hadn't seen in the many years he'd lived with the man he called his grandfather. He rushed up the steps to stop the old man from leaping off the porch and physically assaulting the banker.

Gus had all the finesse of a big burly teddy bear, but he could be downright dangerous if the war stories he sometimes told from his younger, wilder days held a quarter of the truth he claimed. Without the cowboy hat and pearl snap shirts he wore, his barrel build and steely disposition could easily be mistaken for that of an outlaw biker. Especially with the handlebar mustache and silver sideburns he sported.

But something about the banker's stance, something about the way he moved, told Leon that Joseph could hold his own if it came down to it. Leon couldn't pinpoint how he knew, but he knew. Deep down, he knew.

Once Joseph saw Leon's hand braced on Gus' arm, he realized some sort of threat had just been avoided. He took a step forward.

Gone was the slick smile and condescending posture. Leon knew a bully when he saw one. As a little guy with a hot temper, he'd had ample time in high school to hone that skill on jocks who had often misjudged him.

Great, just what I need, either see my granddad gut a stranger, or have a stranger beat down the both of us on our front porch.

Before either party said another word, they heard a deep guttural growl coming from behind the banker. Merle's growl continued to build as he circled the stranger, eventually placing his body between Leon and a perceived threat for the second time that day.

Merle rarely barked. His size nullified the need for those types of theatrics. Instead, he hunched his shoulders and curled his lip, causing him to look more akin to a wolf than a large gray mutt in the moment.

Leon gasped. He couldn't ever recall Merle demonstrating such an intimidating pose, but he didn't call him off either.

The stranger's posture went stone still. He balanced on his toes, leaning just a smidge forward. Leon couldn't tell whether he planned to attack or pivot and run. He didn't seem like the running type.

Merle and the man stared each other down for seconds that felt like minutes. The man wasn't going to allow Merle to intimidate him, and Merle's growl continued to grow until he had spittle running down his chin.

Before things got entirely out of hand, Leon squatted down and grabbed Merle by his collar. The big dog felt the tug and went silent, though the hair on his back still stood on end.

Squinting up into the sun above Joseph, Leon thought it about time to bring things to a close. "Mister, you've delivered your message. Now, I suggest you head back to your bank."

Joseph nodded with a none too friendly smile. All three of them watched the man take three steps backward before pivoting and strutting slowly back to his car. He certainly didn't act like any country banker Leon had ever met.

Before passing through the gate, Joseph stopped, picked up a fist-sized rock, and stacked it with a *thud* on the paperwork above the h-brace in the fence. He didn't shut the gate behind him.

As soon as the engine started, the car took off, spraying dirt and pebbles back onto the old Ford parked nearby. Leon's eyes narrowed as the new dirt kicked up on his mud-covered grill guard. He mumbled to himself more than to Gus, "Well, he didn't have to go and do that!"

"A man like that does what he pleases, Leon, and it typically pleases such a one to do just like that." Then, he growled, "I simply can't tolerate a man who don't know to shut a gate behind his self." Gus spat into the yard for good measure. He was still amped up to the nth degree.

"Well, what was all that about anyhow?"

After a few deep breaths, Gus spoke softly. His age broke through the careful façade he kept and showed a touch of uncertainty in his eyes, "The banks calling our loans, son. The taxman didn't do us any favors either, even with last year's exemptions. Jim allowed us to refinance last winter and gave us a six-month extension on the loan payment this spring. It was on a handshake, mostly. That's why I didn't pay much heed to the boilerplate notices we received in the mail. I've only ever had to do that twice before, and Jim always gave us the other extension to get us through till calves were ready to sell." Gus pulled his hat off his head and mopped his brow with a hanky.

11

"We can't get another loan?"

"This new bank management isn't having it. They've been sneaky. Drove my credit score into the mud. Somehow, though I can't recall how now, the paperwork says I had the old section lumped in as collateral years back. They aim to take it." He swatted at a fly, overly interested in filling the vacancy on his head.

"What about selling off half the momma cows?"

"We do that, and we'll be in the same boat come next year, maybe worse." Gus used his hat to halfheartedly swat at the fly once more.

"Well, how about stripping the lumber in the south pastures?"

Gus paused his fly-catching to look Leon in the eye when he responded, "Wouldn't matter now. The last time we called the lumber company, they wanted a lease inked before they would come out. We ain't got the time to let the lawyers do their dance this time around."

"So, they're just going to take your land? Can they do that?"

"Maybe, maybe not. They won't if I can help it though! Go ahead and finish up with what you've got to do today, I've a few calls to make." He batted at the fly once more with his hat. Then his sour lips split into a grin when its escape path took it right into one of several fly strips hanging down off the eaves. Leon heard it buzz once or twice while it struggled in vain to take off.

Gus sniffed at the air and his eyes twinkled just a bit, "Though, on second thought, that banker feller was on to something. You may want to change yer britches, or at least hang a few more fly-strips if you plan on loafing around out here any longer."

Leon chuckled. That was typical Gus. He could find a measure of humor and a reason to be busy in the midst of just about any situation. They didn't always see eye to eye, but he always knew where the old man stood.

Gus tossed his hat on the porch rocker, fished his cell phone and reading glasses out of his shirt pocket, and shuffled back into the house.

Leon watched the dust cloud from the car's departure in the distance. It billowed up and over the pines once more, but it sure seemed to hang around a bit longer than it did before. He hopped off the porch and went to shut the gate.

D.N. Woodward

Chapter 2

Time flew by and ranch work went on as usual. Leon managed to track down Duke after the banker left, though it took him a solid three hours of searching. The whole incident from earlier continued to stump him, but everything seemed fine when he released the young gelding into his paddocks.

Gus didn't bother to share the verdict of his calls on Wednesday. He stayed busy and Leon didn't see him much over the next day or two. To Leon, this didn't bode well, and he preferred not to push the old man on the subject. Instead, he kept his head down and his hands busy.

Friday morning came around all too quickly. By a quarter till nine Leon had a flatbed goose-neck trailer loaded down with scrap metal for the recycler. A few hundred dollars of scrap metal wouldn't make a dent in what Gus owed to the bank but staying busy was better than doing nothing.

Gus came shuffling out from within the house and joined him near the tailgate as he finished tossing straps over the carefully placed pile of rusted debris from one side of the gooseneck to the other. Gus didn't say much, just stood there sipping his coffee and watching him work.

Leon was happy to see that his grandfather didn't appear to be taking things quite as hard as he had two days ago. Gus even smiled a bit when the pile shifted, and he had to re-tighten one of the straps.

From early on, Gus had been a stickler for the proper way of securing things like knots and straps. But lately, he refrained from giving much advice on just about anything Leon did. After graduating high school that spring, Leon figured Gus either considered him past the age of correction or had simply given up on trying. Regardless, it was good to know the old man still enjoyed seeing a load strapped down proper.

Once done, Leon opened the driver's side door, turned the ignition just enough to run the radio, and tuned into an AM station to listen in on the local pricing reports from past week's live auction market results. He cranked up the volume and returned to stand near Gus by the tailgate.

The morning was mild and overcast. Humidity continued to build rather than dissipate. Leon could almost smell the rain on the horizon.

"Weatherman says we might get a good gully-washer tonight."

Gus took a deep breath through his nose. "You know what I think about weather prognosticators…blind hogs, acorns, and such. But yeah, I'd say he's got the right idea this time. Something big is building."

Leon took a good long swig of black coffee from his yeti mug. Coffee, even in summer, was the lifeblood that kept a ranch running. He tossed his logbook down on the tailgate and prepared to make some notes on the current market prices for 200-300-pound feeder calves. Gus stopped him.

"Son, one way or another, that ship has sailed. No need for crunching numbers. The math ain't gonna change, and we don't have enough calves with enough meat on 'em to cover the note."

Leon nodded. It was a hard pill to swallow but Gus was right. It tore him up to see a piece of the ranch his grandfather loved yanked right out from under their noses.

Gus walked over and patted a familiar-looking blue strip of metal, "I appreciate the job you've done combing these pastures for all this scrap, but did you really need to get rid of this old roping chute."

"Yes, sir, I know what you mean." He halfway shrugged. "But I should have hauled that rusted heap awhile back. Not that I didn't appreciate the time we spent with her, but she's been busted up and patched together with baling wire and crummy welds for one too many years. It's time I found a new hobby."

If Gus was disappointed, he hid it well as he shrugged and checked his phone for the third time in as many minutes, "Well, anyhow, we had a lot of good times with that rusted piece of iron, didn't we?"

"Yes, sir, we sure did… You know, speaking of the chute, something happened while I was working…"

Gus interrupted "Hold that thought son, we got company."

Leon spun around. Gus was right. He could just see a new dust cloud sneaking up through the pines. In another minute or two, Joseph Romano's same black car came rattling up the dirt road for the second time in as many days, followed by the local sheriff's souped-up Bronco.

Leon grinned. Sheriff Tony Vega was practically family to Gus and Leon. Many years ago, he had worked the ranch for Gus on weekends and summers while he pursued a degree in criminal justice. More recently, Tony moved back into the area and won the sheriff's job. They'd seen less and less of him over the past few years.

Tony shut the engine off and slowly shuffled on up to where Gus and Leon stood while the banker shuffled papers in the cab of his car.

Gus called out in a friendly manner, like Tony's presence was a pleasant and unexpected surprise, "Well, hello, Tony, what brings you all the way out here? If you're looking to relive your glory days, I got no horses to break. Leon's done gone and got 'em all eatin' from my hand." Gus meant it as a compliment to Leon, but he scowled for effect, nonetheless.

Tony didn't look up, but a small grin momentarily split his somber lips. Then the grin vanished as he answered softly, "I think you know why I'm here, Gus. The bank's new president, Mr. Ben Heegan, explained the nature of today's visit with me before we headed this way. He also explained a bit about the greeting you all gave that fellow back there a few days ago. I guess I'm here to make sure everyone plays nice."

Gus didn't skip a beat. "So, Mr. President has the nature of today's visit pinned, does he?" He winked at Leon and his eyes twinkled just a bit.

It was the first time Leon suspected all was not what it seemed.

Joseph stepped out of the car, a stack of paperwork in tow. He marched directly up to Gus and asked if there was a place they could all sit down.

Once they were situated at the kitchen table in the main house and Gus had sufficiently fussed over a new pot of coffee, there was only the business at hand left to address. Yet Leon watched, wide-eyed and silent, as his grandfather continued cutting up, telling Tony some of the same old time-worn jokes he'd peddled for years.

Joseph's face held a sneer and Leon could tell he was in no mood to stall-out on small talk. After a few minutes of pleasantries and friendly banter, he cleared his throat and suggested they finish what they came to do. Just then Leon heard another car pull up outside. Gus immediately jumped up and politely excused himself, a big smile on his face. Without him there, the two guests and Leon got up and followed on outside.

A shiny new silver Jeep Wrangler was parked next to Tony's Bronco and two men Leon had never seen before were walking up toward the porch. Gus made a big scene of embracing the older of the two. The man was an inch or two taller than Gus' six-foot frame. He sported short curly grey hair and an olive skin complexion. They were both dressed business casual, with slacks, golf shirts, and Costa glasses. There were a short series of man hugs followed by a healthy dose of back-slapping, like some sort of lighthearted reunion.

Gus then turned and ruffled the younger man's hair, marveling at how he "had grown." The younger man had the same slender but solid build as the older man, though he was a little shorter, about the same height as Gus. He had curly black hair and, Leon noticed, when he pushed his glasses up onto his head, cold blue eyes. They lacked the warmth of his companion.

When all of the antics subsided, and Leon could see Joseph's eyes burning with impatience, Gus turned back around and acted like he had forgotten why everyone was still waiting on an explanation for the additional delay.

"Gentlemen! I'm sorry to keep you in suspense there. This here is the one and only Ethan Adler, and his nephew Reed Whistler! Been a long time since me and Ethan were traipsing through jungles together, but he's the guy I want backing me up if I ever head back!" He went on to introduce everyone there to his new guests.

Joseph stammered, all semblance of patience gone. "We've got business to conclude, and I'll be out of here as soon as it's done. Can't this wait?"

Gus stroked his chin, relishing the moment. Then held a finger in the air like a thought had suddenly come to him. "Well, Mr. Romano, that's just the thing! Our business is concluded."

Joseph's face scrunched up in a puzzled expression.

"If you bother to call your office, you will find that our debt has been paid, in full."

Then, Gus dropped his sunny disposition, and a menacing scowl took its place, "But I want you to know one thing Mr. Romano, you are never to set foot on this property again. Do I make myself clear?"

Joseph's jaw clenched shut and his white knuckles flexed. He wasn't accustomed to being outmaneuvered in such a way. "Crystal."

With that, he marched to his car. He made a call from the driver's seat before he sped off, peppering Leon's Ford with dusty debris once more.

Afterward, they all took a seat on the front porch and had a good laugh at the banker's expense. Leon listened in utter astonishment as Ethan and Gus explained how they had coordinated the private loan from Ethan over the past twenty-four hours. It was just like Gus to keep everyone on edge, right till the very end. It also explained his near absence from the ranch over the last day or two.

The fact that he waited to spill the beans until the banker drove his fancy car all the way back out to the ranch was just icing on the cake. They were all in stitches at Gus' continued antics and banker jokes until Tony finally had to beg off when his dispatcher called. He promised to visit again soon.

Once it was just the four of them, Leon stuck close to Gus, interested in the backstory behind these new *friends* of his grandfather's. He thought for sure he had heard every story about every old buddy his grandfather ever knew at least forty times over before he ever got to high school. The fact that he couldn't ever remember hearing the name Ethan Adler had his curiosity meter just about pegged out.

He delayed his trip to the scrap recyclers and stuck around the house for the rest of the morning, listening in as the two old-timers caught up. Reed remained quiet for the most part as well. Ethan made it a point to brag on him once or twice between every other story, but it was primarily the two older men who did all the talking.

Everything seemed to be going great until Leon went in to fetch everyone some iced tea. As he approached the front door, tea glasses and pitcher in tow, it became apparent the mood had shifted.

Ethan's voice piped up, "...it's well past time, burn it or cut it down and chop it up, I don't care. We are here to see this is ended, once and for all."

"That ain't gonna happen, not on my watch. Time's may be changing, but there's a reason we stand ready..."

Leon pushed through the screen door. "Cut what down, Mr. Adler?"

Gus jerked in surprise. "Nothing, Leon, just an old disagreement between two friends." He tried to smile, but Leon smelled a sour mood forming. Whatever Ethan had just been talking about had them both pretty pissed off.

"I've got an idea. Why don't you take Reed with you into town to drop that scrap and bring us all back some grub? They'll be visiting for the next few days." Gus tried to make it come across as a light request, but Leon could tell it was an excuse to have some privacy with Ethan.

Ethan nodded. "That's a great idea, and it'll give Reed and you both something more to do than listen to a couple of old *has-beens* gripe at each other."

Leon reached up to scratch the hair under his hat. Though he was suspicious of whatever they were hiding, he went along with the request, nonetheless.

Perhaps Reed will help explain whatever those two old birds are crooning over.

# # #

Leon and Reed took the better part of the afternoon to make the run into the nearby town of Bastrop. The market for scrap wasn't bad but, unfortunately, the level of effort Reed put into answering his questions or helping make sense of the simmering argument between Ethan and Gus was halfhearted at best. By the time they turned back into the CW's main gate, Leon realized he had totally forgotten to pick up dinner. By that time, though, he was just too tired and annoyed to head back.

The only nuggets of information he managed to whittle out of Reed were that Ethan and Gus had been close friends prior to and during the Vietnam War, and that Ethan currently worked as a recruiter from some sort of private University located in Idaho. In both cases Reed danced around the details, only providing the bare minimum in terms of dates and places.

When they returned, Gus and Ethan didn't seem to have made much progress over their disagreement. Gus begged off with some excuse that he needed to haul hay to the south calving pasture, leaving Leon alone once more to entertain. Luckily, Ethan took the hint that things were getting awkward and asked Reed to help him get some dinner going.

It was late afternoon before Leon and Merle were able to escape the house to the nearby sanctuary of the workshop, which doubled as his makeshift gym.

The shop's bay door was open to the sunset and Leon had a great view of a massive thunderhead spearheading some rather ominous-looking clouds. The storm slowly crept his direction while he burned his way through alternating sets of chin-ups, push-ups, and curls.

The cooler evening air being sucked in from the back of the barn, ahead of the building storm, was the perfect setup for a tough as nails work out. Leon had learned a long while back that while his metabolism may not have allowed him to stack on muscle and he would never be one of the meatheads that graced his high school with football prowess, he had corded strength to spare.

Pushing back worries regarding all the craziness going on at the ranch, Leon focused on the weather and the workout. Muffling out the questions and concerns nipping at the back of his mind was that faintly electric scent of soon-to-come-rain wafting in on a gusting breeze.

He always loved the build-up to a storm, when the wind changed and calm gave way to mounting chaos just before the actual storm arrived. He could practically taste the electricity in the air, and it served to boost his endurance past normal limitations as he pushed out an extra twenty push-ups on his last set.

Call it Gus' influence, but he always played classic rock when he hit the gym. His radio rocked an AC/DC classic with bells ringing in the background. Adrenaline pumped through his veins, reminding him he was alive. He let all his worries and troubles fade away, embracing the mounting tempo of the music. He even picked up the pace, pushing his body to go further, to dig deeper.

He was so into the moment's exertions he nearly dropped a thirty-pound dumb-bell weight on his foot when a tall shapely figure appeared in the doorway. Wearing a disruptive smirk and trendy workout clothes, his visitor casually gave him a half-hearted wave. The beautiful brunette's name was Shana Weidner, and

Shana was just about the last person Leon expected to see at his shop, but it sure didn't mean he wasn't somehow happy to see her there either.

Shana grew up just down the road. Until leaving home a year back she lived with her stepmother, Daphne Higgins, in an old ranch foreman's house that Gus had sold them for next to nothing years ago. Shana's deceased father was one of Gus's distant cousins, by marriage, but Leon had lost track of how that connection played out over the years. Since about junior high, it had always been enough in his mind to know she was of no blood relation to him. Unfortunately, that was also about the time they had grown apart.

As far back as he could remember, Shana had been one of his only friends, until she got to high school a year ahead of him and simultaneously disappeared into the social hierarchy reserved for beautiful girls in semi-small-town communities. She dated a senior her freshman year and, as far as Leon was concerned, never looked back. When she left for college, they weren't really even close enough to talk much at her graduation party. Since then, he hadn't heard a word from her.

Now, here she was, standing in his shop door, looking at him with those sparkling green eyes, smiling at him with her signature smirk. He racked the weights and killed the volume on the tunes.

"Leon Waldman, just how far do you plan on taking that farm boy strong stereotype?" His cheeks went crimson, and he sputtered to find a retort, but she saved him the trouble. Her eyes shifted down, and she greeted Merle, leaning forward to give a pet.

Leon continued to blush as he shrugged. "I'm a rancher, not a farmer. Anyhow, wasn't planning on company...or any more company that is." He motioned to the Jeep parked out near the main house. "Gus has some friends visiting. But, well, what are you doing here, Shana? Thought you were off at school?"

She laughed, but the laugh didn't reach her eyes, and it certainly didn't hold any of the lighthearted banter Leon seemed to remember from ages ago.

"It's summertime, in case you hadn't noticed. I took off the second summer session to get some things worked out back here. Was headed for a run when Daphne told me the south gate is open and asked if I could let you guys know. Gus' phone isn't working."

Odd, Gus was heading to the south pasture when he took off earlier.

"Thanks. Gus should be down there. Probably forgot his phone. But it sure isn't like him to leave a gate open, even if he *is* only hauling hay."

Shana's smile turned to a frown. Leon couldn't help but notice even her frowns were cute. Wherever her life had taken her the last few years, one thing still bound them together—she loved Gus just as much as him, "That's true, you think we should check on him? I have my 4Runner parked at the gate. Just didn't want to risk trying to drive it over y'all's sorry excuse for a road."

Leon could see the twinkle in her eye at the put-down and decided to play along, "Hey, this road is perfect. Mostly keeps out the riff-raff!"

Shana gasped with a wide-eyed smile. "Oh, I gotcha. Is that what I am these days?"

Leon's smile got tangled up with his blushing once more as he quickly prepared to leave. He already had his running shoes on, so he only needed to throw on a plain gray T-shirt before sliding his ranch-emblemed ball cap on backwards. Though miles out of his league and an inch or two taller than him to boot, the more he thought about it, the more he liked the idea of getting to catch up with Shana.

# # #

Leon gazed out over the horizon where a line of dark clouds continued to build, "I'd say we still have a little light left. The rain should hold off, at least until we make it to the south gate."

He looked her in the eye. "Thanks, by the way, you know you really didn't have to jog all the way out here."

It was her turn to look uncomfortable, "Yes, I did. Gus texted me twice this week. He's been pretty insistent, wanting to discuss something…something about my dad's family, not a big deal, but sort of the reason I'm back, so, perfect opportunity, right?"

Leon didn't know what to say to that. Once again, Gus hadn't mentioned anything to him. He merely nodded and, just like that, they took off down the road. Merle popped up beside them a minute or two later and with his long loping stride, quickly took the lead.

The road cut a rough swath through the pines, totaling a mile and a half from the house to the main gate. Yet, once they got going, any thoughts Leon had of taking it easy for Shana's sake were soundly put to rest. She surged forward, setting a brutal pace. Leon could recall Shana always maintained an athletic physique, but she wasn't exactly a track athlete in high school.

He, on the other hand, was a runner. Weights may not have been his thing, but long strides on asphalt or even dirt roads had always been a comfort of sorts for him. He loved to run. Despite the teasing Gus liked to give him, he had been district champion in the 800. His daily routine still included a long run nearly every evening. Even so, halfway down the road he was actually sucking wind to keep up.

They made it to a dinged up 4Runner in no time flat and Shana drove them down to the south section's gate well before the rain hit. There wasn't much conversation as they both took time to catch their breath.

Once there, Shana pulled into the open gate and shut off the ignition. "If I wasn't willing to take this old girl up the main road, there's absolutely no way I'm taking her down that goat trail."

Leon would have normally bantered back some disparaging remark at Toyota's expense, but his mind kept slipping back to Gus. Something didn't feel right. It was so unlike the old man to do something like leave a gate open, and he absolutely never left a gate open if he wasn't close by. Yet, there was no sign of him or the tractor.

"I guess Merle and I are gonna hike up the road a bit. You're welcome to come along, but we may all be about to get totally drenched."

"Of course, I'm coming." She grabbed a lightweight weatherproof jacket from behind the backseat, "Just to clarify though, *YOU* all may be about to get totally drenched. I'll only be a little drenched." Her grin was infectious and spread. Despite the back-and-forth humor, Leon's gut continued to tell him something wasn't right.

They took a little time to catch up as they walked along, looking for Gus. It seemed life at college wasn't as rosy and easy for Shana as he had assumed. He tried asking her more after she shared that classes were horrendous and most of the guys she knew were animals, but she quickly side-stepped further questions. "Enough of my sob story, I've just got to buckle down more in class is all. What's been going on with you Leon? You heading off somewhere this fall?"

Leon had always considered himself somewhat of a loner, but the past few months had left him feeling more alone than ever before. While others were getting ready to take off in life, he was stuck digging fence posts more often than not. He wasn't happy to hear about Shana's struggles, but it did take some of the sting out of how he had been feeling about things lately.

"Nope, college ain't for me. Gus needs me here," the answer was easy to rattle off, but Leon knew it to be a half-truth the moment it left his lips.

Shana seemed to sense there was more to it as well, but she didn't have the chance to question him further. They turned a corner and saw the tractor down the tree line.

The hay fork out front still carried a round bale, but it was pressed up against a thicket of young pines. The engine was dead, and Gus was nowhere to be seen. They sprinted to the small wreck.

Then, the forest's silence exploded in the echoing bang of a heavy caliber hunting rifle. A moment later, a second gunshot ripped through the unsettled stillness.

Shana turned to Leon. Perfectly sculpted eyebrows were climbing up her forehead as she reached for her phone. Her fingers shook as she frantically tried to call for help. She couldn't get service. Reception was notoriously sketchy out on that part of the ranch.

"What do we do?" Shana's unflappable confidence faltered.

Leon wasn't used to people looking to him when they had problems, but he took a shot anyway, "Run back to your car and get to the ranch house? There are two men there, Ethan and Reed. Tell them what you heard. Oh, and maybe call Sheriff Tony on the way? Tell him he better head this direction."

She snapped back to herself, "Yeah…um, I mean sure, but what about you?"

"Me? Well, I guess Merle and I are going to try to get a look at what Gus is shooting at without letting him put any holes in us. I have a hunch I know where he's holed up." He tried to smile for her sake like he just told a joke. She briefly smiled back but didn't offer anything more when she turned to leave.

She took off toward the gate, moving gracefully in cotton shorts and a pink jacket that read *World's Okayest Runner* on the back. A part of him was bummed they couldn't chat longer. She was definitely still the beauty he remembered.

Then he slipped into the cover of the trees, into a place of familiarity and comfort, a place he understood. Those shots gave him a good idea as to where Gus was holed up. It wasn't far.

He knew most areas of thick cover and heavy timber about as well as any boy could grow to know a place. Merle knew them better. Using that cover they traveled fast enough to make decent time but quiet enough to slip up on an Indian. Leon had always been able to move quietly through the woods and Merle seemed to instinctively pick up on the mood. He flowed through the undergrowth like a shadow at his side, only stopping from time to time to sniff at whatever rogue scents wafted their way.

Lightning lit up the dimming forest ahead, followed several seconds later by the distant boom of thunder. Just then the wind kicked it up a notch and small droplets struck his arms.

Hang on, Gus, we're coming.

Chapter 3

Leon approached where he suspected Gus was holed up. Wind and rain whipped against his face as he crept forward. The deluge pelted down on him from above. It even hit him sideways when larger gusts surged through the pines where he hid. He ignored the discomfort and cautiously inched closer until he came to a stop in some brush on a slight hilly rise.

Downhill, directly in front of him, and out in the middle of an intersection of two widely cut trails, which local ranchers referred to as senderos, stood a deer blind on rusty metal stilts. With each flash of lightning, Leon could see open windows. No one knew the door's combination to the blind but him and Gus, and Gus always kept it locked, windows included. Gus was definitely in there. Leon had guessed right. Though the guess was easy when one knew Gus left a .30-06 caliber rifle up there in a weatherproof gun case, year-round. Gus always claimed to hate hauling a rifle up a deer blind.

Leon was never one to do much of anything without carefully weighing his options. Often, if a quick decision became necessary, he was apt to freeze up, unable to take a step either toward or away from the problem. In the past, this had grown especially challenging when rivalries ignited during roping competitions.

He wrestled with his natural inclination to hunker down and wait things out as he studied the blind below. Would Gus need help? If so, he had to be ready to act when the time to move came.

He looked down at Merle and gave the dog's neck another reassuring squeeze.

He whispered into the mutt's ear, "If it looks like Gus needs help, we help, no excuses!"

Down below, the sendero continued to appear empty. Twilight would come early due to the cloud cover above. Buckets of rain continued to fall. Lighting flashed and thunder boomed as the storm's fury raged right over the top of him.

Still, he waited. He had enough confidence in Gus to know the old man wouldn't be holed up without a good reason. He was thankful at least for the mid-summer climate. The storm's temperature drop was uncomfortable but tolerable.

Eventually, the worst of the rain from the storm's initial band subsided into the ebbing pitter-patter of drizzle. The last of the sun's muted light abandoned him beyond the horizon. The forest was quiet and still.

All of the sudden, from multiple locations surrounding the deer blind, an ear-splitting chorus of howls broke loose. These weren't the types of howls conjured up by local coyotes. These were guttural, bone-rattling, wailing, spooky as all get out, angry howls. Leon felt goosebumps rising from head to toe.

Another rifle shot flashed from the window of the blind, followed instantaneously by the *thh-boom* sound of a well-placed bullet smacking into something solid somewhere off to his right. This elicited more howling from the woods before all the noise abruptly cut out. The forest was silent once more.

Leon didn't dare move. He let his eyes slowly adjust once more to the point where he could just make out the silhouette of the blind.

Then, large projectiles came zipping across the sendero from multiple directions. They converged on the deer blind. Their collisions deafened his ears with reverberations that sounded like several sledgehammers pounding a giant drum.

With the aid of the lightning, now intermittently striking behind him, Leon saw more than one chunk of debris flying off the fiberglass frame. The metal bracing holding the blind aloft clanged and sparked as it too was repeatedly struck. This barrage of pounding was silently executed from the shadow of dense cover.

All hell literally broke loose before his very eyes, and he had no idea what to do about it. Merle's coat quivered against his leg. He knelt and rubbed his dog along the wet tuft of his neck, calming them both and silently hoping Gus would make it through whatever happened below.

The near-constant onslaught of rocks finally busted through the thin metal base beneath the blind. The deer blind lurched, leaned, and lurched again before tumbling down sideways. The pummeling finally stopped.

From opposite locations, on either side of the sendero, spotlights kicked on, illuminating the now shattered remnant of the blind. The devastation caused in such a short amount of time was incredible. The area surrounding the blind was littered with large rocks, twisted metal, and floating bits of dust.

All of that damage from rocks?

Five shadowy figures stepped into the light. Leon was confused at first. From the size of the men creeping out of the woods, it looked like a professional basketball team had just attacked his grandfather. Those guys easily towered a good foot or more above Leon's five-foot-nine-inch stature.

Their bodies were entirely covered from head to foot in some sort of black tactical outfits, but as they moved directly into the light, he could just make out the disproportionate visage of large masks covering their faces. There was something off about them all. Their movement was too powerful, too swift. Their steps were quick yet disjointed.

Cautiously, they approached the remaining husk of the blind. Gus was under there somewhere. Maybe hurt bad. Maybe dying.

Leon still felt the tug of indecision, but something deep down pushed him to fight through the feeling. His racing thoughts bent to a backbone he didn't know he had, at least enough to knock him out of any momentary paralysis. It didn't matter if he went down swinging, he had to do something, anything, and fast.

Fumbling around on the ground nearby, he found two hefty rocks.

Don't think about it Leon, just chunk the rocks, and lose these creeps in the woods, for Gus.

The biggest of the five men had already begun rifling through the remnants of the deer blind when Leon came crashing down into the clearing. It enraged Leon to see the man casually disturbing debris that could be trapping his grandfather's injured body.

He opted to throw his largest rock at the big man. As his arm arched forward, the same tremor intensifying jolt of electricity he experienced two days previously struck. His arm involuntarily let loose the rock along its forward trajectory, but the pain intensified beyond his previous experiences. It dropped him to his knees.

The man originally in his sights managed to halfway turn his direction before the rock smacked him in the padded mask on his head. Still, the contact dropped him like...well, like a rock.

Before Leon had an opportunity to take satisfaction in this first small victory, the four remaining men surged his direction. Merle came leaping out of nowhere and ferociously tackled the one in the lead, fighting and growling furiously as he took him to the ground. Then, before any of the others could make it to him, the remnant of the fallen deer blind exploded upward.

If the wailing howls from earlier turned Leon's blood cold, this terrifying new scream coming up out of the busted blind froze it right in his veins. The scream eked away into a menacing growl.

The men all stopped in their tracks and turned once more back toward the blind. Even Merle and his new chew toy stopped struggling and slid apart to assess the new threat.

There, standing amongst the rubble was a bloodied bull of a man with the fierce green eyes and silver sideburns of his grandfather. Yet somehow this Gus moved with the dexterity of a man at least thirty years younger than Leon's grandfather, and he was angry. He pulled his old hunting blade from its sheath in one fluid motion and smiled a menacing smile as he extended his free hand, palm up, to give them the classic Bruce Lee motion to come get some.

Leon didn't wait around to take the proper time to process what he saw. Instead, he tried preparing himself to use that surging sensation in his chest once more to his advantage. He sprinted for the closest man. As he closed in, he strained to find that electric pulse of power. It never came.

The hooded opponent Leon bull-rushed turned at the last moment. To Leon's shock, he delivered a perfectly timed backhand.

The man's oversized paw of a hand nailed him in the jaw before his rock weighted fist came close to connecting. The motion seemed almost flippant for the towering thug, but the force was extreme. Leon careened back into some brush.

# # #

He couldn't even recall a landing as moments later he gasped for air, flat on his back.

Wow…not my best moment.

His wind and vision were slow to return. When he finally did manage to sit up and regain his bearings, things had further digressed into some sort of comic book nightmare. Gus battled like a wild man, surrounded by the four remaining NBA ninjas in the fluorescent sheen of the spotlights.

His old hunting blade seemed to move like liquid lightning as he blocked and slashed imperceptibly fast at his assailants. Even so, those he fought were nearly as fast, and they made use of their advantage in numbers.

After watching for only a moment, it was obvious to Leon the attackers held back from fatally hurting Gus when clear openings presented themselves, opting rather to attempt to gradually subdue him with their vicious fists and kicks. Leon could see the tactic, though dangerous for them, was working. Gus was already favoring his right leg. As his grandfather sucked wind, one of his four attackers managed to nail his other leg with a well-timed kick. Leon could swear he heard a tendon pop. He knew his grandfather didn't have much time left.

Merle stepped to his side and looked up at him, licking his chops while he waited for direction. It was now or never. Leon pointed to the closest of the four. "Sic 'em boy!" Merle shot out like a cannon, attacking the man he had pointed out, from behind.

Leon moved forward through the shadows, searching for another suitable rock. He was still groping around in the dark when two new figures careened out into the light of the clearing from the northeast side of the Sendero.

He did a double take. It was Ethan and Reed!

Both men swiftly drew stubby, bladed hunting knives from sheaths at their sides and moved to join the fight, squaring off with two of the remaining three opponents.

He could see silver flashes of light flickering off their blades. Leon thought it a bit odd how they resembled the hunting blade Gus always carried. Ethan and Reed were cool customers. Too cool under the circumstances. Almost like they knew what they were wading into before they even stepped out into the clearing.

Nonetheless, Leon wasn't going to sit there and look a gift horse in the mouth. The remaining attackers gave ground as the two men pressed forward.

He finally spotted a suitable rock and rushed forward to help the one creature he now knew needed his help most, Merle. His dog had ripped through the black tactical gear of the man he fought as the man screamed expletives in an inhuman voice, jerking Merle around like a ragdoll.

Then, from back behind them all, a deep, garbled bark of a voice bellowed, "Enough! Someone, stop that mutt."

Before Leon knew what happened, the echo of another shot broke through the chaos around him. Merle lurched sideways and ran several yards into the woods before he fell. The fighting came to a standstill once more. Leon dropped the rock and raced to Merle's side, oblivious to the danger still swirling around him. His best friend lay bleeding, whining softly in pain. Leon's hands shook as he cradled his dog, intentionally ignoring the men nearby.

Vaguely, in the background, he could hear the struggle resume. That same voice growled again, "I don't care if you have to bash his head, get Silberman under control!"

There was a *whack*, followed by the sound of a body hitting the ground. Leon turned back to his grandfather. To his horror, the old man was lying face down on the ground. One of his attackers stood, leering over him, the butt end of his grandfather's hunting rifle clasped like a miniature toy gun in his oversized hand.

Ethan and Reed had their hands full with their oversized attackers, still dancing in and out around them. They hadn't been able to make it to Gus in time.

First Merle, now Gus. Leon was consumed in the agony of pain and loss. His vision went dark as he squeezed his eyes shut. Emotional agony gave way to full-on anger, which burned hot. So hot he could practically feel the heat coursing through his veins.

Somewhere in the back of his mind he both noticed and chose to embrace that same odd tremor of electricity from a few days before. It sputtered to life once more. This time though, it wasn't a flash or a jolt. This time it shook his whole body and held him tight within its clutches.

The pain came searing him, consuming his senses. His head felt torn apart internally. He let loose a scream, but never made a sound. The moment stretched on, lacerating nerves up and down his body. It lasted mere minutes that stretched forward like hours.

When the pain subsided and Leon opened his eyes, his view of the world was different. He could still feel a steady trickle of power in his veins, though the rushing torrent was gone.

He took a moment to gather himself. He must have rolled off the path, into the shadows near where a couple of the men first emerged from the brush. With the lights behind him, his vision pierced the darkness of the forest beyond.

He took a deep breath, and every smell imaginable exploded into overdrive. Though it was hard to identify all the smells coming at him at once, he was able to distinguish an evergreen mintiness in the pine bark of the trees he saw before him to a depth beyond any previous ability. He turned to see the remaining wreck of the deer blind and could sense the musty ick of moldy insulation in the scattered debris. Yet most disconcerting of all, he could almost taste a coppery ferrite aroma wafting off the cuts and nicks of those he saw standing in the clearing. It wasn't appealing in any appetizing sort of way, but it was rich and vibrant.

He took a small step forward and new muscles rippled. Such power, such strength. It was intoxicating and terrifying all at once.

Then he remembered his grandfather, still face down in the dirt. His anger and rage rekindled. The towering figure he first nailed with the rock was just getting up on shaky feet. Leon took a few lunging steps forward and hammered the big bully once more in the head with a curled fist that may have just as well been made of granite. The big man crashed back down to the ground.

Then he turned, searching for the soon-to-be-dead-man with the gravelly voice who had given those sinister orders from the cover of darkness. He spotted movement from deeper in the nearby woods. He stepped around a pair of saplings and confronted another giant of a man.

This man's mask was removed. The sight would have terrified any sane person. Only, Leon wasn't feeling very sane in the moment.

What stood there before him wasn't a man at all. At least, not in the way he would ever describe a person. The creature's face resembled that of a man, but with a strange blend of canine features and short, dark fur thrown into the mix. It held a woman by the throat. Her head was bent over, and hair covered her face. For some reason, the fact that he was physically restraining a woman didn't bother Leon as much as it should have, she was just something standing between him and that creature he needed to take down.

Every B-Horror movie he had ever watched reminded him to turn and run, run for his life. But the newfound power coursing through his veins took his mind beyond where reason was willing to lead. Instead of hightailing it out of there when he had the chance, he popped his knuckles and flexed his fists, preparing to dole out the punishment they deserved.

The creature holding the woman spoke low and raspy through a mouth full of teeth, "Well, this is a surprise!" His rough bark of laughter never touched his eyes, "Jace, hit our friend on my ten with a little UV."

The lights flipped his direction. They hit him dead center. Immediately, white light seared deep into his eyes, burrowing into his brain as if a brain freezes and an ice pick decided to have a party in his skull. The tremor's pain returned with a vengeance and Leon lost himself to its cruel embrace once more.

# # #

Reality came crashing down on Leon as consciousness slowly returned. Pain blossomed across his body, but not the unbearable pain from earlier. This was more of a sore, aching pain.

Barely opening his eyes beyond a slit, he stared up at a dense green forest canopy. The smell of rain faintly persisted in the air. Tall pines swayed to a gentle breeze.

Then memory came back, full force. Gus! Merle! He shot up in an attempt to stand, only to be jerked to a stop by sturdy metal manacles around his ankles and wrists. The manacles were securely fastened to two thick chains connecting his hands and feet respectively, and a smaller chain connecting both sets with just enough extension to allow him to stand up straight. It was like he was some prisoner in a 1920s chain gang!

"Easy, Leon. Easy, son. You're gonna be okay." It was Gus!

"Gus? That you? You okay? Where's Merle?"

Leon could see enough from the spotlight's glow off to the left to make out most of his grandfather's face. His head was bandaged but it was Gus's face alright.

Gus shushed him, "Yeah, son, it's me, I'm okay. Always told you I had a hard head, didn't I?" he tried and failed to lighten the mood, "You've been out a good half hour. And Merle…well, Merle's been hurt something bad. I'm so sorry."

Leon knew it was true, but he refused to believe the words his grandfather uttered. Tears wouldn't come, just disbelief, and anger. Such feelings swirled through his mind and threatened to send him back down the rabbit hole of anguish he had only just escaped. His grandfather's voice pulled him back from the ledge.

"Listen to me, son, I know you're hurting, but we need to focus on the here and now. You understand?"

Leon's mind raced. He had a thousand questions and rage was still threatening to consume him. Yet the steady twang of his grandfather's voice gave him an anchor within the storm. He pulled

37

what little of himself he could together and nodded, there would be time to worry about payback for Merle later.

Gus continued, "Good, I imagine that once your head catches up with your heart there'll be a ton more questions rolling 'round up there, but I'll cut to the chase: I've been a fool son. This wasn't supposed to be possible. These creatures weren't supposed to have known about me or this place, but somehow they do."

"But how—"

Gus stopped him, "Not now Leon. There's so much I want to tell you boy, but time may be short. Whatever happens, keep your head, try not to give in to your emotions until we have a chance to talk again. Here, quickly now, take this."

Leon stretched his hand out as far as the manacle allowed and accepted a silver chain necklace attached to a metal medallion, about four times the size of a dog tag.

"Hide it, quick!"

Not knowing what else to do, Leon shoved it down his shorts, into his boxer briefs.

Just then, a man, not a beast, walked across the clearing, through the light, to where they were sitting. He had a deep, rich authoritative voice that Leon could swear he knew.

"Mr. Silberman. Mr. Waldman. Excellent, you're both up! Unfortunately, this whole op has digressed into one massive cluster. But believe it or not, we weren't here to fight."

"Sure could have fooled me," Gus responded.

The man ignored the snark and continued, "We are simply here to use the Fayden Pine, or the Royal as you call it, and as the steward, Gus, you are going to show us the way."

Gus went white as a sheet and was speechless for the first time in Leon's life.

The man stepped forward. "Do I make myself clear?"

He lifted the nozzle of a pistol and nudged it against Leon's temple. Leon stiffened against the cold metal.

Gus dropped his eyes and nodded. The man dropped the barrel and resumed in an almost friendly tone, "You see there, that wasn't so hard! Now, both of you stand up and shuffle on over with the remainder of your group."

Leon and Gus managed to hobble across the clearing, their movements constrained by the heavy chains and manacles that weighed them down.

Leon immediately saw Ethan and Reed were trussed up the same way as he and Gus. Shana also sat in the mud, cross-legged, her arms behind her back. Her head was down, her face buried behind dark locks. Was she crying or shivering? She looked unharmed otherwise.

A finger tapped his shoulder. When he turned, a sandy-haired man with glasses looked him in the eye. He spoke in a clipped tone, "Your grandfather will be fine, and I've done all I can for your dog. He's stable and alive. Took a nasty hit to one of his back legs...Time will tell."

"Can I see him?"

"I've got him sleeping in the back of that UTV over there. You'll see him soon, I'm sure."

The man wandered off into the shuffle of the busy men surrounding them.

Two large expressionless goons stood holding rifles nearby, guarding his group. They wore the same black combat gear as the creatures from earlier, their masks now removed. To Leon, they seemed much smaller up close.

A number of other men, in addition to the six he counted earlier, were assembled nearby, checking gear, and stowing it in duffel bags and rucksacks. The bags were slowly filled with militarized weaponry and gadgets of all shapes and sizes. Up close, he could see a dark gray embroidery on the sleeve of one of the men. It read *NVG Security*.

Squatting down next to Shana, he gave her a gentle nudge. He spoke softly, "Shana, I'm sorry. I don't even know what I've gotten you into here."

She peeked up at him through a tangle of dark wet hair and gave him a sorrowful smile. "You don't, but I do, kind of..."

Stunned, he responded, "W-what do you mean?"

"Don't be upset, okay? Gus could have only told when you turned eighteen anyway. He never told you then because the chances were next to zero that this...I mean...there was no way anyone could have really known for sure until you turned twenty, even if they had suspected, which they didn't."

Leon didn't understand. "What didn't he tell me, Shana?"

She seemed to ignore his question as she quirked her head to the side, appraising him with a different look than he'd ever seen her use before. "Looks like you may have been a bit older than everyone assumed when they found you all those years ago. Doesn't matter now. You're like us Leon, you're...different."

Ethan jumped in, "Different may be a bit of an understatement. What she means to say, Leon, is after what little we saw back there, it is safe to say you are a skin-changer."

Leon would have thought them crazy, stark raving mad, had he not experienced the mind-splitting pain of some sort of change internally or witnessed a half dozen other things he couldn't explain at the battle royal in the clearing. Even so, there was no good way to wrap his head entirely around that kind of statement. He fumbled for something to say to alleviate the tension building around him. "So, that means we're all like what? Werewolves?"

Surprisingly, Reed answered before the others, "Absolutely not! The concept of werewolves and other *shifter* type fairy-tale stories are misconceptions of those like us, likely brought about by the likes of those Unbladed filth." Reed's eyes flashed contempt as he pointedly glanced back where the men continued to work. "We hold to the original traditions and do not make a mockery of our gifts."

Leon could care less for whatever point Reed was so overtly attempting to make to their captors at the moment. He clinched muddy fists as he pondered whether it was betrayal or apathy that motivated the omission of so many truths by the one man he cared about most in the world. As that world continued to unravel at the seams, he stole a glance at Gus and a bit of anger crept into his voice. "REALLY? You never thought to mention this? You couldn't have just trusted me, Gus, couldn't have clued me in just a bit here? I mean, even if I wasn't like you, did I mean so little?"

"Leon! It wasn't like that son. I was held to an oath! There's no way I could've known you were what you are." Gus strained against his shackles like he might physically push his point across to Leon.

"So, what am I now, Gus?" Their captors continued brisk preparations of some kind around them, but all sound seemed to fade to nothing as Leon waited on an answer.

"Same as you always was. You're my boy, Leon, the one I took in as my own in my old age and called my grandson…the son I never had," Gus responded.

Leon's anger cooled a bit. "No, Gus, not what I meant. What sort of…creature am I? What does it mean for *me* to be a skin-changer?"

The man with the pistol responded as he walked up to their group again, "That's a loaded question boy. Answer is yet to be determined, isn't it, Gus?" He squatted down a few feet from Leon and looked at him like a cattleman eyeballing a young bull at the sale barn.

"Yes, sir, you are a bit of a mystery. No worries though, it sometimes takes as long as a year or two from the time you begin the transition until you turn full-on hairy beast, even though none of us ever really fully transition into whatever creature our bloodlines follow. Most likely you've got the Lupus affinity, though."

At Leon's puzzled look, the man chuckled. "I'm talking about a wolf, boy! In this part of the world, it's rare to meet anyone of our specific heritage not of the Lupus affinity. Unless you're like your granddaddy, that is. Old Gus' momma somehow let a cat into the doghouse, didn't she?" He laughed at his joke. No one tied down cracked a smile.

Leon chose to ignore the headache forming simply by listening to such absurdities. None of it made much sense to him anyway.

Instead, he turned back to the stranger and took another look, desperately searching for a way to change the subject, "NVG Securities?"

The man with the pistol chuckled. "You really have no idea what any of this means, do you? My name is Ben Heegan, and I'm the owner of New Varangian Guard Securities, as well as a few other companies."

He waited like that should have cleared things up. When Leon didn't respond, he shook his head in disgust, "Mercenaries boy. We operate a world-renowned international mercenary firm," he grinned his best car salesman grin and continued, "We're the good guys. We protect powerful interests from terrorist scum throughout the world."

NVG may not have rung a bell, but the name Ben Heegan seemed so familiar. Leon's head shot up when he finally recalled where he had heard it before…from Tony. "You're *the* Ben Heegan, the turd who just bought Lost Pines Credit Union? That creep Joseph Ramano works for you?"

Ben smiled back at him, "The one and only Turd, and yes, you've met one of my employees. He's a prickly killer that one, though he's only human…he remains as clueless as you *were* about all of *this*."

Turning to face the rest of their group, Ben spoke to them all, "I knew Gus was here and I know that he's the steward. I just needed to smoke out Mr. Adler to complete the party."

Ethan spoke up, "Clever. Very clever. But even if you can convince us to help you, you're still missing a piece of the puzzle. The knowledge to prepare the path back was given separately. You're still one man shy. One man, which neither Gus nor I know how to locate these days. It won't work without that additional knowledge."

Ben smirked. "You wouldn't be referring to the Sculptor, a mister Alex Haden, would you?"

Ethan's eyes narrowed. "What have you done?"

Ben crouched down to his level and looked him directly in the eyes, his response came out deadpan serious, "Why, Mr. Adler, Alex was my father."

"Was? No. That can't be, I know...knew, Alex. He was... No son of his would have grown to have done such a thing!"

A note of anger added an edge to Ben's tone. "It wasn't me, you old fool! I loved my father. I wept for him as I watched him die in my arms. It was a territorial young rogue that attacked our home up in Stony River while we slept. Gutted my father before he knew what hit him. Then it killed my mother and my older brother, Dax, before I finally brought it down with a shotgun full of slugs!"

He managed to wrestle control of his emotions once more. "Funny thing, though, while my father was dying, he got my older brother and me confused, and in the process of recalling our family secret, he inadvertently passed it on to me, one who wasn't Bladed.

"I was sixteen, too young for the rogue to have sniffed me out and still in the dark as to who I really was thanks to your foolish rules!"

Ethan's mouth moved like a fish out of water for a moment. "The Blade, Ben, you have to take the Blade!"

Ben stood up again, shaking his head. He spat at Ethan's feet before he answered. "I don't have to have a damn thing to do with you and your superstitions. Their *Blades* didn't do a thing for my parents or my brother when the rogue attacked."

Gus chimed in, "That ain't the point. It's not too late. Take my Blade, Ben. Take it and cure this madness."

"Ha! Keep your britches on, old man. I've got my own Blade now, pure titanium alloy, as well as a few little friends to go along with it. They've served me and my team well in Syria, Yemen, Ukraine...they'll serve us well in Fayden, too."

To emphasize his point, he held up his pistol and tapped a rifle butt poking up through a pack he carried on his shoulders. A few of the men chuckled at his speech as they finished stowing the last of the gear.

"I know you think us traitors to our ancestors, or worse, for not taking up your precious Blade, but I assure you, we're not. We're not lunatic rogues either. We just want the chance to go back where we belong, where we all belong. The chance to take back what rightfully belongs to us. The chance to be free. Hell, you'll be thanking us before this is all said and done."

Everyone was forced up when the rest of Ben's team materialized out of the woods and two more heavily customized UTVs arrived. The men loaded their gear onto the UTVs.

Ben's team was comprised of twelve men, including Ben. Eleven of the twelve looked like typical soldiers. One guy, however, towered several inches above any of the others. He sported a bandaged wrap around his forehead. The man beside him looked to have had an arm heavily doctored, it was in a sling.

Leon saw the big one move in close, leering down at him specifically. He gulped and decided against doing anything to agitate the big guy. That had to have been the one he put down, twice. The other one was likely the one Gus tagged with the rifle.

Ben took a flashlight from one of his men and spread his arms wide. "Mr. Silberman, please be so kind as to show the way before I am forced to put a bullet into the head of one of these fine young idiots."

Gus gritted his teeth but marched forward, manacles jingling with each step he took.

Chapter 4

Gus led the group to an extremely dense area of forest, with a thick barrier of shrubs and brush. He pointed toward the thickest, nastiest briar patch. "In there."

Several men attacked the brush with machetes and chainsaws. Leon gently bumped Shana, standing beside him. "How are ya?"

"I'm okay, I guess. I may know more than you about what we are, but I have no idea what's going on now."

"You said you knew about this? Is this normal for people like...us?"

She shook her head. "Right...so first off, I wasn't exactly off at a normal college. More of an academy for people like us. I came back because Gus said he had some inheritance for me, something to do with my parents. My guess is it had more to do with what's going on now than anything with a dollar value."

Ethan leaned in between them, "Your guess wouldn't be far off, Shana. Gus needed an heir to someday take up his role as steward. I had my nephew, Reed, while Gus had no clue Leon was a skin-changer. He planned to leave this glen, and his knowledge, as an inheritance to you."

Before either of them could fully process what Ethan had just leveled on them, a pair of loaded-down UTVs came rumbling up and stopped beside them. Ben's men furiously worked to clear a path into the brush. Leon took a peek into the back of one of them and caught his first glimpse of Merle. He cautiously reached out and raked his companion's bristled muzzle. Surprisingly, Merle's eyes creaked open, and his tail thumped twice. Then Leon was forced forward again.

The men were through the undergrowth in no time and the party continued forward. Once through, the canopy opened up and foliage disappeared.

Leon's eyes could not open any larger if he tried. He thought he knew the CW like the back of his hand, but he soon realized he had never explored that particular thicket, likely due to the impenetrable thickness of the surrounding forest. He was amazed at what he saw.

Standing alone, in the middle of a grassy depression were three silver barked, majestic versions of the larger loblolly pines found throughout the area. These three trees only stood around thirty feet tall. Yet they were much thicker in girth. They almost looked like their growth was stunted. The base of each trunk was at least fifteen feet in diameter.

Reed fell to his knees. "Trees? This was the big secret?"

So, Reed wasn't exactly in on everything either?

"Yes, the last three Royal Trees still alive, that we know of that is," Ethan said softly.

Gus pointed to the one in the center. "The two on the ends have been used before. The one in the middle has never been touched."

Leon studied the trees as Ben inspected them. He puzzled over what it meant for the trees to have been *used before*. They all looked the same.

Instead of wasting any more time, Ben stepped forward with a heavy-duty camp ax. He cut his arm deep enough to draw blood. Then he smeared that blood over the middle tree's bark. Finally, he struck a glancing blow to the mottled silver bark at the base of the center tree. Over and over again Ben's ax swung, gradually carving away at the ancient bark, scraping off small chunks with each blow.

He worked his way up from a few inches off the ground to approximately shoulder height and slowly sheared away a two-and-a-half-foot strip of thick bark. As his blade bit and scraped it away, piece by piece, Leon's nose detected the pungent fragrance of a rich, sweet smell saturating the air around them.

Ben's Blade was dull and spent by the time he was done. Panting for breath and sweating like a stuck pig, he smiled triumphantly up at Ethan, "Done. Your turn. Do your part, old man."

"That's it?"

"For me, it is."

Ethan sighed. "I'll need to use my Blade."

"Fine, just the wrists, though." One of the men stepped forward to hand him his Blade and unlock the manacles from Ethan's wrists.

"I also need a good reason to do this," Ethan said. His eyes slid from Ben to the tree and back once more, indecision etched across his wrinkled brow.

"Other than the whole bullet in the head thing? Come on, man, really? Just get on with it already!"

Ethan visibly sagged when Ben pointed his pistol at Reed. He dipped his chin in submission. Next, he proceeded to gently take his Blade, grasping it between both hands. He turned to face the tree and shut his eyes. After a moment, he took a step forward and ever so delicately drove the blade down into the wood and sliced down along the bottom edge of the bare wood.

Leon expected the blade to stop as soon as it met the pine's caramel-colored wood exterior, but it sank halfway to the hilt. Using one long, smooth, seemingly effortless cut Ethan sliced out a large rectangular outline along the perimeter of the raw wood. His Blade stayed in the wood until his cut was complete.

When he finished, he tapped the center of the exposed wood with the hilt of his Blade. A small doorway, approximately six feet by two and a half feet, in the trunk of the tree slowly tilted inward, disappearing back into the trunk. Where it was, a dark hole stood before them. The physics didn't add up, but that wasn't exactly much of a surprise considering what just about everyone there had been up to earlier.

The sweet aromatic smell of wood resin and pine needles had grown in intensity throughout the process. Now, even Leon's normal senses were alive with new smells that gave him a touch of nostalgia for something he couldn't quite place. He could only imagine the sensory overload he would be feeling if his current form wasn't quite so back to normal.

Ethan hadn't even broken a sweat. "Quickly, Ben. Get your men going and get on with this foolishness. There's no telling how long the portal will last."

Ben took the Blade from his hands and clamped the manacles back around Ethan's wrists before he leaned forward, "Oh we won't be the only ones going, but don't worry, I plan to leave you some company to temporarily replace the ones we bring along."

Leon saw him motion with his hands. The big man with the bandaged forehead walked forward, crouching down as he passed into the shadowed entrance of the tree trunk. He was armed to the teeth and loaded down with gear. He disappeared as soon as he stepped across the wooden threshold. Others followed closely behind, toting large bags of equipment through the darkened entrance.

"Think of this as motivation for you two to take real good care of our path back. But just to make certain, I'm leaving a four-man crew to help keep an eye on things. Don't worry, we shouldn't be gone long. Once we secure a headquarters around the drop zone, we will begin commuting back and forth to better establish our territory for an eventual full transition from our world to the old world. You people play nice and, within a year, it will be like we were never here."

"Ben, stop. This is insane. You don't really know where this leads. No one has used a Royal in over five-hundred years, and according to our records, that person never returned."

Ben just laughed. "There we have it. No one has ever explored the path home because your fearless Elders haven't had the balls to take the leap! Let's go, boys. Time to make some history."

Leon was shoved toward the tree. He saw Reed tossed forward into the trunk's abyss before any of them realized what was really happening.

Shana went next. Her legs were shaking, but to her credit, she didn't flinch when they moved her forward. Gus was at least able to tell her goodbye and offer a small word of encouragement before her guard hurried her through.

When it came Leon's turn, he at least knew what to expect. Ethan bellowed, "When Reed offers, take the Blade! Take the Blade, Leon!"

Leon reached up and braced himself against the entrance to the trunk. He shrugged off his impatient escort's prodding from behind. Straightening himself, he took a look back and caught a glimpse of the anguish in his grandfather's eyes. Gus' voice cracked as he spoke, "Don't be a sucker for this man's lies boy, come back to me son! Take care of Shana and bring her back as well if you can. The Blade Leon, the Blade is the key!" He gave Gus a silent nod. Then he turned and slowly stepped forward. Just before he crossed the threshold, Gus' gravelly voice rattled the forest, "I love you, boy! Ya hear me? I love you! Don't you forget…"

# # #

The light behind Leon immediately disappeared as he passed into the dark wooden void. He couldn't tell if he was in a tunnel or a cavern, but he felt no walls around him as he fumbled through the darkness. All sight and sound behind instantly cut out when he stepped through the void. He was all alone.

The air was still, and any lingering forest scents were gone. Yet, as his eyes adjusted, he saw a faint light up ahead. Not knowing what else to do, he moved forward, toward the light. One foot in front of the other. A soft muffled *thud* sounded off from each step he took.

It could have been mere moments, or much longer, there was no true measure of time as he trudged forward. However, images subtly materialized before him along the journey. It took a minute to realize they were his memories, from a detached perspective, kind of a highlight reel of sorts. All of them consisting of brief fragments from his life. Each one gradually passed before his eyes as he continued his march.

The first image to appear was the shadow of a skinny blond-headed, almond-skinned child, dressed in rags, half-naked and wide-eyed with fear. The boy was around five or six years old, and he ran as fast as his little legs could carry him, through clusters of familiar-looking loblolly pines.

Light grew a bit around him, and he saw a slightly younger version of Gus with a hired hand, helping that same small boy out of a muddy ditch along the side of a dusty Farm-to-market road.

The realization that he could see a younger version of himself, fell on him like a sack of bricks. All at once, he remembered the gnawing hunger from that day. How it paled in comparison to the sheer fright coursing through his veins. He witnessed his younger self attempted to fight Gus and the other man, Sheriff Tony, when they first tried to haul him up. The indecision that crossed his little eyes when Gus extended a hand to help him brought to his mind a perennial fear Leon thought he'd left behind long ago. Faintly, very faintly, he remembered something he had long forgotten about that feeling of terror. The panic that drove him was for something behind him, something even further back in his past. Yet, try as he might, the memory of that elusive threat continued to slide from his grasp.

Crouching in that ditch, he had been petrified, and though he was soon comforted, that fear never really left. Even twelve years later, Leon saw how every uncertain decision, every half-finished project was at least, in part, a tiny remnant of some long-forgotten terror, urging him to keep moving and stay hidden.

That was the day Gus had given him the name Waldman, claiming it was the only word he could clearly speak. The name Leon, after Gus' grandfather, would come later. Still, that day held all his earliest memories and what lay beyond that day was an empty unknown he could never quite touch.

The light around the vision pulsed and, next, he saw the faces of doctors and strangers who helped him those first few months. The light around him grew a little more with each step he took.

On one occasion he saw his long-dead grandmother, Gus' wife Jesse, during his foster to adopt days. She was tucking him into bed, singing some long-forgotten lullaby as he drifted off to sleep.

More than a year blurred by and slowed until he was once again with Gus on the day he received Merle. He could almost feel the warmth of the puppy as Gus handed him over and told him the adoption was final. Though he could only see pictures of his past, he could almost feel the tremor in Gus' voice as he sat there talking about Jesse, who had passed to cancer a few short months before. How he was empty without her. How she wanted to be there for the adoption more than anything in the world.

He saw the tears in the old man's eyes along with a whiskery smile as he concluded that they were to be each other's family going forward. Leon saw himself embrace both Gus and Merle in that moment. Light broke once more, bright with the colors of dawn. On and on the light grew as he grew.

He saw Shana and him playing as children. Witnessed him and Gus working the ranch. He treasured so many of the scenes zipping by if only he could pause a few of them or rewind and watch others once more! Then there were some he could have elected to avoid altogether. Small childhood cruelties from an insecure young man. Negligence in duties he was asked to perform. The list went on.

He picked up the pace, practically beginning to run. Yet even running, there was nothing he could do but observe every memory as he slogged forward through them all. His lungs burned within his chest and each hurtful remembrance added fuel to his fire.

Just when Leon felt the surroundings could get no brighter, everything paused. He saw Ethan lifting his Blade to sink into the trunk. Time slowed. He studied the dull silver metal. A worn bone handle peaked out beneath Ethan's meaty fist. The cutting edge contoured back to create a form resembling a bowie knife, only with more length and less width. Though deceptive, he knew from the handful of times Gus had shown him his, that the backside tapered near the point and could cut just as well as the Blade's edge. He noticed the glint of Ben's flashlight in the reflection along the knife's outline. It pulsed faintly with its own light.

Leon thought he could almost recall something familiar about the Blade. Something he may have forgotten. It rested at the edge of his memory, just out of grasp. Then, the scene blossomed into a visual inferno, and he lost sight of memory.

Finally, the vision disappeared completely as Leon stumbled forward into the chilly air of a windy gray landscape.

Chapter 5

Leon's lungs were on fire. He took short hacking breaths, gasping for air like a man pulled above water in a last moment's reprieve from drowning. He sputtered and shook, but the pain soon gave way to an invigorating sense of euphoria. It wasn't simply relief that he had made it through. There was something different within the very air around him!

A crisp scent on a muted breeze invigorated him with a sweet fragrance, so fresh. It was both chilly and soothing, like tasting something wonderfully new and a favorite childhood dish, all in the same moment. It was at least a partial fulfillment to the nostalgia he had only briefly felt back on the ranch.

Despite being a bit under-dressed for a mildly chilly day, Leon relished the sensation. He took a look around. It was a misty, foggy day, maybe morning? He couldn't see out very far past a few large stone pillars standing nearby.

Most of the others were there, too. Some were still sputtering, others appeared to be laid out in heaps. It looked like the bags of equipment the men had tossed into the shadowed hole of the tree were there as well, most were ripped open, their contents strewn randomly between them all.

He caught sight of Reed, slumped down on hands and knees with his back to him. Leon could see him panting as well. Shana was one of those face down in the dirt. He rushed to her side.

Reaching out to check her pulse with his right arm, he realized his manacles were gone! Her handcuffs were gone as well! He relaxed just a bit when he felt the steady rhythm of a heartbeat. Then he held his hand an inch off her face, he could feel small but even puffs of warm breath on his fingers. He still worried, but it seemed likely she was simply out cold for the time being.

Not knowing what else to do for her right then, he turned to take a look around. Chalky gray stone ruins framed the area around an immensely large tree and everyone with him. They stood in somber vigilance, like silent sentinels in some ancient open-topped courtyard.

Yet, it was the towering form of the solitary tree that beckoned for deeper scrutiny, holding him captive by its sheer size. It was similar to any one of the three trees in the glen back home, with the exception of its size. It was easily twenty feet in diameter, but without the stunted crown, it soared at least another sixty feet above them all. The difference lay in the canopy. Where the trees on the ranch resembled loblolly pines, this tree looked like something more out of a prehistoric picture book. It resembled normal trees from back home in the way a saber-tooth tiger might resemble a house cat. It was massive and broad. A gaping black hole stood open at the base of the tree's trunk, identical to the one he entered back home.

Just then another man's body shot out from the shadow of that hole. The person wind-milled three or four times before crashing headfirst into the dirt. He twitched and lay still.

It took Leon a second to realize that person was Ben Heegan.

Moron…serves him right!

Leon chuckled darkly at Ben's expense before quickly refocusing his attention back on the tree. Something seemed to move within the bark and, he thought perhaps his eyes were playing tricks on him.

But no, it was no trick of the light. The hole was slowly closing! Inch by inch, scorched bark simply appeared at the base of the hole where darkness existed moments before. Mesmerized, he stood and inched forward to take a closer look. Halfway there the rate at which the hole continued to disappear, increased.

It quickly became obvious there was only time for one decision, to stay or to go. More than anything, he wished he could simply close his eyes and step back through that portal. Back to the world he knew. Back to the home he loved. Back to the security of the ranch and his grandfather. And yet, Gus' last words rang fresh in his mind.

He glanced back over his left shoulder at Shana. She took shallow breaths, so still, so vulnerable. With every fiber of his being, he wanted to take that step forward. But in the end, it was never even a question he could entertain. He wouldn't leave someone he disliked alone in such circumstances, much less Shana Weidner!

He stepped closer and stopped a mere foot or two from the tree. Just as he resigned himself to watch the last of his hope for an easy return home transform itself into a solid wall of charcoal-stained bark, a massive gray body of fur and claws came shooting through the narrowly closing gap. It collided with him and together they rocketed backward, down onto the ground.

When Leon managed to untangle himself from four fury limbs, a cold nose, and a wet tongue, his chest shook in mirth. He shouted in joy and dove back into that fury embrace.

As if encouraged by the greeting, Merle licked him all the more vigorously.

"I wouldn't have stopped you. Wouldn't have blamed you either. But just out of curiosity, what made you stop?" A voice spoke from behind.

He swung around to his right. Not five feet away a brown-haired man sat panting on the ground. He recognized him as the one man who had informed him about Merle back on the ranch.

He ignored the question. "What happened to your glasses?"

"They were gone when I got here. Funny thing though, I don't seem to need them anymore. In a weird way, it makes sense now though, when I see how well your dog is doing." Sure enough, Merle's back leg didn't seem to be bothering him at all. In fact, he bounced and bobbed like a young pup.

Leon tried to ignore yet another impossibility. Instead, he reached down to give the man a hand up. "I'm Leon. You have my thanks for what you did for my dog and my grandfather."

The man looked down. "I'm sorry I couldn't have done more at the time. That wasn't what I signed up for at any rate. I'm Dr. Cooper Schultz."

"Doctor?"

"Veterinarian to be specific, but I do what I can for these animals as well." He pointed to the men spread out around them.

The moment of camaraderie ended before it ever really started. Around them, Leon heard the sound of men stirring. He saw Shana's slumped form moving and rushed back to her side. Reed, despite being a bit grouchy in general, was there in a moment as well. Between the two of them, they helped her to sit up and gain her bearings.

If it wasn't clear before, it quickly became obvious that Cooper was the team's medic. He slowly made his way around the large group, checking men's vitals and giving encouragement where needed.

It didn't take him long to make his way over to Shana. He gave her a thorough check-over before deeming her perfectly fit for duty. By then, Ben was on his knees, weakly calling out for a status on everyone's condition.

As Ben's orders grew more demanding, Leon took in the frazzled state of Shana, she could barely stand on her own. A simmering rage boiled over in his mind. He reached down, grabbed Merle's collar, and handed him to Reed. "Hold him tight, would you?"

# # #

Leaving the meager shelter of his small circle, he walked up behind Ben, "Mr. Heegan, you mind turning around?"

Rising on shaky legs, Ben turned "What can't—"

Leon tried to somehow conjure up his electric current once more, but when it didn't come, he went ahead without its added power. He first struck with a left hook to the right side of Ben's face. "That's for shooting my dog."

A man Ben's size may have been able to shake off that type of blow from a guy Leon's stature under normal circumstances, but Ben was still wobbly. The impact sent him right back on his butt. Even so, to his credit, he rose halfway up in no time.

Leon immediately pressed the point, not waiting for an invitation. He wasn't exactly built to handle trouble, but that didn't mean his grandfather hadn't taught him how to throw a punch. Gus was nothing if not thorough in every lesson he ever gave.

Just as Ben managed to find his feet once more, Leon snapped forward with a left jab. Ben's head snapped back and his nose trickled blood. He didn't stop there though. Punches were meant to be thrown in bunches, and Leon quickly finished the combination, curling his right foot to follow through with a massive right hook that caught Ben in the jaw, just below his left temple. "That's for having my grandfather pistol-whipped!"

Ben staggered back into a low crouch but didn't quite go down again. A few of his men jumped forward to put an end to things, but Ben waved them all off. Leon could distantly hear Merle barking mercilessly somewhere behind him, but it all faded to background noise.

Ben quickly recovered and managed to get his arms up into a fighting stance, waiting on Leon to make his move.

Leon's adrenaline surged. He bounced on the tips of his toes. Another combination would be the expected response. Instead, Leon stepped forward and snapped his leg up in a lighting fast kick.

"This is for Sha..." Everything came to a screeching halt. His leg stopped in midair, a bit shy of the Heegan family jewels. Ben lifted Leon's foot clear of its intended target. He held it high, trapped in a vice-like grip between his hands, and Leon had to hop to keep his balance. He made a tsk-tsk sound between his teeth and grinned a bloody grin back at Leon. "I appreciate spunk kid, but that's not exactly fighting fair." Then his smile disappeared. "For future reference, don't start what you can't finish!"

With that, he flipped Leon around by the leg. A sharp grunt of pain was all Leon had time to convey before finding himself flat on his back. Then, Ben was there above him, mercilessly tenderizing his ribs with the blunt end of a black combat boot. Leon felt only agony as his torso was worked over like a professional soccer ball.

Mercifully, the beating only lasted a few seconds, until Reed's voice broke through the pain, "...I said enough, Heegan. He's learned his lesson! Anymore, and I'll let his buddy here loose!"

Merle practically foamed at the mouth as he continued to fight against his collar.

Ben's foot stopped a few inches from Leon's face. He gave a wicked chuckle as he stormed off and Merle eventually calmed down. Shana and Reed helped him into a sitting position. Leon grimaced, though he was fairly certain nothing was broken but his pride.

He snuck a peek back over to where their designated leader stood. He studied the man a bit harder. Ben wore a black T-shirt. He threw his arms around with animation, barking orders at men who rifled through gear. That's when he caught a glimpse of dark ink. The word 'RANGER' hung in bold letters above three black lightning bolts. He closed his eyes and smacked his forehead.

Reed broke the awkward silence. "Well, it was a nice try, but I don't think you'll be alpha dog anytime soon."

Shana chimed in, "It's not like you didn't get a few good shots in…"

Cooper's head popped up over her shoulder. "She's right kid, that's the closest I've ever come to seeing Ben give an apology. He must feel pretty bad about how things escalated back at the ranch." He shrugged. "You just took things a little too far is all."

Shana glanced back at him with a huff. "Well, I for one wish he *had* been able to take his foot just a bit further." They all laughed, and Shana gave Leon a wink. He found he didn't hurt quite so bad afterward.

Ben soon finished barking orders to his men and returned focus on Reed. "You, Reed, how did you manage to smuggle that knife through the tree?"

"What do you mean?" Reed reached down and unsheathed his Blade.

"Our guns, our equipment, your manacles, nearly everything with metal. It's all simply gone. In addition, two of my men didn't make it through that nightmare." Ben gave an involuntary shiver, and Leon understood what the man felt. Even though some good memories surfaced in that trip through the void in the tree, he wouldn't be rehashing them for anyone, they were just too personal and the hurts they exposed too raw.

Ben continued, "All we have left are a few bags of gold coins and a silver whiskey flask. So, let me ask you again, how did you manage to bring your knife across?"

Leon was also puzzled. He had to agree, the missing metal was a mystery.

"I've got no idea," Reed responded.

Ben took a step forward, and Reed shifted back, holding his Blade firmly in a guarded stance like he might just be someone who knew how to use it.

"As I said, I have no idea why my Blade made it through, but I'm kind of attached to it."

Ben smirked. "Fine. Keep your secret and your little knife, for now, but I'm going to get to the bottom of this eventually." As an aside to the men standing around, "I'm starting to like these kids, they have grit!" The men all chuckled at his joke, but Leon couldn't help noticing his eyes weren't smiling.

A few minutes later, Ben called to get everyone's attention. He walked over to the tree and addressed the group at large, "Okay, men, circle up.

"Here's the bottom line. We knew there would likely be challenges once we got here. I have no doubt we'll find Jones and Jefferson waiting for us earth-side with some hot steaks and cold drinks."

The men laughed a bit uncomfortably at Ben's effort to soften the blow of their disappearance.

"The way I see it, we have three critical challenges to our current mission, but I'll keep this simple so even our civilians can understand."

He held up a finger. "First, we have very little usable equipment. It appears *most* metal objects," he gave Reed a pointed look, "have been lost. We do have food and clothing. So, go ahead and pass out the jackets and such. I can already see the little lady shivering, not that I mind. But let's get her something warm anyway." He winked at Shana.

His men had themselves another laugh at her expense. For Shana's part, she folded her arms over her chest and developed a sudden interest in one of the branches up above, pretending not to notice the remark. Leon's blood boiled again.

"Second, I think it might be safe to say our portal was a one-way ticket. We will need to find an alternate extraction route." The charcoal impact to the bark continued to spread and the green needle-like leaves in the canopy above were already turning yellow.

"This leads to the third and final challenge. This mission's core objective will now be modified. Priority is no longer to establish a headquarters. We are now on RECON, until such a time as we are able to secure passage back for the whole team. No one will be left behind while they are still breathing. That even includes our little slugger over there. Understood?"

Everyone nodded their assent "Cooper and I will stay back to finish sorting the gear with the kids. The rest of you, suit up and head out in two teams of two. I want eyes around the perimeter of these ruins. Let's see if we can find one of the sister trees to this big girl right here." He patted the black bark and as he did flakes crumbled between his fingers.

"Time to earn your money and your freedom."

"Hooah!" at least three of them replied as they all immediately got to work grabbing gear and heading off in their different directions.

Chapter 6

Shana pulled the thick neoprene jacket tight around her chest. Though the buttons and zipper were gone, along with the rest of the metal material brought through the void, the warmth it provided put a stop to her shivering.

On the other hand, Leon was somewhat skipped over when it came time to hand out the cool-weather gear. Likely, it was a not-so-subtle punishment for his earlier spat with Ben. Instead of something thick and warm, he was given long pants and a camo button down to go over his T-shirt. He did his best not to appear miserable and depressed in his current situation, but his teeth were beginning to chatter, and it was hard to appear cavalier with permanent goosebumps.

Shana, Reed, and Leon were all three given the task of rummaging for useful gear through the remnant of the non-metallic equipment that made it over with the team. It was boring work. It was also amazing how much junk Ben and his men were able to bring along. While sorting through what made it through intact, Leon got the impression if Ben could retake the old-world using chewing tobacco and Mountain Dew, they were all in really good shape. He was just glad to see several large bags of coffee beans made it through as well. No coffee would have been simply intolerable!

The weather sure wasn't helping anyone's mood either. A misty drizzle moved in shortly after Ben let his men loose to survey the area. The temperature continued to drop as the day progressed.

Merle, on the other hand, was still doing his best to convince Leon he was a two-year-old pup. The old dog was a near limitless supply of energy and spunk. Almost like the very air around them gave him renewed vigor and youth. And though Leon couldn't be certain, it seemed like his dog stood taller in his new environment as well.

Attempting to ignore Merle's incessant whining for a tug-of-war game with one of Ben's equipment bags, Leon's eyes drifted over to Shana. She was certainly an enigma. How many sleepless high school nights had he spent tossing in bed, wondering how he could get her attention?

He never did quite figure out why they stopped talking. In fact, it was odd to recall that the two of them had ever been close as kids.

On the one hand, it made perfect sense. Shana was beautiful and outgoing, people flocked to her regardless of whether she wanted the attention or not. She carried a unique spark of personality that seemed to say, "I know where I'm going, and I know how to get there." People couldn't help but wish to come along, especially the guys.

He never knew exactly when a rift had developed between them. It just showed up and grew until it was a canyon he never felt capable of crossing. One day, he simply stopped viewing her as his friend. She was something more to him, something he wished was reciprocated.

Yet the more his feelings grew, the further she slid from his grasp. He could vividly recall having trouble finding words to say to her. Soon enough she was busy with high school and before he knew it, she had moved on with life and left him behind.

The thought made him consider things he'd avoided confronting in the past. He'd always assumed it was Shana who left him behind, but maybe he had unknowingly caused their friendship to fizzle?

Recalling the spark in Shana's eyes, the way her nose slightly wrinkled as she smiled back at him the moment she had crashed his workout the day before made him reconsider her disdain for him. It made him wonder if, just maybe, there wasn't some cue he failed to pick up a few years back.

He shrugged to himself.

Leon, you twit, stop reading too much into things. The biggest cue you need to pick up on is the fact that you spend way too much time around stinking cattle and a grumpy old man!

It wasn't that he was unhappy with Gus on the ranch, but even there, as beautiful and peaceful as it could be at times, he often felt something was missing.

He didn't allow himself such thoughts often. As an orphan, he knew he literally hit the jackpot when Gus adopted him. To even think thoughts that shook that boat was to risk the single best thing to have ever happened to him - not that he could remember any time prior, but still…it couldn't have been too good considering the state he was in when he was found.

Such sentiments kept him clear of emotional confrontations, team sports, and nosy teachers during high school. They, unfortunately, did not transfer well into life in the real world. In reality, this was likely why Gus was always encouraging him to get out and try something different.

Definitely going to have to remind old Gus to be careful what he wishes for when I get home!

Shana looked up and caught him watching her. She grinned a mischievous grin back at him, "Leon, I've got something I want to get off my chest. But I want you to promise me you won't be offended?"

He gulped while doing his best, and failing, to avoid a deer in the headlights look.

What could she possibly be about to say that would offend him? Was she actually going to come clean about why they grew apart? Was it something he did? The questions came one on top of another, hard and fast, but he somehow finally managed to nod and give her a less than confident, "Sure, go ahead, lay it on me."

"Why is it that the first thing that came to my mind when I glanced at you just then was you and Gus are the only two people I know who put their ranch brand on everything they own! And not just your cattle! I mean look at that old hat! In fact, I don't remember having ever seen you or Gus when you weren't wearing some stitch of clothing without that CW brand sown onto it!"

She pulled off a concerned conspiratorial glance his way and leaned forward. "Do you have a certain two-letter tattoo somewhere you would rather not disclose? You can tell me, Leon. I'll take it to the grave, promise."

Stifling laughter, Leon pulled his hat off and made an exaggerated show of examining the CW brand centered above the bill. He knew how some guys his age wore their ball caps, with the wide flat brims and decals off-centered or on the sides. His old curve-brimmed ball cap had nothing fancy on it, just the brand inscribed in its unique way. The branded CW letters on the front were a simple mark of pride for him and Gus. Shana was right about one thing though: His hat, along with just about everything he and Gus owned, excluding his person, were custom labeled with the CW brand initials.

He held the cap out in front of him and used his best Gus Silberman imitation, "I don't see a problem. If a man's gonna wear a logo, he ought to wear something that represents his self and what he does for a living, not some jack-nut marketing scheme."

Shana giggled. "Touché!"

"Anyhow, you know how Gus is a stickler about the ranch's brand. I couldn't ditch the CW if I tried."

Shana laughed harder, "Oh contraire…I seem to recall something you may have forgotten. Remember that time we got in so much trouble for convincing the Harper brothers to go Snipe hunting down by Panther Creek? Daphne grounded me for like forever when their mom called for an explanation as to why they were covered in chiggers. But what was your punishment again?"

Leon smiled now as well. "No Cool Water gear for a week. Still a record for the longest I've ever gone without wearing the company colors."

Shana may have actually snorted at that, which just made her laugh harder. Leon laughed, too. Reed even tried and failed to stifle a smile at the ridiculousness that passed between the two of them.

After a few minutes, the laughter faded away and Leon could tell it was a much-needed relief for all three of them. He vowed then and there, to hang on to that hat for as long as they were stuck wherever they were.

Seeing Reed loosening up gave Leon the idea it might be a good time to get some answers. "So, Reed, how about you tell us what you know about this place?"

Reed still struck Leon as a bit of a sour grape. He was definitely on their side, but it was almost like he resented them for it as well.

"Not much to tell. We're in Fayden I assume. This is where our ancestors came from a long time ago, when they were driven out by some Unbladed uprising. I do know this is a dangerous place to be if the stories are true."

"Why were the trees such a big secret?" Shana asked.

"It's a known secret among the Bladed these days that our kind has the means to return to Fayden, to this world. But the reason no one knows the how and where of that means to return is because our ancestors believed the passage between the worlds could threaten our whole existence with people back home.

"Like I said, the stories of this place are the stuff of nightmares. I'm not so sure Ben and his guys really realize what we may be facing. I don't even really know, but I do know this is definitely not a safe place to visit." He made a point of pitching his voice loud enough for Ben to hear the last part but was only rewarded in return with a grunt of amusement from their captor.

Leon winced at Reed's response. He had asked for it, though.

Shana didn't flinch. "Well, you're just a regular ray of sunshine aren't you!"

# # #

A few seconds later, a pair of Ben's men came trucking it out of the mist. The big man, the one who made Leon uneasy, cut right to the point when Ben stood to greet them.

"Heegan, we've found a native dwelling. The area southwest of here bottlenecks into a pinch point, with water on both sides. It's connected to a much larger landmass. The dwelling resides on high ground within that crease."

"You put eyes on anyone?"

"No, but we did see smoke from a chimney of sorts. We are standing on some type of plateau, and the terrain drops down to where the house resides. Jace and I could see a good way down into the valley below before the mist moved in heavy, there were no other dwelling places in sight."

"That may work in our favor. Could it be a defensible base camp?"

They both gave an affirmative.

"Pack up, we head out when the others return."

Once the other team arrived, they were able to confirm that the northern edges of the ruins were surrounded by water. That meant they were standing on a peninsula of sorts.

Leon didn't see how he or Shana had much say in the matter. So, reluctantly, he did as he was told when Ben said they were leaving. In less than ten minutes the whole party had geared up and was moving south.

Light grew dim as the small group passed through remnants of massive columns and giant arches. Shadows slowly emerged to cast a foreboding aura amongst the wrecked remains of some bygone era.

Leon was forced to step around man-sized hieroglyphic fragments and caught glimpses of miniscule shards with intricate carvings of massive, fearsome creatures amongst the wreckage. Initially, the ruins pricked his curiosity. However, the further they traipsed through the quiet city's bowels, the less and less he was inclined to wonder at its origin. It was just too quiet and still. Like they were intruding on a cemetery with broken-down mausoleums the size of small buildings.

Thus, it was a great relief to him when the team shuffled around the last of the fallen stones. Ben called a halt and crept forward with two others to scope out the dwelling just over the next ridge. Leon could smell the smoke from a fireplace nearby.

Shana crept closer to Leon. "Do you think this is a good idea? To just barge in on someone's place out here after dark?"

"No, but they're right about one thing. We need shelter, somewhere safe. At least until we find a way out of here."

"Those ruins back there gave me the creeps."

Cooper spoke up from Shana's right side, "Those ruins were likely once one of the cities our ancestors inhabited before they were forced into our world. Too bad we didn't have more time to explore during daylight hours. Could you imagine what sort of information we might glean from such a place?"

Leon noticed Cooper developing an annoying habit of appearing next to her and butting in on their conversations.

Shana shook her head. "What are you? Some kind of crypto-archaeologist or something?"

Shana had been getting away with those types of subtle digs on guys for years, so long as she smirked with sleepy eyes and a slight dimple when she delivered them. Leon had always admired the self-assuredness of that smile, but sometimes it made him uncomfortable, too.

Cooper chuckled brightly. "Not even close, just a fan of history. I am a scientist, though. A veterinarian medic to be specific."

"Hush up over there!" Ben whispered as he and his men returned.

"The dwelling appears empty, but appearances can be deceptive. When we go in, we go in fast. Slade, I want you and Gunther in beast mode before we head down there. Leon, I'm only going to ask this once, can you keep that dog quiet? I won't have him barking and alerting the whole valley down below if things get chippy."

"He kept his mouth shut just fine until I told him to do something more last night. He'll be fine so long as he's with me."

Ben studied them a moment then nodded and marched back to the front of the group.

The two men he had singled out dumped their gear and shuffled off away from the main party.

Leon hated to admit it, but he had been curious what a *beast mode* transition might look like from the moment Ben mentioned it. However, the noise coming from the direction of the two *volunteers* wasn't exactly encouraging. There were light groanings and snapping sounds. Luckily, it didn't take longer than a few minutes for them to return in the same black suits from the night before. Up close it became obvious that they grew several inches taller between when they left and returned.

Since the sun had fully dipped below the horizon, it was hard to get a feel for the full effect of the change in the dimming twilight. Leon suspected that behind those masks, they had a bit of a wolfman theme going on.

He saw Shana gawking as well, "So, they didn't teach you everything you needed to know about this, did they?"

"No, I mean yes, but what those guys are doing, forcing transitions in the fading light like this is supposedly risky. They say it can be addictive. It can even become a problem for the Bladed, who somehow aren't subject to the demand of having to change on moonless nights, if they do it often enough."

"Chalk it up to another perk from our *heritage*?"

"You're starting to get the picture!"

# # #

As the team crept around the ridge, Leon held Merle tight to his side and ordered him to hush up. He could see a faint flicker of light from a fire through a slatted opening within the quaint cottage dwelling. The cottage sat nestled within a rock uplift less than two hundred feet down the trail.

Despite the fast-approaching darkness, most of the group ignored the cottage and gazed in wonder at an absolutely stunning view, further down into a valley. The sun was just below the horizon, but the last of its rays still cast a rosy glow over the wide canyons below. The scene resembled a tropical version of an Arizona landscape. The difference being, in the backdrop of a darkened sky, ocean waves pelted sandy beaches beneath jagged cliffs and the silhouettes of large clusters of giant palms swayed in the evening breeze, punctuating the horizon deeper inland.

Reed spoke in a whisper. The wind just barely carrying his words to those nearby. "Looks like a prehistoric paradise down there."

Leon frowned. To him and his rancher's eye, it looked like a barren, rough place to make a living. A place more apt to be hot and dry than cold and wet, regardless of current conditions.

Leon only spared a moment to glance over the picturesque landscape. His attention returned once more to the cottage. He was leery of Ben's plan to simply barge in on someone else's home. Such blatant disrespect of private property simply didn't sit well within the framework of his rural Texas heritage.

Unperturbed by any such personal inhibitions and seemingly unaffected one way or the other by the view below, Ben took off for the cottage door before Leon's discomfort had time to simmer and boil over into another conflict. He almost made it there too…until the reason for Leon's bad feeling stepped out from a deep shadow near the entrance and held up an arm to halt his advance.

Leon's curiosity warred with his desire to run and hide at the sight of his first Fayden native. He gave Merle's collar a jerk to let the dog know everything was fine before the first hints of a rumbling growl could fully form in the back of his throat. Then, shrugging off his inhibition, he walked out from the shadows to join Ben and his men. Shana and Reed joined him as well.

I really ought to find a leash, this could get old fast.

Vikings, Arabs, and ancient Scottish highlanders all may as well have played a part in lending the stranger before them a very unique and rugged style of clothing attire. It was a combination of cracked leather, homespun linen, and faded earth tone colors that shouted he was from a vastly foreign culture. Leon didn't need an enhanced sense of smell to tell him the man's outfit hadn't been through a washer in quite some time.

Yet, despite the outlandish wardrobe choices, the man still managed to strike a chord with Leon. His very presence exuded a quiet but confident vibe. Something intangible about the stranger whispered to Leon that the guy could be extremely dangerous.

Despite the disheveled state of the man's windswept white hair and sparse beard, he didn't seem unhinged. Dark intelligent eyes peered out from within a worn and weathered face. Those eyes conveyed measured patience as they rove silently from one individual to the next, sizing up the group as a whole. They neither widened nor squinted as they slowly took stock of the outlandish clothing and gear on the individuals assembled before him.

His relaxed posture gave Leon the impression he was willing to lend them the courtesy of a neutral disposition, but that he would be ready if things went south. His left arm lightly palmed and twirled a small chiseling tool of some sort. He allowed his right hand to rest at his waist, a thumb tucked casually in his belt, inconspicuously close to the hilt of a sheathed blade. Leon did a double-take; the hilt was white bone.

An evening wind faintly whistled up the canyon's entrance, drawing out the stalemate between their group and the native. The man's eyes stopped their roving when they landed on Leon and Merle. He tilted his head and Leon self-consciously took a step back. Perceptive eyes studied him and Merle harder than he had the others until those eyes flickered away, and he spontaneously broke into a smile.

His smile was as warm and friendly as his glare had been toneless and calculating. It was even a bit endearing, in a rascally sort of way, due to a missing front tooth in his bottom jaw. He peppered the group with foreign questions, gesturing wildly at their clothing.

Leon noticed when Ben glanced off to his left, where one of the guys in beast mode stood, hidden in the darkening shadows.

"Wait!" Leon cried.

Ben paused, half turning to look at him, "This ain't the time, boy, unless you know what he's saying?"

"No, well, not exactly. But—just wait." He couldn't simply allow Ben and his team to hurt an innocent old man if he could help it and something about the words the old man used tickled Leon's mind in a familiar sort of way. No matter if the old man looked perfectly capable of dishing out some hurt himself.

He took a step forward and held his arms out to each side, palms up. The man continued to babble but discretely pivoted to address Leon directly. At least he didn't appear to feel threatened. Yet.

Leon began talking. Slowly at first. Then, as the man quieted, he continued in a gentle, easy pace. He introduced the group. Told the man they weren't there to hurt him. Asked him if he cared to share his home. He spoke of simple things in a calm voice. He'd always had a knack for calming animals with a similar type of style, and he hoped some of that might rub off in the present situation. Words mattered less than the truth beneath them and the tone in which they rang.

Eventually, the man dipped his head in acknowledgment, with a still amused expression on his face. He indicated he would like to try talking and Leon nodded in agreement.

The man began his speech slowly, just like Leon had done a moment before. Only, now that his words were spoken slowly and intentionally, the nuance in his language rang beautiful and fluid. The words flowed effortlessly together in a soft poetic cadence.

As Leon listened, it was like a song emerged from within his speech. At first, he thought he might have heard the song before. Then, gradually, the pitch and cadence grew familiar. Finally, the words to the song made sense, like he had known them all along and just needed to be reminded!

The absurdity of the notion lasted only a moment before Leon realized the man talking about how dangerous it was to be traveling through those parts, "…would not have been good for you to have been out—"

"I know what you are saying! I can understand you." Leon stopped talking, his mouth moving like a fish out of water. Had he just spoken in that same fluid language?

Gasps of surprise behind him confirmed he was indeed conversing with the old man.

"But, of course, you can, young man. The question is, why aren't you all able to understand common Fayden, yes?" His cryptic smile told Leon the question was his to know and theirs to ponder.

Ben barged in before Leon could answer, speaking to Leon and directing him to translate, "I'm Ben Heegan, the leader of this expedition. I have many questions I would like you to answer."

It initially struck Leon dumbfounded that he suddenly knew a new language, but there was no time to split hairs. The language was so intuitive, it tumbled off his lips like he had known it his whole life. It was like something had finally clicked into place within his mind. The words came as natural to him as a breath of air. This was yet another mystery to attempt to sort through when time permitted. He translated for Ben.

Before he finished, the old man burst out in laughter. Gradually gaining control of himself he continued speaking to Leon, "This man takes himself very seriously, does he not?" A not-so-subtle wink told them all how seriously the man took Ben's requests.

He addressed the group as a whole, a twinkle shimmering in his eye, "My name is Ferschall, son of Grimm. Your names are yet to be learned, yes? Time is short and darkness is descending. I offer hospitality. Do you understand me?"

Leon shook his head no, but Ferschall ignored him, "Good, we are friends now! You friends are welcome to go on and use my home. Go, rest, refresh yourselves. What's mine is yours for this night. I'll be back later, and we will talk more? Yes? Good!" Leon quickly relayed the message.

Something doesn't feel right. Why would this stranger just give us the use of his house?

Before Leon could voice his concerns, Ferschall briskly stepped forward through the group. He stopped next to Ben. While leaning in conspiratorially and motioning Ben to do the same, he muttered loud enough for Leon to hear and translate once more, "Not too wise to have those pups running loose, you better keep them close. There's big bad trouble out tonight!" Then, right in Ben's face, he erupted in manic cackling laughter once more.

Once Leon finished conveying the message, Ben cursed a few lines that would make a Drill Sergeant blush as Ferschall slipped away into the night. However, it was Shana's comment that made Leon grin as he walked through the door into the warmth of a rustic cozy cottage. "That Ferschall guy has got to be nuts! I like him already!"

# # #

Marveling at the dry warmth of the cottage, Leon shook and stomped the cold from his waterlogged shoes. Outside the temperature still hadn't dropped to freezing, but the combo of chill and wet had taken their toll, and he was extremely thankful for the opportunity to trade the shivers for a dry seat next to a warm fire.

The dwelling's exterior was spartan. It was hewn of rough-cut native rock, with jagged corners and small slit windows. However, the interior carried an entirely different note. Wood trim walls and a drop-down bottom floor bolstered a wide open and welcoming layout that elicited feelings of cozy comfort. The large common area consisted of thick fur rugs over bedrock floors. Artistic designs were hand chiseled into the gray rock walls, and dark wood beam ceiling joists brought the room together. In addition, a well-crafted cave entrance against the far wall led directly into a one-bedroom nook, carved out from the cliff wall against which the cottage stood.

A fire gave off a warm glow as it licked at a few large chunks of ebony wood within a stone hearth, nestled comfortably in the corner. The crackle and pop of the flame would be a welcome balm to soothe frayed nerves when the time came to bed down.

No conventional chairs could be seen, but one chunky wooden boulder sat comfortably close to the fire. The wooden boulder's center was carved to fit the contours of a husky man's semi-resting form, similar to that of large, rounded, lazy boy recliner. Worn and battered arches spoke of years of wear. They lent a smooth, comfortable finish to the seat. Delicate carvings covered the coarse exterior with many of the same type of hieroglyphics observed on the path through the ruins.

However, Leon thought it was the pantry area, which held the most curious feature of all. Stacks of broken and repaired pottery containers rested in tidy piles beneath wood shelving and to the side of a rough, finished stone countertop. Leon picked up one of the repaired pieces and glanced at the intricate colors embedded within the sealed seam along the fractured grooves. The beauty of those colorful seams provided an artistic flair to otherwise unadorned dinnerware. It slowly dawned on him that the repaired shard fragments most definitely resembled some of the pieces he had observed littered about the ruins.

Merle was immediately at home. His sniffer worked overtime to cover all the items in his new domain before he made his customary three circles and plopped down near the fire.

Leon motioned for Shana to join him, "You think our Mr. Ferschall uses the ruins up above for all this pottery? Awfully odd hobby, isn't it?"

"That would make sense. Maybe he salvages this stuff to sell it later?"

They studied several of the repaired pieces and found a few older, nicer piles under some leather hides. Some even had worn symbols and hieroglyphics imprinted within them. Dust covered the pottery despite the thick leather coverings draped over them.

Reed offered his two cents as well, "Or maybe Ferschall's just a crazy old hermit with a thing for ceramics?"

Ben and his men didn't bother to stop and ponder Ferschall's vocational pursuits. They piled up the remnants of their relatively useless gear along one corner and scurried about the cottage, both inside and out, attempting to *secure* the premises.

Eventually, they managed to arm themselves when one of them uncovered several dozen short metal spears in a covered bundle beneath one of the windows. The palpable relief from all those hardened mercenaries at finding a few pointy sticks was comical to Leon and Shana. Leon was also pleasantly surprised to find Reed just as amused at all the Type-A hysterics. Unfortunately, the laughter from the kitchen area reminded Ben of the proverbial burr under his saddle.

"Leon! Get over here, now."

"Okay, what is it, Ben?"

"Don't give me that! I want to know what's going on with you. How do you know the local tongue? Who are you, boy?"

Leon shrugged. "Like I've said before, I don't have any memory from before Gus found me. I'm as surprised as the rest of you that I understand ole Ferschall. I know it seems impossible to fathom, but it's like I've always known the language and Ferschall speaking was all it took to jog my memory."

Ben gave him a long, hard look. "Fine, for now, maybe that's true, maybe you're hiding something. Either way, you are going to begin teaching us that language first thing tomorrow. Clear?"

"I can try." Leon rolled his eyes when he turned back to Shana and Reed.

Ben had his men direct the three of them, along with Merle, into the cave-looking room where they would be confined from mischief *for their own good*.

A few minutes later, one of the men, Griggs, supplied them with a dinner of MRE packets and a preciously small pint of water. The water did more to remind them they were thirsty than to quench their thirst, but they couldn't exactly complain. Until they found a fresh supply, they all had to stretch what they had brought. The three of them made pallets from some thick hides they found in the shadows against the far wall and bedded down for the night.

Once everything quieted down a bit, Leon posed a question that he'd puzzled over all day, "Reed, before I...left, Gus and Ethan both made something clear. They told me to take your Blade when you offered it, said both me and Shana needed to take it. Was this some type of coded message for you?"

It was too dark to see Reed's face, and he didn't say anything, didn't even move for a long while. Just when Leon assumed an answer wasn't coming, Reed spoke up, "It wasn't code. They meant just what they said. Only, it doesn't really make sense, people don't just *take up the Blade*."

"How come?"

"Well, in our world, our identity is extremely important. No one can know what we really are. That's why children aren't taught of their heritage until they are around your age. Then, once they know about the Blade, it takes years to master what you need to know to effectively wield it. I spent close to two years in training before I ever laid a finger on mine and, even still, I feel there's so much I don't know."

"But you only have one Blade, right? How would that even work for all three of us?"

Shana spoke up for the first time, "That's a mystery they don't seem willing to spread around. I've been told there are no new Blades available, but more initiates at the academy pop up with Blades each year. Yet the formerly Bladed instructors all retain theirs as well. Been puzzling over that little factoid for the past year and all I ever get is, 'you'll see.' Really though Reed, just tell him why we all need it, eventually."

"Fine. That, at least, I can do. You see, the Blade provides many different purposes. But the most important thing it does is to allow its wielder to ignore the compulsion to change shape on moonless nights."

"What? So, shifters don't change on the full moon?"

"Again, Leon, we aren't like those stereotypic characters from the movies. Although skin-changers can technically transition anytime, direct sunlight makes the transition extremely painful. Not to mention the eventual mental breakdown it creates.

"Anyone who's ever tried to subdue the effects of sunlight without the Blade is about as safe as a child playing with fire in a hayfield. An Unbladed's exposure to light during transition leads the mind down a wicked twisted path that the body soon follows. The point is, when you carry a Blade, your body doesn't demand that you change on moonless nights, it nullifies the effects of the disease in our blood, though there are some other individual perks as well."

"Great, so until I'm trained up enough to take up the Blade, I'll be stuck being forced to change into some sort of mystery monster on moonless nights? Or otherwise driven crazy by sunny days. Did

I tell you guys I felt a shock in the middle of the afternoon the other day? Am I already losing my mind?"

"Don't get your panties in a twist. Most young skin-changers don't fully transition into their full form until at least their twentieth birthday, and I've never heard of someone getting sun sickness during the transition period. Hopefully, we all find our way back long before—"

Shana interrupted him again, "But I turn twenty next month. So, you will begin helping us to prepare to take the Blade, just in case, right?"

"Yeah, yeah I suppose I can start to show you guys some stuff when things calm down. Now, I need to know something. How in the world do you know the Fayden language, Leon? No one has been back from our world to Fayden in centuries. But back home, in our world, that language supposedly died out over a hundred years ago!"

"I wasn't lying when I told Ben I have no idea! I don't understand any of this, much less the language stuff!"

Reed was quiet for a while before responding, "Fine, we better get some sleep while we still can."

Leon couldn't help himself. "Okay, but one more question. How come Merle was healed and so much of the metal didn't make it through the portal?"

Reed to a moment, then cautiously responded, "Those are two questions and I'm out of my depth when it comes to the question of healing, but I think the missing metal has something to do with the purity of the metals that disappeared. Alloys couldn't pass through for some reason, while more pure metal like the gold and the silver flask had no problem."

"And the Blade," Shana added.

"Sure, the Blade, too," Reed amended.

What in the world is his Blade made from if it's not an alloy?

Leon had never heard of a knife with any measure of durability that wasn't an alloy, but otherwise, Reed's theory kind of made sense. As he rolled over on his side and felt Merle flop down at his back, he reached down and pulled out the metal medallion Gus had given him. Apart from the items Reed had just mentioned, it was the only other metal item he knew of that made it through the portal. Unfortunately, the chain was gone. Only the medallion remained. He couldn't help but wonder at its purpose. Gus seemed to want him to keep it a secret, no matter what.

Sighing under the weight of so many new realizations, he tucked the medallion back down his britches and decided he would wait to study it more before he risked sharing it with his friends. Enough bombshells for one day. And regardless, he didn't feel ready to ask another question he wasn't ready to have answered. His head was already spinning with the information overload from the last day or two.

In the end, bone-tired muscles and a lack of sleep soon won out over racing thoughts. He drifted off to a tumultuous dream of feeding cattle that grew fangs while they chased him into a desert, and of a certain furry four-legged friend who leaped between them and him as they sought to run him down.

Chapter 7

A pounding echoed through the walls and between Leon's ears. It stopped briefly but returned even more forceful. He cracked an eye open and saw candlelight shining through the open archway. It took a moment for him to realize he wasn't in his room at the ranch.

The thought was even further punctuated by the voice of an annoyed woman, grumbling about her need for sleep. And any notion of a typical morning in Leon Waldman's life on the ranch completely shattered once he realized said woman had burrowed up against him, butt to back. It took a few seconds, but it all eventually fell into place. Merle nuzzled close and gave his face a lick as if to remind him he was there too.

Dang dog! Leave it to Merle to ruin a moment...even if it's not really a moment.

The knocking continued until one of the men in the main room gave a command and the door squealed open. Muffled voices could be heard afterward.

"Leon! Get out here!" Ben called out.

Leon gently shoved his four-legged friend aside and crept out of his pallet on the floor. He stretched the kinks out of his knotted back as he stood. His first thought was he really was going to have to do something about finding a softer place to sleep if he was gonna be there for an extended amount of time. His second thought reminded him of how much of a pansy that first thought made him sound.

By then, the voices coming from the main room were multiplying and the conversation's tone took an urgent turn. Reed was unsurprisingly absent.

He reached down and shook Shana until she swatted him away. He never took her for a grumpy morning person, but he'd never woken up next to her either. Both thoughts made him nervous, and he shuffled on into the main room before he gave her an opportunity to set him straight on any other assumptions he might have wrong.

He and Merle ducked out of the cave and stopped in the entryway.

Ferschall stood stone still, straddling an open doorway. His grizzled appearance struck a fearsome note in the candlelight. Gone was any hint of smirking humor in the man they met earlier that night.

The man named Gunther lay unconscious on the floor while Cooper hovered above him, checking vitals. Ben's red face punctuated a solid vein, throbbing on his forehead. The other two men held their metal spears out as if they were ready to skewer Ferschall if he made any sudden movement their direction.

"What is going on here?" Leon surprised himself by unconsciously speaking the question in his new language.

"Ask them!" Ferschall responded.

Leon conveyed the message and still, no one budged. After a moment, Cooper answered him without even bothering to look up from his work as he wrapped bandages around the man's head where an ear appeared to be partially gone, "What does it look like to you, Leon?"

The question was rhetorical. A bit of a soft reprimand for his speaking out of turn. Unfortunately, he still didn't savvy.

"How about someone help me understand?"

Reed pushed off a wall to Leon's right and spoke up, "I'll take a stab at an explanation."

He pointed to their seething leader and the fallen soldier at his feet, "Ben sent his two 'stooges' off to follow our benevolent host after he was specifically warned not to...these *elite* soldiers got in over their heads and Gunther there is lucky Mr. Ferschall even bothered to bring him home. That about sum it up Ferschall, son of Grimm?"

After Leon relayed Reed's assertion, Ferschall nodded appreciatively at the young man. But Ben snapped back before Ferschall could respond, "Those two *stooges* as you put it are special forces combat veterans who specialize in stealth RECON boy, and I won't have you patronize them while one is still bleeding on the floor! Their training, combined with their unique stalking ability, has afforded them a dam near undetectable presence on over forty combat zones on some of the most dangerous conflicts throughout our world." Ben glared up to meet Ferschall's somber gaze. He motioned for Leon to translate, "These men are warriors of great skill. I say the only way anyone got the drop on them was if someone led them into a trap…"

And there it was, the reason for the tension. The accusation hung stagnant in the air for all to taste as Leon reluctantly provided the translation.

Leon watched Ferschall closely for any tell he might give. Yet, he gave them nothing as he once more searched the faces throughout the room.

That man could be one heck of a poker player if given half a chance.

Finally, when Leon thought the tension might boil over, Ferschall responded, with a severe scowl, "I did not betray your men, Ben Heegan. Perhaps you are mistaken in your estimation of their skill, yes? These men move quietly, but not stealthily. Their scent was not completely quiet. They did not keep to the dark shadows but, instead, skirted arrogantly through brighter paths.

"I was heading inland and upwind, to secure a small herd of mountain goats. To bring one back. To feed your group!

"By the time I noticed they followed, they were already under attack. I turned back to help them, yes? By the time I reached them, the Hootsi had claimed them." It took Leon a little while, but he eventually got the message across to the rest of the men in the room.

"Well, what are all these spears doing here?" Ben asked, still refusing to concede his suspicion.

Ferschall responded through Leon, "Weapons are basic currency to the Hootsi. You want a meal, you trade a weapon—you want a wife, you trade many. Nothing is for free in these lands. I've had peace with the local Hootsi clan for many years, but because I offered you hospitality it was my *honor* to save your men. This man I was able to wrestle from their clutches, the other was already taken. I did not escape unscathed, yes?"

He proudly exposed his right arm pulling back a wet sleeve. Leon whistled before relaying the rest of the message. Ferschall had clearly been clawed by a paw large enough to cover most of his large, muscular forearm. The men holding the spears lowered them a bit at the sight of those mangled claw marks.

Cooper glanced up and mumbled something about needing to take a look at that afterward.

Ben let out a long sigh and his shoulders lost some of the tension they had been holding. "You're not lying, are you? Who are these Hootsi? Are they the ones who persecuted the Bladed ages ago? Or are these aggressors a small village tribe? If so, can we beat them?"

When Leon finished translating, Ferschall ran an exasperated hand over his face and chuckled deeply, a bit of that original mania from the night before seeping back into his countenance, "Easy now. We need to sit down and talk. The sun has not yet risen and yet we have much to do. Come sit, let's draw water and boil porridge, yes?"

Leon gave the invitation, then added, "I'm starving. How about you all pony up some coffee as well?" Ben scowled back in response.

# # #

Gunther awoke shortly after Cooper finished patching him up. He was also able to validate Ferschall's explanation. No one walked on eggshells anymore, and Leon was eager to hear whether Ferschall could provide some clarity.

The rich smell of an oat grain porridge and freshly brewed coffee inundated the dwelling, its steamy fragrance enticing enough to draw a certain sleeping beauty out from her cave.

As their meal progressed, Leon marveled that Shana was able to transition so quickly from a stoic grump to her cheery confident self as soon as her spoon hit the porridge. She didn't even seem to need the coffee. Merle was offered some bones from the soup the night before, and he made short work of them while the others enjoyed their breakfast.

Once they all had a chance to savor their porridge and coffee, Ferschall alone retained a look of disgust. Their appreciation for the bitter drink baffled him. He spit it out on his first try.

Eventually, he broke the ice. "There are many things about this area you are not knowledgeable of, yes? Will you allow me to give some advice?"

Ben nodded for Ferschall to continue after Leon's translation.

"The Hootsi are not merely a *village* of people, per se, they are a remnant from an entire race of people. One of the original seven tribes to be exact. This is their land. I live here at their mercy." He paused to let those facts sink in while Leon did his work, then continued. "The years have been good to me, no?" He fluffed his beard and brushed a calloused hand across a worn-out leather bracer as he cackled to himself. Then, he looked around to see if his humor resonated.

When he could tell it didn't, he moved on, "No matter, the point is there are many who will be coming." This got Ben's attention and Ferschall leaned forward in a sinister smile. "Coming for us I mean! There is no way for us to get your man back right now." When Leon's translation drew gasps of anger, Ferschall held up a finger to stall protests, "But old Ferschall knows where to go to get him later. So, perhaps you want to go there with me to get him, yes?"

After a moment, Ben shrugged. "Okay, I'll bite, ask him where we go, Leon."

"North. The Hootsi trade the captives of the North Fang's Kingdom for their own captives once a year. Your man will be sent to North Fang's Capitol, Hollinger, just before fall harvest."

"How long from now till then?" Ben leaned back and stared daggers at Ferschall while he waited on Leon to finish.

"The northern migrations are just now beginning. You have two new moons, maybe longer, no?" Ferschall's strange penchant for ending statements with questions wore on Leon. Although, as a favor to Ferschall, he left them out as he translated.

"Why would they even think he's of this North Fang Kingdom?"

Ferschall looked back at him as if he had made a joke until he realized he hadn't. His eyes narrowed, and he responded slowly, like talking to a slow-witted child, "Because he's of Wolf tribe heritage."

Leon asked the question he assumed all of those in the room were wondering at that moment, "Then what heritage are the Hootsi?"

"They are from the tribe of the Great Cat."

"So, that makes you…?"

Ferschall scowled in frustration, "Your ally, until I decide differently, no?" He mumbled something about polite etiquette before turning back to Ben. "Now, it's my turn to raise a few questions, yes? Where are you from?"

Ferschall held up a hand to stop anyone from speaking as soon as Leon finished relaying the request, "Before you answer, know that I have a hunch, I just want to hear it from one of you, personally."

Shana butted in between bites for the first time, "We came through that massive tree in the ruins above, from another world."

Ben shot her a look that had her staring back down into her bowl before she said another word. Even so, he wasn't fast enough to stop Leon from conveying the message.

Ferschall leaned back, stroking his long beard. A small measure of relief softened the hard edges on his worn face. "It has happened then! It is as I suspected, yes? Regardless, even if your friend could be with you now, where would you go?"

Ben leaned forward. "You know of the Royal Trees?"

"I know enough, yes? Mainly just whispers of rumors passed down from generations before my time. I know to leave that tree alone. Your people, your ancestors were the brave voyagers thought to be lost to us for many years, until one day a man simply returned through one of the ancient trees. He claimed to be from another existence, from a world outside our own."

"What happened?"

Ferschall casually lifted a spoon to his mouth and spoke around the porridge, "Him? He was put to death."

"That's it?" Ben was losing patience between Leon's gasping efforts to keep up.

"Umhmm." Ferschall finished chewing, "Those were dark days, no? Several hundred years ago. No darker than these, but different. Our leaders, our rulers, have grown better at pretending not to be the beasts they truly are."

Reed chimed in next. "Well, the tree doesn't look like it will be taking us anywhere anytime soon. The bark is shot. The whole thing looks dead."

Once Ferschall received the news, his head jerked up. "Impossible! How are you here if the tree has withered?"

Leon knew the response was rhetorical, but he relayed it anyway and Ben answered, "We followed what we were led to believe was an accurate method for opening a path to get here. There were two other trees on our side, why aren't they standing beside the tree here?"

"I suspect those on your side are simply seedlings from three of the ancient Royals here on this side."

"Where are the other Royal Trees then?"

"I don't know. Their locations here have been long since lost to the ages. I only know of this tree in this ruin because this is where some of my ancestors lived, many, many generations back. There are ruins like these all across the remnant of the ancient boundaries of the seven tribes in Fayden. Your trees could be lost for good or standing forgotten and alone, just about anywhere, no? Most believe what you have done to be myth and exaggeration…but not me!" He beamed back up at them from an empty bowl. Bits of porridge stuck to his whiskers, making a mess of his beard.

Ben groaned at the grinning lunatic staring expectantly back at him. "You mean to tell us there is no way to find the location of those trees?"

"Perhaps, yes? There may be one out there who knows their location." he vaguely motioned outside his house.

Ben gnashed his teeth and glared at Leon, like he was somehow responsible for the message. "Out where?"

"Out there, far away…Maybe we will find your answers at the Bladed archives in Hollinger, yes?"

Ben finally nodded as if he had come to a decision. "It's settled then, we travel to Hollinger. Ferschall, how about it? You said they would be coming for you too. Can you be our guide? We don't have much to compensate you, but perhaps we can reach an agreement?"

Leon remembered all the gold that had made it through and frowned at Ben. Eventually though, Ferschall nodded his acceptance, "It just so happens I need three strong backs to help carry my most valuable pieces from several years' worth of work restoring pottery, yes? Would you be willing to share my load along the way?"

Ben smiled a genuine smile as he motioned toward Leon, Shana, and Reed, "I suspect these three will be just perfect for the job. I can assure you they will have no complaints about pulling their weight to ensure they help to find a ticket home." He slapped Leon on the back in a playful gesture, but a dark look passed across his face as he turned to look each of them in the eye, daring anyone to contradict his decision. Leon thought twice before relaying Ben's response, but eventually gave in to the glare in the man's eye.

"Great, it's settled then, no? Let's get moving as we have much to do if we are to be loaded up and across the border by night."

"How far is the border?"

"Not far, not far. We must travel inland before we travel north, yes? It will be a close call, but we should be able to make it there before nightfall. Otherwise, we will be hunted and killed by many Hootsi. No doubt the word has spread, and they will be preparing for a fight."

"There is no way to reason with them?" Leon asked.

"Ha-haha hehe," Ferschall cackled," No! Not after what I did to free your friend last night. They will fight us all to the last man, then maybe ask questions later, yes? Only enemies honorably captured, are ransomed in Hollinger. Others, who surrender, are made slaves, or are executed as punishment for such dishonor. It is their way, no?"

Shana stopped Leon before he could give Ferschall's last line, "Why exactly would there be Wolf Tribe people down here on Hootsi territory?"

Ferschall scrunched up his nose as if the answer tasted bad in his mouth, "Why not? They're mostly slavers and bandits that come here, they take men, women, children, and loot, yes?"

"And I'm assuming the Hootsi do the same? That is why they trade prisoners each year?" she continued.

Leon smacked his forehead once the reality of the situation dawned on him, but Ferschall answered somberly, "Hootsi don't trade for their own warriors. Those Hootsi men unlucky enough to be captured have dishonored the tribe and are banished, yes? Hootsi always attempt to trade for the women and young ones of their tribe who have been taken. The gathering at Hollinger every fall is the one time of year there is a truce between all Tribal Kingdoms."

"And yes, they raid as well. Though their raids are blood raids, meant to visit vengeance on those who dare attempt to take from them. So, all the more reason to hurry, yes? We must cross the ancient border quickly…especially because of her." His eyes fell at last on Shana.

"Why her?" Leon asked.

"Leaving Hootsi lands with a woman in hand is a crime punishable by death, yes? All more reason to conceal her before we leave."

D.N. Woodward

Chapter 8

The mid-day's sun cast rippled shadows over miles of wide-open canyons through a patchwork sky of cotton clouds. The previous day's haze had been washed away and Leon continued to marvel at the rough, arid scenery surrounding him.

For Leon, the rocky landscape's distant profile sparked memories of the old cinematic westerns he had been forced to endure at Gus' side for years. Yet on closer inspection, rugged exposed hillsides of red granite outcroppings were peppered with the foreign sheen of deep sapphire and purple tinged mineral deposits.

Even more surprising were the clusters of trees that had resembled tiny oases along the shoreline the night before. Instead of the swaying palms he expected to encounter on their path, Leon found those hamlets were actually comprised of giant thick-barked trees, more reflective of some Jurassic era scene from a science book than the tranquil Mediterranean palms he had expected to encounter. They were grouped in small circles, and their massive canopies swayed hypnotically in the morning breeze as he and his companions marched inland.

Leon mentally paused in his appreciation of the new scenery. He realized that, while zoned out on the sights below, he had momentarily forgotten the grudge he carried against Ben and his merry band of mercenary thugs. The prior moments notion, that they were his companions, forced him to consider something undeniable. He would need to continue to rely on Ben and his men for survival, and Ben's crew would likewise probably need Leon and, by extension, his friends to help them if any of them were likely going to make it home. They were, for better or worse, all in it together.

In any case, Leon was thankful Ben's men temporarily traded him and Shana the heavy pottery packs Ferschall intended them to carry. Despite the fact that they were all loaded down with Ferschall's stash of spears, the lighter, less encumbering backpacks they received in return contained a few useful remnants of scavenged gear. Ferschall's packs looked sturdy enough, but they were laden down with mountains of pottery and certainly weren't made for a swift hike over the jagged foothills they were ascending.

Despite the fact that Leon couldn't quite get a bead on why Reed could be such an arrogant turd at times, Leon's estimation of him increased considerably when the Blade carrying grump shrugged off Ben's offer to have one of his men carry his gear as well. Much to Leon's surprise, Reed proceeded to hoist that bulky pack across his shoulders. In fact, he then took off near the head of the party, easily matching the pace of their special forces' escorts.

Leon was also thankful Ferschall had provided a supple leather skinned tunic to wear over some type of thin woven fabric before they left. It was trimmed with a thick leather belt. His cross-country shoes and hat definitely gave the group cause to laugh after he finished his wardrobe upgrade, but he was happy to at least be comfortable once more. The new threads were certainly warm, even if they did make him feel a bit like an Arab Viking. The best part was he now had a hidden pocket for Gus' medallion.

Even with the lighter packs, the pace they kept was grueling. It was more than a bit humbling for someone who cut his teeth on manual ranch labor and made a hobby out of long distance running to realize he was completely out of his depth with those around him.

Leon glanced back at Shana. She appeared to be in amazing shape, but, in general, she wasn't doing any better than him. Her head pointed down as she trudged up the hill behind him. She had been clothed in a similar wardrobe to his, and he couldn't see her facial expression due to the hood Ferschall insisted she wear to hide her hair and face, but Leon could clearly hear her panting and grunting as she struggled to climb the last few feet.

He moved toward the front of the pack, "How much longer are we going to keep this pace?"

Ben answered, "Until we are safely across that border."

Leon frowned, "Fine, but we need a break soon. Just a moment to regroup. Maybe get a bit of water?"

Walking nearby, Ferschall motioned for him to translate and Leon obliged. "Yes, yes, but first, let's get off the top of this hill."

The surged over and down into the next canyon. Ferschall led them to a shady area and told them to rest for a few moments while he scouted around.

Shana looked up at Leon and smiled conspiratorially, "Thanks, I'm sure you could have kept going for quite some time."

Leon smiled back. "Ha, glad I had you fooled then. They must feed you guys some heavy-duty Wheaties at that school of yours I don't remember you being such a trouper."

She smiled back. "It's been a few years Leon, there's a lot of things I bet you don't remember about me."

Leon was sure Shana meant the comment to come across innocently, but he couldn't help it, he blushed. Was she flirting with him, or just giving him a hard time? It had always been so hard to tell with her.

Shana winked in good humor and continued, "Wish I could take credit. The truth is our bodies go through lots of changes the closer we get to the full change-mode. The rest of these guys are probably grinding their teeth we aren't another few miles down the road by now. If they're built anything like some of the instructors I know, they could keep this up for hours. I bet they've still got a ton of gas left in the tank."

Leon didn't say anything as he took his turn chugging water. What would he be able to do once he became whatever it was he was supposed to become? The question was certainly exciting to ponder. A bit frightening too if he turned out anything like Ben and his men.

Ferschall returned after a few minutes.

"We have shadows on our tail."

When Leon gave the news, Ben and his men jumped to their feet. "Where?" Ben demanded.

"Relax, calm yourselves, no sense in letting them know we know they are here, no? Besides, they won't attack until the sun dips over the last hill, unless we give them a very good reason. This is one of their honor traditions, they are a very…sporting…people, yes?" He gave a pointed look at Ben, waiting for Leon to catch up, "We simply have to move peacefully, at a brisk pace, and we should be to the border bridge in time. We can re-evaluate once we are across."

A few more hours passed them by before anyone caught a glimpse of their pursuers. The first sighting occurred just after they turned North, while taking a path through a narrow, twisting series of canyons. Leon heard Cooper gasp beside him and followed his hollow-eyed stare to the cliffs above them. There, his eyes met something his mind told him didn't seem possible.

Leaning out from within the shade of an extended rock outcrop a bare-chested, darkly-tanned man stood, still as a statue. He leaned against an even larger mottled-black cat. The man held a short spear, similar to those from Ferschall's house. He was obviously a warrior. Even had he not been armed, Leon would have known it instinctively on some level.

He wore no beard, but short brown hair stuck up above his head. His body was lean and chiseled, scarred, and sculpted to mirror the arid landscape around them. The cat at his side was the size of a small quarter-horse. Leon couldn't be sure, but he swore the cat wore a saddle and harness of some type.

The warrior's impassive face gazed stoically down at them all. Half his face was covered in dark, swirling war paint that swept down across his chest. He held a long thin spear, similar to the ones Ben's men found in Ferschall's cabin the night before.

Slowly the group came to a halt as they all glanced up to catch their first glimpse of their pursuer. Ferschall, at the head of the party, turned around at the audible chorus of their combined gasps.

"Hmmphh. Are you all planning on feeding his pride till his neck can't carry his head, or are you interested in making it to that border? Young Dimple's needs more self-confidence like I need another bag of pottery, yes? Now move!" he continued on, grumbling incoherently.

"He says not to worry about that guy," Leon conveyed to the group.

Leon reached back and gave Shana's arm a gentle squeeze. But his gesture went unnoticed, and his hackles rose just a hair as he observed her cheeks were flushed while she stood gawking up at the young Hootsi. They picked up the pace once more. He hurried to catch up to Ferschall. "You know that man?"

"Of course, I do, he's First Warrior of the local Hootsi sect. Got his name as a joke because he so rarely smiles. Personally, I have no idea if he actually has a pair of dimples...as I've never seen him smile." Ferschall smiled encouragingly at his attempt at humor and shrugged when it didn't stick.

"What sort of man rides a giant cat?"

"The sort that doesn't like to walk, yes? He's not a bad fellow most of the time, but not someone any sane person would tangle with either." At that Ferschall let loose one of his irritating cackles. It bounced off the canyon walls and caused Ben to glance back in irritation.

"I'm mostly sure he's the Tom who gave me these fancy new scars last night." He lifted a bandaged arm to demonstrate his point.

Leon fell back in the pack to his position beside Shana and Cooper. How could their group, lightly armed as they were, hope to fend off seasoned warriors mounted atop some type of war cat the size of a full-grown horse?

An unsolicited answer came screaming back from those cliffs high above. The mid-day's stillness was broken by the high-pitched blood curdling roar of a giant panther. Leon had to yell at Merle to hush as he attempting to respond in kind and came up a little short.

"You're just embarrassing yourself boy. A desperado like that would have eaten Geronimo and all his renegade Apache warriors for breakfast!"

The plodding pace ate the day away. The hills grew higher with every mile they traveled until Leon saw mountains in the distance, further north by northwest. They were encased in shadow and smoke with definite hints of volcanic activity.

It didn't help the morale that there were several more sightings of Hootsi warriors perched above their trail, lazily resting along cliff walls, watching them with cat-like smugness, but it did provide a sort of motivation that quickened their pace as a group.

To that point, only three enormous cats of varying earth tone colors accompanied the warriors. None of them attacked, they simply stared down with a casual disdain as the group passed below.

Leon knew the odds of making it in time would be close, but onward was the only answer he had. So, he put on his best game face. He dug deep. He encouraged Shana when she grew tired. He leaned into his work and the miles sped by as they raced the sinking sun.

# # #

At last, everyone made their way up a small rise and peered over to catch their first glimpse of their destination. Leon couldn't help but feel a bit deflated. An abandoned and crumbling stone bridge stood above a wide rift in the valley's floor. He could just make out the rushing roar of a fast-moving river below the bridge.

The land on the opposite side of the river was just as empty and desolate as the Hootsi's side seemed to be. The divide certainly didn't look to hold much significance, though Ferschall assured them all that no serious offense had been committed and the Hootsi would not pursue them across the border without a very good reason.

Leon turned to help Shana up the crumbling trail behind him. She saw him extend his hand and glanced up to take it. Just as her eyes left the trail, the rocks below her shifted. Leon could only watch as a horrified expression of panic flashed across her face. Her eyes locked with his. She windmilled momentarily in mid-air before tumbling backwards.

His heart erupted in an electric pulse and his hand shot out to grasp her coat, but fast as he was, she was already beyond his reach. The effort dropped him to a knee in momentary agony as the day's waning light dug furrows into his eyes.

She rolled back down the hillside a good twenty feet before coming to a stop on her back. The rest of the group rushed to the edge to check the commotion.

As she struggled to sit up, she reassured everyone, "It's okay, guys. Really, I'm fine. Those stinking rocks are slick though!"

"Up! Get up, Shana! Run! All of you run for the bridge! Go!"

Ferschall's voice held the first notes of panic Leon had yet heard him utter. He shouted the instructions to the others.

Looking down at Shana, the reason for Ferschall's change in demeanor washed over his mind. Her hood was lost in the tumble. She stood, a tall unmistakable feminine silhouette against the hill. Long dark hair billowing out behind her in the evening breeze. Their prior misdirection would be obvious now for any Hootsi watching closely.

Ferschall urged them all again, "Go! Go! Go!!"

This time there was no need for translation. Understanding dawned on everyone at once. A couple of the men near the front took off for the bridge.

Leon shouted down, "Come on Shana, we have to go."

She clamored back up the hill in a few more seconds. Alongside Leon, Cooper, Ferschall, Reed, and surprisingly Ben, were still there to meet her at the top of the hill.

No one said a word, they all turned and sprinted for the bridge together. Merle quickly moved to the front of the pack as they tore toward the finish line.

Back behind them, Leon could hear the rising wailing cries of wildcats screaming into the wind. Their earlier taunts carried long aggressive notes of dominance, likely meant to intimidate. These screams exuded violent fury. They were short, piercing, and angry.

The two men who took off first, quickly made it to safety across the bridge. Leon estimated his group had another two hundred yards to go. The others were holding back to keep pace with him and Shana.

Then, seemingly out of nowhere, Leon spotted a Hootsi mounted on a great cat. He simply popped up ahead of them, moving parallel to the rift and converging on them from the right side of the bridge. He called Merle to his side to prevent the dog from confronting one of the cats, with whom he was woefully over-matched.

Leon could only continue to pump his legs, eyes forward, not daring to look behind to see who pursued them. Ferschall's legs were spry for an old man, with his long stride he remained out in front with Ben. Without slowing he reached behind his back and pulled out one of two metal spears he carried. Then he grabbed the second and tossed it to Ben. Ben caught the spear and flicked an arm in acknowledgment.

Ferschall shouted his instructions to Leon, who quickly divulged them to Ben, "Cover the group from behind, when you get to the bridge. If you must strike, aim for the riders, not the cats."

Focusing on their wild sprint while keeping a close eye on Shana took most of Leon's concentration, but the scene in his periphery held an otherworldly quality so surreal he couldn't help but to continue snatching little looks while racing along.

The rider came sprinting in from their right, at least twice as far as them from the bridge, but his ruddy feline mount was lightning quick and closing fast. They would all make it at about the same time.

When Leon glanced over again, Ferschall started angling away from the group, toward the rider. He veered to the right, ahead of the others. Once in position to intercept the rider he stopped and jabbed his spear down into the ground beside him. Leon rushed by with Shana and the others but not before he saw the rider and cat slow from a sprint to a stalking approach to meet the old man who stood between the two parties.

The bridge may have appeared crumbly from the hills above, but it was massive. There was plenty of room for them all to safely surge across. At the halfway point, Leon slowed down and turned to see how Ferschall was doing. Ben turned as well.

The light of the setting sun partially blinded their ability to fully appreciate the scene before them, but it was a forlorn conclusion that their group would soon be overrun. In addition to the rider facing off against Ferschall, at least two dozen more were pouring up and over the last hill. Ben turned and began barking orders to his men, something about suiting up. Someone tossed him more spears.

Leon remained firmly planted where he stood, gripping Merle's collar, watching the scene as it played out before him. Ferschall's adversary dismounted and approached him in a crouched stoop. He clutched a long, curved sword comfortably in his hands.

Ferschall drew his blade and, to Leon's eyes at least, it cast a much longer shadow than it should have. The men saluted one another and initiated a single combat demonstration of martial skill, too fast and furious for an amateur's eye to follow.

What was obvious was that Ferschall moved with surprising speed and agility, like being pushed and pulled up by an unseen wind. He made impossible twists and dips, barely missing being mortally wounded in several instances by the warrior he faced. Yet he held back and pulled his swings when opportunities to strike crippling blows presented themselves.

The other Hootsi were no longer closing in on the bridge. They appeared to have intentionally stopped at exactly where they were when the two adversaries began their duel. A few reared back and tossed their metal javelin's. Metal spears struck within mere feet of Ferschall while he fought, likely in an attempt to distract the older man. It was a testament to their skill and accuracy that no one came close to hitting either of the two as they battled.

Ben gave Leon a nudge. "Here, take this." He handed him a spear. "If things go south, I don't believe a man should be left to face a battle without a weapon in his hands, even a *new guy* like you."

Leon considered the offer a moment before taking the spear.

Reed stepped up on Leon's left, gently shaking his head from side to side in disbelief as he too watched the fight. A moment later, Ferschall flicked his Blade through the parrying-defense of his opponent. The longer sword of the Hootsi shattered in two. All motion ceased and the man gingerly dipped his head to expose his neck in defeat.

To Leon's surprise, Ferschall cackled in laughter before belting out loud enough everyone in the vicinity to hear, "Mighty Hootsi warrior! I will not dishonor myself with your blood. It was my honor to dual with you, no? Though I prevail, you have caused blood to flow from my sword arm." He held up his injured arm. Leon guessed that the dressing had come undone during the fight, but the blood from the re-torn wound dripped to validate his point.

Ferschall continued, "I ask a boon!"

The warrior responded in disbelief, but quickly regained his composure and bellowed his response "Ask your boon, son of Grimm."

"Might I have time to heal in order to more fully give honor to my grandmother's heritage before we conclude our struggle?"

The warrior turned back toward his allies in deference. Of all of them, only one other Hootsi was mounted, he and his dark steed stood much closer than the others. Leon couldn't quite be certain, but from the sheer bulk of the cat he rode it seemed he was the First Warrior they had seen that day, the one Ferschall called Dimples.

Dimples dismounted and slightly bowed in Ferschall's direction. He then proceeded to throw up the peace sign. He beat his chest, pointed at them all, and threw it up again. Finally, he pulled out a knife and cut a small streak across his painted chest, above his heart. Ferschall, for his part, repeated the gesture back to the man, with the exception of the self-mutilation. Leon thought about throwing up a peace sign as well, but wisely decided against it.

Ferschall turned without another look back and slowly walked toward Ben, Leon, and Reed. As he approached, he spoke roughly. "This isn't a staring contest, children, let's get some distance between us and this border, yes? Things aren't over. That fight just bought us a two-day head start. Once two days have passed twice our number will cross the river and a Hootsi blood hunt will begin."

Ben stepped forward and stopped him," Before you fought that man, you put aside your spear. Why?"

Leon's explanation seemed to anger Ferschall as he replied, "Honor. One spear, one man. It was a challenge for man-to-man combat. No other Hootsi could interfere, and I prayed you all were smart enough to know not to make any stupid moves, yes? It was a risk, but it paid off well enough."

Leon sputtered and blurted out, "Why didn't you just tell them Shana wasn't taken? You had their full attention! We could have straightened out this whole misunderstanding!"

Ferschall's sidelong glance had a frosty glare. "You have much to learn Leon. I told them as much and more when I issued my challenge. Had I died, or killed my challenger, you would have all been free to go. As it is, I chose a different path. One we will all travel together."

After Leon managed to explain the nature of the struggle, Ben spat back with contempt, "From now on, while you travel with us, you will inform me before you make decisions which affect our collective path! Do I make myself clear?" Ferschall's amused nod a few moments later seemed to appease the irate leader.

"Now let's get moving further north and away from this bridge. I don't care what those savages promise, I want a defensible position before we bed down this evening."

Chapter 9

The next morning, Leon awoke well before the sun. One of Ben's men, Jace, was up as well, his back to camp, patrolling the shrouded landscape beyond. He glanced over his shoulder at the small commotion, but quickly turned to resume his position when he saw Leon's familiar leathers. Everyone else remained soundly asleep. Leon ventured off to the edge of camp to take care of some morning business, though he dared not wander off too far.

When he returned, Ferschall was there, hovering above a small fire, working to stoke a flame he had somehow produced during the short time Leon was gone.

Once the fire grew, its kindling crackling sufficient to his liking, Ferschall adjusted a wooden stake, holding thin strips of meat, above the blaze. They hissed and sizzling quietly above the smoldering heat.

"You actually had the time and energy to go hunting this morning?" asked Leon.

"I did."

Leon studied the man as he took a seat close by. Ferschall's calloused hands and wrinkled brow told a story of a life lived hard. Lines crossed with scars in many places, but he was convinced that, for a silver headed old man, Ferschall could still go toe-to-toe with just about anyone he'd ever met, present company included.

"Any idea how much farther we are from a town or a city?"

Ferschall studied the fire for a long time before answering. "Many more days. I had hoped to move slowly. To catch a large caravan to the east. Now, perhaps we should reconsider, yes?"

Leon rubbed his hands together over the fire, "So, what are the options?"

"We move northwest and skirt those Anderle mountains you saw in the distance yesterday, continuing up around the silent forest, until we make it far enough north to intersect the Brindle River. Or we can move northeast and hope to join up with a traveling caravan heading north."

"What about directly North?"

Ferschall grimaced. "There dwells a truly savage nation, hostile to all who venture too near her borders. The Vin do not welcome any within their forests. Even those of the North Fang Kingdom steer clear."

"Well, which of the other two routes is the safest then?"

Ferschall looked up at him for the first time. "These are Fayden lands son, there are no truly *safe* routes? Only decisions which lead to consequences, yes?"

Leon grabbed a small stick and fed bits of it into the fire as he broke it into smaller and smaller pieces. "Okay, so what do you recommend we do?"

Ferschall studied him thoughtfully "I recommend you all take up a Blade and begin preparing to use it."

Ben stepped quietly from the shadows, "I don't think I like you two conspiring together. Tell me what the old goat is saying boy."

When Leon summarized the conversation, Ben gave a throaty chuckle, "Even here, after all that has happened to our people, such superstitious madness remains! Listen Sensei, I hate to disrupt your little moment with Grasshopper, but he had a point that I'd like you to answer a bit more directly. Which way do you recommend we go?"

After Leon translated, Ferschall cleared his throat, "I believe we should head for the mountains."

"Why?" Ben gripped a small stick, stoking the flames with the short end as he waited on Leon between statements. His question was clear.

"The Hootsi won't venture very close to the cliffs that run along the edge of those mountains. They won't pursue us if we stick to the game trails along the base. It will be a much longer route, and there is an arid climate to contend with, but that route gradually curves north, avoiding the Still Forest. Further north, we will eventually make it to a place where you can ride the river down to Hollinger, yes?"

"How long?"

"Maybe…by the time your friend arrives."

"What could possibly be their reason for just giving up?"

"The Hootsi?" Leon interrupted to get Ben to clarify.

"Yes, the Hootsi"

Leon relayed the question, "Many of the beasts that live in those passes are…challenging. But one creature in specific will target their mounts as a threat to its territory." At their blank expressions, Ferschall continued to explain, "*A Hootsi leader who allows his mount to die in service to him is no longer a Hootsi man, yes?*"

Ferschall quoted the last line like a well-known saying. Leon couldn't imagine what sort of creature could easily take out one of those giant cats, but he by no means wanted to meet one any time soon.

Ben continued the discussion. "That honor system of theirs can't be healthy for the general population."

It took a few minutes for Leon to find the right words to convey *general population*, but he eventually succeeded, "In a sense, you are right. There are far fewer Hootsi than those of the Wolf Clans to the north. There are also far fewer great cats than men to ride them. Yet, honor makes the Hootsi much more dangerous in many ways as well, yes?"

"And the danger on the eastern route?"

"It's a gamble, there should be caravans moving through this time of year, but will we meet one in time? Do you really want to risk your life and the lives of your companions on a throw of bones?"

Against his better judgment at not exactly knowing what they might face in the mountains, Leon chimed in his support for Ferschall, "Ben, this is a no brainer. We didn't see any sign of caravans yesterday, and we covered all that ground between here and the ocean."

"Repeat that to the old man, just like you asked me."

Leon did as requested, and Ben turned to face Ferschall. When it was clear Ferschall had nothing to add Ben answered. "We didn't see anyone because the caravans will be coming from further east, won't they Ferschall?"

"But—"

"That wasn't an ocean's shoreline grasshopper, that was a lake. Big moon, big waves, right, Ferschall?" Then, more to himself, he continued, "However, I find it more interesting that Sensei here just let the two of us go on thinking it was an ocean."

Leon tried to soften the blow in translation, but Ferschall ignored the insinuation, "I admit, I don't like the idea of making a race for the caravan route, but if that is the direction you wish to take, I will go along, yes? We are in this together."

"How reassuring." A bit more than a touch of skepticism crept into Ben's voice.

Soon the others were awake, and everyone helped themselves to Ferschall's roasted skewers. As the sun's first rays peaked over the horizon, Leon and Shana shouldered the packs originally meant for them. Ben's men needed the ability to move should anything else decide to attack their group.

Surprisingly, despite their size and weight, Ferschall's packs were well made and fit their backs comfortably. Each pack was outfitted with thick leather straps built to be tied securely around their waist to balance out the bulk of the weight on the shoulders.

Once again, the morning breeze lent a cool, invigorating touch. It blew in from the north with a cool herbal fragrance and seemed to carry away some of the soreness from their aching limbs as they packed up and set out.

The sunrise itself coalesced in a beautiful display of golds and pinks, smeared across a partially clouded sky to the east. Once the sun rose beyond the hills, Leon could see the terrain changing. Deciduous trees, more similar to large hickory hardwoods he had known back on earth, were present in patches here and there. There were fewer rocks and more grass as well. Even the hills took a more rounded, less jagged shape.

The group traveled further north for several more miles.

"Leon, I want you right here next to me. From now on consider yourself the language teacher for the whole group. I'm going to give a word and you're going to give the Fayden equivalent. We are going to keep doing this, day in and day out, until we all know enough to converse adequately. Understood?" What point was there in answering? His agreement was implicit.

Eventually, around mid-day, Ferschall drew them to a halt. "Ben, this is where we must make a decision. We can either go west to those smoking mountains there in the distance, or we can head northeast through those hills till we come to the lowlands where the caravans travel. Once again, I recommend we head to the mountains, yes?"

Ben studied Ferschall for a long moment. Reed shifted uncomfortably, grumbling under his breath over why Ben continued to deliberate on such straightforward advice from someone solely responsible for getting them as far along as they were. Only Leon truly understood the dubious countenance Ben held, as he studied their native friend and ally.

"We go east."

Ferschall didn't say a word to contradict his decision when Leon made it known. He shrugged in deference, gave a good-natured nod to demonstrate his acquiescence, and turned the group east.

Leon watched Ben as Ben watched Ferschall. At Ferschall's calm and respectful acceptance of Ben's decision, the muscles in Ben's cheek twitched. It was a momentary glimpse into what Leon assumed was some serious second guessing on Ben's behalf

Regardless, the decision was made, and their path was set.

# # #

Two more nights passed as Leon and his companions continued their pursuit of a north-bound caravan along the eastern route. Once they reached packed earth indicative of past caravan trails, Ferschall steered the group north, hopeful they would see some type of large procession very soon.

To Leon, it all looked like pristine grasslands with small hardwood groves clustered along shallow creek bottoms. He couldn't help but think how it would make such excellent rangeland for grazing cattle. Best of all though the land was rich with wild game and that, paired with Ferschall's uncanny hunting skills, kept them from Ben's MRE packs more often than not.

At first, Ben had tried to confuse their pursuers by covering their tracks and planting fake trails away from the party. But when Ferschall explained the Hootsi mounts could follow a scent trail as well as any wolf, Ben dropped the tricks and began scheming with his men on 'contingency plans.' Not that they bothered sharing any of their thoughts with the remainder of the crew.

However, as the other four mercenaries grew more secretive, their resident medic, Cooper, grew less reserved. He traveled a step behind Leon and Ben, spending his time with Reed and Shana for most of their journey. Though Leon didn't hear all of their conversations, Cooper had no qualms sharing a wealth of knowledge regarding much of the fauna and many of the animals they saw.

The biology of Fayden oftentimes felt familiar, but with rare exception Fayden plants and animals tended to grow much larger than those from back home. In addition, they saw several animals present within Fayden which Cooper claimed had gone extinct ages ago on continents across the world back home.

Cooper's friendship came with other benefits as well. Gradually, Cooper's subtle suggestions helped Ben trust Leon and his friends with more and more responsibility. He even allowed them to collect firewood in the evenings, so long as they kept Merle close and didn't stray too far from camp.

At the end of the third day following their departure from Hootsi land, they stopped to make camp on a slight draw, near a creek. Ben wanted to get a brief rest and to push on early the next morning.

A little daylight still remained when Shana told Leon she had no energy to help him gather wood that evening. So, he left her at camp and went out with Merle to scour the area for logs and sticks to use for kindling. It was his first time to be truly alone in days and, despite the ever-present concern for danger in the wilderness around them, he relished the opportunity for a little elbow room. Once far enough away from the others, he pulled out his grandfather's medallion to inspect it more closely in the ebbing light of the fading sun.

The first thing he noticed when he held it in the light, were tiny gems lodged perfectly within seven different locations across the medallion's surface. Almost all of them were a deep green color. One gem, however, stood out from the rest, near the middle of the medallion. It held a transparent golden yellow sheen. The only other large feature present on the surface was the off-center hole cut for the chain, near the top of the medallion.

Leon held it up and looked closer at its surface. The actual metal of the medallion had a gray-blue color, etched in detail so fine he had to hold it very close before the odd angles and shapes revealed a design. The etching formed a picture of sorts. Once he unraveled the scene as a whole, it was easy to spot mountains, rivers, forests, lakes, and quite possibly an ocean along the far-right side.

A map of sorts? A map of the seven tribes?

His pulse quickened, and he looked from side to side while listening for the muffled footsteps of anyone approaching. Once certain he was still alone, he turned it over. The other side's surface ran flat. The gems could be seen from that side as well. Tiny calligraphy writing decorated the areas below or beside each gem. The writing had been artistically crafted, but Leon couldn't make any of what it said. Apparently, his inherent knowledge of the common tongue didn't extend to knowledge of the written word.

For some reason Gus wanted him to keep the tiny map hidden. Though on some level he believed he could trust Ferschall to help decipher the medallion's meaning, he didn't dare pull it out near Ben and his men. They would simply take it, and he would be left on his own, entirely at their mercy. For now, at least, he had leverage.

Leon decided he would just have to keep his secret a secret from everyone until a better time presented itself.

# # #

The weather on the third day carried a chill, but the sky was clear, and the wind was calm. If Ferschall and Ben could finally fully agree on one thing, it was that the Hootsi would be close on their heels very soon.

The party continued their steady progress north through the morning hours, until Ben called a halt as they moved through a pass snaking back up into the mouth of a gorge which sat at the base of a rocky uplift.

"Leon, get over here. Ask Ferschall how far this pass extends into that outcrop?"

Ferschall scratched his chin at Leon's question, "It has been years since I traveled this way, but it should not go very far, why?"

"What about those smaller passes up into the canyon to the west there?"

"Tributaries during the rainy season. They all most likely lead back into dead ends at slightly higher elevation, yes? We would be playing into their strengths if we attempted to outrun the Hootsi up those canyons. That's their native terrain. Now let's go, we must move faster."

Ben ignored his demand. Without bothering to provide an explanation, he walked back to his cluster of mercenaries and quietly relayed instructions.

When he finished, Jace took off and begin climbing up into the cliffs above. The rest of their group threw down their packs and peeled off their outer clothing. They donned their black combat gear.

Leon sidled up to Cooper, "Doc, what's going on?"

"Ben's done running. We're going to make a stand."

Ben turned, "You too Cooper. I need everyone suited up. You kids hand over those extra spears. Leon, tell Ferschall I want him to take you kids up that trail into the ravine, move as far up the trail as you can. Don't come looking for us, we'll come get you when it's all clear."

Ferschall wasn't as easy to command and expressed his disagreement, "What are you planning? The Hootsi are not men to be trifled with, they are born warriors, very dangerous, very tricky, even apart from their corrupted forms. The Anastashe cats their leaders ride are legendary. Now come, stop this foolishness. We should continue North as fast as possible, yes? Perhaps there's a caravan just over the next hill."

When Leon gave his response, Ben stepped up close to Ferschall. He didn't flinch as he looked up into his eyes and held the old warrior's stare. His face turned red, and a vein showed on his forehead. "Old man, WE are VERY DANGEROUS MEN. Men not to be trifled with...born warriors, very tricky. Now ..get going!" One or two hooahs from behind him echoed the sentiment.

Ben reiterated his command in Fayden for the first time "Go Now!"

Leon had no idea what Ben and his men planned to do against over twice their number, but he knew it wouldn't do anyone any good to argue any further. He touched Ferschall's sleeve, "Come on man, let's get on up into these hills." Ferschall calmly stood his ground a moment longer before allowing Leon to pull him back toward the others.

Reed didn't bother to take a side. He said nothing and made no effort to indicate he cared one way or another. He stood, reclining his back against a small tree, patiently scraping the bark from a branch, as stoic as ever. When eyes turned his direction and silence demanded an answer, he dropped the stick causing it to clatter down the dry creek bed, then turned and started up the trail.

Shana on the other hand, held her emotions on her sleeve. If Reed's departure was ice, her response was fire. She squared up, hands on her hips and addressed Cooper. "So, that's it, Coop? He's going to order you to make some foolish last stand and you're just going to do what? March along like Davy freaking Crockett to the Alamo?"

Cooper, for his part, fiddled with the hem of his sleeve. He couldn't raise his face to look her in the eyes. Over the past few days, he had spent a lot of time with Shana and Leon, and they had both begun to see him as someone outside Ben's inner circle. Someone they could almost trust. Now, Shana was calling him out, right in front of his boss.

"Easy now Shana. Those guys at the Alamo were outnumbered by like twenty to one, these odds are much more in our favor, right?" His attempt at levity failed miserably, so he regrouped and approached from a different angle, "Ben can be a bit…spunky? But the man knows what he's doing, why don't you head on up with the others?"

Leon watched as Shana went from heated concern to fiery disdain in the measure of about two heartbeats. "You're a fool Coop." She turned and hurried up the trail to catch up with Reed.

Cooper finally lifted his head. He caught Leon's eye before he could follow. "Look out for her, will you? Tell her I'm sorry too."

For some reason, Leon's stomach did a full-on somersault before he saw red, "Just so we're clear Doc, looking out for her is already *my* job! I've known her my whole life and I'll go down swinging before I let anything happen to her, you savvy?"

Leon didn't wait for a reply as he and Merle turned and moved up the trail behind the others.

Ben whistled through his teeth as he slapped Cooper on the back. "I think she likes you Doc. Better watch out for little brother though. The kid's got an attitude brewing under that quiet country demeanor!"

"He ain't her brother, Ben."

"Exactly Coop! Exactly! Now come on and suit up; get your mind right. We move out in ten."

Chapter 10

The winds whistled and groaned as they twisted down the barren rock walls of the ravine. Leon couldn't help but flinch each time one of those shrill notes carried through the pitted rock. Yet, he and his friends remained hidden, comfortably tucked away amidst the sandy gray crevices near the very top of the ravine, while the rest of their companions were awaiting a Hootsi attack, back at the base of the gorge.

When Ferschall started in again on why they should all take up the Blade, Leon left the immediate vicinity of the group. He was all for taking up the Blade at some point, whatever that meant, but even Reed had admitted it would be years before he was ready.

What a putz! We may not have another hour, much less another year!

Ferschall's pressured pitch frustrated him. They didn't need the distraction. They needed to be focused on the here and now — he certainly didn't want to be reminded of what he would eventually have to face in the form of his own corrupt nature, if by some miracle he did survive the Hootsi.

He and Merle climbed up onto a shady ledge tucked quietly away from everyone else. He pulled out his medallion just to feel its weight in his hand. Apart from his hat, it was the last vestige of Gus left to him. Holding it close helped him pretend like perhaps Gus wasn't so terribly far away.

Merle seemed to sense his mood and leaned in for a lick. It was classic Merle. He stooped in to hug that fur coat but paused when his nose caught wind of a steady dose of dog musk. Merle needed a bath, they all did. He gave him a pet instead and pretended to ignore the furry stench.

Is it simply my mind playing tricks or has Merle grown a little taller?

No, there could be no denying it. The dog had grown at least an inch or two taller. His fur had changed as well. It now grew longer, tougher…wirier?

He sighed. Everything he knew was changing. Even before being swept up into Fayden, change had been brewing. What would be left of his old life if he ever returned? Would he even have a life to go back to at the CW? The hard work and isolation of ranch life wasn't easy, but it was consistent. This new world was beautiful and mysterious, but also unpredictable and dangerous.

"I've been meaning to ask you about your companion here. The pup is from your world, yes?" Leon stiffened like a boy caught with his hand in the cookie jar, his head swiveled to meet Ferschall's broad smile. Tightening his hand around the medallion, he tried to return the smile.

"That's right. But he's no pup. My Grandfather gave him to me years ago. The day I was adopted."

"Adopted? Hmmm, I see." Did Ferschall stare at him with a bit more interest than normal?

Hard to tell, Ferschall's a weird dude. At least he isn't still pushing the Blade topic.

"You are partly wrong, you know?"

"Oh?"

"Mmhmm. That is no ordinary hound, yes? That is a *Bladed War Hound* if I guess right."

Leon laughed. "A *Bladed War Hound*? What are trying to say Ferschall?"

"Again, if I'm right, he's from an ancient bloodline of hounds, bred for a unique purpose. Those beasts required specialized training, yet the pup seems to have bonded well with you."

"Well, I don't know about all that. Gus told me he got him from old Dean Foster's place, just down the road. I do know this *pup* is at least ten years old, he's not a spring chicken—that's for sure."

Ferschall stooped over and scratched a spot behind one of Merle's ears. Merle groaned appreciatively and rolled over on his back as if to invite a belly scratch.

Leon snorted.

"Ha! There's your *War Hound* in action Ferschall. He's just a lazy old ranch dog most of the time. He was a real worker back in his day though."

"You may only see him for what he was in your world. I see the product of what his ancestors, over generations, were bred to become in ours. His kind is rare, if they even exist at all these days. Don't take him for granted, yes? He may not be as old as you suppose."

"Well, whatever he may be, he's my best friend. I'll keep him safe either way."

Ferschall responded with another wide-eyed smile. "Want to show me what you have in your hand?" The question nearly caught Leon off guard. He squared his shoulders and slid his free hand over his fist. For some reason, he wasn't in the mood to share his secret with anyone else just yet.

"Not really."

Ferschall mumbled to himself as he shimmied away, back down to the others. Leon held up the Medallion once more to study it in the light before tucking it away in his pocket.

A few minutes later, Shana slid down next to him. "You look like you're ready to pick a fight. Promise not to bite if I pet Merle for a bit?"

Leon chuckled. "Sure, knock yourself out. Watch out, though. According to our native tour guide, Merle's a Bladed War Hound. Whatever that means."

Shana just laughed as they settled into a comfortable conversation, recalling stories from when they were kids and giving each other a hard time as they remembered conflicting events from different perspectives. Leon had just begun to forget the anxiety of their situation and to enjoy himself when an odd sound carried over the wind, giving him pause.

Motioning Shana quiet, Leon concentrated. At first, he could only hear the same whistling wail he had been hearing for hours. Yet, he could have sworn he had heard more than simple wind screaming through the rocks moments before. Then, just as the

113

wind briefly died, there it went again. The sound of a screaming cat could be heard clearly without the gust of a stout breeze to drown it out.

When he leaped from his ledge, Ferschall was also listening intently, ear cocked in the same general direction. Leon eventually found his eye and arched a brow.

Reed beat him to the punch, "I think someone should check on things down there. I'll be right back."

"Wait!" Ferschall shouted. Once Reed stopped, he continued speaking through Leon, "No one leaves our group. We all go or no one goes, yes? It's too dangerous to split up at this point.".

Leon started translating, then stopped, grimacing as a new sound that echoed up from down below.

Ferschall held up a finger to quiet them all, before resuming, "That was a Hootsi warrior signaling the rest of the pack, they've obviously found our trail up the gorge and will be closing in on Ben and his men soon. If you all are intent on accompanying me, we do it my way, understand?"

There were nods of consent all the way around, though it was more of a rhetorical question.

Ferschall immediately laid out the ground rules. "I go first, followed by you, you, and you." He pointed to Reed, Shana, then Leon, respectively. "We move quietly and stay down in these crevices as much as possible, yes? You all hold still where you are, even if I have to slip around a corner to get a better look at something.

"Don't move unless I come back and wave you forward. If I come running back up the ravine, don't pause to ask me any foolish questions. Just turn and run. Everyone, sprint back up to that shallow cave over there where we'll stash our gear. Leon, you and Shana be ready to dive in and get set to throw what few spears we still have while Reed and I make a stand with our Blades. Understand?"

When Leon finished communicating his instructions Shana raised a hand.

"What?"

"How do you throw a spear?" Leon translated.

Ferschall threw his hands into the air. "Pointy end forward!"

They slowly backtracked a quarter mile down the trail. The slope wasn't especially steep, but the adrenaline paired with all the hurry up and wait created quite an intense hike.

Ferschall signaled a fast stop about once every ten feet until he eventually found a vantage point to his liking. After a few long moments, he glanced back over his shoulder and gestured for them to quietly approach his shaded ledge.

Leon cautiously took a peek and could immediately recall that particular portion of terrain down below. The gorge continued to steadily rise from the trail at the bottom, but cliffs collapsed down at steep angles from either side, choking the passageway leading up the ravine.

From the shadow at the bottom of the far cliff, one enormous black-clad figure stepped out into the afternoon sun just as a mob of Hootsi warriors, accompanied by two Anastashe riders, slowly rounded the bend. The big man held several spears in his arms. He stopped and quickly drove them all down into the ground before him. Then, he lifted his head back and let loose one of those wailing howls Leon first heard the night Gus had been attacked. Even hidden well out of reach, in the middle of the day, Leon felt goosebumps form up and down his arms.

Ferschall's jaw dropped, "Impossible."

If the Hootsi were surprised, they did a great job of hiding it. With practiced discipline, they all stopped at once and lifted their arms to shake their spears in the air. The two riders on cats simultaneously leaped forward to charge their giant foe in some unspoken command.

The man in the suit stood motionless one moment and then, in the blink of an eye, spears were flying at the Hootsi, being released in a rhythm like a piston in an engine. The scene was hard to comprehend at first. Leon grew up hunting with rifles, but he occasionally used a bow. The speed at which those heavy metal spears sliced into the ranks of the charging enemy stunned him. In his estimation, those bolts moved much faster than any flash of fletching ever flung from the sixty-pound-draw on his old compound bow.

Even so, the cats dodged the first few throws. Soon enough though, spear points found their mark. Painted Hootsi warriors screamed in horror as the two magnificent mounts went crashing down. The feline steeds thrashed about, biting down, and pawing at the burning pain buried within their chests. One even found the heart to slowly continue a shaky slog forward. Awful, ear splitting wails of dying cats and screaming Hootsi drowned out the sound of the wind. The lengthy bolts did their job in the end and both cats went still under the penetrating weight of sharpened iron.

After their initial surprise at the speed and lethal accuracy of the lone warrior, a few of the Hootsi near the back of the pack quickly spread out, clearly preparing to bull rush their opponent. However, before they could make their move, two more enormous black-clad men leaped behind them from the cliffs above. The two new additions to the fight effectively blocked an escape. The Hootsi were forced to fight a battle on two fronts.

The lone warrior, still blocking the path up the ravine, continued to zip spears into the ranks of the enemy. Yet when they charged, attempting to overrun him, several were immediately cut down by even more bolts coming down from the cliff above.

Then, from directly behind Leon and his friends, Leon heard the skitter patter clacking of rocks and pebbles being dislodged. He turned and momentarily lost his breath.

Three monstrous panthers were racing down the ravine. Above each panther rode a savage Hootsi warrior. The Hootsi warriors atop their Anastashe steeds were fluid pictures of grace in motion. They leaned back as their mounts dove forward, weaving headfirst through a rugged trail of boulders, leaping and dodging obstacles in their path.

Each of the warriors clenched a spear in their free hand. They were so close Leon could see the white in the knuckles of the one leading the charge. The rage in his eyes remained fixed on the devastation below. He and his men rushed past like a soft breeze on padded paws the size of dinner plates. Leon could smell the hardy scent of cured leather from the saddles they rode, it was there for a heartbeat and gone like a forgotten dream before he could even blink. Leon couldn't help but respect them for such a demonstration of physical prowess and noble pride.

Then tragedy struck. Before they could make it another twenty feet down the ridge, a series of spears came slashing through the air, across Leon's periphery, from somewhere in the shadows of the rocks above.

The first three targeted the rider's mounts. The timing was such that each spear connected mid-leap. The panther's graceful descent was shattered. Their bodies crumbled, careening off rock faces and crashing down, head over heels. They disappeared from his sight down the belly of the ravine, and their Hootsi riders were thrown from their saddles.

Within moments, another one of the black-clad skin-changers stood from a well-hidden location further up the ravine. He loped down the hill after the fallen Hootsi. For the first time, Leon could clearly see the thick mask covering the mercenary's face. A tinted visor built into the fabric stretched over the eyes. It looked like polished plastic or glass, but it gave no reflection in the sun's light.

Further down, one of the three fallen Hootsi jumped up and launched his own spear. His throw sailed true, but wounded as he was, it carried nowhere near the force of his larger opponent. The mercenary in black didn't even bother to dodge the javelin. He simply knocked it away with one of his own at the last moment. Without breaking stride, he flicked his arm in a blur of motion. The Hootsi fell to a knee, the spear stuck through his belly. He made an effort to rise, but the wolfman was on him in seconds, swiftly ending the struggle.

The scene down below played out in a similar fashion. The two men from behind converged on the remaining Hootsi. They pushed the warriors up the gorge to face their lone companion.

The solo warrior stood his ground. Though he didn't leave his position to attack, he let no one pass him by either. He moved with such speed and skill that not one Hootsi was able to touch him. Twice, they tried to rush him in mass, but spear thrusts from above continued to disrupt the effort. The third time, however, there was no help from above.

Just before the solo soldier was overrun, the man who slew the three riders made it down into the pass. When he took the side of his ally, the few remaining Hootsi retreated up against a cliff and the fight moved out of view.

Leon made no further attempt to witness the inevitable conclusion. He turned his back to the ledge and slumped down onto the bare gravel. Pushing his hat up with fingers that felt numb, he scratched at his head. He couldn't quite wrap his mind around what he had just witnessed. Everything seemed so senseless, he could barely grasp the gravity and scale of what had just gone down.

Shana was already curled up at his side, sobbing quiet tears. He put his arm around her to give comfort, and she folded over on him in a tight hug. Her tears continued to flow less quietly.

Leon looked to the others for answers as he held her. Reed still watched the battlefield below, blinking, wide-eyed. Leon couldn't help but think he looked like a man attempting to solve a puzzle missing a few pieces.

However, Ferschall's response concerned him the most. Visibly shaken, his back was to the scene below. His jaw was clenched, and the knuckles of his right hand were white where they gripped his Blade handle. His eyes smoldered in stormy torrents of emotion.

Leon had known, going into things that afternoon, that he and his companions were being hunted and that they were all in a dangerous situation, but in those last few moments of the fight it was sure hard to know how to feel about the outcome.

# # #

A half hour passed before Ben came looking for them. He was still dressed in his black tactical gear. His overly long sleeves and leggings were rolled up neatly to fit his smaller, human frame. He wasn't wearing a mask. Leon noticed his free hand rested on the elaborately decorated pommel of a Hootsi sword in a leather sheath at his side. He smelled awful.

Before he could speak, Ferschall lashed out at him through Leon, "What have you done?"

"Isn't it obvious? Like I tried to tell you before, we aren't prey, Mr. Grimm, we are predators. Besides, we wouldn't have had to do what we did, had they not been attempting to kill us all after you let that fool go free!"

Ferschall continued on a moment later, an abhorrent look in his eyes "I'm not talking about that, though that's bad enough. I'm talking about your ability to change in daylight, yes? What have you done? How do you not all have sun sickness at this point? Have you no idea what you will soon become!?"

"Easy Ferschall, no one's going rogue. It's called tech-no-lo-gy. We use this clothing to fully protect us from the sun's…well just tell him no light touches our skin. Overlapping neoprene straps and Kevlar padding keep us completely protected. Our faces and eyes are also fully protected. While wearing these suits it is dark-thirty to our senses." He waited while Leon did his best to convey the general idea before continuing, "This is what we are able to create, to achieve, in our world. It's an enhancement of our natural abilities, and back where we come from, it is a small sample of the power we wield."

Ferschall's shoulders dropped as he let out a breath he had been holding, "He's wrong, Leon, it's twisting what is already twisted. It should not be done. Tell him I would like to speak with his prisoners."

Ben dropped his eyes for the first time. "There are no prisoners."

"What?" Ferschall's voice held a cold edge.

"Not one of them bastards gave up. They don't quit, I'll give 'em that." He lifted his face once more, and his voice broke as he spoke, "Also, Jace is dead."

The news hit Leon hard for some reason. "Jace? How? You were all so much faster, so much stronger!"

Ben looked even more dejected after Leon's statement. "Sure we were. But let that be a lesson to us all as well. No one's bulletproof. One of them must have snuck up on him from behind. Not an easy thing to do, but what's done is done."

He continued, "Of the three Hootsi Cooper stopped up here, only one managed to escape. At the time, Coop assumed he wouldn't pose a problem. He didn't have time to stick around as I was a little outnumbered down below."

Shana gasped. "Coop was the one watching over us up here?"

A small twinkle worked its way back into Ben's eye. "That's right, princess. What do you think of our mild-mannered doctor now?"

Shana stammered, not knowing how to respond.

Ferschall interjected, oblivious to the new direction the conversation had taken, "We should at least grant them the respect of covering their bodies, yes? I assume you also want to bury your friend?"

"Yes, we need to give Jace a proper burial." Ben agreed.

"Fine, but then I must insist we move on, out of this area and back onto a level landscape before nightfall."

Ben shook his head no, "We're nearly finished with the bodies down below. But we can't simply move on, not yet at least. That's partly why I came up here. I'm going to suit up once more and search the trail for the one who got away."

Leon could faintly hear the sounds of dirt and rocks being tossed and stacked down below. The racket was distracting and the reality, unsettling. To think that so many people who had been up and running, talking, breathing, such a short time before, were now being laid to rest for good. It took him a while to convey Ben's message.

Ferschall shook his head firmly. "That's exactly what he would want you to do. Lingering here is not a good idea."

"Okay, so how about you tell us what exactly we are supposed to do about him?" Ben asked.

"Leave him. Even if you can manage to follow a scent trail over windblown rock using your magic *tech-no-lo-gy*, you won't catch him before nightfall. Then, you may be surprised how the tide might turn. I underestimated you and your men. So did the Hootsi. Don't make the same mistake." Ferschall lifted his arms, pointing out the desolate landscape around them, one with thousands of places to hide from or ambush one's enemies.

Surprisingly to Leon, Ben slowly nodded his agreement, "Okay, tell the old man we'll leave, but not because I'm overly worried about some renegade Hootsi. The faster we can make it to this city of his, the better. The men won't like it after what happened to Jace, but they at least know how to take orders."

It seemed odd that Ben gave in so easily to one of Ferschall's suggestions. Leon could only figure he'd had a hard day and was too tired to argue. At least that's what he hoped. Ben was very good at playing his cards close and the man didn't make decisions without being a step or two ahead, always with an angle he could exploit.

"Wait here while I fetch the rest of the crew. We'll all go on up together and gather your gear. Our group remains together from here on out." Ben made his way back down the gorge and the others remained silent.

Something dawned on Leon as he continued to replay everything that happened over the last few hours in his head. He turned to Ferschall, "Ben used us as bait, didn't he? He somehow knew they would send scouts up the trail to find us, and he had Cooper waiting, hiding nearby the whole time!"

121

"It seems so. The man has good fighting instincts, yes? But he doesn't truly understand Hootsi."

"How so?"

"Those three Cooper attacked were the leaders of the raid, not the scouts. We would have been cut down had we stayed where we were and allowed them to attack from a position of stealth, regardless of Copper being nearby. The Hootsi must have known they were walking into some sort of trap. They just didn't expect it to matter. On their cats, they could have easily evaded a few bolts thrown by normal men. At night, they would never have attacked so brazenly" He sighed. "No one could have predicted what resulted."

"I thought they were supposed to be some real tough warriors, though. Ben and his men sawed through them like a pack of wolves cutting through a herd of sheep."

From the way Ferschall's eyes twitched and narrowed at the irony of the metaphor, Leon knew his patience was nearly gone, "The Hootsi are uniquely terrifying to encounter within their element. We were extremely fortunate, yes? Had they arrived this evening or had Ben and his men not been able to change in daylight, we would have no doubt been easily over-matched and at their mercy."

"But why were the leaders after us without their men?" Leon asked.

Ferschall blinked at them all for the umpteenth time that afternoon. "Their leaders lead, yes? It would have been a tribute to their honor to sneak in and take out as many of us as possible, from behind enemy lines, without help. They probably meant for the men below to posture and toy with our warriors until their deed was accomplished. Also, they were likely competing to be the one to 'liberate' Shana."

He made a placating gesture toward Shana, and the coloring faded from Leon's face.

Ferschall continued, "As I've said, the Hootsi value their honor above all else." Seeing Leon's distress, he added, "They would not have done anything dishonorable to her. They would instead have taken her home, unmolested, and given her over to one of their worthy young men in marriage."

"Well, I'm glad we got that cleared up," Shana responded with an icy tone when Leon interpreted.

Despite a sudden desire to push the conversation away from the direction it was headed, another question popped into Leon's head. "What if Shana's not a Hootsi type skin-changer? How would that even work?"

Ferschall threw his hands in the air, "Has no one ever bothered to teach you anything about anything? This is not the time for such questions!" With that, he began climbing back up the Ravine, undeterred by Ben's prior directive to stay put.

Leon gave an edited version of the tail end of the conversation to Shana and Reed.

Reed responded, "Different skin-changers can marry and have babies. The babies' affinity always follows the male's bloodline. Back home though, when skin-changers marry humans, they simply aren't able to have babies."

Shana put an end to that line of the conversation, "Really guys, the birds and the bees? You really want to toss that around right now?"

She demanded Leon stop Ferschall before he got too far ahead.

"Hey, Ferschall, what about the guy who escaped? Shana wants to know if he'll be okay?"

Ferschall turned his head back to face her and held his arms up flippantly. "What about him? He is now *shunned*. He will not be allowed home."

"Why?" Leon asked.

Ferschall sighed in defeat and turned back to them once more. "Because, least of all, he allowed his mount to be slain in combat, yes?"

"So, that's it? Those guys are just dead to their families and friends whenever their pet cats are killed?"

"I said that was least of all. Those mounts are the Anastashie, no? They are the dwindling remnant of the fiercely protected Great Cats of the Nondo Dessert. They are rare and stealthy beasts, and they require a rare talent as well as the better part of a man's youth for most Hootsi riders to train. It is said *a Hootsi on an Anastashie mount at night is the hunter of hunters*."

Leon swallowed as he moved in on the conversation. "But you battled them alone when Gunther was captured?"

Ferschall chuckled as he shook his head no. He held out his fist and extended a finger for each point he made, until he ran out of fingers, "True, but the Hootsi knew my scent. They did not consider me an enemy until I was already upon them. Those who attacked were a small hunting party of four men, yes? All but one were young warriors in training. The moon was out. None were mounted. As it was, I would not likely have escaped with your companion had I not so confused them by swiftly attacking them from behind and knocking their leader out of the fight before they could form up!"

Shana pressed Leon for a translation, then asked, "So, the Hootsi love their giant cats so much they value them above their own people."

Ferschall growled, "How can I make you people understand? Explain to her that the cats provide them a tangible reminder of a long-lost former glory, a dimmed vision of what they were originally able to become. The Hootsi are skin-changers, no more, no less. But yes, they value the Anastashe as symbols of their ancestors, those originally gifted with the true form of the greater desert panther."

Leon pushed his hat up and rubbed his fingers through his curly hair. "This place just keeps getting weirder and weirder!"

Shana added, "Ask him if he knew of any of them well? The ones down there, I mean."

Ferschall softened when Leon relayed her request, "Some, yes. I think the one who got away was our young friend, Dimples. Though I did not know him well, his father was one of the few

Hootsi who offered to trade with me when I first came to live near them, years ago." Ferschall hung his head. "Such a proud young warrior. He maybe could have killed me that first night, even though I had the drop on him. He hesitated. I didn't." Ferschall took a deep breath and marched away without allowing for further response.

Leon felt some measure of grief for the soldier he had so recently come to know as Jace, yet he couldn't help but feel another tiny bit of sympathy for Ferschall's disgraced acquaintance as well. His men were all slaughtered, and he was homeless. If he survived, he would have a hard, lonely life ahead of him. It made Leon wonder if perhaps there were indeed fates worse than death.

# # #

From a rocky alcove, perched high above the fray, three stoic faces crept back from the ledge. There, they had observed the entirety of the lop-sided struggle. Their expressions were stern. Two of the three faces were youthful, though their dark eyes were malevolent. They feigned boredom like they were entirely unimpressed. The third had the unfazed look of an experienced leader. Despite wearing a patch over one eye, his good eye was better equipped to see the full picture of what had just occurred below than those of his subordinates.

They stood, dressed in well-tailored light tan leathers, the colors blending in well with the surrounding landscape. A solitary rust-colored scimitar sword stitched to their leathers was the only insignia present on their clothing. It had been sown into a patch on the right shoulder of each man. Two carried heavy longbows. Their leader wore only a curved sword with a black pommel at his side.

"Now, that was a pleasant surprise, and surprises are few and far between these days," the sword-bearer commented.

"Captain, those fools are tainted." One of the men carrying a bow motioned down below. "Shall we cut them down now? End them? Before they digress further into madness?"

"Typical wolves, they used about as much finesse as a butcher with a cleaver," he spat as if naming them for what they were put a foul taste in his mouth. At that, his subordinates laughed. And though he grinned right along with them, the smile never reached his eyes.

"Even so, they didn't seem so far gone that they warrant immediate intervention. No, there was still a touch of something measured and deliberate about their tactics." said the captain.

"And if they digress further?" said the other.

"Well then, they will be but a small pocket of rogues. Even the Fang Kingdom should be able to handle putting an end to them. For now, I say we watch from afar.

"Adrial, follow discretely and keep eyes on them. I'll return with reinforcements as soon as our gifts are delivered. If the wolves are still lucid at that time, maybe we arrange to have a few words?" The captain's dark blue eye remained implacably hard as he spoke.

His gut whispered to his head something was off. Perhaps it could be leveraged to expedite his ambition? Just like dozens of seemingly unambiguous situations in his past, he would use that strange tick in the back of his mind to skirt the danger and find the gain. Or maybe there would simply be lots more killing for him to dole out. Either way, he would be the one to get to the bottom of whatever was off with those wolves below, before any feckless superior had a chance to claim credit.

"And the Hootsi who escaped?"

"One disgraced Hootsi? He should already know better than to cross our forests. Either way, that man is cut off, scorned. Without his mount, he is of no further concern. He'll be dead before the next moon." The captain's hand fluttered as he spoke, dismissing the thought entirely. He had larger priorities to address than allowing Adrial to spend another day or two hunting one mangy Hootsi.

The men walked back up the trail to where their gear had been stowed. As they approached, the captain glared down at the back of another under his command. This fourth man had been a constant source of irritation over his six-month mission. He wore a uniform identical to the other three, but he was far from being counted as one of them.

The man was supposed to be watching over their two captive women.

The captain stopped and observed his guard's movements more closely. He gently washed the blood from a wound on the brow of one of the two. The women were old and feeble. Even so, they wore long sturdy wooden braces over their shoulders with shackles binding their hands tight against those braces. Linen strips, tied across their faces, held gags firmly in their mouths.

"Rezzin, what in all the sacred glades of the Quiet Forest do you think you're doing?" he reined his anger in, just barely, and proceeded more warily, with forced warmth in his voice, "How many times have I told you not to baby the prisoners? Your persistent efforts at stirring false hope for those condemned are no doubt crueler than Adrial's whip."

The captain had to constantly remind himself not to push too hard against the feeble-minded young man. Lately, that effort had grown considerably more difficult as the fool was less than useful at any task given. Sure, he was deadly accurate with that bow of his, one of the most accurate bowmen to join the Ranger's Guard in a long while. Yet his mind was weak and insolent, unable to carry out orders with the type of cold indifference that made the Guard infamous within the six realms of Fayden.

What had become clear during their time together was that Rezzin wasn't just going through some phase, he was damaged goods. The captain had taken to giving the nitwit under his command backhanded compliments at every new vestige of weakness he exhibited. The fool no doubt knew something wasn't right but was too blinded by fear and insecurity to see the truth of the matter. However, only one truth mattered to the captain in the end, if he ever wanted to become General Argile, he needed to keep himself ingratiated with the nitwit's father.

The young ranger dropped the cloth like he had been struck with a forging iron, while his comrades laughed from behind. His scarred cheek grew white along the seam of an old battle wound and red everywhere else. He quickly rose but didn't make a move one way or another, literally caught red-handed in the act of attempting something utterly taboo among his peers.

The captain continued, oblivious to Rezzin's discomfort, "Good news, everyone. False alarm! What we saw was no rescue party. Just some idiot tribal dispute. It's over and there's nothing more between us and home."

The other two guards smiled expectantly back at the women with an evil glee in their eyes. Then, they chuckled at the mournful sounds of despair from the gagged women.

Rezzin still attempted to hide the red in his face while he busied himself packing up the supplies from their camp the night before. If he hadn't been the son of one of the highest-ranking officials in the Silent City, Captain Argile would have found a way to lose him long ago on the patrol. But Captain Argile was no fool. An accommodating report for Rezzin would be an accommodating advancement for himself, and so the young Ranger was doomed to continue his advancement up the ranks of the Ranger's Guard.

The warmth in the captain's voice went cold as his true derision surfaced. "To think, you people traded Ageless beauty for useless hunks of metal!" He turned to address his subordinates, "Come on men, let's get these old 'teachers' moving. It's hard to tell from their stink, but I don't think they're dead yet and I don't want them dying on us out here before they have a chance to learn the sorts of lessons the Vindarri give their kind for the type of seditious insolence they spread."

Another one of the Rangers lifted the prisoners to their feet and ordered them both forward. Both women winced as the renewed motion caused the wooden staves resting over their shoulders to aggravate the chaffing on their wrists. The despondent slump in their shoulders was only intensified by the familiar weight that each of them felt against their right hip, where their bone-handled Blades swung loose in leather sheaths, well out of the reach of their bound hands.

The small party moved west, and a lone figure returned to his watchful perch above the ravine.

Chapter 11

Three days following the massacre in the gorge, Leon and his companions came upon the first flowing water larger and deeper than any of the knee-high creeks they had previously crossed. Ferschall called it the Murk Water River, though the crisp cool waters appeared clear to Leon and the others.

Upstream, across the river, Leon could see the beginnings of a massive forest. It rose a quarter mile to the west and spread to the north and the west as far as one could see. The water rushing down along the periphery of that forest churned and foamed with the spray of rapids. Navigating such waters would pose a nasty challenge for anyone venturing to cross upstream. Downstream was much calmer, but the distance between opposite banks continued to widen the further east one traveled.

"Ben, you could walk up and down this river from sun-up to sun-down either direction and you would not find a more optimal place to cross, yes?" said Ferschall.

Ben nodded his understanding before Leon had a chance to translate. Leon continued to marvel at how the man was a sponge when it came to language. If he had been intimidated by Ben's physicality before, he was downright terrified by the depth of his intellect.

For nearly their entire time in Fayden, Ben had been insistent that Leon practice the Fayden language with all of them at every possible moment, and yet he alone could grasp and retain each new word or phrase after hearing them only one or two times. Recently, Ben had even begun communicating directly with Ferschall and Leon was being called upon to translate between the two of them less and less.

His clipped response was strained but the meaning was clear enough for Ferschall to comprehend, "Maybe, but we no want wet things. It deep here."

Ferschall stroked his beard and spoke slow, "If you give me a few hours, and lend me a hand, I may be able to furnish some crude rafts from some Shephard's Grip I saw growing upstream."

Ben scowled in response and pretended to mull it over before reluctantly agreeing to the offer. Leon rolled his eyes at Shana. When she arched a brow, he gave her a nudge, and they wandered off from the main group.

"I'm getting so tired of having to suffer through Ben's skeptical BS," he told her.

"I don't know, Leon. He's a jerk, sure, but at least he's turned out to be a pretty smart guy, and he's got some sort of an idea for how to get us home, right?"

Leon sputtered. He couldn't believe she was taking Ben's side! He pushed his hat up higher on his forehead. "Maybe he does, maybe he doesn't, I do know he's been throwing his weight around for no good reason since the very start. The man thinks the sun comes up just to hear him crow. Ferschall's the one really running the show if you ask me."

"Well, good thing no one's asking you, right?" her voice was huffy as she flicked her hair and signaled for Cooper to join them. Then she turned back and gave him her signature tell for a subtle dig—sleepy eyes with a slight dimple. How many guys had he seen her melt with that look? He tried not to give her the satisfaction of seeing him react to it like every other guy she ever used it on, but his own face betrayed him, and he grinned back like a cur dog begging for a bone before she turned to Cooper.

Way to go and give her another reason to think you're a dope, dope!

When it was all said and done, Ben gave them all a few hours to rest and relax. For the first time in over a week Leon, Shana, and Reed weren't being forced to do something for someone else.

Though the temptation to lounge around and pepper the others with questions while Merle sniffed and sprayed every bush was a truly inspiring proposition, Leon forced himself to consider the big picture. Thinking back to his last moments with Gus, he remembered his primary goal for the unforeseeable future. He had been tasked with protecting Shana and making it back home with her in one piece. His constantly expanding litany of questions concerning where they really were and why they were really here, would have to continue to remain bottled up for a later time.

For the time being, the most sensible thing to do would be to begin learning to better protect himself in his new reality. And there was one person who had promised to teach him. Leon stood and turned to Reed. "How about you start those lessons you promised?"

Reed, engrossed in whittling on some walking stick he had picked up that morning, paused mid-cut to answer without looking up, "You mean the Blade training? The first free day we've had in over a week and you want to begin Blade training?" He cut another long smooth strip of soft bark and glanced up in Shana's direction. "You too?"

Something in the way in which he pounced on the question instead of attempting to fend off further conversation with his normally antagonistic disposition made Leon leery.

But before he could renege on the request Shana answered enthusiastically for them both. Her hair bounced as she nodded with naïve vigor.

Reed's expression morphed into a suspiciously nefarious smile. "Fine, but don't complain if it isn't as exciting as you might be expecting. I don't train quitters." He looked them both in the eye, deadpan serious. "The first thing you need to learn is how not to be so weak and ill-equipped for fighting."

Leon wasn't buying the put-down, "Just how do you propose we learn not to be weak? We've been doing nothing but hard physical exercise for days on end. Apart from the fact that we're a little short on free weights out here, I'm in the best shape of my life."

Yet another larger smile spread across Reed's face, "Glad you brought that up! We won't be hiking or lifting weights…" He reached over to one of the nearby packs and handed them each a metal spear before digging through a separate bag and fishing out a sturdy rope. "You guys will start with some core work while I devise some other fun activities to strengthen those arm and wrist muscles. Think of this as your first steps in a daily routine. Now, have either of you ever heard of flutter kicks or burpees?" Shana shook her smiling face no, still excited to begin, while Leon simultaneously groaned.

Me and my big mouth!

Flashbacks of high school coaches yelling at him during mat drill exercises in the off-season fluttered through his mind. Reed cracked his knuckles, "Excellent, now go change into those workout clothes you were wearing when we first got here, and Leon, when you get done why don't you demonstrate a dozen burpees for Shana before you both get started building up those doughy little belly muscles? Now move!"

They both quickly fished their workout clothes from their heavy pottery packs and trotted off in opposite directions to change. A few moments later, Reed's voice carried through the bushes, "And Leon, I want to see full-grown man push-ups and air under those feet when they leave the ground, or you'll have to show her again!"

Leon groaned once more under his breath as he wrapped his Medallion up in his travel clothes and ordered Merle to guard the pile.

This is going to be a real peach of an afternoon.

# # #

What Leon soon discovered was it didn't matter how in shape he believed himself to be, Reed's version of being in shape was miles beyond his own. Both he and Shana were made to hold metal spears throughout the duration of a killer conditioning workout before Reed tied a loop in a rope attached to a pair of homemade pulley systems on a nearby tree with a pottery pack lashed to the other end. Hoisting those packs with that rope forced them both to use arm, back, and shoulder muscles Leon didn't even realize were there.

To top it off, burpees continued to be a persistent theme throughout the remainder of the workout. These were done on bare knuckles so he and Shana wouldn't drop their stinking spears. Leon could only cringe at the transition from milk toast mellow Reed into some stranger with the persona of a deranged army drill sergeant.

The one saving grace to all the pain they allowed Reed to dish out came just after Ben's men returned with Ferschall. By that time Reed had nearly broken them. He was goading them to finish a torturous wrist exercise, screaming out something about how it was his pleasure in life to turn their rat claws into meat hooks.

Obviously, the initial reaction from the other men was pure hysteria. Gunther actually fell to his knees he laughed so hard. Even Cooper cracked a smile. But the laughter ended when Ben strolled down from a nearby hill, where he had been on lookout, and suggested that the challenges of Fayden might be better met if a certain group of soldiers did their part to maintain company conditioning standards.

Soon thereafter, it was agreed that the team would make camp along the side of the river and, to Leon's amazement, Ben put his three remaining men through a much more advanced sparing session, complete with their own much more rigorous military core workout.

Leon and Shana retreated to sit in the shade of a nearby tree, which smelled like peaches but sported wicked-looking three-inch spines up and down its trunk. Reed stalked up the hill and took Ben's place, keeping watch.

Ferschall claimed a place beside them before long. Leon didn't hear him come, just looked over, and there he was. Ferschall was like that, though.

As they watched the antics playing out before them, Ferschall chuckled softly at Ben's blunt and colorful approach to the art of motivation, but he didn't seem overly impressed at the level of activity that ensued.

What would Ferschall consider strenuous exercise?

If Reed's definition of physical conditioning was miles beyond his, Ferschall's had to be a whole 'nother order of magnitude beyond Reed's.

Eventually, Ferschall's chuckles wore thin. He turned to Leon and spoke softly. "How come you two were allowing Reed to guide you in those arm exercises?"

Leon was still amused at the antics before him and answered without taking the weight of the question into account, "So, we'll be ready to take up the Blade someday. Reed says we are way behind in our training. We still have a few years of work to do before we are ready to use one."

When Ferschall didn't respond Leon pulled his eyes away from the action. Ferschall sat frozen beside him, staring at him, slack-jawed.

"What? I don't want to turn into some monster if I can help it. What's the matter now?"

"Leon, I thought you've been ignoring my invitations because you despised the whole idea of taking up the Blade, yes? Why in Fayden would Reed think such a thing? What exactly does he feel he needs to do to prepare you two to take up Blades of your own?" Ferschall's voice had gone from soft bewilderment to raspy concern in no time flat.

"Hey hoss, don't shoot the messenger. Two weeks ago, I was living on a whole different reality, oblivious to all of this Blade talk. Besides, there aren't any Blades available for us…unless you want to give me yours?"

Leon meant it as a joke, but the anger in Ferschall's voice melted into a wispy note of sadness. He spoke with the reverence of someone granted a great honor, "Leon, of course, I would be willing to give you my Blade. There's obviously a lot you two haven't been told, yes? I don't know what strange customs the remnant in the lands of Sanctuary have developed, but I can tell you there is no reason to wait for years if you are willing to take up the Blade now."

At some point, Shana had tuned in on their conversation. When Leon brought her up to speed, she responded, "Do it, Leon. I want to watch and see what all the big hoopla is about."

Ferschall's eyes shifted back to Leon and it was all he could do to simply nod his agreement.

"Wonderful, follow me up the hill. Though Reed has an odd notion as to how these things work, there is no denying he carries a Blade as well, yes? I want him to be there for this too."

Ferschall stood and, without another word, made his way up the hill. Leon gave Shana a questioning look. She shrugged and took off after him. It took Leon another few seconds to consider everything before he did the same.

As Leon rushed up over the crest of the hill to catch up with his two companions, he collided into Shana's back, and they barely missed bulling over Ferschall. They both laughed as they steadied themselves.

Yet Ferschall and Reed stood stark still, ignoring them. They were frozen in place, staring downriver, far to the southeast. Following their collective gaze toward where the river grew flat and wide, Leon observed a densely crowded, slow-moving mass of creatures, still a mile or two away, gradually inching their direction.

Ferschall was the first to break the silence, "Well, Leon, unfortunately, this conversation will just have to wait a few short hours. Tell your friends that if we don't cross now, those water pigs could hold us up another day or two, maybe longer."

Reed asked what was on everyone else's mind, "Are they dangerous?"

"Most definitely. But that's not our concern today." Ferschall's response drifted off with him as he raced back down the hill. Reed was right on his heels.

Shana looked at Leon with obvious exasperation, "Is it just me or does everyone and everything around us have bad timing?" She sported a coy expression, looking over at him with those unreadable eyes of hers.

The wind blew a tuft of loose hair across her cheek. Leon so wanted to reach up and tuck that stray strand gently behind her ear, to wrap his arms around her and draw her close but, for some reason, the gesture wouldn't come. It just didn't feel right.

"Couldn't say, timing's never been my thing."

Chapter 12

Ferschall wanted to press forward ahead of the mob that approached. Ben refused once Ferschall confessed that the horde wouldn't likely be dangerous. He wanted to at least make contact before heading up the trail.

Leon and his companions were still drying off on the far side of the river when the first of the horde lumbered up along the river's shoreline. A thin-framed, short-statured, heavily bearded man casually rode Indian-style atop a colorfully designed large platform mounted securely to a harness behind an immense creature, mostly submerged beneath the water. The back third of the barge was stacked high with boxes and crates of varying sizes lashed securely together. As the water grew shallow near their bank, any expectations regarding the "water pigs" Ferschall previously described quickly dissolved at the realization that the submerged beast was actually some sort of giant hippopotamus.

The bearded little man spotted them shortly after they saw him. He was dressed in loose pants made of faded purple fabric but wore a plain tan and yellow leather vest over a hairy little chest. Several layers of multicolored seashell chains hung 'round his neck in loose hoops while still others hung from braided loops in his hair and beard.

Once it was clear their paths would intersect, he proceeded to pull a large spindly white seashell to his lips, then blasted out a long note to the horde following in his wake, back down the river. Similar notes echoed back upstream from the ranks behind.

Leon and the others remained perfectly still while the nervous little guy sprang to his feet. Reaching back into a boxed compartment behind him, he produced a long three-pronged spear and a thick hide-covered shield. By simultaneously tapping his bare feet in an odd rhythm on the platform below, he somehow managed to draw his mount up from out of its slow, plodding gait. His quick, agile stomping sounded much like the pitter-patter of a snare drum.

Leon couldn't help but chuckle inwardly at how the little man resembled a tiny, angry, river-dancer. However, his mirth was short-lived once the Hippo below began responding to the foot drum.

The enormous creature rose from the water until its nose was a few feet from the shoreline. Then, what appeared to begin as a yawn grew until a menacing mouth full of gnarled tusks were fully exposed. Each ivory canine measuring well over two feet in length.

Leon marveled. The creature was practically the size of a small elephant, or a tank, back home. Its enormous girth expanded as it heaved in a deep breath and groaned out in a low bass octave, which steadily built until its rumbling became an infernally aggressive roar. Even standing a few dozen feet away, Leon could feel those basso vibrations making his nose itch until his eyes watered. All the while, the little man continued to stomp about in growing intensity. Strangely, the rhythm sounded more like a war drum in the presence of such an intimidating backdrop.

In that harrowing moment, all eyes went to Ferschall. Ferschall had explicitly warned them prior to and during their hasty river crossing that first meetings with the approaching hoard could be *tricky*. Of course, he also managed to take full opportunity to remind Ben what happened the first night they met, back when his advice wasn't so well-heeded.

He immediately stepped forward, lifting empty hands, and casually sauntering out toward the water's edge. His head was bent toward the ground, but the gesture was so carefree and welcoming it was almost like he intended to invite an old friend over for dinner. Then when he looked up to address the snarling little man, he stopped short and broke into uproarious laughter.

"Ferschall...Ferschall Grimm? That you?!" The little man sitting up on his perch still floating behind the hippo squinted down inspecting the man belly laughing before him before breaking out into a fit of laughter all his own. He laughed so hard he dropped both his spear and shield. Then, in a completely unexpected move, he took a few steps back, made a running leap, sprung off the hippo's back, vaulted off its still upturned nose, somersaulted through the air, and landed upon the riverbank in an all-out sprint, only to stop once caught in the outstretched arms of Ferschall. Though the little man appeared normally proportioned, he hovered just over five feet tall on tippy-toes, and when Ferschall scooped him up in a massive bear hug, he all but disappeared from view.

"Ferschall! Where you been, you big oaf? Never mind! I'll call off the guard. Hold on." He pulled up his horn once more and gave three short toots and one long bellow. "Don't you worry, nobody has forgotten you, you old tramp. We are going to have a big party, yes?"

From that moment on, the afternoon slid by without much in the way of explanation from Ferschall or his new friend. He did manage to convey that the current horde of individuals gradually arriving in greater and greater numbers were somehow distantly related to him. It was later learned that when he mentioned he was related to the horde, it might actually have meant everyone in the horde! And it seemed each of those distant *cousins* were just as happy to see Ferschall as the first had been. His temporarily forgotten companions were thus forced to wait patiently as a long string of over-enthused reunions played out before them. Every new rider to wobble up elicited all manner of renewed exuberance, though the conversation remained consistently humorous.

It generally started with, "Ferschall, son of Grimm? That you?"

"Ah, my favorite cousin thrice removed, yes?! How is your dear mother?"

As soon as the yelling, jostling, and back pounding ended another would show up to take it up again, and on it went.

Shana was the only one who found it cute when Leon explained that they were surrounded by a hundred little mini-Ferschall's with the same annoying speech proclivities as their older, larger, cousin. If there was any question where that linguistic tick stemmed from, it was quickly put to rest after the first dozen reunions.

141

Leon could only feel grateful when the group's initial gathering point moved further upriver from the shoreline. Apparently, even their overzealous little visitors noticed that their original greeting point had become more of a mud wallow than a riverbank.

Soon, the sloping shoreline was filled to the brim with dozens of oversized draft hippos, which mulled about under the direction of the pitter-patter foot stomping from obnoxiously loud little men who all seemed to scream orders at one another simultaneously. It was synchronized chaos.

The platforms turned out to be amphibious wagons with wheels. They could be pulled behind the hippos once out of the water. Each wagon had been loaded down with all manner of bundled goods, but especially interesting to Leon were the small holes punched in several of the larger boxes stacked within the piles. Many of those boxes appeared to be reinforced with steel framing.

By late afternoon, a couple hundred of what Leon initially guessed were giant guinea pig-looking critters made their grand entrance. These creatures turned out to actually be the much-anticipated water pigs. Though each *water pig* measured half a ton in size, and they looked nothing like pigs, they did manage to squeal and grunt as they climbed up out of the water.

Luckily, Cooper was able to dispel the notion that the oddly random Fayden size increases could account for an eight hundred percent mass increase in a common guinea pig before any such implications had time to sink in and cause Leon to truly panic over what else might be lurking about. He informed the group that the creatures were more likely massive cousins to what were called Capybara, basically the biggest rodent alive back home. They were still big, but only four or five times the size of their earthly counterparts from South America.

The sun was well on its way down the horizon when a string of campfires came to life along the ridgeline overlooking the shore, creating a half-moon arc around the herd of livestock drawn up into a mob at the water's edge. The bulk of the horde had arrived, yet wagons continued to trickle into camp.

The very last of the horde to arrive were the oddest specimens of the day. Little men stripped down to some sort of swimming trunks waded up into camp on foot, leading humongous hippos on long leashed halters. These were handily the two largest hippos yet witnessed. Instead of pulling simple wagons mounted with goods, these hippos actually pulled a tiny house.

The house toting hippos slowly made their way up the little rise until they and their mini-house were drawn to an abrupt halt on level ground. Leon snuck away from the boring proceedings surrounding Ferschall and made his way closer to the activity to get a better look at the amazing sight.

Once the hippos were both essentially parked on level ground, several more little men raced up, shoving large chunks of wood beneath the wheels below the house to serve as chocks, locking the house in place.

At about that same time the harnesses were removed, and the hippos were signaled to slowly move forward. They were led back down the hill. Surprisingly, all coordinated activity took place in less than two minutes and ran as smooth as Swedish clockwork

Knowing a thing or two about training herd animals to work, Leon could appreciate the relative level of ease with which the little men were able to handle the large hippos. Especially considering how everything he'd ever heard about hippos highlighted how extremely volatile and dangerous they are.

As soon as the main house was set, more little men led the hippos with wagons up onto solid ground and the process was repeated many times over. Brightly colored tents soon popped up on each wagon platform. Once the work was done, the wagon drumming continued. All drumming throughout the camp gradually coalesced into a single rhythm that carried a steady cadence, and the hairy little men took license to hoot and holler out bawdy songs as the smell of sizzling meat slowly wafted from one fire to the next. Merle was too nervous around the hippos to leave

Leon's side and together they moved back closer to the man of the hour. But before they could get there, Cooper waved them over.

"Leon, I've been meaning to ask you about something. Do you have a moment to spare?"

"Sure, Doc, what's on your mind?"

"The other day, just before the Hootsi attacked, I was watching over all of you, and well…I saw you inspecting something, almost like you didn't want anyone to see. Whatever you had, it looked to be metal? I didn't think anything of it at the time, and then things went nuts, but it's been tickling my mind ever since."

Leon licked his lips and tried to remain calm on the outside. Internally he was shaking like a leaf. The medallion was special, but if Ben caught wind of its existence, he could just as soon kiss it goodbye. All his instincts told him he definitely shouldn't allow Ben to hold all the cards.

"Easy, hear me out, Leon. I haven't mentioned it to anyone else, and I'm not going to force your hand now. Just know that if you have something useful, you should share it with everyone, okay?" Cooper gave Leon a friendly pat on the shoulder, "I'll give you some time to bring it up to the group in your own way. Believe me when I say that although Ben is a hard man, he rewards trust and loyalty. I know you two didn't get off on the right foot, but I think, if you give him a chance, you'll come to see he isn't your enemy."

# # #

Ferschall remained preoccupied for another hour, though he did attempt to introduce his reacquainted family horde with his current traveling companions. Ben took position front and center and pretty much ignored the rest of them. The little men, for their part, were simply too busy and too worked up at meeting the long lost "son of Grimm," for anyone to really get a cohesive explanation.

When Leon's patience could take no more, he eased away from the excitement and once more made his way over to take a closer look at the tiny house. He needed to get his mind off the ultimatum

Cooper had given and a miniaturized cottage, pulled by giant hippos, was the perfect distraction.

Standing far enough away so that he wouldn't draw any more attention to himself than necessary, he couldn't help but admire the detailed craftsmanship of the small structure. The architecture was unique but not outlandish. He just couldn't put his finger on the type of material used to construct the colorful façade.

He shook his head in disbelief at his train of thought as he chuckled to himself.

If only Gus could see me now. Ha! Out on a trail drive with a dangerous cast of tiny ginger people, herding overgrown rats up rivers behind overgrown hippos.

If he ever made it home to share the story, Gus would either envy every moment or claim BS and never let him hear the end of it!

Leon was startled from his contemplation by a sarcastic and petulant voice pipping up from behind. "Are you done gawking there, big fellow, or can you lend a hand?"

He turned to see another one of Ferschall's relatives dragging a hefty bag with one arm and several thick bone-looking poles of varying length in the other. Leon didn't mind helping but, in general, the little horde members had all behaved indifferently to everyone but Ferschall. Nonetheless, after a brief moment of deliberation, he decided to give the guy a chance, and he reached out, offering to take the bag.

The little man unceremoniously dumped both loads of gear into Leon's hands.

"That'll be fine, thanks. Now come help me and I'll see about securing you a choice cut from the water pig feast this evening, yes?" The little man said, already walking ahead.

Leon had been smelling the beginnings of that feast as he strolled through camp. Why not take a chance? "Ugh, okay, sure. By the way, my name's Leon, umm, Leon Waldman."

"Well then, Leon, umm, Leon Waldman, pleased to meet you. I'm Sveddleton Haberkorn the third." The curt little cuss resumed his trek toward the house without looking back.

Leon flinched at the guy's blunt disposition but hurried to catch up anyway.

"I go by Leon."

"Fine, fine, I go by Sved." He didn't seem inclined to offer further conversation and Leon felt no further inclination to seek it.

Along the way Sved exchanged gentle ribbing with several other little men stoking a nearby cookfire. Leon noticed in passing that he gave as good as he got.

When they arrived, Sved pointed out where to drop the poles and held his arm out for the bag. Then, snatching it back, he shook it until several coils of thin braided rope tumbled out. Leon stood there watching him weave the poles in amongst the rope until his curiosity got the better of him.

"So, you know Ferschall as well?"

"Nope, but I plan to by the last song tonight, he's my second cousin, twice removed, after all."

"Really? Ferschall's related to you, too?" His sarcasm was ignored if it was noticed at all.

"Sure he is, by his father's mother if I hear right. Use to live with our clan, but he's been gone since before I was born."

This was more news than anyone else had bothered to share all day. Leon took a closer look at Sved. The firelight was a little ways off, but the little man wasn't nearly as old as his demeanor and candor would have first led him to believe. His hair was just as red as all the others, but his beard was quite a bit shorter than most.

The little men were a quandary to Leon. In a place where everything seemed to be larger than on earth, the little men were much smaller. They weren't off in any other way, they were simply a smaller, evenly proportioned, version of a normal-sized man.

Sved dressed in the same swarthy sort of manner they all seemed to be clothed. One notable difference though was a bandoleer's harness with slots for knives of all sizes running across

146

his chest. Leon studied the harness while Sved leaned forward to finish his work on the rope. That's when Leon saw the tip of a white bone-handled hilt, just barely poking up over the back of his neck.

"Hey, you're Bladed!" Leon meant the comment to come across as friendly and interested, but when Sved's posture went rigid he worried he had said something wrong.

"Right you are, Leon...umm, Leon Waldman. What of it? I carry many Blades."

"No man, it's not like that! Listen, I plan to get one soon as well. In fact, as soon as Ferschall comes across some extras I think he's going to give me one, or he may even lend me his until then. So, anyhow, we're all good, right?"

The little man was finally at a loss for words. His expression held a completely bewildered look.

Just then the front door to the tiny house opened, revealing the warm flickering glow of candlelight. A woman's teasing voice spoke up, "Sved, is that you? Oh my... Who's your tall friend?"

A similarly tiny, yet extremely captivating young woman stepped out of the entryway and hopped gracefully to the ground. She possessed the same short, slight stature as her brethren. The similarities, however, ended there. Her wavy hair was cut stylishly just above her shoulders. It reflected a light auburn shade of red from the candlelight and nearby fires. While she wore a more ornate yellow vest across her chest, it was stretched firmly atop a thick off-white linen undershirt. Leather leggings and boots rounded out her thin and curvy look.

She just stood there grinning up at Leon and Sved, waiting for a response. Her smile, from cheek to cheek, was contagious in a mischievous sort of way, but her dancing blue eyes and dimpled cheeks gave her away as a true beauty.

"Well, Sved, are you going to introduce us?" Her voice came off smooth, without a hint of the shrill sound Leon might expect someone her size and gender to emit.

"Leon Umm Leon Waldman, may I introduce to you Haddianna Haberkorn, my aunt, once removed." Leon cringed at Sved's continued, and likely intentional butchery of his name.

"Leon Waldman is fine, Sved. Very nice to meet you Haddianna. Oh, and this is Merle." Reaching down to give Merle a pet, he remembered manners long since drilled into him by an over-zealous grandfather and removed his hat.

Haddianna gave Leon a wink, "What a lovely beast! And Sved, you've managed to bring your dear old auntie a man of manners at last!" Because her eyes remained locked on Leon, he couldn't decide whether the lovely beast part referenced him or Merle.

"Dear old Auntie...do better math...five years younger..." Sved mumbled, still fumbling with the rope. Haddianna just laughed in response and reached out to give Merle a good scratch.

Then she turned back to Leon, "I like your hound, so I think I'll like you as well. You may call me Haddie, yes? Good, that settles things doesn't it? We're friends. So, let's all go meet this long-lost relative everyone keeps going on about before I simply die of hunger."

She grabbed Leon by his arm and marched off, practically dragging him in a beeline through the camp toward the blazing glow of the largest fire, a few hundred feet away.

Sved threw his rope contraption down and groaned. "Haddie, just when am I ever supposed to fix that leak up top? All you do is complain..."

He looked around, realizing he had been talking to himself. Then griping under his breath, he quickly caught up with Haddie and her new friend as she continued to pummel Leon with an endless barrage of questions without ever stopping for an answer.

# # #

A lively conversation was in full swing when Leon and Haddie arrived at the big fire. Leon's first instinct had been to slink back and take it all in before joining the commotion, but Haddie plowed forward with a surprisingly tight grip on Leon's arm, right up to where Ferschall and Ben were locked in serious discussion with three other little men. Their beards were colored more white than red, and their demeanor lacked the energy and exuberance of every other horde member Leon had yet encountered.

"Father, is this the renowned cousin I've heard so much about?"

One of the older men, Leon assumed it must have been Haddie's dad, let his shoulders slump at the sound of her voice.

"Yes, dear. This is Ferschall, son of Grimm. Ferschall, may I introduce you to my only daughter, and most rambunctious child, Haddianna Haberkorn."

Haddie smiled wide as if the remark was the most reaffirming introduction her father could have made. She momentarily let loose of Leon's arm to jump forward and embrace her distant cousin in a dramatic squeal of a hug.

Ferschall laughed a deep, full-bellied laugh, with that crazy cackle of his but hugged her back just the same.

Ben spoke up in broken Fayden, "You talk danger now? No attention pay to servant of me."

Leon frowned and Ben scowled back at him, like he had somehow interrupted some big important conversation of his own volition! Haddie completely ignored the scowl on the veritable giant of a man standing next to Ferschall. "Cousin, might you already know my newest friend, Leon Waldman?" She didn't bother introducing Leon to her father and his friends.

Leon answered wryly, "We've met."

"Enough!" Haddie's father cut in, but one of his companions beat him to the punch.

"Haddie, why don't you take your new friend and grab a bite to eat. I'm sure all of you are hungry. Then, maybe afterward, you and Sved can gather up a foraging party to help collect more firewood for the trek north? We'll be starting out under a waning moon, and we will need all the wood we can gather in case we don't make it to the south fork of the Somber in time."

Haddie's father gave his friend a silent nod of appreciation.

For her part, Haddie made a pouty face. "But I only just met cousin Ferschall! Daddy, what would mother say if she heard I was so inhospitable?"

Ferschall shook his hairy beard in mock seriousness. "Haddie, you and I will travel together tomorrow, yes? What will we talk about then if we've said it all tonight?"

Haddie cut sharp eyes from Ferschall to her father. "Come on, Leon, I can take a hint!"

Leon looked pleadingly around for help as he was systematically hauled off toward the nearest cook fire. Ben only bothered to cast back an irritating smirk before turning around and returning to his conversation with the little men.

"Hey, Leon! Wait up, who do you have there?" Shana came striding up from the other side of the fire, pulling Cooper and Reed along behind. Leon felt a twinge of jealousy as she playfully tugged at Cooper's shirt to hurry him along. Shana had been gradually warming to Cooper over the past day or two and it looked like she had finally gotten around to forgiving him for his part in the fight with the Hootsi.

"Oh, how wonderful! Leon, you didn't tell me you had friends. And another girl, too! Yay!" As Haddie clapped her hands in excitement, Leon thought it futile to offer that he hadn't had much chance to tell her anything at all.

He dutifully translated between the two girls, until Shana responded, "Yes well, Leon is kinda shy if you haven't noticed. My name is Shana Weidner. This is Reed Whistler and Cooper Schultz." Leon rolled his eyes at the offhand comment, but Haddie cut him off before he could craft a proper response. She introduced herself and Sved, still lurking behind, directly to Shana.

Haddie and Shana immediately hit it off. It was a bit comical to see their hand gestures and body language mirror one another, despite their significant size and language differences. Shana stood taller than most women Leon knew, hovering just around six feet, while Haddie was at least a foot shorter.

However, Leon's annoyance gradually melted away as he relayed messages back and forth. It was truly amazing that two girls, from two different worlds, with two different languages, and practically nothing in common could still manage to chatter aimlessly like long lost sisters within a matter of moments after meeting. It wasn't until Merle began whining due to the pungent fragrance coming from the barbeque nearby that the guys were able to move them along so everyone could grab dinner.

The water pig's shredded meat wasn't overly appetizing to look at, but when paired with roasted veggies and a wild river rice under a spicy sauce, it practically melted in their mouths.

"Son of a biscuit, that's good!" Leon went back for seconds and thirds. The cooks were tickled at his appetite and piled his plate higher each time he returned for more.

After dinner, Leon was ready to crash, but Haddie had other plans. She had no trouble convincing Shana to accompany her on a hunt for firewood. The guys eventually all went along too, giving just enough protest for the ladies to feel they had won a small battle of sorts. Leon took solace in the fact that the noise coming from all the drum beating and dancing would have kept him up anyway.

# # #

Away from the fires, the night was breezy and cool. Just west of camp was the beginning of a dense hardwood forest. Plenty of dry kindling rested within the tall forest's borders, nestled beneath a dark swaying canopy of thick vegetation. Much like most things in Fayden, the hardwoods stood a few hundred feet taller than any Leon could recall back home.

Sved brought up a draft hippo and hitched it to one of the open-top wagons. Several littler men, armed to the teeth with knives and tridents, insisted on joining them, simply to keep everyone safe. Those guys all moved deeper into the woods to scout around and generally keep an eye on things while the youngsters were working.

The crew gradually moved a couple hundred feet into the forest. Before their party spread out in search of woody debris,

Haddie suggested they pair up into teams of two and make a competition of the job.

Much to Leon's annoyance, Cooper and Reed acted quicker than he expected in asking Shana and Haddie, respectively, to team with them. He found himself paired with Sved. His only consolation being that Reed had quite an entourage of red bearded chaperones lurking behind Haddie at all times.

Leon noticed Sved was quick, too…quick to claim the role of torch holder once they started. Together, the two of them traveled deeper into the woods. Leon worked to haul wood back to the wagon while Sved lit the way and played the part of a one-man peanut gallery.

"You certain you don't want to grab one more chunk before we head back? You look like a big strong lad, but maybe not, no?"

"Hey, be sure to grab any logs you see with the big fluffy mushrooms like this one here, they make an excellent soup when boiled with Water Pig vitals."

"Can you hurry up? I'd like to make it back to my wagon deck before morning."

The constant stream of suggestions and complaints were actually kind of amusing at first, and Leon would have normally given as good as he got, but the fact that he had been stuck with a dude while the two prettiest girls he knew were paired up with other guys didn't help his lackluster sense of humor.

While returning to the deeper part of the forest after delivering their third load, Merle caught a scent that evoked a growl. Leon initially tried to shush him, but Merle's back hair stood on end. He was crouched low to the ground, pointing off deeper into the darkness of the still forest.

"Sved, hush up. Merle senses something. Where are those scouts supposed to be?"

"Hmm, that's probably one of them now. Bardo was out this way, I think. Hey Bardo? That you out there? Bardo?" There was no response. Just a gentle breeze that kicked up, causing the branches above to creak and groan.

Sved turned back to say something more to Leon when something large landed with a *thud*, directly in front of Merle.

They both jumped back. Sved lowered the torch and gasped. His eyes flashed fear, darting to and fro as he peered up into the shadows of the limbs above. Laying at their feet was the deathly white corpse of a little bearded man.

"Run," Sved whispered.

"Is that Bardo?"

"Head to the riverbank. Go, now."

"What about the others?"

"Just go!" Sved raised his voice for the first time that evening.

He raised a horn to his mouth, but an arrow from the distant canopy above struck it, knocking it from his hands. Whoever took the shot likely wasn't aiming at the horn.

Leon dropped the wood in his arms. He took one last glance into the canopy. Small leaves were crinkled dry, drained of moisture as if fall had come early that spring.

"Come on, Merle!"

Sved didn't wait around either. He led the way forward, away from the hippo with the firewood and toward the riverbank. He was surprisingly nimble and quiet as he navigated the woods.

The trees around them felt more and more menacing in the stillness of night. Leon could still hear the rhythmic beat of drums in the distance. He didn't have time to consider why Sved wasn't taking them directly back to their camp and safety.

Just when he could see the steep drop off the riverbank in the distance, a scream split the air from a direction behind them and a bit further upstream. Leon's heart stopped cold. "Sved, stop!"

"No time. Come on, Leon!"

"We can't, that was Shana! Just give me the torch if you're afraid." That seemed to sober Sved a bit. He set his little shoulders and drew the bone-handled Blade from the small sheath behind his head.

"We go quietly, we get who we can, then we get out of these woods, yes? Haddie and Reed were much closer to camp, and there were at least six well-armed warriors watching over her. They should have been whisked away to the safety of camp at the first sign of trouble."

Together the two of them and Merle crept quickly back in the direction of Shana's scream. Then, Merle caught another whiff of something. He lurched forward, bounding into the darkness ahead. Leon tried to catch him, but Merle could be a pigheaded brute when he locked in on something.

Sved and Leon picked up the pace, following the sounds of him crashing through forest vegetation. They barged through a thick cluster of saplings and tumbled out into a small clearing. Merle was already positioned in a less conspicuous spot, crouched over like a bird dog on point, preparing to attack.

Chapter 13

A torch at the center of the clearing was all but burned out. It gave off enough light for Leon to see Shana being forcefully restrained. A man with his back to them casually held her by the neck. He had her pressed against a tree. Her face was pale white and by his posture, he appeared to be entirely ignoring her distressful gasps for air. Her attacker's body was covered in what looked to be light leather armor.

On the other side of the clearing Cooper, or who Leon assumed was Cooper, was in full wolfman mode. His clothing had been stretched and torn, but enough remained intact for Leon to tell it was him. Already cut and bleeding, inching back, paws out, Cooper looked to be in bad shape. Two other men stalked forward, toward him, each angling in from a different direction.

Leon rushed the man restraining Shana. As he came dashing forward, the man whipped his head around. Leon was caught off guard. Though he looked like a normal person from behind, his face told another story. If the long pointy ears weren't enough, the culmination of haughty disdain and cold red eyes nearly caused Leon to turn away in fear right then.

It was only Shana's wide-eyed look of frozen pain that spurred him forward. Ben had held her similarly once before, and there was nothing he could do to help then. At least this time, he could personally intervene.

As he closed the last few feet between himself and her attacker, his chest beat with that tangy electrical current he hadn't felt in several days. This time, he was prepared for the pain and welcomed the charged embrace.

Dashing in over the last few meters, he cocked an arm back to pulverize the face of the man holding Shana. At the last moment, he rotated his hip for extra torque as he let loose a haymaker that should have put the ghostly white creature down for a good long nap.

Instead, his hand smacked into an open palm with a leathery sound that mimicked a fast ball hitting a catcher's mitt. His punch's momentum had been stopped dead in its tracks. Steely fingers wrapped around his fist, trapping it in a vice-like grip.

The touch instantly immobilized him. His chest pumped out more of the electrical current to combat the void, forcing power out through his veins in response. The sheer volume of raw power he produced shot through him in intoxicating waves. Leon's face contorted. His body began changing, the power outpacing the pain.

Then, it all vanished. Almost like the current had been sucked right out of him. The man-thing, holding his fist, threw back his head and laughed in manic glee. Leon could see his red eyes rolling back in ecstasy, savoring the power he had just stolen like some sort of supernatural addict.

When he spoke, his mouth was inches from Leon's ear. The voice was just a muffled whisper, barely loud enough for Leon to hear, strained and laced with utter astonishment, "A child of the lost tribe? I've heard stories, but never tasted such…such power! I will be offered a boon of unequaled value, I will be—" He never finished the statement.

Merle tore between Leon and Shana, right into the throat of the creepy attacker. The pale white apparition screamed a short gurgling shriek before going quiet. Merle ended him with a double shake of his powerful jaws. Just that quick.

Leon wanted to cheer, but his voice failed him. Instead, his legs buckled. He fell to his knees and slumped back against the rough bark of the tree. Shana slouched down beside him.

All the dark colors of the forest were spinning, bleeding together until cold fingers brought the spinning to an end. Shana shook him again, just as quickly bringing him out of whatever sort of trance the man had put him under. "You still with me Leon?"

"Always," he responded.

"Good, come on, we've got to get up."

156

In response, he squeezed her hand to convince her he was better but didn't attempt to scramble to his feet right off. He swiveled his head until he spotted Cooper. One of the attackers was distracting Cooper while the other had his sword lifted, ready to deliver the final blow.

Leon did the only thing he could in the moment. He stuck two fingers in his mouth and whistled high and shrill, the way he did to get a lazy steer moving.

It worked a little too well. The two goons abandoned the wolfman when they realized what Merle had accomplished. They came running, swords held above them, outrage in their eyes.

Leon was preparing himself for a mercifully swift ending when Merle dropped the ghostly corpse at Leon's feet and threw himself in their path. Crouching low on corded muscle and growling like a rabid hound, he looked every inch the danger he threatened to impose. Blood covered his jaws in the growing light of the torch's flame. That dwindling fire had managed to ignite a small cluster of dried debris and it was spreading. The whole thicket would soon be consumed in flame and smoke.

The men came to a skidding halt and split apart, each moving forward toward a different flank. They both were taking Merle seriously and Leon didn't blame them after what he had just witnessed.

Then, from out of the shadow of darkness, a ferocious little red-bearded man burst onto the scene. He threw a silver Blade at the one on the right. The Blade struck, buried to the hilt in the shoulder of the creepy white man-creature. Its shriek was cut short as it formed on its lips, and it fell like it had been hit with a taser.

In the moment of confusion, Merle attempted an attack on the man on the left, dodging and diving below wild swings from the curved sword. Cooper simultaneously came in from behind, ending the injured one's spasms with a slash to the neck from one of his dinnerplate-sized paws.

Sved freed his Blade from the dead man's shoulder and the two of them closed the distance on their last remaining attacker. Just when it seemed they had the goon cornered, he crouched low and leaped up in an impossible vertical jump that would make an NBA star green with envy. He landed gracefully on a branch in the canopy of trees above.

Sved held his torch high. The pale apparition screeched down at them as it moved effortlessly away, gliding over and around other branches, off towards camp. Leon saw limbs wither and leaves crinkle in every spot where a bare hand touched down. The fleeing man-thing continued to make an eerie screeching sound that carried in the air. There was only one conclusion he could draw—it was calling reinforcements.

"Quickly, to the river! The forest isn't safe! Go!" Sved ushered them all forward.

Cooper came limping up and gingerly sniffed at a cut on Shana's arm. He towered above the rest of them, almost seven-foot-tall in his current state. Despite him being a snarling hairy mass of cuts and anger, he apparently understood Sved. Completely unshaken at his physical transition, Shana pushed him forward, and he immediately took off in the direction Sved pointed. She hurried on behind him.

Leon called for Merle. The dog came trotting up, tongue lolling, obviously pleased with himself like he had just penned a whole mob of angry momma cows, all on his own. Leon moved him along but didn't hold back on any much deserved 'attaboys either.

# # #

The five of them reached the riverbank without further harassment and Leon saw why Sved wanted to head that way. The forest stopped around twenty feet shy of the bank's edge and there were plenty of rock outcroppings where they might be able to take shelter and hide near the ledge. As they looked down Leon could see it was at least a twenty-foot plummet to the water below.

"Let's move along this ridge, quietly downriver, until we clear those woods, yes? Shouldn't be but another couple hundred yards."

Now that they were out from under the forest's canopy, Leon could see clouds had moved in, blocking the moon. There was only a sliver of light to see by, but it was enough that he could make out the distorted profiles of rocks impeding their path. Sved obviously thought the light was sufficient because he tossed his torch down into the currents below.

Cooper took a position at the back of the party while Sved led the way. They moved forward at a brisk pace until Sved held up an arm to stop them all.

At some point, Leon couldn't exactly remember when, the drums had gone quiet, and horns had begun to blow. Sved scrambled back to confer.

"Camp is in chaos. Looks like the horde's attempting to retreat back downstream. They're under attack!"

A whooshing sound interrupted his report. Leon looked back over his shoulder. The small fire from the torch back in the clearing was obviously growing, and fast! Half the forest appeared to be caught up in flames. A steady north wind drove the inferno their direction. It drove the shadows away and lit up their position against the backdrop of the riverbank.

"What do we do, Sved?"

"I-I don't know." The little man's eyes skittered between the camp ahead and the flames behind.

The quietness around them erupted in the same eerie keening sounds they heard when the creepy white-haired guy from earlier had fled. Then, nearby trees withered and died as five white-haired phantoms stepped from the forest's edge, surrounding them in a crescent formation.

Cooper, still in his wolf form, didn't hesitate. He charged the one standing in the center. The creepy white-haired guy didn't even bother drawing his sword. He simply reached out and snatched the wolfman by the neck. His hand was coiled firmly below Cooper's overgrown Adam's apple before anyone saw it move.

Cooper stiffened and whined like a dog with his paw caught in a door. He fell to his knees as his opponent grinned down savagely into his eyes. His body pulsed. His form blurred and contorted until the unmistakable contour of a shrunken man in raggedly torn clothing took shape in place of a raging beast.

One to his left spoke through clenched teeth in defense of the attack on his companion, "How dare you? HOW DARE YOU!"

As Leon looked over the faces of the crowd before them, he couldn't help but notice that of an archer closest to Sved. He was much larger than his brethren. He sported an ugly puckered scar down his face, from just below his eye down beneath his chin. They all looked scary, but he had an especially intimidating charisma going for him. He would be one to keep an eye on, come what may.

Then, the one who had spoken, screamed in that unflattering sound they tended to make and jumped back when Merle growled deep and advanced a step. At a flick of the leader's wrist, two others knocked arrows and drew bows in one fluid motion.

Leon jumped out and grabbed Merle, hauling him back into his group by the scruff of his neck before things got ugly...again.

"Fools! None of you will receive the kiss of a quick death. Torture is a naïve word for what I intend to do to you until you confirm its origins!" He pointed a shaky white finger down at Merle as he spoke.

Then, the smaller of the two archers lurched forward, driven to the ground by a force from behind. Leon saw Reed's curly dark hair sprouting from beneath the archer as the two of them struggled together on the ground. But the battle was over before it started. Reed had led with his Blade and it had done the work for him. Whether the man-thing was paralyzed by the Blade, or dead, it was hard to tell. Either way, the time for talking was over.

Sved immediately took the opportunity to flick his Blade through the air and into the shoulder of the scarred-up archer. He fell like a sack of potatoes, just as quickly as the first. Leon let go of Merle and together they attacked the leader who had been talking so big a moment before. Merle caught an arm in his jaws and shook the ever-living fight out of their would-be torturer while Leon let his fists fly. He knew Merle was doing all the heavy lifting, but it felt good to finally land a few solid combinations on an opponent.

Shana leaped forward and struck the one still holding Cooper with the blunt end of a thick stick she had collected from the forest floor minutes earlier. He hissed but she growled back louder. Gone was her soft surly voice, and in its place was a beast's raging fury. He slipped back a step, and she pressed her advantage, literally beating the creepy white guy's face into a pulp with the thick wooden stump until he crumbled.

Their final foe leaped into the cover of the trees. Leon tried to follow but couldn't even reach the lowest branch.

At about the same time, Cooper made it back to his feet and was staggering about in a stupor, dangerously close to the riverbank's ledge when an arrow struck him in the shoulder. He spun around in a sharp spasm of pain and fell back into the water below. Shana screamed like a wild cat. Without a moment's hesitation, she raced after him and dove off the ledge before anyone could stop her.

Leon ran to the edge and stopped short. He was torn between following Shana and helping the group behind.

It was Sved's voice, which drew him back from the water's edge. The little man cried out in pain. He had cast himself over Merle, just before the goon in the trees above let loose another arrow. He paid a steep price, going down hard with red fletching protruding from his thigh.

For the second time that night, Leon's heart beat with an electric current. He grimaced as pain lanced through his body. Luckily, the pain wasn't debilitating the way it had been in the past. It was there and gone in an instant.

Opening modified eyes and looking deeper into the tree line, he could clearly see the white apparition repositioning and knocking another arrow, aiming once more at Merle. He could also faintly glimpse a stealthy shadow stalking it from a branch above. Somehow, he could smell them both, individually, from where he stood. They both reeked of danger.

The fingers of the apparition twitched as the shadow descended. Leon roared and dove for Merle. Time seemed to slow as he somehow managed to grab his dog and roll.

A heartbeat later all was quiet again but for the breeze in the trees, the crackling blaze of a distant fire, and the echoing clatter of an arrow as it ricocheted off the rocky ledge and careened over into the dark void of the river below.

The shadow and its prey fell with a hollow *thud* onto the forest floor. Neither one arose. Leon glanced down at Merle who was staring up at him with concern in his eyes. That concern gave him the motivation he needed to let go of the pounding energy. When he did, the ever-present urge for more power lost all hold on him.

When it was over, he reached down and gave Merle a pet.

"Well, boy, that hurt worse than a kick in the nuts, but at least we're still sucking wind."

Chapter 14

Leon's boots squelched with each step he took as he scaled the steep bank of the river as quietly as he could, which wasn't exactly quiet at all. But the fighting was over and, even if it wasn't, he was so bone-tired it just didn't seem to matter anymore.

While navigating the muddy incline, he did his best to protect the small skin of water slung across his shoulder. Despite the cool evening air, he was covered in sweat by the time he finally made it back to what was left of his small group. It was his third such trip down to the water's edge in search of Shana and Coop and his legs continued to shake, even after he slumped to the ground. Exhaustion was an understatement, though the filth of the mud, blood, and smoke continued to aggravate his already strained nerves.

Lifting his ball cap, he scratched his curly blond head. It was hard to process everything that had happened over the last few hours.

We're literally up a creek without a paddle!

At least Reed looked to be pulling through, slowly but surely. He was still too groggy to be of any help in planning their next move. Though he did give an amused grunt when Leon wiggled several fingers up and down in front of his face and asked him how many fingers he was holding up.

Sved's leg was something different though. It looked bad. His face was pale, and his eyes were closed. Leon could tell he wasn't asleep by the shifting grimace beneath his beard. He was just hanging on, hoping the pain would ease.

Leon had been certified in one short first aid course back in high school. He wasn't exactly a wealth of knowledge on the subject. Therefore, cutting away the purple cloth from around the wound, rinsing it with some water, and continuously applying pressure to the injured area was the best he knew to do. The arrow didn't appear to have hit bone, but he worried any attempt to remove it by force might nick an artery.

Then there was still the question of the shadowy figure who just happened to jump down out of nowhere to take out the last archer, just in the nick of time. He could tell there were two bodies lying next to one another, out in the forest where they fell, but the shadows were thick that far back. He took a few moments to rest until he was no longer sucking wind.

Cowboy up, Leon. Time to get a better look at what we're dealing with out there!

Gritting his teeth and creeping back into that cursed forest didn't seem like a good idea, but it was something he knew needed to be done. So, he pulled his shoulders straight and stepped forward into the darkness once more.

Thankfully, Merle had no such qualms and jogged out ahead to sniff out their quarry. As he moved closer, Leon was better able to make out the vague silhouettes of the two bodies in the undergrowth. They were both still unresponsive. The archer was obviously the one with the long straight whitish-blond hair. But who was the big, dark-haired guy? There definitely hadn't been anyone over five feet nothing with the horde earlier that evening, apart from him and his companions.

Reaching down to check for a pulse, it was quickly apparent the dark-haired stranger was still breathing. He turned and fumbled around to check the archer, but none too soon realized his hands were touching a corpse. Leon jerked his fingers back and tumbled over onto the big guy.

A few seconds later, and he finally released a ragged breath he was holding like somehow the man's condition was contagious. Leon had never before been exposed to as much death as he had over the past few days, and he still wasn't quite used to the reality of the finality it brought. Even worse, the notion of touching a corpse in some dark spooky woods carried the creepiness factor through the roof. Regaining his composure cost him some time but it wasn't like he was on a schedule.

Dragging the big fella out of the smoke-filled forest was another matter entirely. If his legs were shaking before, they were practically jelly by the time he got him out into the light of the moon, currently playing peekaboo between batches of clouds.

When Leon saw the man's face all his annoyances melted away. He literally dropped him as he fell to his knees. Merle's savior was none other than the last surviving Hootsi warrior, Dimples!

Leon scratched his head frantically once more. He really needed more time to figure things out. Returning to Sved's side, he fished out some rope from the man's pack.

This Hootsi may have helped us out but I'd be a fool not to hog tie him till I know what he was up to with that stunt. Time to put Gus's knot-tying lessons to the test!

# # #

Testing the bonds on the Hootsi once more and grunting in approval, Leon finally took a breather. Other than the condition of the folks around him, he had two significant problems to ponder.

Number one, the fire they started a short while back was now raging just to the west of him, spewing dark smoke everywhere. The only reason he hadn't yet been forced to take a plunge into the river below because the wind had changed and was presently gusting from the river at his back. The wind was a fickle ally though. He was holding tighter to the hope that his nose proved true in regard to the faint scent of rain in the air.

The second, and perhaps more serious of the two problems at hand, was the fact that the goon Sved initially stuck with his Blade was now nowhere to be found. Leon had only just recently realized the man-thing had vanished sometime after he had returned from hauling water. There was no sign of that puckered scar in any of the shadows he searched.

They had been extremely lucky twice already that night. He doubted their luck would hold a third time if Scarface managed to make it back with reinforcements before he could figure out a way to escape with all the injured bodies around him.

This wasn't the first occasion he'd had reason to wish for Gus, but it was certainly the sort of pickle the old man would have sorted with his own brand of pragmatic efficiency. With a heavy heart, Leon conceded the fight. He was no Gus Silberman.

As he slumped down beside Merle to further consider their dilemma, no good answers sprang to mind. Instead, thoughts he had successfully put off for over a week escaped from the corners of his mind, where he had, so far, managed to keep them in exile.

If those creepy white guys were skin-changers, and Ben and his men are skin-changers that make wolves look like poodles, and Gus is the sort of skin-changer that makes a cougar look like a house cat, what kind of man-creature-thing does that make me? And what's happening to my dog?!...He's getting huge, and he just killed that dude! ...

Once he started with the questions in his head, they didn't seem to have an end. In all of his short life, he hadn't had much cause to consider death on a personal level, but for the last few days, death lingered closer to him than white on rice. It was crouching in anticipation, waiting around every corner he turned.

He suspected he had only minutes before death would come calling one final time. This time he would be on his own, and he was all out of ideas on how to put it off his trail.

At least, maybe Shana made it somewhere safe.

It was a pitiful thought to cling to, but at least it was something. His feelings for Shana went back so far that he couldn't tell what was real versus what he'd built up in his mind. Did he really care for her, or did he simply covet the idea of being someone somebody like her could come to care about?

Regardless, when it came to the topic of Shana, the only sure thing he could put in the bank was that he would fail in the unspoken promise he made to Gus. He wouldn't be around to help her find a way home. He wouldn't be around to see the pride in Gus' eyes or the gratitude in Shana's.

A tear slid down his cheek. He couldn't decide if it was there on behalf of Shana or his own miserable ineptitude. Either way, it seemed a pointless gesture, and he wiped it away before he gave into a trickle of hopelessness that could become a torrent.

His new reality was becoming starkly apparent to him at last. Ben and his men were clearly outgunned in this new world. Sure, they were scrappy, deadly even, and smart, but it was only a matter of time before they were all eventually brought down by the harsh nature of the dark world in which they ventured. He clenched his fists as he fought off a twinge of anger over the injustice of it all. But, being raised a rancher, Leon knew day-to-day injustices had nothing to do with life or death. Everyone and everything eventually had to face an end. Oddly enough, the thought of failure struck harder than the threat of imminent demise.

Sitting there in a far-off-world, knowing time was short, Leon realized just how precious he valued his life. He hadn't ever really known what he wanted out of life. Sure, he knew he wanted to live, but he had no inkling of what he wanted to live for when all his chips were about to be called. The absurdity of such piss-poor timing made him chuckle.

Timing's never been my thing.

He remembered saying that very thing to Shana just a few hours ago. His chuckle morphed into a belly laugh. He laughed until his eyes watered, and his gut hurt. He laughed until tears ran down his cheeks, and he could laugh no more.

Hopelessness may weigh him down, but he knew he couldn't let it freeze him solid. He buried his morbid thoughts, struggled back up to his feet. Not knowing what else to do, he decided to salvage what he could from what he saw around them.

When Leon stooped to grab the ornately curved sword off the dead leader, Sved's breathless whisper from behind stopped him, "Don't grab that...when you can take this."

Leon looked back at the man. He was laying on his side, slightly propped up on one elbow. His free hand was lifting his bone-handled Blade in Leon's direction. How he'd managed to get it back from the fella he stuck was beyond baffling. The fact that he was feeling strong enough to be more like his disagreeable self was good, though.

"Yeah thanks, but keep your Blade bud, you're still gonna need it. This one should work fine enough for me...even if I haven't got a clue how to use it. Better you lay back and get some rest while you can."

"No, Leon." Sved paused and squinted up at him. "No one's ever explained it to you, have they? You don't understand what I'm offering you? This is so much more than just a Blade." There was no accusation or condescension in his tone.

"What do you mean? What is it that no one has bothered to tell me about that stinking Blade?" Leon couldn't keep the cynicism from his voice. No one had bothered telling him anything, much less anything about the Blade.

"This Blade, it is many things to us who take it. But primarily, it is meant to shield us from the corruption that inflicts our world; the corruption that inflicts us, yes?"

"I get that, but what is it? What makes it so special?"

"It's hope? It's a shard left for us from a legendary hero who stooped to free us from the result of the corruption. He was something so much more than you or I could ever be. He's gone now, but he left us this shard of his power in the form of a Blade.

"You can take it too, Leon. It won't completely remove the corruption from your body, but it can circumvent the corruption's power over you."

Sweat was pouring down Sved's brow. It was obvious the effort of explaining these things to Leon was taking a toll on him in his current condition. But Leon was finally getting answers, and he pressed him for more as he knelt beside the little man.

"What about needing to know how to use it beforehand? I get that it's a special tool, but I wouldn't know the first thing about how to use it Sved. Reed says we need at least two years' worth of training. I doubt it would do me any good to take your Blade from you now, even as banged up as you are."

Sved's eyes held a touch of anger at that. "No, Leon, don't worry about all that, you just need to admit you need help, yes? You just open yourself to the Blade's power. Trust it to do what you can't do for yourself. It will change you more later, but this is the first step. You don't have to try to prepare yourself to wield it. If so, none of us would ever be ready at all!"

"That's it then? Just take it, huh? But what difference does it make now? Honestly, man, we aren't likely to make it out of this fix we are in, you know that, right?"

"You'll never know until you try. Never underestimate what it has the power to do. Listen, Leon, wars have been fought and nations have toppled over the power this Blade carries, yes? Powerful folks have been attempting to extinguish its presence from this world from the moment it was first passed along.

"Most folk these days don't think there's anything wrong with their moonless form. They see the beasts and the twisted monsters we become as powerful pinnacles of our true forms, not as corrupted forms of who we were once meant to be. This Blade won't make you into something you don't want to be, much the opposite, it saves you from those effects that twist and corrupt. It at least gives you the option to choose what you become and when. The fact that we have no other option at hand just means there's no reason why you shouldn't give it a try, no?"

Leon shrugged. Sved was right. What did he have to lose? Gus at least had always carried one, it couldn't be all that bad. If there was even the smallest hope that that ancient hero's help was really able to save him now, why not?"

"Okay, Sved, I bite. I can trust this hero and his Blade can cure me. What do I do?"

Sved flipped the Blade around so the handle was extended out toward Leon. "Not a thing. Just take it."

Leon reached out and hesitated. "What will happen when I do?"

"Only one way to know, yes?" There was irony in his voice as his brows rose in question, but his eyes held an earnest sincerity.

Leon took a breath. He reached out and gripped the handle. It was warm to the touch but didn't feel exactly the way he somehow expected it might. When he gently pulled it up, he was prepared to feel something…powerful, painful? He was totally surprised.

All he felt was a slight tingling sensation in his hand. It spread down his arm and into his body, right to the core of his chest, to the center of where that electrical pulse always seemed to coalesce. Then, it was as if a tension he didn't realize he carried dissolved. The sensation was strange, it stole his breath away, and it took several moments before he could look up again.

He glanced at Sved. Despite the pain in his thigh, the small man grinned back up at him through his scraggly red beard.

Then Leon noticed something amazing. Sved was holding his Blade just as he had been when he extended it out to him. Leon compared the Blade he held to the one in Sved's hands, they looked identical, but where had the second one come from?

"Sved, I-I don't understand? How did this happen?" He held out the Blade in his hand.

"That is the question, Leon! That is the question that has puzzled and amazed learned men for many, many years. That's the power of the Blade - its power is never diminished no matter how many times it is shared! Just know that that Blade there is now yours. No one can ever really take it from you, and you can't ever really give it away. If you lose the Blade, it just sort of pops up on you or near you when you need it again. Welcome to the life of the Bladed!"

Leon didn't feel any more or any less himself. He couldn't tell that anything significant had really changed. But for the first time in forever, he was hopeful. He pushed up his hat and scratched his head as an unexpected smile graced his face.

Then something rustled above. Merle growled low. His snout pointed up, toward a branch extending out from the nearby forest. When Leon locked eyes on what Merle saw, he froze.

From high above Scarface blinked back down at him. His legs were balanced on a limb. His arms held a bow with an arrow drawn.

Leon didn't even dare breathe. He could almost feel an itch in his chest, right where the arrow would go.

Chapter 15

Leon closed his eyes and took a deep breath, waiting on the inevitable. When the seconds continued to tick by, and the arrow's bite held off, he glanced back up into the trees.

Scarface wore a wilted look of astonishment. The arrow was still notched, but the bow was no longer drawn back in imminent threat.

Leon took a chance and cautiously stepped forward. He spread his arms wide to show he wasn't planning on tossing any more knives around.

"We never intended this to happen. I don't know why you guys attacked us, but we were only defending ourselves. Take what you want and just leave us alone, okay?"

The man's expression went from slightly puzzled to extremely perplexed, but when he spoke his voice was deep and steady, "You took the Blade just now and it didn't hurt you? You feel...no enmity? No bloodlust?"

His statement made zero sense and Leon sensed the questions were rhetorical in nature, but he answered anyway, "No, sir, there was no pain. If anything, I feel better than I've felt in a long time, and as to the blood lust, I'm way too tired to fight any more of you tonight."

The man's eyes shifted to Sved, "And you, you stabbed me with that Blade! What bewitching spell did you cast to cause it to make me feel such...confusion? Why...why can I not draw on my power? What have you done?" He reached up and palmed the area between his leather armor where the Blade had found purchase during the fight.

Leon still worried the bow might rise again at any moment. Sved, for his part, remained conscious. He waited patiently until it was clear the man would allow him to answer, then he rose back up onto his arm once more, "I've done nothing to you myself. I've got no more magic in me than this dirt between my fingers, yes? It is the Blade that holds the power, and whatever the Blade's prick may have coaxed you to feel, I'm afraid it isn't permanent. If the Blade's presence temporarily cut you off from your power it's likely because you were seeking something beyond that power, deep down. My guess is there must be a part of you who questions the purpose of such power. The Blade...it persuades you to feel differently about things, no?"

The man's countenance took a visible hit. His shoulders sagged as his gaze dropped. Eventually, he nodded an affirmative.

Not waiting for a response, Leon called out once more, "Hey, mister, why don't you come down and talk? I'll call my dog off. He won't bother you. We're done fighting. Believe me when I say we never even wanted a fight to begin with!"

The man studied them with another inscrutable expression on his scarred face before disappearing back into the canopy.

Leon called Merle to his side and ordered him to sit and stay.

A few moments later the man stepped out from the shelter of the trees. He was hunched over a bit as if he was still experiencing some residual pain from whatever it was that the Blade did to him. He took hesitant steps forward, watching them with the eyes of a cornered animal until he stood before Leon and Merle. It wasn't lost on Leon that he moved without making a sound. For his part, Merle remained calm, silently panting at Leon's feet.

"I'm Leon Waldman, that there is Sveddleton Haberkorn, and that's Reed Whistler over there, he's still coming around. This is my dog Merle. Oh, and over there, well, I think his name is Dimples. Can you tell us who you are, why you attacked?"

"Rezzin Harl. We didn't know who was who when we attacked. Only that the Otterkin Horde was harboring fugitives. Your group was in the way." He spoke the last as if that fact alone completely atoned for the earlier battle.

He continued, "We were dispatched for the Day Walkers."

"The Day Walkers?" said Leon.

"Those wolves who are able to transition during day. We came to capture them, to bring them back to the Silent City, to learn their secret, and to determine whether or not to deem them rogues.

When your group wandered into the woods, the captain split our party. Our unit circled around and sought to subdue the one with you while the main force attacked those with the merchant horde."

Sved jerked up at the last but grunted in pain as soon as he did, "So, the Vindarri decided to wipe us out, just like that? We carry a written permit for our caravan, sanctioned by the Thrall himself! Would the Vin so easily revoke their own writ?"

"The goal wasn't to eliminate your horde, just to capture the Day Walkers. They will push the horde back downriver until they capture or slay the remaining Day Walkers. My guess is they will continue the pursuit for another day or two afterward though, just for the sport of the chase and to drive home a lesson for future consideration."

Leon cut in, "So, the other Vin? They are coming back, eventually?"

Rezzin's face turned grave, "Yes, sooner or later, they will be back this way and will expect me and the others to be here waiting with the last remaining wolf."

Leon cut eyes to Sved, "He means Cooper. Cooper, Ben, and the rest of that group have specially crafted suits that allow them to transition during daylight. That's how he defeated the Hootsi raiders on our way here."

"You're telling me that man who was talking with Ferschall back at camp took on a Hootsi raiding party with a handful of men and won?"

Leon nodded. "That's not all. That big guy over there was one of the leaders of the party. He alone escaped, but he lost his Anastashe mount during the raid. Ferschall said he would be dishonored and unable to return to his tribe. You think he might be looking for a little payback?"

Rezzin squatted down near Sved, "I think he was looking for more than vengeance. That woman defending the Day Walker. If I'm not mistaken, her scream before she dove into the river gave her away as a Hootsi, did it not?" Sved nodded thoughtfully, and Rezzin shrugged. "You men keep strange company!"

Shana might be a Hootsi?

Leon hadn't considered it at the time but her scream, just before she dove in after Cooper, did sound a lot like Gus when he came bursting up out of the old deer blind back at the ranch, and they both sounded similar to several of the Hootsi warriors when they chased their group across the bridge.

He took a closer look at Rezzin as the blond Vin studied Dimples.

"Sorry about your friends?"

Way to go, Leon, remind the man of why he was about to make you pincushion a few minutes ago!

Rezzin snorted in disdain. "You think we would be talking if those men were my friends? I've been forced to serve the whims of the Vin War Council for years, but no love is lost between me and the others who serve. I've dreamed of an escape for far too long. When you all took out the rest of my squad, my death was all but sealed." He shrugged. "I am a dead man walking."

Leon felt he was taking the situation much more philosophically than he would have thought possible.

"They are going to kill you just for being a survivor. Are you sure you folks aren't related to the Hootsi?"

His response was curt, "The Vin do not suffer disgrace as lightly as the Hootsi. They will make an example of my suffering before I am ended."

Leon felt a chill. He thought the Hootsi took their honor to a level beyond anything rational, but the Vin were downright insane!

Rezzin's eyes wandered down to the Blade tucked neatly into the belt at his side. Leon didn't think twice, he lifted it and extended it out to the Vin, hilt first, just as Sved had done for him, "I'm guessing you heard our conversation a few minutes ago. So, you probably know about as much about this as I do. You just trust that our hero from long ago passed along enough power to cure you, and you take it. Anyhow, I know this probably isn't why you told us all that, but it can't hurt to give it a try now, can it? It's yours if you want it, no strings attached..."

To Leon's surprise, and Sved's astonishment, Rezzin made an unexpected decision. He reached out and gingerly grasped the bone handle. When he pulled his arm back Leon was amazed all over again. Even though he was expecting what happened to happen, it was still surreal to actually see the Blade so seamlessly duplicated.

For a few heartbeats, Rezzin marveled the way Leon had marveled. Then he suddenly fell to his knees. A small hiss escaped his lips and his body trembled as tears slid down the sides of his face.

Leon looked to Sved. "Sved? Is he okay? What's wrong?"

Sved fell back on his back. He gazed up into the sky. "He'll be fine soon enough. We all carry a certain amount of residual scarring from the effects of the disease in our blood. Most of us don't even notice it's there. It grows as the disease corrupts until we first lift the Blade. After letting it build for years, it can shock a person's system to feel it dissipate."

A few minutes later, Rezzin took a deep satisfied breath, like he was tasting fresh air instead of the smoky haze that surrounded them. He looked uncertain but refreshed. He rolled his shoulder that was pierced, tentatively testing its ability to function. Then he smiled with a dawning realization that he was no longer encumbered by the prior wound.

Sved spoke up once more, "Whatever you were, whatever you may be, you won't ever be without the Blade again, Rezzin. Just remember that from now on."

"I have been a Ranger Guard of the Vin for many years. From the Wild Forest here to the far reaches of the Southern Islands, I've helped to further our tribal ambitions with violence. Many, many times I have wondered if we were in the right to do as we have done but it wasn't until tonight, until I had no other options, and until I saw what happened when you took the Blade, that I dared to hope that the Blade was truly a blessing and not a curse."

Leon gave Rezzin's shoulder a gentle pat. All in all, the moment was a little awkward, but he figured things could have gone so much worse!

Sved cringed like his leg was starting to get to him again, but he gritted his teeth and responded, "The way I see it, we have three choices if we can just figure out a way to get moving in the next day or so, yes? We can cross the Murk Water and head back toward the Hootsi border, we can continue toward Hollinger through the northern plains, a path extremely dangerous for such a small party this time of year, or we can follow the Murk northwest, further into the Wild Forest, to the borders of the Ageless Folk and skirt well north of the Silent City's territory. Leon, what do you think?"

Leon had no idea what the Silent City was, but he guessed it was somewhere in the kingdom of the Vin, which Ferschall had already warned him about. He also knew it would be suicide to return the way they had come. Finally, he knew being stuck out on flat plains with injured people was an all-around horrible idea. "We should follow the river west. Seems like our only choice if we want to try to stick together and avoid capture."

Sved agreed and Rezzin nodded his approval as well.

Leon suddenly felt the need to divulge a little more to his new companions. "Guys, I'm glad we are going to make a run at this together, but I've got to ask you something. Either of you ever heard of a Royal Tree?"

The blank looks he received in return were enough of an answer.

"Well, I had to try. Regardless, Reed and I and, hopefully, Shana, need to find one. I was told that they may have that information at the Bladed Archives in Hollinger?"

Sved chuckled till he grimaced, and Rezzin shook his head in disgust. "Who told you such a thing?"

Leon started to see where this was going, and he didn't care for it one bit. "Ferschall, he told Ben and his men that their best bet to retrieve their captured man from the Hootsi would be in Hollinger and that we could all get more information about those Royal Trees there as well."

"Well, he wasn't lying about the Hootsi. Your captive friend should be heading that way in the next month or so, as long as he doesn't dishonor himself between now and then, yes? But the Bladed Archives part doesn't sound right. To my knowledge, those archives burned to the ground generations ago. The spot where they once stood has been nothing more than a historical marker for many years now.

"Hey now, don't go looking like a water pig stole your dinner, maybe Ferschall knows something we don't, yes? What I can tell you is that if anyone knows anything about any Royal Trees, it is the matriarch of the Haberkorn Horde, Madam Hazzel. If we can make it far enough west through the Wild Forest, perhaps we can find a northern route that will take us into the territories of my people, no?"

"I'm not from around here, what is the Wild Forest, and who are the Ageless Folk?" Once more, both Sved and Rezzin gave him odd looks.

"Just where are you from, Leon?" Sved said.

"About as far as you can get from where we're standing right now, from a place called Texas." They both blinked at him, understandably unfamiliar with any such location.

Sved broke in, "Leon, those who make their home in the Wild Forest have cut themselves off from the outside world. There are many stories of this tribe, but my people are only merchants and none of us have successfully established trade with the Ageless folk in generations."

"So, no one really knows if they're still there?"

Rezzin responded, 'Oh they are there. The Silent Forest runs adjacent to the Murk River further west. The Vin War Council still convenes with the leadership of the Wild Ones, as my people call them, from time to time."

Despite the pain, Sved's eyebrows rose at the new information.

"Great! So, you have contacts over there?" said Leon.

"I'm afraid I don't. Some Vin have claimed to come and go among them, but many who have ventured beyond their borders are never heard from again.

"They may not be our biggest threat though. There are outlaws and fugitives who rob the caravan trails and retreat to the sanctuary of the eastern reaches of the forest. Then there's the wilderness itself, the terrain grows more rugged and the wildlife more violent the further in we go, but there is one upside to taking this path…"

"I'm almost afraid to ask…" Leon muttered.

"Most all tribes avoid the forest's interior, and the Wild Forest is the largest of all forests in Fayden."

# # #

Fortunately, the wind from the south remained steady and the forest's fires never drew close to Leon and his new companions. In addition, a light misting rain blanketed the area for a few hours before sunrise, smoldering the flames before they grew beyond control. Leon suspected they were out of danger from any lingering forest fire for the time being.

As it turned out, Rezzin had some knowledge on how to deal with arrow wounds. He safely had the arrow out of Sved's leg, and the wound cauterized before the first rays of sun broke the horizon.

At Rezzin's request, they pulled the stiff bodies of the fallen Vin out to the edge of the river and tied large rocks to their chests before sliding them down into watery graves.

Rezzin sighed as he nudged the last of them off the bank, "It's better for everyone that the fate of those men remains a mystery to any who return."

Rezzin also helped Leon to move Sved and Dimples back into the shelter of the trees and to disguise all traces of the battle at the edge of the clearing. By that time Reed was doing better and took Leon's explanation for everything that happened earlier with calm resignation.

Afterward, everyone managed to get a little sleep while Reed offered to keep watch. Leon noticed he positioned himself facing the direction where he had last seen Haddie. If he felt guilty or worried, he didn't say.

When dawn broke, the early morning fog paired with the residual smoke from the smoldering embers of nearby fires provided little visibility. Leon rolled over and gazed up into the canopy of trees, at least as far up as the mist and smoke would allow. So peaceful. The swirling mist gave those giant hardwood branches an uncanny mystique.

How is it such a beautiful place is such a freaky nightmare?

As he lay there, he realized he was resting comfortably on bare earth. It was amazing how quickly he had acclimated to sleeping rough. He wasn't even sore from the spare pebble or two he had missed when he cleared his small spot the night before.

Sved was also awake by some miracle. His head lay propped on a pack, just a foot or two from Leon's. He coughed, and his voice was so hoarse it came out like a whisper.

"Leon, we need to think about how we're getting out of here. You need to go check the camp. Maybe find supplies, yes? They left in a hurry and there should be stuff left behind. I'll need a crutch, something to help me get around. Why don't you take Reed? Probably better that you two aren't here when the Hootsi finally comes around?" Sved continued in delirious chatter, his voice barely audible over the creak and sway of the hardwoods in the morning breeze.

Looking up like that at the canopy above served to remind Leon of some of the last moments he had alone with Gus.

Could it really have only been a little over a week since we parted ways?

Sved nudged him. "Leon, you hear me, yes?"

"Yeah, Svedster, I'm on it." He climbed to his feet and Merle shot up beside him, already eager to get going. He looked down at the surly little man, "Now don't go wandering off anywhere while we're gone."

Sved grumbled at the poor excuse of a joke. But Leon didn't give him time for a retort. He nodded once to Rezzin and walked over to where Reed stood peering out into the fog. He had long since recovered from his addled state the night before. Now he just looked pensive and sad.

"Reed, how about we go see if we can't find something to scavenge from what's left of the horde's camp before we get moving? Sved says we need to find a way to head out soon if we plan on giving these Vin the slip before they return."

Without a word, Reed grunted, turned, and walked back through the woods, toward the previous night's camp. Leon watched him for a moment, then jogged to catch up.

"Hey, man. I get it, this is all one crummy trip down the rabbit hole. But, for better or worse, you and me, we're stuck in this together!"

"True."

"Well, how come you do that then?"

"Do what?"

"Shut down, slink away into your own thoughts, disconnect? Come on, man, you've got to know what I'm talking about? You do it all the time!"

"Listen, Leon, you are handling things pretty good, okay? I know this is new to you and believe it or not I'm actually glad you took the Blade when it was offered. I've just got a lot on my mind. Are we good? You need a pep talk or something?"

"No, we're good...I guess. Just...well, never mind. Anyhow, what happened to you last night? Did they get Haddie?"

The color drained from Reed's face. At first, Leon thought he had made him upset, but then he started talking, "All those scouts with us came busting through the brush all at once. They grabbed Haddie, dragging her back toward camp without a word. Before I could even drop the firewood to follow, the Vin had me surrounded. I would have been dead for sure if they hadn't responded to some strange call from where your group was holed up. The couple were more interested in Haddie's entourage when all the others split. I decided she was in good hands with all those guards and took off to help you guys." He shrugged. "You know the rest."

He didn't seem in the mood to discuss things further and Leon couldn't blame him there. They continued marching forward in silence until they came to the still smoking remnants of the camp at the edge of the woods.

# # #

One of the colorful little barges had rolled into one of the cook fires. It was still smoldering. Lying beside it were the bodies of two small men, arrows protruding from the back of each corpse.

After that, the swirling fog lost its wild mystique for Leon. It became dense, oppressive, and ominous as they spread apart and quietly scoured the area for supplies and survivors.

Leon suggested they sneak down close to the river to see if perhaps Shana and Cooper had taken refuge along the shoreline somewhere. Unfortunately, they could only see clearly enough to scour their side of the river's shore and there was no sign of a living soul present. After over an hour of searching, Reed insisted they go back up into the remnant of the camp to search for supplies and survivors.

Leon was rolling up some spare rope when Reed popped up behind him and tapped him on the shoulder. He jumped so hard he nearly took a tumble.

"Dude! You nearly gave me a heart attack!"

"Well, pay more attention. Finish that and come here."

He led Leon several paces away until he came to more small bodies. Leon looked down at them and noticed two of them looked familiar. "That one there is Haddie's father! The guy next to him is one of the other leaders of the horde. I talked to them last night before we left."

"I thought I recognized them, too."

"But no sign of Haddie?"

Reed's expression faltered, "None. But if this guy was their leader, we had better get back and let Sved know what's happened."

They turned when they both heard a sound nearby, like something scraping against wood. They froze. Even Merle froze where he stood. After a moment, they heard it again.

Leon spoke up, "Ughh…who's there?" Reed thumped him in the shoulder. Merle growled, and Leon shushed him as well.

After a moment, there it was again, a thumping and scratching sound.

Leon walked toward it. It was close enough that if it was one of the Vin archers, he was done for anyhow. He couldn't see anything at first, but the closer he got, the more he could distinguish an odd shape just up ahead. It was another one of the hippo barges. This one was a much tinier cart than many of the others they had seen. It was actually still lashed to a dead hippo. The hippo was also small in comparison to most he had seen the day before. When he sidled up beside it, he noticed another dead Otterkin man lying face down on top of the cart, his body was slumped over a large wooden crate on the back. Had the box just moved?

There it was again! It moved once more like there was something inside attempting to get out. Leon rushed over and respectfully lowered the man to the ground. There was nothing more they could do for him.

When he turned back to inspect the box, he couldn't help himself from feeling a small thrill of excitement. The day before he had suspected the horde were transporting some animals on a few of the barges when he had seen the boxes with the air holes. Now he was going to get a peek at what sort of creature they might be carrying.

Merle walked up and sniffed the box before making a half-hearted effort to give it a low growl. Then he moved on to sniff around the hippo.

So, you don't think it's much of a threat do you, boy?

Leon quickly discovered the box was still locked from the top. He pulled out his new Blade from where he had it tucked in his belt and pried the nails off from one of the side panels.

Reed spoke up from behind, "Are you sure that's a good idea, Leon?"

"No, but aren't you curious what's in here?"

"Not really, no."

Leon ignored the Debby Downer attitude. "Whatever it is, it'll die if we don't at least free it."

"Let's hope it's thankful then. Let me get up there out of the way before you open that thing up! No telling what sort of creature they may have hoarded away in there."

"I'm not going to let you live this down if it's a giant chicken!"

"Haha... Okay, I'm clear, go ahead and open it up if you must."

Leon pried the last nail away and pulled down the board, standing just off to the side in case anything came barreling his way.

When no rampaging creature came leaping out, he took his first look inside.

He was speechless. He tried but couldn't form a word.

"Leon? Hey, man? Leon, what's in there? Is it dangerous?" Reed could see Leon's expression, and he could hear some soft chirping noises but still couldn't see a thing. He shuffled around slowly until he had an angle where he could get a glimpse as well.

He froze.

Standing huddled together at the back of the box, on hay and broken eggshells, were two very odd-looking animals.

"Leon, you got any idea what these creatures are?"

Leon's eyes sparkled with newly discovered fanatic obsession. "I don't know for sure. I mean, I've only ever heard of them from storybooks when I was a kid, but these don't exactly match up against any description I've ever heard."

"Descriptions of what?"

"Bodies and back legs like Lion cubs with the heads, beaks, and front talons of large raptors? These aren't supposed to be real, but this whole world is geared that way, isn't it?"

"What way? What are they?"

"They appear to be griffin chicks...err, cubs?"

#

"Leon, we seriously don't have time for this."

"Just give me five minutes with them. Somehow, and I don't know how, I feel like I can make this work. I think I can get them to come along."

Each of the two griffin cubs was about a quarter of Merle's size. They were coated in silky fine feathery fur colored white with a rich tan dappled mix of spots. Leon noted their coloring held an odd similarity to the coloring pattern on the hides of longhorn cattle from back home.

That, however, was where similarities ended. Their beaks and claws held a dull metallic sheen, with razor-sharp edges. The wings looked oddest of all. They were there, they just didn't have any feathers on them. More like ungainly little stumps.

The griffin cubs were obviously brand new hatchlings. Their eggshells were broken into pieces at the back of the crate. Leon couldn't smell either of the cracked shells, which, if they were like any of the chickens he had ever seen hatch, meant they were fresh. He suspected they may have even hatched the previous night, during all the commotion.

He held a hand out to each of them. In each hand was a partially burnt slice of water pig from a nearby campfire.

They sniffed at the offering, each one making small chirping noises. Finally, the larger of the two took a cautious step forward and snatched the meat away. That was all it took to melt the ice. Soon the smaller one followed suit. While they distractedly picked at the chunks of meat, Leon slid his hands forward to pet them both.

Just as his hands met their fur, a warmth from within his chest bubbled outward. It was similar to the electric current he was used to, but this had a different taste. It wasn't painful either. In fact, it felt great. The warmth spread out into his hands and onto the cubs. To Leon's amazement, both cubs stopped what they were doing and nuzzled his hands affectionately.

"Um, Reed? What just happened?" Reed was nearby, going through whatever food stores were still lashed to the wagon.

"What do you mean?"

"When I reached out to touch these guys, I sort of felt that weird power thing push out from my chest. Only this time, it wasn't that electric push, you know? It was more of a warm, soft push. If felt…more natural?"

Reed was by his side in a moment. "Can you do it again?"

"I don't know, maybe?"

He reached out and touched them once more, when he did, he thought about that warm feeling. Out from his chest it pushed, and the cubs responded accordingly.

Reed reached up and rubbed his forehead. "You've found a gift, Leon. It's not one I know, but there's no doubt about it, your gift has something to do with animals."

"A gift?"

"It's from the Blade. The Blade doesn't only stop the corruption from making you transition on moonless nights, it also unlocks and enhances unique gifts. Some gifts are more based on extensions of inherent tribal abilities. Others…well, others are unique to each person. Most folks spend years attempting to discover their gifts, many never realize all the gifts the Blade provides. Looks like you took the fast track…once again." Leon could hear the dry disapproval in Reed's voice, but it didn't answer the questions floating in his mind.

"So, my gift is to make little cuddly creatures…cuddlier?"

"No, Leon, I suspect your gift is to make those mythical beasts somehow less apt to tear into us once you run out of water pig, but maybe it makes them cuddlier as well? The point is, the gift grows with the gifted, you just have to use it to strengthen it and better know its limitations."

Reed reached out to give one a pet and almost lost a pair of fingers when the cub snapped at him with a ferocious little screech. He gave all three of them his signature glare and tromped back to the other side of the cart.

The new knowledge got Leon thinking. "So, everyone has at least one gift then?"

"Yeah. Pretty much."

"Well, what's one of your gifts?"

Reed was silent though Leon could still hear him working. He absentmindedly scratched the cubs up under their beaked chins, and they actually purred back at him in a cooing sort of way.

"Come on, Reed. It's just us two here. I get so little information from any of you as it is, I'm just trying to learn how this all works."

"Okay, I guess no one's given you much to go on."

"You think?"

"But since you opted to take a Blade as woefully unprepared as you are, I should probably try to teach you what I can. To start with, all Fayden Tribes once supposedly came from six or seven different families, with different attributes that manifest themselves in different forms.

"Before you ask, I have no idea what Tribe you come from. Your hair itself is odd enough, I don't know of any tribe that has curly blond hair and darker-toned skin. Every Fayden person back home has a dark shade of hair color. But the redheaded folk in the horde we met yesterday kind of threw me for a loop too, so who knows, right?"

"Fair enough. But how about you just tell me about you. I think we're past the point where it's not polite to ask, don't you?" Reed nodded in agreement.

"I'll tell you, but first I've got an idea for how we can put some distance between us and all of this without having to haul everything on our backs. Help me drag this cart over there. I'm thinking that if we can rip off all that extra wood on either end, the exposed frame may be light enough for us to maneuver around on our own."

"Kind of like a hand cart or a rickshaw?"

"Yeah, that's the idea."

Turned out that Blades were useful for ripping up boards, too. No matter how hard Leon pried on a board, the edge of his new Blade never chipped, it didn't even seem to grow dull. Half an hour of prying and pulling later, and they were in business. The wheelbase wasn't but about three feet wide and removing all the extra wood really lightened the whole platform. The going wouldn't be super-fast, but it would be maneuverable in the forest and at least they would be able to bring Sved and the cubs along now.

As they finished scavenging for gear and supplies, Leon found the pack he had been carrying for Ferschall. He was interested to see that Shana's pack was missing. He was pretty sure Shana wouldn't have come back for it, she hated having to lug that thing around. Which meant Ferschall likely made it out of there in time. The best part though was when he saw that the pack containing the remaining coffee rations was right there next to it. He wouldn't have to worry about his caffeine fix for quite some time.

He considered abandoning the hefty mound of pottery, but for some reason, his feet just wouldn't allow him to move along and leave all of Ferschall's work to waste away beside the river. He scooped it up, then threw the pack, along with the coffee, on the cart.

It's not like any of us are going to be going anywhere in a hurry, anyway.

When they were fully loaded, and Leon had fed the cubs once more, they started back toward the others. Leon pushed the cart while Reed walked behind, doing his best to wipe away any trace of their passing with a heavy fur blanket.

# # #

They fell into a slow plodding rhythm. It was then that Reed finally offered up some explanation, "You may be interested to know that Gus and his family are related to the Hootsi. Ironically, that's probably what Shana is as well.

"Ethan traces his roots back to the Lupus or wolf Tribe. But here's the catch, even though he's my mother's brother, I trace my bloodline through my father's clan."

"What is your father?"

"My father was from a small and obscure clan in our world. In fact, I am considered by many to be one of the last of our kind.

We've been called many things over the ages, but most know us as Fae folk." Reed sounded so serious. Leon almost couldn't swallow down his chuckle in time.

Instead, he turned back to Reed with a straight face and said, "So, basically, you're telling me you're the long-lost relative of…Tinkerbelle?" Reed even had to chuckle at that.

"Ah-ha! You do have a sense of humor!"

"Hey, man, of course, I've got a sense of humor, and I get it, the weirdness of all of this just keeps getting worse. But you have to remember, most of the fairy tales back at home are just made-up stories constructed around bits and pieces of truth that people have experienced.

"My tribe was never very large in our world. So, there's just not as much information available about the types of gifting my people receive from the Blade."

"So, you don't know how you're gifted yet?" It dawned on Leon how insensitive he had been regarding his gift earlier.

"No, I mean I know two basic gifts I have, but I haven't discovered any personalized gifts yet."

"You want to share?"

"Well, the first one is simple, I help things grow. Plants, for example. I can push to grow much more quickly than is natural. Animals are more nuanced, but I think I can do the same, I just haven't had time to really experiment. Some of this is new to me as well.

"My other gift is endurance. Though I'm not as fast as some, I have incredible stamina and can keep going for much longer than other people, even other Fayden people. We are like the distance runners of the ancient Tribes."

Leon considered what Reed had shared. He definitely could have used that endurance gift during track season last spring. But it made him consider something else nagging at him, "Okay, so we have this Blade that saves us from having twisted versions of powers we really don't understand, it gives us these awesome gifts in return, and it basically protects us from turning into monsters. What type of monster are you…without the Blade I mean?"

"The answer to that is likely not what you're expecting. Unlike most of the other tribes, Fae folk don't change halfway into any particular beast. We are known to take on a different look, though" Reed shrugged. "It's hard to explain, but you'd know if you saw.'

"How come more people in this world don't take up the Blade?"

"Good question. The best answer I have is that most folks don't see their natural power as twisted, they simply see it as powerful and useful. Pound for pound, us Bladed don't have the same strength at night as someone who is transitioned. The Unbladed also develop abilities, those abilities are simply twisted versions of the gifts we employ and can be extremely strong starting off. Many choose to use that power for their benefit.

"But the biggest problem for an Unbladed person is when that person pursues their natural power beyond the confines of the night, and they begin to ignore the painful effects of daylight on their body, it drives them insane."

"Those people are the rogues you all keep talking about?"

"Exactly. It's lunacy for Ben and his men to do what they've been doing. The first few times exposure to the sun may simply be painful, but over time the pain stops to be a deterrent and begins to create an addiction. That's when the crazy starts.

"Rogues can become extremely strong with beastly agility. Though they prefer to hunt with at least a little light in the evening or early morning. They can, on rare occasions, be dangerous in daylight as well. For this reason, most rogues become most active and reckless on a full moon. Even other Unbladed work together to quickly put those individuals down.

"Back at home, in Fayden society, you don't have to take up the Blade, but when Unbladed go rogue, we have specialized teams ready to eliminate them as quietly as possible."

"That bad?"

"Let me put it this way, I don't know for certain, but I suspect that every fairytale villain you've heard of likely had a rogue it was based off because when they lose their sense of humanity, they become the stuff of nightmares."

"What about our gifts? I just used mine a few minutes ago! Will daylight affect us as well?"

"Daylight doesn't affect our use of the Blade's gifts. I suspect if you tried to transition into your more twisted form, it could have an effect, but Bladed people have no need to ever do that type of thing."

Leon continued plodding along as he considered what Reed had shared. It helped to resolve so many puzzling observations, but it also brought up so many more questions. The questions would have to wait, however, because they were getting close to the rest of their party.

Angry voices shouted back and forth a little further up through the wood. The sheer size of the forest's trees allowed them to maneuver their hand cart through the barren undergrowth, but they couldn't quite see what was going on up ahead.

Chapter 16

Reed signaled for Leon to leave the cart. Leon called Merle to his side. Then, with the griffin cubs stashed securely in their wooden nest, Leon joined Reed to investigate the shouting.

When they were just a few dozen feet away from the commotion, they paused to listen.

"Please, believe me, I had nothing to do with that wound in his leg!"

"Get back! I said get back!" It was a familiar voice. Haddie's voice!

Reed heard it, too, because he immediately broke cover and rushed out into the open.

"Oh, Reed!" As Leon followed behind, he saw Haddie latch on and cling tightly to Reed's arm.

"What's going on here? What's happened to Sved?" Leon looked from her to Rezzin.

"That's what I've been trying to tell her. I think this man has an infection. I need to brew him some gristle tea to break the fever, but she's been insistent that I stay away."

"It's okay, Haddie, Rezzin is with us now. I can explain while he works to get Sved fixed up." Haddie squinted at Rezzin but didn't move to intercede either.

Leon, at least, was relieved to be over that hurdle. Then he remembered her father's corpse in the clearing and groaned inwardly at what needed to be shared.

"Come on over here. Umm…why don't you sit down?" He shifted to English and addressed Reed, "Hey, man, can you grab her something to drink, maybe a bite to eat?" He gave Reed a knowing look, and Reed returned it with a sad nod.

"Haddie, Reed and I went back to the camp, but the horde is mostly gone, chased downriver by the Vin."

"Oh, that's horrible, but as long as they have access to the river, they should be fine." A quiet sob escaped her chest, "They killed everyone with me, Leon, everyone! I thought they must have killed Reed too, I'm so glad you all made it!"

"How'd you escape?"

"One of my escorts, I think it was cousin Mendleton, told me to hide in a hollow stump while we were being chased. I was so worried for everyone, but he made me promise I would stay until he returned. Only, he never did. I stayed there all night."

At the last, she broke down and heavy tears streamed down her cheeks. Leon, having grown up with a crusty old cowboy like Gus, simply didn't know what to do with a sobbing woman whom he had only just met. He awkwardly patted her back until Reed plunked down next to her and wrapped an arm around her thin shoulders in a gentle embrace.

"I'm so sorry Haddie. But there's something else you need to know." Leon paused, not knowing how to continue. He figured there was no good way to say what had to be said so he opted to just spit it out, "Haddie, when we went back to camp, we found your father…"

"Why didn't you say so? Where is he now? How come he didn't send some men back with you to at least help…" Leon held up a hand to stop her.

"No, Haddie, we found his body. He and…well, lots of folks from the horde. They're dead. I'm so sorry to be the one to tell you…"

Haddie's face contorted in anguish while a silent sob shook her body. Then she melted as Reed pulled her in close. Leon put a hand on her shoulder and gently squeezed before deciding that Reed, despite the language barrier, offered better comfort than he knew to give.

He got up, made sure Rezzin had everything he needed for helping Sved, then shuffled over to the Hootsi.

Dimples was awake. Tied up tight, he wasn't going anywhere any time soon; yet he missed nothing with a silent, wary expression in his intense green eyes.

As Leon approached the man, an overpowering scent of blood and musky body odor hit him. Here he thought he had been living rough! Dimples was the sort of guy who made a mountain man legend like Jeremiah Johnson seem civilized by comparison.

"Can I get you some water or something?"

Maybe a bar of soap and a couple dunks in the river?

Dimples studied him stoically, eventually nodding yes.

Leon slowly fed him from one of their skins, one little swig of water at a time, so he wouldn't sputter too much.

"I'm Leon Waldman. Can you give me your name?"

Dimples opened his mouth to speak, then closed it as if considering something, when he continued his voice was deep and raspy, "Your people have already taken my name. I have no name left to give." Leon cringed.

"Listen, man, I know it doesn't seem like it, but those guys weren't my people, and neither me nor Reed," he pointed over in Reed's direction, "had any part in what they did to you and your friends. We were their prisoners as well, for all intents and purposes."

The man studied Leon for a long while, before giving him a silent nod.

"Is there something I can call you then? Ferschall mentioned you had a nickname...Dimples?"

He scowled in disgust but shrugged. "Dimples is about as good as I deserve. Sure, call me Dimples."

Leon couldn't quite figure out what to make of the guy. "Well, anyway, I'm sorry I tied you up. I just wanted to make sure you didn't wake up thinking we were your enemy. Like I said, I had nothing to do with what Ben and his men did to you and your men."

Dimples just shrugged again, so Leon continued, "In fact, I wanted to thank you for what you did last night. You saved my dog for sure. That guy would have put an arrow through him if not for you."

No response.

"Regardless, I'm just glad I was able to find you and drag you out of the woods before the smoke from that brief forest fire got you first, it turned pretty smoky in there for a while. Until the rain snuffed things out at least."

Leon knew he was rambling, so he stopped and simply grinned down at the man, thinking he had found some common ground. Only Dimples continued to ignore all the social cues for his overtures of friendship.

"Where are the men who fought me in the canyon?"

"No idea. The Vin were after them. They may have them now for all we know. They shot the one warrior with us, and he fell into the river during the fight last night."

Dimples' countenance shrank, shame crept into his eyes. "I have no way to reclaim the honor that was lost and nowhere to go. Kill me and end this sorry excuse of a Hootsi man."

Leon coughed up the water he had been attempting to swallow. He wasn't willing to let the warrior give up on himself that easily. "Look, Dimples, you don't know for sure that the Vin have the folks you are after. Even so, what were you planning to do? Kill them all?" Dimples nodded in a matter-of-fact fashion, but Leon ignored him and pushed forward.

"A tough old herder I know, one who shares the same blood as you, used to tell me the only way to keep the taste of revenge fresh on your mouth is to take a long pull off a bottle of hate every so often. But the problem with hate is that it's poison to a man's soul. I'm not telling you to give up seeking justice for your friends, but I'd like to offer you another path, for the time being at least."

Dimples looked up. Leon could tell he was trying hard and failing at not appearing interested.

"Come with us, Dimples. Come with us into the Wild Forest. We are heading to skirt the borders of the Ageless Clan. You've been stranded out here just like me. Come with us, and let's find a new path together with these people. You just might be surprised where that path leads."

"I will kill those men if we see them again." He glanced at Leon to see if he would protest.

"When that time comes, you're going to have a decision to make, and I won't get in your way if that's what you're asking."

"It has been said the Wild Forests are an Emerald Ocean that leads to western skies. My people speak of legendary beasts and magical creatures that inhabit these forests. If my life is forfeit, I think I would like to see these sights before I am no more."

"Ferschall sure seemed to think you were an honorable person. If you promise not to hurt us, your word is good enough for me." Dimples nodded. "Good. Now that you're with us, you should know we have to leave before the Vin return or we're all as good as dead. So, want to help me bring in some of the supplies we scavenged? Then maybe get yourself something to eat…or maybe have a bath before we head out?"

Leon could tell Dimples was taken by surprise when he sliced his bonds and helped him to his feet. The man was still apprehensive, but who wouldn't have been in his shoes?

Together they helped drag the cart into their improvised camp. When Dimples heard the growling and cooing and peered in to discover what was in the kennel, his whole demeanor shifted once more. For a few brief moments, the stoic warrior disappeared. To Leon, he suddenly looked more like a kid standing before the candy aisle. The guy really treasured animals with claws and talons.

Chapter 17

As they traveled into the depths of the forest, Leon once more resumed his role as a language teacher for Reed. This time, Reed was an intense and avid student. Leon could tell that a certain redhead who gave praise at every small step along the way was as good a motivation as any. Though Reed wasn't the uncanny student that Ben represented, he was quicker on the uptake than Leon would have thought likely.

Still, the trip wasn't easy. On their first week of travel, Leon suffered insomnia each night over fear that the Vin would find them, that they would come screeching in from the branches above like demon phantoms with red eyes and cold fingers reaching out to clasp him and steal his power. Rezz did his best to put his mind at ease when Leon woke up shouting for the third night in a row.

"Leon, the Vin are flesh and blood, same as anyone else. Tribal talents have allowed many of my people to master the art of absorbing life's energy. It is true my fellow tribesmen are dangerous warriors, but they are not all astute trackers, and fewer still would care to follow us into these woods." Leon wanted to believe his new ally but thought he walked a fine line between making a point and undermining it with his own unique skill set. Rezz was an exceptionally skilled woodsman.

Both Rezzin and Dimples worked together to use all their considerable knowledge of woodcraft to hide their tracks and cover their trail. In the end, it was the lively rhythm of forest sounds that followed in their wake and gradually ate away at his anxiety. It took time, but Leon eventually came to believe there would be no pursuit.

The endless green of the forest, both above and below, capsulated Leon and his traveling companions, giving him an appreciation for the perspective of an ant in an earthly garden. Its dark depths spoke of an immeasurable vitality that continued to impress upon him a need for wary vigilance. But the bulk of the unease it engendered was displaced by the wonder it created through the sheer magnitude of foliage it housed and the diversity of species it held.

The loss of Shana continued to weigh heavy on Leon's heart. Many times, he questioned what it was that held him back from diving off that cliff behind her. Was it loyalty to Reed and Sved? Was it jealousy at her growing affection for Cooper? Or was it cowardice, plain and simple? He wanted to believe it was the former but was never very good at pinning down his own motivations. Whatever they were, what was done was done. He held tight to the hope that she and Cooper somehow made it far enough downriver to join the protection of the remaining horde.

As they traveled, Rezzin, or Rezz, as Leon took to calling him, continued to look after Sved's injured leg, treating it with forest herbs and clean cloth as best he could. He even attempted to teach Leon some herbal lore. "Leon, this small mossy plant is called Reaver's Relief. It grows in densely wooded areas throughout Fayden and when ground up into a poultice and applied to a wound, it can help to prevent infections..." Leon marveled at the knowledge the Ranger Guard possessed and tried to learn as much as possible each time the man offered advice.

Initially, Sved moaned the days away in agony from his perch atop the cart. Haddie fussed over him a couple of times a day, and Leon had mixed feelings when she did. His turn to push the cart would either be punctuated by Sved's grumbling or her steady stream of questions.

After about a week the moaning and grumbling dwindled. Leon almost wished it hadn't. If a return to good-natured sarcasm and snark were any indication of an overall improvement in the health of an injured person, Sved was quickly progressing into a glowing specimen of vigor.

Reed made some significant changes as well. As his proficiency with the Fayden language grew, so he and Haddie grew more inseparable. In an ironic way, it actually made perfect sense that the one who could never seem to pipe down would be so smitten with the one who never would pipe up. Leon made sure to explain such profound observations to anyone willing to listen. Yet, despite the constant ribbing, Reed took to wearing a smile more often than a scowl. It was a win for everyone as far as Leon was concerned.

By far though, Leon's biggest surprise was Dimples. Upon his very first introduction to the griffin cubs, he had become infatuated with the furry creatures. He claimed he knew of no one before who had ever managed to tame such a beast, though many of his clan had tried over the years. He marveled each time Leon fed them and picked them up or held them close.

It came as no surprise to Leon that Dimples was the first of any of his other traveling companions which the griffin cubs allowed to come near. With time, they even tolerated allowing him to feed them, though they would snap at him if he attempted to touch their silky coats.

Still, Leon could somehow tell they would soon come around to allowing the Hootsi to touch them as well, and it made him glad. Each small milestone seemed to give the broken man a tiny sliver of hope in an otherwise hopeless existence.

The wooded path they traveled was a slow slog, and much to Merle's endless delight there were constant run-ins with exotic looking beasts that had to be chased away, but they were surrounded by beauty the likes of which Leon had never imagined. Spring was in full swing. The air was sweet with the new life of the forest. Carpets of exotically pungent wildflowers bloomed vibrantly in every open meadow they passed. Even the canopy above blossomed with flowering vines.

Their pace was light, and their days were long. Small creeks and streams provided ample locations to bathe and refresh themselves. The forests held an endless supply of delicious foods. These combined aspects worked to lighten the tension within the weary shoulders of all the travelers.

Reed even had time to resume training Leon on how to use the Blade, though his lessons were often punctuated by criticisms and correction from a certain little man with a bum leg. Despite the admonishments from the peanut gallery, Sved did add to Leon's training by instructing him on the basics of throwing his Blade, something even Reed agreed could be handy to know. Still, the majority of Leon's lessons were adjudicated by one of Reed's more volatile counter-personas, seemingly inspired by Gunnery Sergeant Hartman.

The exercise routine each evening was a test of endurance, but the Blade training afterward was worth the pain. Leon found the art of fighting with Blade was similar in form to a dance, just deadlier. The steps came easy when the pacing had a flow. Leon had always been a decent country dancer.

"Blades lack the reach of swords. This provides advantages and disadvantages. For instance, in tight settings fighting with a long sword may be a detriment. Then again, fighting one on one in a wide-open setting places the Blade wielder at the disadvantage. And finally, fighting without shield and armor requires speed and dexterity for compensation. It is therefore just as important to learn to pick the setting for the fight as it is to learn the styles used to wield the Blade."

Leon thought about what Reed said. Something just sounded off until a realization struck. "Ferschall didn't seem to adjust the setting when he fought the Hootsi."

"Ferschall didn't have a choice. As it was, he was extremely lucky he only got away with a few small nicks."

Leon thought back to the fight. At the time, it seemed obvious to him that Ferschall was in complete control of the fight for the entire duration of the struggle. Almost like he had been sparring with the man to appease the Hootsi clan's honor. Ferschall had just as much admitted to it after the struggle. However, Reed was the more experienced fighter and Leon deferred to his judgment.

"Focus, Leon. Take your stance, Blade up. I'm going to attack with an overhead swipe, and I want you to deflect the blow."

Leon tried and failed. His mind just wasn't in sync with how he needed his body to move.

"Come on, man, you're about as useful as a chocolate teapot right now!" Reed shouted before continuing with forced restraint,

"You had this down yesterday. Focus! I'm going to attack. I want you to defend and counter. Remember, most Bladed fights are over in seconds. Your first counter may be the only one you get."

So far Leon had only ever been able to parry Reed's blows. The counters he had been trained to throw were easily deflected by his new instructor. Thus, once again, his parry absorbed Reed's blow and yet when he stepped into the next move with a backhanded slash, his feet were kicked out from under him, and he hit the forest floor with a painful thump.

"Leon, I know you can move faster than that, how come you won't commit to your attacks? You need to move with purpose! Stop tip-toeing through the daisies!"

"I don't want to hurt you, man," Leon responded.

Reed's sour face broke out into a feral smile. "You think you can hurt me? Leon, I've been training to fight since I was ten years old, since well before I knew of our blood heritage. My instructors were masters of five unique fighting styles. I welcome the challenge, but a simple farm boy who's never even held a Blade before a few weeks ago won't be hurting me anytime soon. Now get up and focus! Let's do this again."

Leon simmered. Not so much at the disrespect that Reed exhibited in not acknowledging the difference between a rancher and a farmer, but more at the idea that Leon was somehow less worthy to wield the Blade. There was more to the Blade than its usefulness as a mere token of power, or even as a weapon. There was a connection there, he had felt it the moment he lifted the hilt.

I just need to find that connection again, let it feed into me!

Putting aside his annoyance and focusing on his Blade instead, he readjusted his grip on the bone hilt handle. He reached for the flutter of connection he had felt off-and-on over the past few weeks. Only after he found the trickle of power emanating from his Blade and into his arm did he adjust his stance and nod that he was ready.

Reed's Blade darted forward in a right-handed straight jab. Leon didn't think, he just acted. He stepped in and to the right, slapping Reed's Blade with his own as he moved. In the same fluid motion, he sliced inward toward Reed's shoulder.

The shoulder moved out of reach before he could connect. Some part of his brain told him Reed would be countering, so he continued to pivot, even as he slashed to the right, and then left, dropping down into a crouch as he did.

At the last moment, just before he was so low, he would need to roll forward to maintain his balance, a rush of power flowed into him, from his Blade. It pushed his hand forward. He tried moving the Blade to the right, but the power's surge steered him to the left. He didn't fight the surge. His hand snaked out so fast he couldn't turn his head quick enough to follow its arc. His hand twisted as it moved and when it was fully extended the flat side of his Blade connect with something solid.

He came up grinning. Reed stared at him dumbfounded. "Do that again."

Once again, Leon reached for the connection, but all he could picture was Reed's red face. Before he knew it, he was flat on his back. Things became painful afterward, and the night's sparring went an extra half-hour longer than normal.

#

At just a little over two weeks after their encounter with the Vin, the group saw changes within the forest. First, their path transitioned from gently rolling terrain into rougher grade slopes. Then the river they followed took a switchback and vanished around a bend to the south. Sved insisted they continue northwest. So, they left the comfort of the river.

Afterward, Leon felt they moved uphill more than downhill as they steadily gained elevation, into more of a hill country-esque type area. The forest fauna grew older as the trees grew even larger. Shady deciduous hardwoods gave way to sprawling evergreens. Sved claimed this was good, that it meant they were drawing closer toward the border valleys, where they could finally turn north. He claimed to know of a cousin of a cousin who had skirted the forest boundaries of the Ageless Tribe, much as he planned to do and returned to tell the tale.

Leon attempted to bury his growing anxieties under the struggles of learning new things from his travel companions. Reed's blunt approach to training continued to hammer him into a well-conditioned fighting machine, but it wasn't his favorite. By far, his newest found passion was archery.

He grew up an avid hunter in a place where hunting was encouraged. Yet, his previous style of hunting, the old Texas deer feeder near a deer blind equipped with propane heater style of hunting, couldn't much hold a candle to the true art of hunting practiced by Rezz. When Rezz went out solo, the camp seldom went without fresh meat. He could stalk his prey through all manner of terrain. He had the kind of accuracy that transcended talent. The kind that could only be reached through a lifetime of consistent practice.

All it took was an invitation to tag along on one hunt and Leon had the bug. He begged his new friend to teach him to hunt and shoot like he did. Despite the fact Leon knew how to use a compound bow back home, it took over a week of consistent practice with the longbow and a never-ending tutorial on the basics of spot and stalk tactics, before Rezz felt confident Leon was ready to give it a try. The morning Leon went out to lead his first hunt was the day everything went wrong.

Leon's heart raced as he struggled to control his breathing. He had what Gus had always called Buck Fever, and he had it bad, for good reason. He tried to relax where he rested, crouching comfortably on a knee behind a clump of ferns, arrow knocked, ready to draw. He was finally in perfect position.

The dappled red and slate gray hide of the stag, standing not twenty yards away, belonged to a true forest king. His sheer size would give any Canadian elk a run for its money, and his antlers were gnarly and dark, they looked almost blue in places. Such a prize would feed their party for a long time to come.

Just one last step! Come on, big fella. One last step, and we will be eating venison stew tonight!

As if on cue, the stag moved gracefully forward into position and raised its head sniffing at something on the breeze. Leon gasped. He had the perfect heart shot from an exposed broadside position between two saplings. Then, in the split second it took for him to silently draw his arrow back, the buck bolted.

Leon released the tension on the bow and, hands shaking, set it and his unused arrow down against a nearby bush. Disgust swelled up from deep down in his gut. He pulled his hat off and threw it down as well. Then he vented his frustrations to the forest at large, "Son of a biscuit!"

It had taken him and Rezz two hours to circle into perfect cover to make the shot. Now, as far as he knew, their quarry was in another county, and they had a long, empty-handed, jog ahead of them if they were going to be able to catch up with the rest of their party in time for lunch, which just happened to be leftovers from Rezz's more successful boar hunt the day before.

He reluctantly turned to Rezz to face up to his failure. The man was already grinning back at him, "Chin up Leon, just about everyone comes up empty-handed from time to time. The fact is, I have no idea what you could have done to spook the old forest father. It just happens that way sometimes...not to me of course, but to most people." His wink spoke volumes.

Leon grinned back and prepared a good-natured comeback when Rezz went taut and tilted his ears into the wind. Leon froze as well, not knowing what was going on but having come to trust the man's well-honed senses within the forest environment.

Rezz whispered, "Gently, slowly, reach down and hand me the bow. Do it, now."

Leon complied and did as he was told. Using slow, deliberate movements, Rezz took it and the quiver from Leon's shoulder, "Now, when I say go, I want you to climb up the nearest tree you can find. Don't come down until I tell you all is clear. Understand?"

Leon nodded.

"Go!"

Leon sprinted for a sturdy tree ten feet away. The zip of arrows and the thrashing of something large in the trees made his heart thump in double time, but he didn't stop to look. He was ten feet above ground before he paused to take a glance at his surroundings. Everything was still. Even the birds had gone quiet. Rezz was gone.

He waited for what felt like an eternity but was actually closer to five minutes before Rezz came racing up out of nowhere, silent as always. He paused beneath Leon's tree, never allowing his eyes to pause in their scan of the surrounding forest.

"Down now, we have to go."

No explanation was offered, and Leon knew enough not to stop and ask. They tore through the woods. Rezz looked to have seen a ghost and considering the source, that was enough for Leon to suck wind and pump legs as fast and for as far as they could carry him.

When they finally caught up with their companions, Leon was running low on adrenaline and nursing a cramp in his side that wouldn't have let him breathe even if he wasn't out of breath already. Rezz wasted no small talk.

"There's a troupe of Fridgit Hunters somewhere behind us. We were stalking a stag when they caught our scent. I killed one before the two stalking us could attack, but the other gave me the slip. We need to move."

From the astonished looks of the others and their immediate responsiveness, Leon could tell things were not good, though he couldn't understand what could cause such concern. Reed caught his eye and gave him a questioning look, but all Leon could do was shrug helplessly to indicate he had no idea.

After a minute or two, he was able to breathe normally again. Then, just as his pulse shifted down out of high gear, the whole party took off at a light jog. Leon groaned before he set off once more.

This was not how this day was supposed to go!

# # #

Merle turned back twice to growl at something following in the shadows and twice Leon had to call him back. Minutes turned to hours, and still, they jogged. It would have been impossible for Leon to carry the pace up and down hills through rural terrain just a few weeks ago, but his legs could now just manage. Sure, his muscles wanted a break, but now that they traveled at a steady pace and not the all-out sprint Rezz had demanded, his stride felt longer. He even took a turn pulling their cart.

It was nearly evening when they first heard the leaves rustling behind them, along their flanks. Sved relayed the directional orders to the group, "Veer toward the middle of that meadow, then stop. Just stop. Otherwise, they will simply run us to ground, yes?"

"How far west have we come?" Leon asked.

"Further than I had planned. Much further," Sved answered.

"I had hoped they would give up the chase. I was wrong. If we are lucky, it will be an hour or two before the whole troupe catches up and perhaps another hour before they work themselves up into a frenzy to confront us. But they won't attack without the alpha, so let's hope he's at the back of the pack. We will make our stand here tonight, yes? We need a big fire. This cart will have to serve for kindling. Me and the cubs will just have to limp along with the rest of you from here on out."

An hour later, as a sturdy fire crackled, Leon and Reed sharpened the tips of a few of the longer wood beams they were able to salvage. In turn, Haddie and Sved heated the already shaved tips of another pair on the fire's embers, hardening them to solid points. Rezz and Dimples stood with their back to the fire, searching the nearby woods for any sign of impending attack.

"How do you know so much about these creatures, Sved?" Leon inquired.

"Where I come from, we live near the same western mountain range you see there, only further north. Every so often, a troupe will wander down out of the high country into our marshes. When they elect to claim one of our islands they can be challenging to remove."

Though the frightening countenance of their pursuers had been generally explained as the group worked, nothing could have prepared Leon for his first glimpse of the alpha behemoth when it came strutting calmly from the woods a few minutes later. The beast was all business. Flinging dirt and debris into the air before him, he flipped over a boulder the size of their cart, before beating on his chest and roaring his challenge into the night sky.

Leon's mind simply couldn't come to terms with that mountain of muscle and mean as it readied its attack. The beast stood over eight feet tall. It had the same general shape and build as an African gorilla, but its fur was long, and its coat was tinted a pale russet color. If any such thing as a Sasquatch ever truly existed back in his own world, Leon was certain it would have cowered at the monster standing there before them.

Per their plan, Rezz and Dimples moved forward to meet its advance. Rezz pummeled the beast with arrows that only seemed to enrage the creature while Dimples ran forward to meet it halfway between them and the edge of the woods. It charged.

Dimples stood his ground. At the last minute, he reached down and pulled up their longest spear. While tilting the pointy tip up, he planted the other end in the ground and stepping back, bracing it with his foot. He moved so quickly the beast had no opportunity to completely avoid an impact, but it somehow managed to twist its mighty bulk around, mid-stride. Instead of taking it in the center of the chest, the makeshift spear lightly grazed its hip.

Everyone watched in horror as the beast ripped the heavy spear from Dimples grasp with one arm. It slammed it into the ground, pounding it to splinters. Then, it reached for Dimples.

The Hootsi, who had assumed his cat-like form, was only just able to slip from its grip. Meanwhile, Rezz retreated to the fire, firing arrow after arrow the whole time. The arrows provided enough distraction to give Dimples some breathing room, but they didn't carry the amount of force necessary to deeply penetrate the thick hide of the beast.

Their whole plan hinged on being able to quickly take down the troupe's leader. They hoped that by doing so, they would dissuade further aggression. Instead, the alpha was only momentarily distracted as it swatted at the feline figure dancing around him.

Dimples did a fair job of keeping the alpha busy. But he ran a fine line, where any misstep on his part would mean a quick and painful end. Leon realized just how hosed they really were when the alpha beat his chest once more, finally opting to ignore the hissing nuisance at his side. More giant shapes materialized from the forest at the edges of the fire's light.

Merle snarled and the griffin cubs shrieked their diminutive threats behind him. Somehow, in the midst of the chaos, Leon felt an itch at his hip. Absentmindedly reaching down with his right hand to scratch it. His hand brushed against the bone hilt handle of his Blade. As soon as his fingers wrapped around that hilt, a tingling sensation worked its way up his arm. In that moment, he turned his head and saw Haddie, clinging to Reed's arm. Her innocent look of terror sparked an image of Shana's face. Shana was beyond his reach, but his new friends were there with him. A plan quickly fell together in his mind. Any other time and he would call it crazy but, somehow in the midst of the chaos, it just felt right.

Leon turned back and told Merle to stay put and guard the cubs. Then, in what he considered either the single most courageous or perhaps most foolish moment of his young life, he tossed the longest spear they had left a good dozen feet out in front of him. He leaped forward, roaring a challenge to the alpha as it continued to swipe at the slippery Hootsi.

The alpha's menacing glare turned its focus his direction. That raging force of nature locked eyes with him. At that first glance, Leon thought his knees might turn to jelly. To keep from running away screaming, he did the only thing he could think to do, he sucked his teeth, spit, and belted out one of Gus's favorite John Wayne movie quotes, "Fill your hands, you sons of…"

The beast moved from zero to rabbit-on-crack in no time flat, and just like that, the best one-liner he knew fell silent on his tongue. The alpha came trucking it in on all fours, and Leon gave the beast his full concentration. His focus seemed to slow time a tad. He noticed little things, like how the creature threw turf behind him as he charged forward, like some sort of thoroughbred racehorse careening down the last stretch of the derby. The closer he came, the bigger he grew.

Then, Leon turned on the jets, sheer adrenaline overpowering his every instinct to freeze. He made it to the spear in time. He bent down and grasped the rough wood tightly in both hands. He gritted his teeth and crouching over in a four-point stance, he let loose his own battle cry. His raging scream morphed into a growling roar as warmth spread throughout his whole body. Muscles hardened and expanded under his resolve. Surging power rippled through his veins. But that power tasted differently than in the past. It didn't consume him. His new energy felt like it was being fed to him through the stinger on a power washer rather than flowing from him through the nozzle on a firehose. It was condensed, but it didn't carry him away. The pain was missing too. In its place, he only felt resolve.

At the very last moment, he swung the pointy tip up to greet his charging adversary as he exploded forward and upward. What he failed to account for was the spear being a few feet too short to simply impale Bigfoot's big brother. It left him no room to avoid contact.

The ensuing collision was violent, violent like a freight train smacking into a mountainside kind of violent. When the creature's hairy shoulder plowed into his chest, Leon felt bones snap, but he continued his surging advance with every ounce of momentum, screaming till all the air had been pushed from his lungs.

A few moments later, as pain seared through a busted rib cage, Leon could hear nothing but the steady thrumming of his pulse. The world wobbled in and out of existence, spinning to-and-fro as he stumbled sideways, somehow still on his feet. It took a few moments before everything stopped spinning. When it did, a clear starlit sky coalesced in his vision. He could see stars upon stars. They weren't his stars, the ones he had grown up with back on the ranch, but they were beautiful, peaceful, so aloof from his struggles far below. He barely had time to ponder the glowing violet streaks of light that soared across his vision before the pain flared, and he gave up the fight for conscious thought.

Chapter 18

Dawn's light filtered down through weary eyelids far too early for a sensible person to stir, but before Leon could even contest any promptings to open those tired eyes, a litany of smells and sounds nudged his mind back into some semblance of working order. Birds of all types sang in melodies that blended together to form a soothing rhythmic sort of background noise. His nose caught a whiff of heady herbs and aromatic spices with a hint of wood smoke from a fire nearby. Those smells lingered in the air, cooling the back of his throat, and easing the painful rise and fall of each breath he took.

He rubbed a hand over his face and took a deep breath. Bad idea. That was when blinding pain decided to remind him of the fool he had played the night before.

"Ach, No! Short, shallow breaths Bonehead. You just try to relax where you are." The command brokered no refusal, but even so, Leon didn't have much of a choice due to the shattered state of his chest. He was painfully aware of every lump and dip in the cushioned support laying beneath his back.

"That's it, child. Let Olwena tend to her business, and she'll get you back to yours…eventually…so long as you keep them busted ribs still…foolish boy…" An airy old woman's voice continued to mumble and wheeze as Leon heard what sounded like bottles jostling and pans clanging a few feet away.

Soon, the sounds died down. As he opened his eyes and peeked around at his surroundings for the first time, a wrinkled-up chestnut brown face popped up above his own, startling him and causing another inadvertent intake of air that sent needles through his chest. Frowning lips somehow found the strength to lift themselves into a snaggle-toothed smile.

When Leon closed his eyes again the old woman whistled in sympathy and ordered him to remain still while she tended his wounds.

Cool and gentle hands pressed down against the skin on his chest as they applied warm compresses and massaged tender bruising. She asked him several annoying questions like "Needed you awake before we could begin. Does it hurt here?"

"No."

"Here?"

"No."

"Here?"

"Ouch, yes!"

She simply cackled and moved on to another area where the process started all over again. Just when Leon had decided to tell the old croon to take a hike, she placed both hands firmly against his lower ribcage and gently pressed down. Something passed through from her to him, and broken and cracked bones shifted back into position! The pain was unbearably intense for a split second, then it melted away in blissful relief as her touch receded. She continued the process up one side and down the other. The on-again off-again process of sudden intense pain followed by instant relief brought tears to his eyes. Still, he savored the momentary remission each time the hurt subsided.

When her hands slipped from his chest and did not return, Leon opened his eyes once more and turned his head to look on his benefactor with new respect. There before him stood a plain-looking older woman in a shabby rawhide dress with a colorfully beaded scarf. She was still smiling at him, but there was something deeply mournful in those eyes. She held up a withered hand and waved off the concern in his eyes.

"Sorry, child, I'm fine... I... You just reminded me of someone for a moment."

"You sure? You certain whatever you just did didn't take too much out of you? Thanks, by the way."

She at last straightened up and looked him in the eye, "Nonsense! Wasn't magic that healed you, child. Magic takes something from whom it's used on so that the user might take something from some other fool. What I did was give to you what

214

was given to me. You ought to know that! Now, no thanks are necessary, just promise me you won't be getting up to bumble into something and undo all my hard work. I'll be off to find you your visitors before their bleating requests to see you start up once more."

At a blank-faced nod from Leon, the little old woman bounced through the doorway and disappeared behind a heavy linen flap.

Leon took the moment alone to look around at his surroundings for the first time. He couldn't be sure, but he seemed to be housed within an oversized, hollowed-out log the size of a shack. The room wasn't overly large, but it was comfortable and snug. Wood walls curved and dipped in no true form or shape with no visible seams. The windows were similarly uneven, they all consisted of natural, albeit enormous, holes formed from knots in the wood. He saw a rusted cooking stove with a vent hood piped out of one such window, but the shelter was otherwise bare bones. He lay his head back, resting on fur blankets, thrown over some sort of crude straw mattress.

When am I going to stop being surprised by what I see here?

No sooner had he relaxed than the doorway peeled back and five people, two griffins, and one overly large hound all spilled into the little room, crowding around his bed. All at once, there were squeals of excitement, questions of concern, sarcastic anecdotes, chirps, whines, and a general demonstration of relief by all parties involved. That is, until Olwena hollered out above the racket, "Enough! Quiet yourselves or I'll throw you all out again!"

No one moved, not even Haddie. Of all the amazing things that had yet happened that morning, Leon considered the last to perhaps take the cake.

"Good. Now, as you can see, the young bonehead is feeling much better, but he needs his rest. Say hi, say bye, and get out. You'll all have plenty of time to visit later."

They quickly gave their goodbyes and gradually trickled out the entrance until only Reed and the critters were left. Reed wore a smile, which automatically put Leon in a defensive state of mind.

The man rarely smiled unless Haddie was around, which she wasn't. And even then, he tended to hold a grin about as long one would palm a hot potato. A pit grew in Leon's stomach.

"What don't I know, Reed? Am I horribly deformed in some way and you get to be the bearer of the bad news?" He made a show of patting his face in earnest disgust.

Reed shook his head but remained smiling. "I hate to break it to you, but no, that mug of yours looked like that long before last night."

"Wow, man's got jokes! Must be something really serious. Go ahead and spit it out then."

Reed leaned in. "I found my people! They are here, in these woods!"

"You found more of the Bladed remnant?"

Reed scrunched up his brow as his smile faded, "What? No, I meant people like me, the Fae!"

Leon chuckled, but the effort still hurt. He settled for a smug grin instead. "So, you're telling me you found a whole colony of grumpy Tinkerbelles? Fantastic! Just what I needed to hear!"

"Seriously though Leon, this is amazing. Back when I told you my kind were rare, I meant really rare. Like so rare I've never met another skin-changer like me. I never even really knew my father. This is something I've dreamed about. Something I never thought possible! This is a chance for me to better know where I come from, who I am!"

Leon could see just how excited Reed really was over the whole ordeal, so he opted to lay off.

"Well, man, I'm happy for you, really I am."

Reed then glanced over his shoulder at Olwena.

"Mind giving us a moment, I need to talk with Leon privately."

When Olwena drew a breath to rebut his request, Reed quickly pleaded, "Please! This is important. It won't take long, I promise, I'll only be here a short while longer."

She squinted back at him for another few seconds before huffing and exiting through the door. While she took her leave, the griffin cubs hopped up on the bed and snuggled down to nestle in for a nap against Leon's legs.

Reed turned back to Leon and a cautious frown replaced his prior mirth. He reached into a leather toggle hanging from his belt and pulled out a metal medallion.

Leon knew what it was immediately. Reed held the shimmering medallion up into a ray of morning light.

"What is this, Leon? Where did it come from, and why were you hiding it from everyone?"

"Does everyone know?"

"No, I was the first to your side when you went down. It must have jostled loose when you fell. I found it resting halfway out of that small bag you carry on your belt. I snatched it up and pocketed it to give to you later. Didn't think anything of it until I took a closer look this morning."

In a way, the fact Reed was finally privy to the presence of the medallion was a weight off Leon's shoulders. He had considered sharing the medallion with him several times over the past few weeks, but somehow never found the right opportunity. Part of him wondered if he wasn't simply hoarding it away to himself as a final memento from Gus.

Looking back, he knew he had been foolish not to trust his new friend. Perhaps Reed even knew something of its purpose and could use it to help their cause. Leon quickly relayed the story of where it came from and how it came into his possession. When he finished Reed was just as perplexed as him.

"So, Gus never had a chance to tell you what it was, only that he really didn't want it to fall into Ben's hands?"

"That's about the short of it."

"We need to find someone who can translate these inscriptions on the back. I bet that's the key to understanding why it's so important."

"But that's just it, how big a secret is this? Who can we trust?"

"For starters, we only consult someone Bladed. How about we start by bringing Sved and Haddie in on this?"

Leon absentmindedly reached out and scratched Merle behind the ears as he considered the idea. Reed was right, they had to start trusting someone, and if they couldn't trust their two Otterkin companions, who could they trust. "Do it. Take it to each of them individually and show them."

Reed's smile returned. "Will do. Now, get some rest. We need our Fridget Slayer up on two feet for his big award ceremony."

"Hold up! What award ceremony? And did you just call me a Fricken' Slayer?"

"Ha, no, not Fricken, *FRIDGET*. I guess we all assumed you knew! Leon, you took out that alpha Fridget singlehandedly! That beast was insanely dangerous, it's a wonder it didn't turn you into a skid mark when you two collided.

"Regardless, to the Ageless Tribe...err, I mean to my people, what you did is some big mojo. As I understand it, that troupe has been plaguing their borders in this part of the forest, ambushing people, and generally causing mayhem for several months. In fact, they were gathering for a big hunt when we showed up. They saw our smoke and assumed it was another attack on one of their own. A war party of ten Fae raced to our rescue when you did what you did. They all saw! They were so impressed they are throwing us a banquet, in your honor, four days from now! Rest up champ, you've got a party to attend!"

Leon was stunned. Reed just smirked, but as he left, he turned back. "Hey, what possessed you to attack like that anyway?"

He gave a halfhearted shrug, and Reed had the last laugh as he lifted the flap through the doorway.

From zero to hero, just like that!

Leon relaxed back into his bedding. It was wonderful to be able to breathe normal again. He lifted his hand from Merle's ear and allowed it to flop down at his side. Fingers brushed against the warm bone-handled hilt of his Blade and Reed's question played back through his mind. What had given him the notion to do such a thing? Deep down, as crazy as it seemed, he knew he had only chosen to act on what the Blade somehow suggested.

He considered the implications as he drifted off to sleep.

# # #

Reed walked with a tempered sense of wonder through the makeshift forest gathering area where more and more of his father's bloodline arrived each evening. He spoke polite greetings to the random guard standing watch here and there, and their replies of cordial respect gave him a heady sense of belonging. His full immersion in the Fayden tongue was finally paying off. He might miss a word every now and again, but he could at least carry a conversation with any he met.

Welcoming fire pits, gaudy tents, and ferocious dogs were scattered throughout the gathering area where he strolled. Each new group of Fae to arrive brought dark-haired working dogs on metal chain leashes. They were intimidating to look at but behaved well enough. The dogs were all hooked to travois contraptions, used to haul the materials for the temporary housing of the Fae.

Their tents went up quickly. Each one was unique to the family or clan it represented, yet all exhibited true craftsmanship. Silver stubbed tent poles were decorated with sparkling emerald gems and matching canvas walls in varying patterns. The canvas walls themselves were bejeweled in archaic picto-patterns that added context and color to the nightly greetings and well wishes of a beautiful, carefree folk, both quick to laugh and eager to smile.

The camp came truly alive each evening as fires were lit and delicious smells blossomed from cookpots. Forest companions were reunited, and the music of woodwinds and laughter swept through the meadow's clearing.

Every woman he met was a beautiful raven-haired, almond-skinned flirt. They all shared knowing smiles with each other upon his introduction, teasing him and pretending to pout when they learned he and Haddie were sort of an item. Thankfully, Haddie and the others stayed closer to where Leon was housed, further back in the woods and away from the nightly ruckus in the clearing. The last thing he wanted was the saucy redhead getting fired up over the willowy Fae as they played their games. He didn't believe they were intentionally fickle, but he also wasn't eager to see how any such exchange would play out.

The one thing that had surprised him in a not-so-glamorous way was the work ethic he witnessed, or rather the lack thereof. It was obvious his people were not morning or even early afternoon people. Each day they slept in late after their nightly bouts of carousing. It was so universal that he wondered if their culture had some nocturnal predisposition.

Few guards were posted during daylight hours, but there was little around to guard against anyway, so he supposed it didn't make much difference. Though he was a disciplined morning person thanks to a childhood spent with an uncle who thought sleeping late was a cardinal sin, he remained ecstatic at the reality of walking shoulder to shoulder with folk so similar to him in so many ways.

Haddie had certainly noticed a change in him. She teased him over his ever-present smile. And what was not to smile about? He walked the very forests of his father's ancestors with folk he could at last claim as his own, he was kind-of-maybe-sort-of dating the best-looking redhead he'd ever met, and he was set to be one of the honored guests at an upcoming feast!

He had even given in to the promptings of his forest kin, donning their traditional clothing attire. Now, as he strutted about the forest clearing in an entirely new wardrobe, he couldn't help but toy with the notion he might truly belong somewhere for the first time in a very long time.

His outfit consisted of coarse tan trousers, stitched together along their outer seams in a frilly patterned design. A soft russet-colored shirt was tucked in beneath a leather belt that bubbled up roughly in spots, resembling some sort of thick avian leather. The shirt had been made of some material that felt like silk on his skin but was thick as leather. It hugged him close to his skin, tight beneath a mossy green vest from the same skin of the creature that sourced his belt. The outfit was trimmed out with knee-high leather boots. Though he suspected he must look something like an extra from a Lord of the Rings movie set, the mental picture it drew in his mind didn't bother him a bit. Haddie claimed the get-up made him look dashing. Who was he to disagree?

Just then, as his thoughts turned to Haddie, the old hag, Olwena, stepped out into his path.

She clucked her tongue at him, "My, my! Aren't you just a Crowley-Pie's summer-crust? Prancing about with your feathers out like a field cock on a lover's limb." She tsked. Then her eyes narrowed within her wrinkled brow as they darted to her left and her right. She leaned in, "Come with me child. We need to talk."

Leave it to that old sour puss to steal his thunder and shatter his peaceful morning walk. He considered ignoring her, after all, he did still need to talk to Haddie and Sved about the metal medallion. He had put it off too long on account that it would probably require the full story of how he and Leon actually arrived in Fayden. Still, though, she was some sort of Fae healer, and she was doing a wonder treating Leon's wounds.

Better to see what she needs now so she'll let me be later when the parties kick off again this evening.

# # #

"Okay, fine. What is it, Olwena?"

She didn't answer. Instead, she turned down a shadowed trail back into the woods. Not given any choice in the matter, Reed followed.

After a good five-minute hike, Olwena stopped and stuck her arm into the knot of one rather large hardwood. Just when Reed wondered if she was strangling a squirrel in there, there was a *click*, and a small door within the tree's bark swung outward.

"Quick, get inside!"

Reed stepped into the small hollowed-out space and Olwena latched and locked the door behind them. Reed couldn't help but laugh. "Really, old woman? What is with all this mystery?"

"Shut it boy. Shut it and listen close." She struck a flint and lit a lamp nearby, then she turned and watched him silently a minute too long. The flickering light from the flames wick, lit up the lines on her face, creating deep shadows on her rough appearance. When she finally did begin to talk, there was a sadness there he hadn't quite noticed before.

"You don't know much of Fae folk, do you, son?" Reed just shook his head, and she nodded like it was a foregone conclusion.

"I'll just cut to the chase then. How many Fae have you seen wearing a Blade like you have there?" Reed reached down and touched the bone hilt handle at his side but remained silent.

"That's right, none! These people may be our kin, but they aren't our people." At this, she reached down into the rags she wore draped around her and pulled out a Blade just like his own! She must have seen some of the hurt on his face because she reached out and squeezed his arm.

"I haven't given up on them, child, don't get me wrong. But they can be a cruel lot, and they aren't all here to throw your friend a banquet, that's for sure. If you knew just who those old crones were that have been flirting with you child, you would do well to run from their empty appeal."

"What? Then what's going on with all the parties? And what crones are you talking about…everyone I've met but you has been young!"

She tilted her head, studying him curiously, "You really did grow up an orphan from our people, didn't you? Think, child, why would the ancients call our people the Ageless tribe?

"Several of those 'young' flirts you are so smitten with are the same old bats I knew as a child. Our people possess the power to extend youth well into old age." Her eyes grew somber and lost any hint of playfulness. "All is not what it appears to be within the shadow of these woods!

"Now, as to your first question. They call it the Convergence. It only happens a couple of times a year. Tomorrow night is the first moonless night of spring, it's a bloody tradition of the border regions, where Fae gather together for a big party and a hunt. One with past horrors I care not to dwell upon.

"They don't persecute Bladed of the Fae Kingdom here, but they don't tolerate different ideas either. I keep my mouth shut and my head down, and though they know I'm Bladed, they leave me be. I think they only let me stick around all these years because I'm skilled at setting bones and healing scrapes. But the true answer to your question is twofold. First, they will want a sacrifice to bless their superstitious vanity, and second, they will need a Wild Hunt to quench their thirst for blood. Your group is poised to offer both."

Reed sputtered, "Sacrifice? Wild Hunt? As in they're going to kill something?"

"Not something, someone! And not just they, you! You've been prancing around like some long-lost toe-licker all week.

"Now don't look at me like that child, I get that you likely don't have much family, not many of our kind ever leave these woods. Only...you need to understand, these folks aren't your mama's kin boy!

"Still, there's no denying you're Fae, through and through. I suspect they've decided to feel you out for citizenship. Problem is, they don't just let people into our little forest kingdom. Come tomorrow evening you will be asked to make a choice. Kill one from your former life to gain your spot here in this new one, then join them on their Wild Hunt, or join the Wild Hunt from the other end of the sling, if you know what I mean." Reed could only stare back at her in horror.

"Who? Who do they want me to sacrifice?"

"Whoever you chose I suppose? Leon, I think, would be their preference though. The sacrifice of a man who tamed griffins and took down an alpha Fridget would be a big boon, by their standards, for any spring Convergence."

"What about everyone else? Haddie?"

She wouldn't meet his eyes at the question, and instead, turned to grab a box behind her. "I'm not in favor of any of it and I have a plan. But listen close and try to focus. I want you to put all of these concerns aside for a moment and focus on doing something for me." She reached into the box and scooped up a small ugly baby owl, half molted.

"This here is a baby forest bandit. He must have fallen from one of the moon nests deeper in the woods. I only happened upon him last evening, while I was out hunting my healing herbs. There are few of these creatures left in this part of the forest. They've been hunted hard for the silver in those talons.

"He may not look it now, but his kind are fierce and silent hunters. Rarely seen, even by Fae. They are famous for their aerial acrobatics. Their kind weave silently through treetop canopies and ambush unsuspecting prey each night. Only, this one has a broken wing. See here? He will never learn to soar unless it is healed."

Reed just stood there still trying to process everything she had said before. "What? What has this got to do with anything?"

"I'll tell you, but before I do I want you to pick him up...just like this. I want you to hold him in your arms." A protest was still forming in his mouth when Olwena's sharp tongue beat him to the punch, "Just do it, boy! This is important!"

Reed held the bird in his arms. He secretly had a soft heart for small things that suffered, and the little bird peering up at him tugged upon those strings.

"Good! Now close your eyes. Focus on your Blade. Touch its injured wing, consider its hurt, and..."

The old woman's voice faded into the background as something happened. Despite his anxiety Reed's mind turned to the Blade at his side. Normally, when he needed the Blade's power, he would focus on that power until it sent him the help he needed. In those instances, it would generally respond quickly. Though, thinking back, there had been many occasions where he demanded its power but only received a trickle. Regardless, this was different. This was something new, something beyond his experience.

Being on such uncertain ground took him back to those first weeks after he first received his Blade. He could remember his initial fascination with the subtle power it held. Recalling those first days of discovery and wonder, Reed affectionately rubbed the thumb of his free hand over the Blade's pommel. His grip softened, as he subconsciously coaxed it for support, just as he had back then, imploring it to lend to him...what exactly? What was it Olwena wanted him to do for the pitiful creature?

He stood there pondering the situation, a man out of his depth, though Olwena remained blessedly silent for once. Then, just as he was ready to accept failure and throw in the towel on the whole exercise, a tingling sensation pricked his thumb. It strengthened into a warm pulse. The warmth flowed into him from within the Blade. Yet it was siphoned away as soon as it arrived, seeping through his arm and into the chick he held.

He ignored the feeling and focused instead on the bird in his hands. In his mind, he pictured the wing's bone realigning and fusing together. It was like opening a book and understanding the words without ever having learned to read. The sensation lasted mere moments, but when it was over Reed couldn't help but smile. He opened his eyes and stared with amazement at the owlet. His eyes could have been playing tricks on him, but the owl looked a tiny bit larger, and its broken wing was straightened!

"Oh, child! That's even better than I dared hope! You're blessed, boy! Blessed with both the gifts of growth and fusion!" She continued to cackle, her happy little laugh wheezing and chortling as she spun around gathering supplies and stuffing them into a sack.

"That's great and all...but how does this help me with the impending sacrifice?"

"All in good time, all in good time, child! I had to throw you off your guard to see if you were gifted like I suspected and, of course, I needed to relay everything I told you before. I didn't know if it would work, but it did, it did!"

At last, she spun around and slipped a sturdy pack's straps across her back.

"So, what now?"

"Now? Now, you help me rescue your friends and escape this infernal forest!"

Reed cracked a smile. "And then?" She waved her arms at him.

"Tomorrow will take care of itself, boy, we have more than enough on our hands today! Meet me with the rest of your party at Leon's cabin, but don't make a scene. I've been babying that child, but his ribs are healed and he's fine to travel. We make our move while the Forest sleeps this afternoon. Tomorrow's feast is a moonless night, and we have miles to put between us and them before then!"

"What about Sved?"

"The Otter-boy?" She waved away his concern, "I already mended that nick on his leg. I'll say that Vin friend of yours knows his business with forest herbs, there was no infection in the wound, so my healing was a simple matter."

She stopped him as he moved toward the door. "That's important by the way."

What's important?"

"Your gifts are fusion and mending not healing."

"Meaning?"

"Meaning your Blade will allow you to mend bones, seal veins, and fix damaged flesh, but you are powerless against infection and disease. Come on now, let's get moving. You head back to camp, act natural, and get the others packed and gathered for when I return."

"What about this?" Leon held out the owl.

Olwena waved him off once more. "Keep him, he's yours."

And just like that the old woman flung the door open and scurried off into the forest.

As Reed made his way back through the gathering area carrying his small bird on his shoulder, his former smile was nowhere to be seen. Yet, deep within his heart, there was consolation. He may disdain what his people represented, but now he at least knew his roots. He also knew just a little bit more about who he could truly choose to become. And, despite initial reservations, he had a teacher who might just be able to help him learn more. Nope, he wasn't smiling, but there was a certain spring to his step that wasn't there before.

Chapter 19

"For the last time, Leon, I don't know what this is all about. Reed said he would explain everything once we're all together, yes? Be patient!" It was odd hearing those words, coming as they were from Haddie.

"I know, this just isn't like him is all. He's more of an, 'I reluctantly go with the flow and pout about it,' kind of guy. Not someone who gives orders and makes vague warnings about the safety of the group."

Rezz spoke up, "Could this be about the movement in the mountains?"

"What movement?" Haddie and Leon spoke at once.

"Last night, a few of the guardsmen were sharing a fire at the edge of the clearing, near my bedroll. I heard snippets of them talking about how beasts were fleeing down through high passes north of the forest's western edge, right through the borders of these woods. One said the troupe of Fridgets we fought came from just such a place." Rezz leaned in for effect, "Another talked about a Fae scout who claimed he caught sight of an army of invaders moving north, beyond the western Reach." The mood took a somber turn.

Just then, Sved came stomping in, followed close behind by Reed.

"Finally! Reed, what's got your panties in a knot? And...wow, what's that on your shoulder?" A small creature on Reed's shoulder bobbed its head, giving him a vicious stare down.

"That's an owl Leon. Yes, that's right, I can have animals too. But there's no time for this now. Get up and get dressed. Has anyone seen Olwena?"

Everyone shook their heads no, but Leon sputtered, "What do you mean, 'Get up and get dressed?' Can't you see I'm still officially on injured reserve?"

"Not anymore, the old woman says you're all better now. She's just been babying you to keep you down and laying low. Doesn't matter though. We have to get out of here and soon! Those people out there aren't who they've been pretending to be. And they aren't getting ready to throw you a banquet either, that's for sure. Guys, we are all in serious danger. I'll explain later, but when Olwena arrives we have to be ready to book it! Make sure you all go through your packs. Leave anything you don't need. Tomorrow night is moonless, and we have to put some miles between us and them before then."

The cabin went stone cold silent, with the exception of Leon. He gingerly rose to his feet, stretching from side to side, testing Reed's claims.

Finally, Sved spoke up, "I had forgotten the lunar cycle." His eyes shifted over to Dimples. "You are going to have a tough go of it with us out there on the trail my friend. It's a long way from the security of home, no? You lose your head out there and there won't be anyone around to point you back to the group."

"I have no choice. Don't worry little man, I have never entirely lost control before."

To Leon's surprise it was Rezz who spoke up, "But you do have a choice, my friend." Rezz unsheathed his Blade and held it out, hilt forward.

Dimples took a step back. Leon thought he saw momentary indecision in his eyes. Then Olwena burst through the door and into the dwelling.

"Come quick, all of you. Time to leave, now!" She was dressed differently for the first time. She wore worn and faded travel gear, similar in build and function to the shiny new threads Reed wore. She didn't stick around though. She disappeared back out as quickly as she came. Everyone geared up and followed suit.

Creeping single file across the meadow in broad daylight wasn't exactly stealthy, but the gaudy tents stood silent, their canvas walls occasionally flapping in the afternoon breeze. The Fae still slept off the prior night's festivities. Olwena led them through to the north side of the camp. Even the griffin cubs could sense the need for quiet movement, muting their constant whistles and grunts for the time being.

Looking at them in the light, Leon could finally see just how much they had grown. They were both just a hair smaller than Merle and Merle was currently larger than a Great Dane. It wasn't surprising, though. Those cubs ate everything in sight! Their baby fuzz had been replaced as well. Leon could see hints of thick feathery manes sprouting throughout the top halves of their bodies, while back halves grew fur that had already turned silver and curly, similar to Merle's thick hide.

Just as their party made it into the shelter of the woods on the far side of the glen, a friendly but firm challenge rang out, "Hey, you there! Wait up! Where would you all be off to in such a hurry?"

Olwena tugged at Rezz's sleeve. "Put an arrow in him, now!"

"He's not just going to shoot someone for no reason," Hattie protested.

The Fae guard came jogging to catch up. Leon thought he saw movement from within some of the nearest tents.

"Olwena's right, Rezz. Put him down. We have to go. Now." Reed's tone meant business.

When no one responded, the man charged forward. He fished something out of his pockets and twirled a long strip of leather above his head. It was some sort of ancient slingshot. His face no longer held a curious, friendly smile. Even from thirty paces away, Leon could see his sneer.

With a final look of resignation, Rezz drew an arrow and let it loose in one fluid motion. The man fell to his knees, an arrow through his throat. The leather strip in his fingers slipped loose and a stone went sailing…right into the canvas wall of one of the tents. The racket the incident created was sure to wake the camp. Everyone took off behind Olwena into the woods.

Olwena left the main trail, bushwhacking through the woods in a northward path. Leon quickly lost track of his sense of direction in the canopy of the woods, but not Olwena. She set a break-neck pace and didn't lay off the gas. For an old woman, she could fly.

Hurdling logs and dodging limbs didn't throw her off her stride. Reed still carried Ferschall's pottery pack, along with an owl glued to his shoulder, but he didn't show any signs of slowing either. The griffin cubs were managing to keep pace fairly well, too. And though he managed to keep up, Leon could see Haddie and Sved already sucking wind.

"Wait! Olwena, we can't keep this speed. We have to pace ourselves. We'll never last!" he yelled.

"Keep moving, children! Just a little further!"

And so, the group continued their mad dash through the Forest Kingdom's borderlands.

Crossing over another hilly incline Leon felt certain they had lost any potential pursuit. But his stomach turned at the sounds of hoots and hollers of sadistic laughter followed by angry barking from much further back up their trail. They had broken away with small lead, but the Fae were relentless.

"They're coming!" Reed shouted.

"Faster now, just a little further!" Olwena encouraged.

No one had the wind to argue. They drove harder and dug deeper until they broke through a clearing and Leon observed four of the most menacing looking birds he had ever laid eyes upon. They stood close to the same height as an ostrich but had longer legs, larger torsos, thicker necks, and hooked beaks that looked capable of crushing coconuts or puncturing tires. Large bundles of speckled brown plumage were balanced over those sturdy legs. Wicked bone ridges curved up from above their eyes, over their heads, disappearing down into their girthy necks.

Dimples piped up, "Thunderbirds?"

"Yes, kitten. Thunderbirds. The only creatures alive who can give the Fae a proper foot race!"

Rezz grimaced as they all drew to a stop just shy of where the birds were standing, tied to a stump. "They are horrid beasts. They peck and kick, and for days you will reek of bird…"

Olwena cut in, "I don't need any sass, Vin! They give us an edge. We can't afford not to take what we can get. Now, which of you two little pond rats wants up first?"

Sved scowled at her in reply as he stepped forward. "Let's get this over with!"

Olwena helped both Sved and Haddie into their saddles while providing a brief tutorial on how to control their steeds. Leon was ushered up into a seat on the third and their collective packs were trussed up on the fourth.

The Thunderbirds gave deep murmuring chirps that sounded more like grunts and lightly pranced in anticipation of the race to come beneath the weight of their riders. The griffin cubs, and even Merle kept their distance from those powerful club toed feet.

Do I dare lay a hand on the bird's neck?

Sved somehow managed to pick a fight with his new friend about the same time he settled into his saddle. Turning the same shade of red as his beard, he dressed the beast down with his tongue while it did its best to peck at his legs, all while they both spun in circles. It took Olwena stepping in and smacking each of them before everyone settled down.

Yep, time to dare.

Concentrating on the Blade's power, Leon felt a gentle thrumming pulse go from his hand into the bird. He could sense the bird letting down its guard for him, just as the griffins had done. It was like he gained its trust immediately. He gave a gentle nudge forward. The bird complied, responding instantly to his prompting almost like it could read his mind. He smiled.

This may not be too bad!

A moment later, the loud *thwack* from a rock slamming into the pack atop the fourth bird, as well as a chorus of eager barking and howling from behind, got them all moving. Everyone, including the Thunderbirds, leaped into the cover of the nearest trees.

Merle growled, creeping back toward the clearing when Leon called him to his side. He was just as irate as his dog, realizing several pieces of Ferschall's pottery were now likely ruined, but the last thing they needed was to get bogged down in a fight right then.

Rezz returned fire with his longbow, but the old woman ignored the threat as she brought Sved and his mount under control once more. Then, grabbing the reins to the fourth mount she told the group, "We move north until we reach the Somber River trail, then east."

"Somber River Trail?"

She had already begun running, and called back over her shoulder, "You'll know it when you see it. If we can make it far enough away from these cursed woods, we just might have a chance."

# # #

From there on out, their race through the woods was more an Olympic marathon than a sprint. Sved and his Thunderbird held themselves to an uneasy truce while generally keeping pace with the group. Rezz came trailing behind, sending devastating shots into the midst of their pursuers anytime a Fae hound came too close.

Yet it was Olwena's knowledge of the forest that gave them their greatest advantage. She knew every turn and corner that allowed them the most direct route. She led them up creek bottoms and between hills. She made turns and cuts in and out of trails that none of the others would have suspected were there. Their pursuers tried flanking the group twice but always failed to cut them off and slow them down in time.

After about three hours of steady running, the sounds of pursuit could no longer be heard. The old woman called a short break. They all took a moment to catch their breath and have some water. She made Rezz agree to trade places with Leon when Dimples declined, but there was little conversation otherwise.

Before the break ended, Leon took a moment to calm their pack bird. Once he was sure it wouldn't freak out, he whistled. The cubs came running to his side. Placing them carefully up onto the packs above wasn't too hard. They were significantly lighter than they looked. He had no doubt that, if wasn't for his link to them through his gift, they would be off and away from the big bird in a heartbeat.

It was for their own good, though. He didn't know how they had made it that far, but it was obvious their legs were spent. Merle, on the other hand, still kept pace like some sort of husky sled dog! The old mutt had truly proven himself to be the war hound Ferschall had once proclaimed. He snorted at the thought of 'me 'I told you so' Ferschall would give him if he were there.

"Let's get moving."

That old woman is relentless!

Another few hours of flight brought darkness. The moon wasn't quite absent just yet but was a near enough sliver to make travel difficult. Olwena had Dimples guiding the group further northward while she and Reed fell back. Haddie and Sved slid from their mounts and led the giant birds by their reins. Sved's bird seemed to be too tired to give him further trouble for the time being. Leon led the other two.

When Reed and Olwena came to a stop for a third time in as many minutes, Leon gave Rezz his reins and went to investigate their delay.

"Good, now push here and here."

"Like this?"

"Yes, see how that limb there pointed in the right direction from the start? It does the work of covering the gap doesn't it?"

"Yeah, wow, that's much easier than bending the others…"

"What are you two doing?" Leon could see his friend's young owl twisting its neck from side to side from its perch as Reed worked at something before him.

"What does it look like boy? We're blocking off the paths behind us through this Needlebrush." She gave a soft chortle. "It's something our pursuers won't be expecting. The power of growth is a rare gift among the Bladed. I've only ever heard stories of others with such a blessing!"

Reed was oblivious to her praise, still concentrating on the task before him. Leon tried leaning over a shoulder to watch what he was doing. Even from within the dim starlight filtering down through the forest canopy, he could see the branches of a large and thorny brush twisting and growing, closing off any easy access through behind the path they traveled.

Amazing!

Reed had said he could help things grow over time, but this was different level stuff! "That's incredible! Way to go Reed."

Olwena smacked his shoulder, "He's just doing what needs done. Get back up there with the group, child. We'll be along soon enough."

Leon rubbed his shoulder. That old woman was as thorny as the prickles on the bushes below. Still though, it was good to know they had an edge.

Reed kept right on working with Olwena continuing right there at his side, coaching him in that sharp cutting voice of hers. Reed didn't seem to mind though. He soaked up every word like an old bull on a salt lick.

After a few more hours of a slow slog through thick pockets of brush, the forest around them faded. The trees stood smaller and less clustered. Eventually, the group broke free of the heavy canopy. Though the light was limited, they felt a thrill stepping out into a true end to the forest. Leon could see tall grass swaying in the wind and disappearing out of sight beyond a small rise further north.

"We did it! We made it to the Somber trail!" Olwena seemed so surprised it made Leon suspect she wasn't quite as sure of their escape as she let on when the race first began.

"Where to now Olwena? You said east?"

"Yes, the Somber River turns more north than west as you head upriver. The path that direction narrows dangerously close to the woods the further west you move, but it widens as one moves east."

"East it is!"

"Sved, how do we get to your lands from here?" Leon was curious to know.

"We cross the Somber, yes? I'm not sure how far west we traveled on our run from the Vin, but I think we should continue east for a few days, at least before we turn north once more."

Their path settled, the weary travelers turned east. Everyone was bone-weary, but no one wanted to risk sleeping so close to Wild Forest. Leon was comforted that they carried plenty of food on the pack bird. They all had a chance to scarf down an early morning breakfast or hard bread and dry fruit as they moved along.

A full and beautiful sunrise broke through a dotted horizon several hours later. Rich green grass swayed in the morning breeze and dew twinkled on the needles of the nearby evergreen trees, glistening in the first light of dawn. The mottled collection of clouds in the sky created a brilliant tapestry for color. It was as if a wide-open canvas bled forth above, from muted gray into brilliant pinks and majestic purples all of which paved the way for the first rays of the morning sun.

Leon turned back to look behind them. There he spied a towering mountain range in the distance. The words of one of Gus' most cherished songs came surging up to the tip of his tongue.

"*I've seen the morning burning golden on the mountain in the skies.'* Never knew what that really meant until now," Leon whispered in English.

While Reed was the only one who understood what he said, the others seemed to know what he meant. They all slowed to a stop, basking in the imperfect perfection of the scenery before them.

Then, misfortune, the sorry mistress that she was, decided to rear her ugly head once more. A sharp voice cut through the gentle breeze and shattered the quiet tranquility, "Stay exactly as you are!"

A small missile struck Rezz in the arm when he attempted to heft his longbow. The bow fell and Rezz sank to his knees in agony, holding his injured shoulder. From quite a distance away, and all around them, Fae warriors rose up out of the long grass. Each one swung a long thin leather strap above his head, just itching for someone else to make a move.

Olwena hung her head and mouthed silent protests, while the rest of the group help up their arms in surrender. Leon called out to Merle and the cubs. They stood down as well.

The Fae leader laughed at her dejection as he approached their group. "You useless old wretch, did you really think you could slip through the fingers of true Fae so easily? Look at me!" She lifted her chin to meet their captor's eyes, before he continued, "We have tolerated your fool-hearted sympathies for far too long, but no more!" He rolled the next words in his mouth, savoring their flavor before spitting them out at her through a cruel smile. "You are deemed a traitor to the Kingdom and will join the others in the Hunt tonight."

"Gladly." Her answer was spoken softly. It was the only response Olwena gave.

"It was all a lie, wasn't it? The banquet, the honor, everything! Do you even know what that word means, honor?" Disdain came dripping from his tongue as Reed addressed the men he had so recently considered "his people."

The man laughed even harder, before slapping him across the face, knocking Reed to his knees, "The irony you fool is that we would have gladly taken you in." His smile disappeared, "Better that we all now know the truth of the matter - you were never worthy of the secrets of the Endless Forest! Still, you will serve us in your own way. Take them to the trees and secure them at the edge of the wood! Someone, get a cook-fire going and get me some grub. It was a merry chase, but that was just the appetizer boys!"

Chapter 20

The morning passed quietly. It wasn't until late afternoon that the first few Fae hounds, hauling bits of the Convergence tack, came trickling into the new camp. A drafty breeze birthed a windy gust, which could soon be heard bending branches as it rustled through the trees above. The winds soon brought a chill that blew cool as dark clouds rolled in from the north. A storm could be seen in the distance, surging down off the mountain peaks, coming hard for the forest's edge.

Haddie spoke up over the building storm, "I take it they must have guessed where we were heading from the very start. I just don't get how they guess so quickly! Olwena?"

"Should have crossed the river when we had the chance, yes?" Sved added.

"It's getting late, almost dark. Hey, Olwena, what are they planning?" Leon asked.

Only the old woman didn't answer. Gone was her snark. Gone was her barbed tongue. She stood there with the rest of them, rocking her head and humming tunes inaudible to the others, staring out into the darkening green fields that lay so terribly close, just beyond the shadow of the trees where they were bound.

"Pipe down, all of you. And leave her alone. Another pack of dogs just arrived. Looks like they're setting up more tents." Reed's positioning provided him the best angle to see into the new make-shift camp. Everyone else hung limp or fought against the leather lashes around their wrists. The Fae bindings held them in standing positions, arms spread and tied around opposite sides of thick tree trunks in a manner that made it look like they were all hugging individual trees within a small circular mot of hardwoods. Even Merle and the griffin cubs were with them. They lay hogtied and whimpering in the center of the mot. Yet the Fae adopted the owl as a sort of mascot while they worked. They took him with them when they left, and he was nowhere to be seen. The Fae had a sort of twisted sense of humor.

A few minutes later and Leon heard the clanging, stomping, and exuberant approach of a large group of people. He could hear the crowd growing and expanding until he was sure there were dozens more individuals clustering near their trees. He still couldn't see what was happening, but he could guess.

The whole stinking 'Convergence' must have finally shown up.

A smooth and polished tenor voice shouted through the mounting noise. "Friends and fiends! Welcome! Welcome to this year's first Convergence of the Eastern Wood!"

Everyone applauded. There were catcalls and whistles, wild whoops, and crazed laughter. It was a celebratory atmosphere, but a certain restless energy, above and beyond the celebration, permeated the minds of the people surrounding them, transforming the gathered group into a boisterous mob. Leon could taste the building tension.

"I can only tell you that this moonless Hunt will be one of the greatest of our modern era! Not in all the forest, in over a thousand moonless nights has there been a hunter's quarry such as we have gathered before us tonight!"

Applause and exhilarated screams erupted again. At this point, people were screaming of their own accord in mounting blood lust, oblivious to the speech. The crowd's murmuring rose but the voice rose higher, above the increasing din of racket.

"The Hunt will ride the wind with the coming storm, and just as in days of old, when Fae ruled pockets beyond the boundaries of these ancient trees, we will run them down beneath open skies!"

The crowd was thoroughly enlivened. It erupted with intoxicating screams and shouts of inaudible passion. The man continued his speech, but it was at that time that Olwena decided to come out of her trance. She shouted above the noise, loud enough for Leon and all his companions to hear her, "When they cut your bonds, run! Run faster than you've ever run before! Skirt the forest, run west then north, into the storm, cross the trail, then swim the river if you can. The waters will be running swift, but try, try to cross. They will kill us off, one by one, but you must not slow or stop. We all must run for the hope that one may yet escape!"

Leon couldn't see her, but he could guess she had been staring at Reed as she belted out that last part. He couldn't tell if she was manic or hysterical, but it didn't matter. He would run like she said. What choice did he have?

As the man's speech reached its climax, his promises grew abhorrent and the nastier they were, the more enthused the mob became. Finally, he concluded by saying, "And our forest queen has sent her very own son, Dirk, here to lead the hunt himself! Remember! His is the first stone cast and his shall be the last kill! All others are for you my people, but his is the first and the last!"

There could be no more coherent words voiced above the crowd after that. The screaming and shouting were deafening, the mob was in full meltdown. Guards came and removed them from their trees. The guards' visage was changed. Each of them wore dark purple face paint, curling across their skin in outlandish patterns.

Leon was hustled to the edge of the clearing and made to stand with his back to his enemy, facing out into the grassy plain beyond. The only weapon they took from any of them was the longbow from Rezz.

The big Vin Ranger was placed beside Leon. He turned his face and smiled at Leon with that wicked-looking scar that had once made him feel such fear. Leon thought how far they had come that the same old scar now gave him a small measure of comfort.

Rezz took that moment to speak, and though his voice broke as he yelled, his words carried over, barely audible to Leon, "Don't look so sad my friend. Freedom tasted sweet while it lasted, did it not? I am glad I took the Blade. No regrets. You hear me, brother? No regrets!"

Leon couldn't entirely fight back an uninvited feeling of guilt that accompanied those simple words. He nodded back, but quickly turned to his other side and saw a different expression on the face of Dimples.

The Hootsi's mouth twisted in a snarl, carrying visceral disdain on the verge of unbridled rage and anger, as well as something feral, something he hadn't yet seen in the man's eyes. Then it dawned on him.

Dimples isn't Bladed. He's about to completely lose it, just like the Fae.

Leon had no idea what to expect from a Hootsi warrior in Dimple's state of mind, but the man was at least as dangerous as anyone, or two, of those heathens behind. He took a sidestep closer to Rezz but was yanked back into position by the guard holding him in place.

Leon winced, but not Dimples. Dimples threw his head back and laughed. It was a laugh of contempt. Perhaps it was his way of thumbing his nose at what was about to happen? Yet, having grown to better know the Hootsi during their time together, Leon could hear the feigned mirth in the man's voice. It was steeped in pain and regret and loss. As it trailed away, it morphed into a cat's scream and ended with raging spittle as he bellowed out some battle mantra to an odd rhythm, working himself into a higher frenzy. The words were garbled in the noise, and Leon had no inclination to ask for clarification.

The guard tried to silence him as he thrashed about, but Leon saw hesitation, even there, in the guard's eyes. The Hootsi's violence had pierced the Fae's blood lust. He must have sensed something in Dimples' dark charisma that gave him pause.

The Otterkin were brought up next, both on the other side of Rezz. They were wide-eyed and pale-faced. Leon tried to get their attention over all the noise, but they were too far away to hear him, or too dazed to acknowledge his yelling.

Finally, Reed and Olwena were brought forward, next to Dimples. Olwena looked resigned to a morbid fate, ready to accept whatever was to come. But Reed, Reed carried abhorrent disgust in his very posture. Only, Leon couldn't tell if the disgust was aimed against his tribe for their barbaric proclivities, or if it was aimed at himself for his recent desire to be one of them. Either way, what did it matter? Even Merle and the cubs were tossed out onto the grass beside them all.

What was about to happen was obvious. The Fae meant to run them down like animals. It was to be a game, a bloody sick, and twisted game.

The hands of guards reached out from behind each of them. Those hands carried sharp knives. The knives came to a stop. Sharp edges rested against knotted bonds.

# # #

After a long wait that further stretched the nerves of Leon and his companions, the tenor-voiced man finally gave a command. Or at least that was what Leon suspected he did. In reality, it was more like he screamed something incoherent, his voice rising once more over the wind and the wild taunts from behind. Their bonds were all simultaneously cut.

Leon immediately leaped into action. He whistled high as he planted cut and darted northwest. Merle and the cubs immediately found their place at his side. He could hear his companions running close beside him as well.

He kept listening for the sounds of footsteps and jeers from behind, but the mob's screams faded into the wind. The seconds continued to tick by, and still nothing. There was little to no light left, the sun had descended beyond the mountains quite a while back, and Leon could barely see where he went. He started to fall behind.

Then for some strange reason, he let his hand drop down to find solid comfort in the old bone-handled hilt. He pulled the hilt and drew the Blade from the belt at his side as he ran. A tender pulse sent a comforting feeling that passed over him. Its tingling warmth sank into his head. His eyes adjusted until they were able to discern shapes and shades of color in the muted light. Was this another gift he had just discovered?

Olwena roused him from his thoughts, screaming at them all as the pace of the group faltered, "Run faster! Faster you foolish children!"

Something wasn't right. The feeling built in Leon's gut. It built until it forced him to double up and stumble left.

A dark purple streak came slicing down through the air a half-second later, just where his head would have been. The hair on Leon's arm stood on end as the projectile bounced once and disappeared. It was a rock, likely sent his way by one of those long leather slingshots, but it was something more as well. The Fae had done something to that rock. To be hit by one like that would be bad, real bad. He drove his feet forward and picked up the pace.

Then more rocks crashed down further back behind him. He guessed they had crossed out of range and chanced a glance back. The dam holding back the mob broke loose in that instant, the painted Fae came pouring out into the clearing, their black hounds racing before them. It truly was a Wild Hunt.

He turned back, focusing on breathing, on pumping his arms, and lifting his legs. His pace was all he could control.

Olwena had been leading the group but dropped back to encourage the others. Leon ran beside Sved, doing his best to hasten the little man to move those tiny legs. He and Haddie were small, but they were quick. Leon's hope was that as they put more distance between themselves and the mob, they could begin angling more to the north, toward the river. Once the Otterkin made it to the river, they would be the ones with the advantage. Then, out of the corner of his eye, he saw Olwena fall back behind Haddie who had started to lose step. Reed ran by her side, but it wasn't doing much good. The last thing Olwena screamed was, "Don't stop!"

A heavy purple streak collided with her head, and she plowed headfirst into the tall grass behind.

Reed hadn't seen her fall. He had been trying to encourage Haddie to move faster. Leon remembered her last words in the clearing and though it tore at his very soul, he kept quiet, kept going. Olwena was gone, of that, he was sure. He had seen the rock penetrate in a way that left no question as to the outcome. He was sick at the thought of leaving her behind, but what could he do?

Was it truly better to not distract the others in the moment, or was it cowardice creeping in on him once more?

Purple streaks fell all around them after that, and he no more time to ponder moral implications. Their collective impacts released a strong odor that had a distinct resonance of rusted iron and ozone. Still, they ran.

Rezz ran up front, a little ways north of Leon. A missile smashed into the leather bracing of his hurt shoulder and spun him around. The injury caused the Vin to stop and pivot back to his attackers.

As Leon came even with Rezz, the man's eyes shifted into his own, and he smiled, raising his Blade in salute before racing back into the mass of death behind. Leon was stunned. His legs kept running but it took him a good second or two to process what he saw. Had his friend just opted to give his life to help buy them time?

When realization dawned, the weight and guilt of leaving another companion behind came crashing down against his conscience harder than any of the purple missiles from above. His run trickled to a jog, before it faded to a stumbling halt as he prepared himself to turn back and meet his demise. But it was at that very moment that he saw a light up ahead.

Beautiful bright campfires were growing in the distance! Reed was already locked in on it. Screaming to encourage them all, he shouted, "To the lights! Head to the lights!" No one but Leon understood him, but they all saw where he pointed. Then Reed lifted Haddie into his arms and took off with renewed speed. The two of them soon left the rest far behind.

Despite lacking Reed's wheels, Leon turned on the jets once more. If he could get help, perhaps he could still save Rezz. Purple flashes continued whistling past the remaining members of the group until Leon heard something he had hoped to never hear again. Howls came from the camp. Yet, right then, the bone-rattling sound of wolves was music to his ears as their haunting wails tore through the night, momentarily silencing the taunts and jeers fast approaching from behind.

Looking around once more, Sved was there, but Dimples was gone. Leon held back and matched Sved, stride for stride, as they raced toward the lights.

Up ahead, he could see large, powerful shapes cutting through the grass toward them, coming from the direction of the lights. Many, many, shapes!

"Sved, what's going on up there?"

"The wolves! They must have seen the Fae slinging their colored stones. To them, it's a challenge. Get down, we don't want them to confuse us with those behind."

Soon after Leon and Sved dove down into the grass, a solid wave of massive shapes of furry fury swept by. Fortunately, they were ignored. Leon popped up and pushed on soon after, keeping his eyes forward. The ensuing fight behind sounded epic. It was sheer madness.

Just as they broke free from the sounds of clashing bodies and the ensuing shrieks of pain, and Leon could taste their deliverance, one last purple missile came streaking up over the top of them. It overshot both Leon and Sved by a good margin, but when it came down, a griffin cub screeched. The missile drove itself deep into the griffin's back and the cub tumbled over with one last shriek.

The pain of the small creature was just too much for Leon. Too much death for one night. Leon screamed in anguish and fell to his knees beside the cub. Sved stopped beside them too.

"Come on, Leon. We've got to go! Can't stay here! Carry him, yes?"

Leon scooped the small cub into his arms as gently as possible, and they hurried forward at a much slower pace, still making their way toward the lights.

# # #

It hurt to hear the cub's mewling chirps of agony. They tore at his heart. Still, Leon held tight to the hope that if they could just make it to the light, he could somehow find help to save his little friend.

As they drew closer, he saw large carriage-type vehicles begin to materialize. Silhouetted movements from people near campfires could also be spotted. A feeling of relief took root in Leon's belly. It grew for a short time until Merle stopped several yards ahead and growled. The dog's snarling nose was aimed in the direction of the fires ahead.

Leon kept moving but Merle leaped out in front to block his way. He dodged around him the first time the dog did it, but the second time it happened Leon stopped, finally remembering the lesson he'd learned with Merle and the rattlesnake at the old roping chute, back at home.

"Sved, hold up. Something's wrong. Merle wouldn't be doing this if there wasn't some sort of danger ahead."

The two men crouched down in the grass. The wind was still gusting from the north. Leon lay the injured griffin down to try and make him comfortable. He could see where a small rock was lodged between his wings, near the spine in his back. The flesh around the injury continued to darken. Leon pushed feathers aside and witnessed violet streaks extending out from the wound.

Sved peeked over his shoulder and gasped aloud, "That rock must have been imbued with Death's touch."

When Leon looked up at him with questions, Sved shook his head. "Didn't even know it was a real thing until now. Only ever heard bits and pieces from stories meant to scare us kids when we were disobedient, yes? When my uncle returned from these forests safe and sound, I chalked the stories up to forest tales and never considered their merits again."

"What is Death's touch?"

"It's like what the Vin do, only the Ageless Tribe can't kill directly like them, yes? When they change shape, they can only imbue stones or other such items with the power to break apart those connections that hold flesh together. It was said that the forest warriors collect those stones after battle and use them for their own twisted purposes. That's really all I know."

"Is there anything we can do? To save him?"

"No, Leon. I'm sorry, I don't think so. I doubt even Olwena could help our young friend. Best to just make him comfortable, yes? He doesn't have long."

The other griffin cub came over and sniffed its sibling. It made quiet chirping sounds and nudged the dying cub's side. Leon felt hot tears sliding down his cheeks. The north wind dried them as fast as they fell.

He couldn't just stand there and do nothing. So, he used his Blade to dig the stone out from the griffin's back, taking care not to cause more suffering for the cub or to touch the stone himself.

Still, the damage was done. Shortly thereafter, the cub breathed its last. Leon used the Blade once more to dig a hole and bury the stone several feet away from where the dead cub rested. No matter what happened the rest of that night, no Fae would be collecting the Death stone that had cost his griffin cub its life.

When he returned to Sved's side, he saw they were not alone. Dimples was there. Merle's hackles were up, and he was on high alert, but he wasn't attacking. Leon calmed the dog with a hand to his back.

Dimples had completely changed, and this was the first time Leon had seen him in his current form up close. Short dark, midnight-blue hair covered his face and extremities. His ears were pointed, and his facial features were contorted, making him look more feline than human. Leon couldn't help but notice there was blood on his chin. No telling what he had been up to, or whose blood stained his chin.

He bent low and sniffed at the griffin cub. When he glanced back up, Leon shifted uneasily. Dimples' eyes were no longer his own. The whites were yellow with vertical green slits down the center. Somehow though, Leon could tell that the Hootsi mourned the little griffin's death with the rest of them. There was at least some measure of humanity in there somewhere.

"Come on, everyone. Let's go find Reed and Haddie up ahead."

Dimples objected, the same as Merle. He motioned them all to follow him instead. Leon looked at Sved in question, and Sved nodded back in agreement. So, they allowed Dimples to lead them. The other cub whined in mourning but followed when Leon placed a hand on its back and gently bid it come using his Blade.

Dimples took them southwest, toward the tree line, then cut straight west before those cursed woods drew in too close around them. They crept north through the swaying grasses once more until they came to a stop on the banks of the Somber River, northwest of the wolves' camp. Leon could see the churning waters below and knew immediately why Olwena hadn't wanted to cross further east. The river's rapids were raging with snowmelt from higher up in the mountains to the west.

The wolves camp was much closer to the trees growing along the edge of the Somber than to the forest beyond. The winds of the storm would make it challenging for any of the skin-changers still in camp to be alerted to their presence, so long as they didn't get directly upwind.

Leon and Sved used the cover of those trees to sneak in close and get a better view. That's when Leon saw what Merle and Dimples were sensing. The large carriages weren't made for carrying supplies, they were cages. Heavy metal bars held all manner of creatures, and many of those creatures walked on two legs. Two of the cages even held human captives.

"Slaver's caravan!" Sved gasped. "You see the guards, yes?"

Leon looked closer and noticed normal-looking guards stationed up on top of each wagon cage. He confirmed he saw them.

"Those are Bladed, but they are traitors to all that we know." Sved spit into the dirt. "What these men do is evil, more so than even the crazy Fae from the woods beyond. They sometimes capture their kind in the borderlands and cut out their tongues to keep them silent if they return low on stock for the markets at Hollinger!"

They retreated further back from the camp and Leon consulted Sved once more.

"What can we do?"

"Nothing for now. I think I should go for help, yes? My people are not powerful, but we are wealthy. Reed and Haddie should be left alone until they get to Hollinger. We can buy them back before they are sold there."

"How far to Hollinger? And how do we know they even have them?"

"I know they do, I saw a shock of red hair in the women's cage near the big fire, but to answer your first question, it could be three to four weeks, depending on the slaver's greed. Wagons move slow and these types are easily distracted by easy pickings, yes?"

"So, you think we should just leave them, shouldn't someone trail them back, just to make sure they aren't lost when they arrive at the markets?"

Sved scratched his head thinking.

"Could be a good idea but trailing a slaver's caravan through the border lands is a dangerous proposition. Still, the markets are a big place, it's not implausible that we could miss them when they arrive. What did you have in mind?"

"Leave me behind. You need Dimples to help you make it home. I have Merle and this little guy here to help me stay hidden. I can do this, Sved." Sved didn't want to give in, but in the end, Leon convinced him of the necessity of splitting up. They couldn't afford to lose sight of the caravan.

He handed Leon a small stone pendant from somewhere in his pockets. "Take that to the first Otterkin trader you see near Hollinger. Ask them to help you and tell them that the Haberkorn clan will be in their debt if they do. I can't promise, but perhaps it will make a difference, yes? It should at least get word back to us on where you were last seen."

The little man grinned and turned to the Hootsi. "Come on Dimples, there's a storm coming, and the waters might rise if we twiddle our thumbs too long, yes? Let's go see how well a big

Hootsi cat can swim!" Dimples gave a rumbling growl of displeasure but nodded once to show he understood.

Leon stopped them and grabbed Sved's shoulder.

"Thank you Sved. You're a brave man and a good friend, you too, Dimples."

"Bah, you're the one fool enough to follow a slaver's caravan, I'm just running home to my family with a full-grown lion to watch my back!"

The two men shook hands and Leon drew him in for a hug with a hearty back thump before he released the little man. Sved and Dimples melted down the river's slope and faded into the darkness below.

Leon and his two remaining companions moved upriver, further away from the camp.

With Merle's help, Leon eventually found an outcrop on the drop-off leading down the riverbank. It seemed high enough to weather any flood surge and it was out of the way of the rain. The three of them huddled down together for a chilly night. Leon felt comforted he at least had two warm bodies to snuggle up against and a semi-covered rock ceiling above while the winds cut hard and continued to blow.

They were all worked up and skittish due to everything they had seen, but when sleep came it came hard and fast. Leon didn't even wake when the storm's rains finally broke. However, the crescendo was over-promised and under-delivered; the downpour was nearly done before it started.

Chapter 21

The next morning Leon awoke to a rustling disturbance in the bushes nearby. Whatever was there, was slowly working its way toward him from further down the embankment, near the river. He rubbed the sleep from his eyes and drew his Blade.

He did a double-take when he saw his lone-surviving griffin cub was the cause of all the ruckus. The cub swayed on its feet as it stumbled up over rocks and brambles, carrying an oversized fish in its beak. The griffin's wings, which were sprouting small silver feathers, were stretched out in an effort to counterbalance the weight upfront. Leon let out a long breath and dropped to his knees in relief.

"You little turd, don't you go sneaking off like that anymore!" He was perturbed at the creature, yet he couldn't stop a smile from breaking free when the cub stumbled over the slimy tail hanging down below his chin. "Bit off more than you could chew, didn't you, boy? Come here, let's see what you've got!"

He gave the cub lots of praise and attaboys while he used his Blade to fillet the prize. He and Gus were devoutly opposed to eating much of anything not blessed by a flame, but he was half-starved and the sushi he swallowed, though bland, settled his grumbling belly better than expected. Merle ate his portion after one or two disdainful sniffs. The cub, however, simply swallowed the scraps, bones and all.

A thought struck him as the cub's belly bulged. "You know, I never gave you or your brother a proper name. I'm sorry that it's too late for him, but maybe not for you?" He squinted down at his fierce little companion, "Considering your newfound talent, and your surly disposition, how does Ahab suit you?"

The griffin looked up with a cockeyed tilt of the head and cooed through his silver beaked nose. Leon snickered. "Captain Ahab, it is!"

He stood up and stretched his legs. Dawn had come and gone, though it was still relatively early that morning.

"Okay, boys, it's time we take a look around, but we've got to be extra careful." Thinking things over, Leon reached out to each of his pet companions. He had been exercising his gift over the past few weeks. Now, he decided to turn things up a notch.

He focused in on what he thought they ought to do and, very gently, coaxed the Blade to lend him what he needed. The result was immediate. His gift allowed him to communicate the need for his companions to stay hidden and to help warn him if there was danger lurking nearby. Then, he sent them off to scout. Amazingly, they complied!

A few minutes later, they both returned. Somehow, he perceived they were encouraging him to follow. He took off after them and it wasn't long before they were all peering out from the cover of some brush along the riverside. He could just make out the last remnant of the slaver's caravan as it disappeared over a rise to the east.

"Wow, they don't waste time, do they?"

Leon sat tight with his two companions watching for any signs of movement. He gave it a good two hours before allowing them to venture out into the area where the caravan's camp lay the night before. After using the Blade once more to ask them to sniff around the general vicinity and to look for anything out of the ordinary, he also broke cover and went to explore.

There wasn't much to see. The fires were doused and the ruts from the wagon cages continued in single file. They definitely wouldn't be hard to track over the coming days.

It wasn't until Ahab came trotting up with something in his mouth that Leon called them both back to him. When he saw a familiar metal etching reflecting the morning sunlight in the griffin's beak, his heart skipped a beat. It was Gus' medallion! For the second time that morning, he lavished praise on little Ahab. Reed must have lost it or cast it aside when they took him.

Bet he didn't go down without a fight.

Reality, however, came crashing home for him when he glanced up into the sky. Off in the distance, he could see ravens beginning to circle the area further east, where all the fighting had gone down the night before. The cold hard truth of what those carrion would mean put a short end to any momentary excitement.

The thought of burying dead friends turned his stomach. He could count the number of funerals he'd ever attended on one hand. Still though, he knew his companions would at least attempt to do the same for him, had their fates been reversed. It was the least he could do to honor their sacrifice.

He found the slain griffin cub first and carried the little animal's body into the scattered remains of a much larger scene of death. Slavers and Fae lay side by side on a trampled and bloodied field of battle. The slavers had obviously won the struggle but had chosen to leave the bodies of their fallen there where they fell. The smells of that battle, now warmed by the morning sun, forced him to regret his breakfast, but he continued until Merle led him to where Olwena lay. She had rolled onto her back and her eyes wide open, gazing up into the clear skies above.

Leon lay the body of the griffin cub down next to her and folded her stiff arms, Blade in hand, over her still chest. He sent a request through the Blade, asking Ahab to stay and guard them both from the winged opportunists nearby while he went on to search for Rezz with Merle.

Merle spent an hour sniffing the battlefield while Leon searched the area he thought he had last seen him. Only, they never found the body! Hope surged.

Maybe he made it?

When he returned, he dug a large grave for his two fallen companions, right there in that grassy field. He used his Blade to break the earth and his hands to carve away the dark soil. Deeper and deeper he dug. The work exhausted him and the cool breeze from the day before had mostly died away with the storm. Still, though, something about the hard work and the sweat it cost him, gave him a release of sorts. He was proud to be able to do this last service for both of them.

Recalling the way Olwena looked so longingly toward the open plain the day before, he thought she might prefer to be buried there, outside the shadow of the forest, beneath an open sky.

When the hole was deep enough, he gently laid them to rest. Many of the dead slavers nearby wore heavy leather armor. He removed several heavy pieces of that armor and pilled it up over them before he packed the dirt back over them.

That ought to at least deter any coyote size scavengers.

Done at last, he sat down and rested. Words wouldn't come at first, so he lay back and stroked the fur and feathers of his two remaining companions. Eventually, the numbness in his heart dissipated enough for him to carry on and his voice broke as he gave a short, improvised eulogy.

"Olwena was a rough shell with a soft center, she didn't deserve to die like she did. Even the little griffin, in his own way, was a true and loyal companion. I hope, wherever they are, that they're at peace." All he had to offer were simple words from a heavy heart, but simple words were better than no words at all. He lingered a little while longer beside their grave before moving on.

As picked his way across the field of battle, he couldn't help but notice the rich clothing of the Fae warriors. New clothes like that would certainly be nice. He was still wearing the thick rawhides Ferschall had originally provided, and his footwear wouldn't last much longer. He certainly wasn't eager to strip clothes off the fallen enemies. Although, maybe there was no need for those types of measures?

He traveled down the tree line, to near where he suspected the Convergence camp still stood.

#

The Fae camp was tucked far enough back into the trees that it had most likely been hidden from the slaver's caravan when it passed by earlier that morning.

Once more, Leon sent Merle and Ahab in ahead to scout things out, but they both quickly returned as if to say, "Come on in, you'll be fine."

As he slunk from the cover of the trees into the camp, not one item looked to be disturbed from where it was the evening before. It seemed likely that everyone in the camp had been pursuing him and his friends when they ran headlong into the slavers.

Leon assumed any survivors were still racing back through the woods to find help. As such, he didn't waste time. There was no telling how long the empty camp would stay empty. He scavenged through a few of the richly adorned tents at the edge of the camp and found a treasure trove of useless items within. Though he did manage to find a few piles of clean clothing that looked like they would fit, he was quick to bundle up what he needed and to discard what he didn't.

Near the back of the camp, he came across one of their four Thunderbirds. Its reins had become tangled in the branches of a nearby tree. They prevented it from escaping like he assumed the others had done during all the screaming and howling the night before.

The bird made a throaty warning sound when he got too close and tried to kick him when he stepped around its back to check the gear. Leon could only assume it was Sved's dear friend from the day before. He quickly reached out and calmed the bird with his gift. The effect was immediate.

I'll never get tired of using this on surly critters!

Several of their packs, including Ferschall's pottery bag, rested nearby. Taking the initiative, he loaded the bird with plenty of supplies and food. On a whim, he threw Ferschall's pottery up on the pile as well.

I've been lugging it this whole time, it may be worthless, but that old man seemed to think it was worth something to him. Anyway, it'd be a waste to leave it now!

Then, in an impulsive decision on his way out, he decided to check out the big tent at the center of camp.

When he ducked in through the soft canvas flap, he spotted movement in his periphery. Diving into a crouch, he drew his Blade. The tent flap fell, and the tent went dark. He reached out for his Blade the way he had the night before, and his vision cleared enough to take in the surroundings. His frightful nemesis was only a young bird, perched eye level on an antlered hook, hanging fashionably off the center pole. The items in the tent were opulent when compared to the others he had entered.

This must belong to that queen's son.

The tent smelled like the hippie's head shop he had once visited out of sheer curiosity when some friends talked him into a trip to Austin, but its decorum was over the top in every way. After fumbling through the mass of pillowed cushions that lined the floor and kicking over more than a few half-empty canteens containing a residual fluid that gave off an odor of something stronger than water, he stumbled across a small ornate leather chest next to a bedroll in one corner of the tent. The chest wasn't even locked!

Jackpot!

Inside was a box of glowing amber stones, a heavy leather-bound book, and a few pounds of metal blocks that looked suspiciously like gold. Not wanting to waste any more time, Leon grabbed the chest and bedroll as he headed to the door, but turning back, he paused. Something about that little fuzzball on the antler perch looked familiar.

He stepped closer and studied the bird. A thick woven leather strip secured its leg to its roost. It hissed at him when he got too close. Then, when he stepped back, it bobbed its head, staring at him with wide eyes. Leon drew recognition from that look. It was Reed's owl! It had to be! For some reason, it looked a bit larger and older than it had the day before.

He carefully approached the bird and observed the blue-violet feathers which were sprouting through the baby fuzz on its body. It was still awkward in appearance, but he could tell it would soon be a magnificent-looking creature. Reed would certainly want him back.

What the heck, I've already got a zoo waiting outside, may as well add another.

He reached up and used his gift on the wide-eyed bird. It immediately calmed and allowed him to remove the leather bindings that held it to its perch. When he held out his arm and whistled, it gladly hopped right up onto his shoulder. Its talons dug into his rawhide shirt but didn't pierce the leather.

Just as he was about to leave, he made one last discovery. A small but well-crafted canvas rucksack lay leaning against the wall. Without a second thought, he scooped it up and brought it out, lashing it securely to the mounting pile on his pack bird's back.

Not wishing to push his luck any further, Leon led his little caravan of critters out into the afternoon sun, across the grassy trail, and into the sheltered shadows of the far trees growing along the Somber. Though he desperately wanted to clean himself off in the river, he forced his way forward and continued east for another two hours, until the river widened some, and he could see a shallow, gravel-bottomed pool that backed into a beachy hamlet. That clear water was too enticing to pass up, and he itched to get out of his blood-stained clothing.

"We can make some ground tomorrow and catch up just enough to keep an eye on that caravan. Now, though, it's bath time!" Merle slunk away at the mention of his least favorite activity, but Ahab stuck around. The cub seemed thrilled at the prospect of a swim.

The water was as cool as it looked, and though he had sent Merle to keep watch, Leon was glad Ahab stuck around. Oddly, the griffin was a veritable fish in the river!

Leon bathed and used the sandy bottom to thoroughly scrub himself, including his old CW hat. That hat suffered from a sweat stain at least an inch thick. It desperately needed the cleaning. When he finished bathing, he used his Blade to shave a splotchy beard that had been making his neck itch for days. Afterward, he threw on a clean undergarment and both him and the griffin relaxed on the pebbled beach till the sun's rays no longer warmed their bodies.

His new clothes fit rather good considering they were looted from the camp in such a hurry, but the rucksack proved to hold the greatest treasure of all. It contained a small field tent. The tent was made for one, so the critters were out of luck, but it would keep him dry and comfortable if he hit more bad weather. Plus, its mottled earth-tone appearance proved to be a perfect color for blending in with his wooded surroundings.

Must have been what the prince used when he traveled to the Convergence. Oh well, he sure won't be needing it now!

Taking some small measure of comfort in the little victories of the day, Leon settled into the task of feeding his animals and preparing his camp for the coming night. He definitely planned on following the slavers, just not close enough for them to catch his scent.

Chapter 22

Later that night, Leon tossed and turned on the bedroll in his new tent, restlessly struggling to find rest. A fire hadn't seemed prudent, but the bedding was warm and there was no doubt the tent was comfortable. Comfort wasn't the problem. A cold and empty camp was a lonesome place for a man to be alone with his thoughts, especially so soon after the tragedies he had so recently endured.

Sleep had come blissfully swift the night before, spurred on by sheer exhaustion. This night was different. Insomnia mocked him with dark thoughts of loss and despair. No matter how hard he tried, he couldn't fight off those lingering apprehensions. So, at last, he kicked aside his bedroll, hopeful that fresh air would still his racing mind.

He flung open the tent flap and stood to stretch his tired back. Touching a hand to his Blade brought his vision into focus. Was it him or had it become easier to call upon the Blade's gifts?

Reed's owl hooted down at him from a limb somewhere above. The Thunderbird was out, eyes closed while gently rocking in the wind like some drunken feathery sailor. Merle and Ahab were curled up next to one another beside the tent. They both lifted their heads and gave him questioning looks, but he waved them off and asked them to stay. "Just need a little time to myself fellas, I'll be back soon."

Leaving the wooded cove of his riverside camp, Leon walked back out onto the treeless trail. The new moon was barely a waxing sliver, but the stars that night were something special. The sky was clear, and all those thousands of tiny twinkling beacons lent their collective light to create a humbling glimpse into the great expanse beyond. He took a few steps and plunked down on his hind end.

As he sank comfortably into the grassy carpet, he continued his stargazing. He had never seen a sky so bright, even back home in Texas. It stirred a longing in his chest and one of Gus' many cowboy poems came bubbling up in his memory. He recited it quietly to himself.

"As I gaze up into moonlit skies,
On a night which I despise,
I stop and think and realize,
There are many, many cries."

Tears finally found purchase through the dry cracks in the corners of his eyes. He let them come, weeping alone in the tall grass. Hoping beyond hope that he would someday be able to look up into a starry sky with Gus by his side once more. He knew better though. He knew the world of Fayden was a hard place, a merciless wilderness.

But the stars! All those stars above whispered small promises of beauty and hope against the dark void where they hung. Slowly the hurt in his chest softened until it was only a dull ache. He took a few deep breaths to further settle his mind and to relax, content to lay there a little longer, watching the night sky and remembering the good things about the faces and voices of all those he had lost over the past few weeks. The smell of the morning dew rising on clean grass around him helped to further still his thoughts.

His hand fidgeted over the now-familiar bone-handled hilt at his side. He drew the Blade and held it up above him. Starlight flashed in its reflection as he turned it first one way and then the other. He relished the calming sensation that came from simply holding that bone hilt handle close. He didn't know much about the Blade, but for some reason he wished…he wished he might know more. There were mysteries hidden in puzzles in his new world, yet the Blade always seemed to rest unobtrusively at the center of every new revelation.

He was so lost in thought that a raspy chuffing noise didn't register with him as it drew close. It wasn't until a large shadow loomed over him, partially blocking out the starlight from above, that he hollered in fright and attempted to roll aside.

A paw the size of a ten-gallon hat brim came down on his shoulder as he scrambled to roll away. It easily rolled him back onto his back, where it settled on his chest and held him firm. Foul breath from a great toothy mouth huffed in his face, slinging slobber down his forehead and blowing his hat right off his head. He couldn't move, and he dared not cry out again.

The terrifying standoff was interrupted by a deep-throated growl from nearby, followed by a not so threatening squawk-growl.

Good ole Merle! At least he and Ahab still have my back...for all the good that'll do me now.

Leon tried to tilt his head back to see what was going on, but the grass limited his view to the toothy maw above his face. The beast lifted its head to face his dog and Leon could better see what pinned him where he lay. They were all in big trouble!

Crouching over him was a bear on all fours. But not just any bear, this bear was so large that Leon would have had to look up an inch or two to look him in the eye, even if he had been standing on his own two feet! It responded to Merle's snarl with a dismissive chuff, clearly less than impressed and equally unafraid of the dog's aggressive tactic. It didn't even acknowledge the griffin. Then it swiveled back to Leon.

Things were heading downhill quickly until a rich, smoky smooth voice spoke up from above the bear. "Easy Grumpy, you can eat them later if they don't behave, but I want to ask this fool in the grass a couple of questions first." The phrase was spoken in such a literal manner that it brokered no humor.

The woman then addressed him, "You alone out here? Don't lie! You won't like Grumpy when he's...well, when he's grumpy."

"Yeah, just me. Me and my animals I mean."

The bear backed up. "Sit up, let me get a better look at you. Call off that hound."

Leon called out to tell Merle that he was okay, but through his Blade, he sent both him and Ahab a silent request to be ready. Then he eased himself up into a sitting position, careful not to make any sudden moves.

He took his first full look at the bear beside him and, in turn, the woman riding above. Frizzy blond hair framed exotic features on a wary face, both of which were further accentuated by high cheekbones and a square but feminine jawline. She wore a light smattering of some type of dark red facial paint beneath a stenciled maroon leather headband. It gave her a severe look, fierce enough to match the bear she rode. The strange woman wore a gray fur poncho wrapped tight around her neck. Her arms, which extended out the sides of the poncho, were fitted with dark maroon leather wrist guards. What he could see of the flourishes and swirls on the wrist guards matched those on her headband. Hers was a wild sort of fierceness. Leon felt awkward and meek in the shadow of a woman whose every attribute served to meld danger and beauty in such a balanced blend.

As she stared down at him her eyebrows rose, until a frown slipped through her solemn demeanor. Leon saw sadness mixed with confusion in that frown. More perplexing were the implications. What had he done?

He subconsciously wiped the back of his wrist under his nose and made a half-hearted attempt to brush his curly mop of hair back up off his brow. Still, she didn't seem to notice any of his normal self-conscious ticks. She just sat there on that giant bear, slack-jawed, looking almost as stunned as him.

"You are Bladed." It was a statement, not a question. He still held his Blade in his right hand.

The woman studied him a while longer. Then she climbed down and made him face away from her as she searched him for other weapons. He had nothing on him at the time but his Blade, so he didn't protest.

"Who are you?" she asked as she reached down to frisk his boots.

"Leon Waldman."

Leon couldn't help but notice that, when he turned back around, she stood eye level to him, but she seemed so much taller. After she was satisfied, he didn't have any other weapons, he took a chance and offered an olive branch. "Can I ask your name?"

She remained silent for a bit longer. Then she reached out and gripped his wrist. Her grip was as bone-crunching solid as they came. Nearly made his eyes water once more.

"I am Kyra of the Stonebreakers clan."

She didn't waste any more time on pleasantries as she dropped his hand. Instead, she went straight to the point. "What are you doing here and why are you alone?"

Though everyone Leon had met since his arrival spoke common Fayden, he had noticed subtle variations in every new Tribe he encountered. The Fae spoke in lilting patterns, the Hootsi in a firm, direct manner, and the Otterkin, in a scattered, pondering voice. Kyra's words flowed with strength, in a steady, rhythmic cadence. They called to him and bid him listen at the same time.

# # #

Leon spent the next hour answering Kyra's questions and explaining his story as best he could. He did, however, leave some significant portions out, and opted to start his narrative back at the moment Ben and his men stumbled into Ferschall. He didn't lie, per se, just mentioned that he was a stranger traveling from southern lands.

Kyra, despite being initially suspicious, was a good listener and only interrupted to get clarification or to ask for more detail. When Leon came to the part of the story that included the last few days, and he explained the results of their run-in with the Fae, he thought he saw a hint of empathy flitter across her eyes.

However, at the mention of the slavers, her expression turned to granite. Whatever quiet coals she kept smoldering below her calm demeaner erupted into blazing fury at the mention of the capture of his friends. For a few terrifying moments, Leon worried Grumpy might get the wrong idea about the nature of their conversation. His chuffing escalated to a rumbling growl until she placed a hand on the big bear and calmed the situation.

Once Kyra regained composure, she told him her story. To his chagrin, her story held much more loss than he could have dreamed possible. Though she held back on specifics and only gave facts, he could piece together the words between the lines.

"My family and our clan are some of the last remnants of a nearly extinct tribe of people. We lived on the far western side of those mountains," Kyra flicked a hand back at the towering peaks to their west. "Well, outside the protective borders of Fayden. We were shepherds, raising Slowfoot Grazers in the foothills of those mountains." Leon didn't know exactly what sort of animal she referenced, but he suspected it was some sort of ruminant livestock and opted not to interrupt.

"Over the past two years, an army of foreigners slowly formed along our territorial borders. Last year they began attacking our people. Our clan was one of the strongest of the mountain clans, but we were no match for the thousands upon thousands of invaders who pushed us out of our hillside homes and up into the refuge of our summer hunting camps, in the high mountain meadows."

Kyra shuddered but bravely continued her story, "My parents and most of my clan were killed as those invaders continued to hunt us down. My three brothers and I alone escaped through the mountains last winter."

"You came through the mountains in winter?"

She nodded back. "The high passes are hard but not impossible if you know how to cross them, even in winter." She let out a long sigh. "Still, it didn't do us much good. Those filthy slavers attacked us the day after we made it over!"

"How did you escape?"

"Pretty simple really. Grumpy and I were out hunting mountain herbs when I heard the shouting. When I went to investigate, three of the slavers broke off and ran me down. Lucky for me, they only sent three. By the time those three realized I wasn't alone, it was too late for them. Grumpy ruined their day and carried me up into the high country, clear of their trackers.

"I know little of the people of this land. It was always forbidden for any in our clan to venture here, but the choice was either come here or die there. All I know now is that I will follow that caravan until I rescue my brothers."

"How long have you been trailing them?"

"A little over a week. They were moving north along the east side of the mountains when they found us, then turned east to follow this river the next day. I only move at night and lay low during the day."

Leon's heart melted for the girl's situation. Beyond that though, he thought her plan for following at night showed some shrewd strategy. It was a much better tactic than what he had been considering, which included little if any planning at all. He decided to make her an offer.

"Here's the deal, I'm going to try to get my friends back when the slavers reach their destination, the North Fang capitol called Hollinger. How about we team up to track this bunch and you help me to stay hidden along the way? Then, when we get there, I'll do what I can to see about freeing your brothers as well as Reed and Haddie? I've got friends who should be there when we arrive to help buy them all back, and if worse comes to worst, I've recently come into some wealth of my own."

Initially, Kyra didn't seem to like the idea of waiting to free her brothers, but she apparently knew enough to admit she stood little chance of saving them without being captured herself. The practicality of the offer eventually won her over. They would work together until they made it to Hollinger.

"There's something else I need you to answer." She stood stock still while she waited for Leon to respond. It was obviously a pretty loaded question.

"What's that?" Leon asked.

"What Clan is your father?"

"What do you mean? I honestly don't even know my Tribe, Gus, my grandfather, adopted me as a child when he found me near some woods, and I have no memories before that. He raised me in…well, like I said earlier, in a place that wasn't within the borders of Fayden."

"Well, you might not know who or what you are, but I'm sure I do…your hair gives you away. You may be small for our kind, but there aren't many of us left where I'm from and, I don't know, maybe my clan's just big for our tribe?" Her words were crafted so as not to give offense, but Leon didn't care a lick about that, his palms grew clammy over the notion that she might be able to answer a question. *The question!* The one that had eluded him for so long.

"What exactly is our kind, Kyra?"

She searched him with a questioning glare. "You don't know?" It was his turn to freeze in place, "You are of the Lost Tribe, Leon…you're a Bearskinner, there's no doubt in my mind."

Hadn't that Vin said something about the Lost Tribe before Merle ended him?

"A *Bearskinner*, huh?" Leon tasted the word for the first time and pondered the implication as she continued.

"Our kind were once the pride of the seven Tribes. Father told us stories as kids of how we were revered as the warrior champions of Fayden. Then we were betrayed. People thought we were stoking some rebellion to enslave the other tribes, but it was a lie, and it tore the kingdom apart. Each of the tribes withdrew into themselves, but for a time they all rose together against us. Thousands were killed, or murdered, however you want to look at it. Now, there are very few of us left. Our people are scattered, and our heritage, disgraced.

"I grew up in exile, but if what I've been told of this land is true, we will not find much sympathy for our kind at this Hollinger place you mention. The only fact we may have going for us is that Bearskinners have not been present in the territory of Fayden for many generations. Maybe people have simply forgotten us?"

His head buzzed with the repercussions of what Kyra had just divulged.

She continued, "I don't believe its random chance that I found you, another Bladed Bearskinner," she pulled a Blade out from under her poncho and held it up for him to see as she continued, "out here in the middle of nowhere. Perhaps something more is at work? Even so, we've got to weigh our options carefully, not take too many chances, you understand?"

He didn't. Leon was still lost in thought. "So, a Bearskinner...that means we are...bear skin-changers. Our ancestors could somehow take the form of a bear, like Grumpy."

Kyra nodded a slow yes, but he already knew. Somewhere deep down in his gut, he had known all along. It just never clicked into place until she put it into words. Somehow, he managed to find the strength to turn the conversation back to the task at hand.

"Thank you, Kyra. Seriously, you don't know how long I've waited to hear someone explain all of what you just parsed out." He paused to gather his thoughts, then continued, "So, we may not be well received in Hollinger, but we've got to try, don't we?"

She nodded. "Yes, we've got to try. There's just one more thing."

"What's that?"

"War is coming. As soon as the higher passes thaw, I expect the giant tribes will be marching on the border walls."

"Who?"

"Giants."

"As in really tall people?"

She nodded back with a flat expression before arching a brow, like she knew he really didn't understand what the word meant, "Their kind is at least as tall as Grumpy when he stands." She gave the bear a wordless *thump* on his shoulder, and he rose on two hind legs. He was almost twice again Leon's height.

Leon swallowed. "They're coming here to raid these lands? You're sure?"

"There are thousands of them. They are an unstoppable force of nature. They can't be reasoned with or appeased. They only come to take and to tear down."

For the first time that night, Leon saw a flash of fear in her eyes. "The faster I rescue my brothers, the faster we can flee."

# # #

If he couldn't sleep before, there was no way Leon could go back to sleep after hearing all of what she had to say. He quickly broke camp, stowed his gear, and took one last look at his peaceful river cove. With a shrill whistle, Reed's missing owlet came hoping out of a tree to plop down on his shoulder. Its silky blue feathers reflected a dark luster in the starlight, but its body was still that of a small pudgy owlet.

Leon shook his head. Reed's gift must have pushed the little owl's plumage well beyond the pace of normal development. He hoped its little body would catch up someday. He still suspected the small owl would grow to be a beautiful bird.

Before they started on their way, Kyra whistled at the full extent of his traveling zoo. She was especially amazed at the little griffin.

"I've never heard of one taming a griffin!"

Leon laughed. "This coming from the person riding a giant bear!"

She shrugged. "Many Bearskinners have a bit of a natural affinity with bears. It's a gift linked to our tribal heritage. My gift for taming animals doesn't go beyond bears, though few do." Was that new appreciation in her eyes?

"Well, he isn't exactly *tame,* but I bet little Ahab grows on you." She scrunched her brow and gave him a look.

"Leon, tell me something? Do you have griffin flocks where you are from?"

Leon chuckled. "No, ma'am, no griffin flocks in Texas."

"Then you have never seen a full-grown griffin?"

Now it was Leon's turn to shrug, "No, he and his brother came straight out of a crate. He's an awkward little creature, though, isn't he?"

"Awkward?! That *awkward* little creature will grow in a few years to have a wingspan of twenty paces and to stand taller than Grumpy! The wild flocks of the southern Anderle range would sometimes move north and raid our pastures when I was a child, they were supreme stalkers of the sky. Even our larger herd protectors, like Grumpy here, were hard-pressed to defend the calves when griffin flocks chose to attack."

Gulp.

Considering Kyra mentioned her people herded some sort of large hairy creature using ginormous bears, he suddenly had a new and different appreciation for Ahab.

Guess that solves what the Hootsi were afraid of along Ferschall's western trail!

"Um, no. No one bothered to mention that in the fine print when I adopted him. He's a good boy, though, aren't you, Ahab? Aren't you? Who's a good little griffin…yes you are!" His baby talk turned muffled as he reached down and patted the griffin, causing him to dance enthusiastically back and forth around his legs.

"Perhaps because they all assumed someone who knew enough to tame a griffin would know enough to understand what they were taking on." She held enough of a poker face that Leor couldn't tell if it was a matter-of-fact statement or thinly veiled disdain.

Either way, he tried to pretend it would all work out in the end, though he knew his little friend could someday become a huge liability. If he ever did find a way home, there was no way he was gonna be able to bring something like Ahab along. He would need to think more carefully before attempting to tame any more animals in the future, but there was no way he was giving up on the cub just yet.

"So, you know I can tame animals with my Gift, and I know you can befriend bears…anything else you can do? I mean, we may as well know what each other can do if we're going to be working together, right?"

Kyra flinched, obviously not used to his friendly bantering tone of the conversation, but she soon recovered and eased into a thoughtful response, "The Blade…it does give me a little extra strength when I need it. It isn't the limitless kind of strength an Unbladed person can leverage on a moonless night, but I hold my own."

Leon thought back to her handshake. Her hand around his wrist had been like a steel vice when she squeezed.

So, no arm wrestling the bear girl if you want to keep your man-card, got it!

"I told you one of mine, what about you? Anything else the Blade allows you to do?"

He paused as he considered what to say, "So, when it gets dark and I have a hard time seeing, I touch the Blade, and it's like I can see in the dark." Leon looked over expectantly, waiting to see what she thought.

"Well, yeah. But that's kind of a given, right?"

He gave her a look, and she held up a hand, "Sorry, I keep forgetting you are new to this. But yeah, seeing in the dark is another gift most Bladed can access."

"Most?"

"I just know that all of us in my father's clan had the ability. They said it was normal."

Well, that explains why no one else had a hard time running through the dark field the other night.

Leon's thoughts turned to Grumpy. The furry beast plodded along beside him, large as an ox. "Are all mountain bears as big as him?"

"Some are, but not many. Grumpy's special. He's only three years old!" she said grinning from ear to ear. "I raised him from a cub, but last winter I kind of accidentally figured out I had one other gift."

"Well, don't hold back now. What is it? I just want to know, in case it is something that can help us, in case we have to fight." He pointed forward, in the direction of the caravan they pursued.

"It's not likely to be much help if that happens, but I don't suppose there's any harm in sharing." She shrugged, "I can help things grow beyond their full potential. It's not a flashy growth gift. I was taught that most of those are limited to only allowing something to grow into what it is meant to be. Those gifts usually work really fast to grow something into its full potential. You can barely see mine at work at all, but over time, it makes quite a difference. Grumpy was a runt!" She beamed up at her furry giant.

Leon thought of Reed and his gift. He had a feeling he knew why his owl's wings were coming in so quickly while the rest of him hadn't yet changed. He immediately asked her to use it on all his creatures.

"Sure, I agree, but only on one condition."

"What's that?"

"That you allow me to test it out on you as well!"

He couldn't decide whether she was messing with him or not, but he agreed just the same.

What am I getting myself into here, Leon?

# # #

They continued walking along together into the wee hours of the morning, sometimes in companionable silence and at other times comparing the menial day-to-day work of the different forms of animal husbandry they practiced in their previous lives. Leon could tell Kyra was clearly as fascinated as confused at the concepts of training horses and roping cattle, but she remained polite and didn't probe too deep in her questions.

He couldn't help but wince every now and again as he thought about how much Gus might have thoroughly enjoyed hearing the woman talk about the types of things she took for granted as she casually reminisced how *easy* she had it as a herder on her Clan's lands. By comparison, his normal ranch work on the CW sounded more like a seat in the lap of luxury...something Gus ardently attempted to convey to him throughout his teen years.

He did continue to avoid broaching the subject of his passage and arrival through the Royal Tree. Not that he didn't feel like he could trust her, he just didn't want her to think he was crazy so soon after meeting her.

Eventually, just before sunup, they stopped and made a small camp when Merle, who Reed had sent ahead to scout, returned, and warned them to go no further. In the sunrise of that first morning together, Leon finally saw Kyra in the light of day. He had just offloaded his kit from the Thunderbird and turned to ask her something about saddles when he was stopped cold in his tracks.

She shrugged out of her fur poncho and tossed it down on a nearby rock. Beneath the poncho, she wore a sleeveless pale linen smock trimmed and lined in a tight leather vest above rawhide leggings that ended in furry boots. She took a moment to stretch her legs before reaching up to untie her gear and unsaddle Grumpy's tack.

She turned, and he caught a profile view of her face. Those exotic features he had noticed in passing upon their meeting the night before coalesced into smoky blue eyes, full lips, and a square jaw. She used a water bag to wash away her facial paint, which she had explained was a design to display her clan symbol when on the warpath, and Leon noticed the absence of the paint served only to accentuate those natural features.

There are certain things a guy can't help but notice in a glance and while he wasn't one to stare, Leon was definitely noticing all of those things. Kyra wasn't just a natural, albeit aloof, beauty the way he initially presumed, she was a total knockout. The amazing part was she seemed clueless as to the effect her beauty might have on him, much less any other man.

He must have gone a bit wobbly on his legs because when she turned back to toss down the riding leathers and saw him standing there with his nose to the clouds, pretending to enjoy the morning air, she gave him a skeptical look. She then suggested they take turns standing watch during the day and insisted on taking first watch.

Things are bad, but they just got a little more bearable!

The next day bled into the next as they continued their journey together. Kyra remained distant and pensive, but Leon learned it wasn't due to any fault of his own. She was just a young woman whose youthful vigor was worn thin by all the tragedy and trauma she had been dealt in life. His heart broke for the hurt that she carried buried so close beneath the surface. He could only really glimpse its presence at times in the way she would hug Grumpy or cry in her sleep, but it spurred him to crawl out of his shell in an attempt to get her to crawl out of hers. In fact, traveling beside her at night, without the distractions daylight provided, somehow made it easier for him to focus more on conversation meant to foster her interest and encourage her laughter. The tension he might normally feel when visiting with pretty girls faded a little more with each setting sun, and they never ran out of topics to cover.

Their nightly activities grew into more of a routine as well. Leon and Kyra traded turns sleeping in the dark confines of his solo tent each day. Ahab continued to gain proficiency in catching fish from the Somber and, at the break of dawn each morning, Leon went hunting with Rezz's longbow. Out on the grassy plain, he was able to consistently take down some type of large furry critter that looked to him to be a toothy relative of a prairie dog the size of an actual dog.

Kyra made her unique contributions to their meals. She used Grumpy to sniff out tubers growing along the riverbank and sporadically taught Leon a bit of general knowledge regarding which types of berries and herbs were safe to eat. She even showed him how to render oil from a juicy seed she called a dimple-berry. She would pile the berries up in a pot and boil them down on the rare occasions they felt safe to light a fire.

Then she would seine out the pods, so that, when it cooled, she could scoop out the oil floating on the surface. She used some of the oil to fry meat. The rest she mixed with strong herbs and flowers. Her herbal concoction would dry into a thick sort of paste that she claimed was useful as a shampoo. She kept her florally scented paste stored in a leather pack.

Perhaps most exciting of all in his new routines were the daily sparring lessons Kyra insisted upon. Leon knew the basics of how to hold a sword and move his body to block or defend himself from his work in the forest with Reed, but Kyra had a whole lifetime of lessons from a father who she described as a master with the Blade. She wasn't quite as fast as Leon and, unless she focused on using her gift, he was the stronger of the two, but where he edged her in

275

physical abilities, she dominated in using what she called *modified technique.*

The odd thing about her father's fighting philosophy was that it wasn't some prescriptive formula he had to learn to learn to fight, it was more of a framework. It provided a solid base that freed him to use his creativity with the Blade as his weapon. At its core was the precept that proficiency only ever came through practice paired with an exploration of one's boundaries.

Every afternoon he gained at least one new insight into how to use his Blade. Often those insights came at the price of a pound of pride and a nice welt but, nonetheless, he was thankful for every bruise he earned.

"Leon, loosen up. Don't try so hard to guide the Blade, let the Blade guide you!"

The comment was one she used often. It was also nearly the exact opposite of what Reed had attempted to hammer home during their sessions in the forest.

"Come at me again, but this time try to surprise me."

Leon wanted to laugh. Surprise her? Nothing surprised Kyra. He'd been trying to catch her napping for days and yet she somehow met and defended his every ploy.

He backed off and did his best to study the surroundings immediately around her with his peripheral vision. It was that strange time of twilight where the sun sometimes sets and turns the air a rosy color. Kyra was bouncing on her toes, standing beneath a sturdy hardwood that had provided shade for their camp throughout the day. Just above her head, he saw the feathered form of Reed's little owlet watching them both. Working on a whim, he sent a pulse through his Blade.

Leon stopped bouncing and pointed up, feigning a look of terror in his eyes. Just then the little owl let loose the most wicked sounding Hoot it had ever attempted.

Kyra flinched so hard she nearly fell over. By the time she regained her balance, Leon was barreling down on her, preparing to execute the type of form tackle that would have made his high-school football coach wish he'd have taken the time to recruit him.

Unfortunately for Leon, Kyra had grown up with three brothers who had attempted similar such distractions at least a hundred different ways while their father drilled them growing up. She didn't try to fight against the take-down, she went with it and then used Leon's momentum against him.

Before he knew what was happening, he was rolling down the riverbank, then sputtering to stand in knee-deep water. He didn't try to surprise her again that night.

On evening's when they lingered within sheltered terrain that felt safe, with wind gusting in the right directions, they would wait until just before dark to light a small fire, usually somewhere down in a crevasse along the river bottom. There they would cook food and listen to the early evening sounds along the river's shoreline. Then, just in time for sunset, they would smoother the coals and take turns individually bathing downriver from camp, washing their clothes of the smoky scent of their fire before drying off, packing up, and continuing their nightly pursuit. Luckily, Leon's salvage run in the Fae camp managed to provide him with more than one change of clothes, and Kyra's packs contained multiple sets of clothes for her as well.

Three weeks came and went in the blink of an eye for Leon before the caravan's trail finally took a turn, leading them to cross a crumbling gray stone bridge, which sat straddling the Somber. There was an obvious trail leading up from the east, and the bridge looked to be used frequently enough that they decided to stop and make camp a ways up the river before crossing.

The next evening, Leon left the remaining animals in their makeshift camp with strict orders to stay put. However, he did take Merle with them across the bridge to scout out the hills to the north.

Leon had been working on using his Blade to strengthen his connection with all their animals, but the connection he shared with Merle was deeper than the others. The Blade sharpened Merle's understanding of Leon's directives, but a lifetime of trust and companionship buffeted their relationship to the point where a simple thought was all it took to convey a complex request. Merle led them to a distant hill and stopped.

Peeking over the crest and down onto a small town centered on a rather steep pass between two larger hills, Leon could clearly see a line of caged wagons dotting the road, awaiting permission to enter through the exterior of a tall wooden gate which blocked entry into the pass. He studied things carefully for a few minutes then motioned Kyra. They crawled back down out of sight before either dared speak.

"Did you see all those great roundhouses and that towering wall around them? You think that's Hollinger?"

Leon had traveled alone with Kyra for a long time, yet he sometimes forgot how sheltered her life had been prior to their meeting. Though he hadn't seen what a *big* city looked like in Fayden, he was certain the small village below wasn't where they were headed.

"I don't think we're there yet, but I do think we are going to start seeing more and more cities like this. We might be able to dodge around this one, but we are going to need to figure out a way to intermingle with folks, eventually. Come on, we can't go down there till the caravan leaves anyway so that gives us a day or two to figure things out."

Chapter 23

When Leon made it back to camp, he rummaged through his pack until he dug up the last of the coffee. Somewhere along the way, in the endless forests, he had weaned himself off his favorite drink with the recognition he would eventually run out if he didn't conserve. Not that the effort did him much good. He stared down into the near-empty pack containing the last remnants of his once plentiful bounty and took a heavy-hearted sniff of the pungent aroma that he would miss more than just about any other thing he'd left back at home. Presently, one of his greatest fears was about to become reality.

"What is that?"

"This? This is the stuff dreams are made of…black gold." He opened the bag and Kyra scrambled over to peek inside as he inhaled deeply.

"Those are beans, Leon."

"Way to steal my thunder!"

"Thunder stealing? You make no sense sometimes."

"Look, we use these beans to make a delicious drink where I live. And though it pains me more than you can imagine, I've got an idea for how we can use the last of my beans to help us blend in more naturally."

"You want to use magic beans to get us into the city?" He could hear the skepticism in her voice. It would have been funny if the stakes weren't so high for both of them.

"Help me find a couple of rocks. I need one that's flat and another that's heavy and round, we have some beans to grind! Then, I'm gonna show you a trick I heard about from a girl at school a few years ago. If it works, you can say you're sorry for doubting me by letting me take you out to dinner when this is all over. Deal?" Leon tried to throw out the dinner invite casually, like it was no big deal but held his breath in anticipation as he continued to sort through the remaining contents of his pack.

"Leon, you do realize we have dinner together every night? You are so odd sometimes…" Not even realizing the metaphorical puppy she kicked, Kyra stomped off in search of his rocks.

Soon, though, Leon had an improvised pot of cowboy coffee boiling in Kyra's large cookpot. After allowing the beans to boil for a few minutes, he pulled the pot off the small fire and poured some cold water gently over the top to let the grinds settle. Next, he took a cup and scooped up some of the dark nectar for his selfish edification. Squinting through the heavenly steam that rose off the top of the cup, he took a small swig. It was as delicious as ever, but he exaggerated a bit more than necessary for Kyra's sake, making his eyes roll back in his head, and exhaling with as close to a sound of satisfied bliss as he could muster.

She quickly took the cup when he handed it over. She tilted her head back and took a large sip, followed immediately by spewing the steaming brew out onto coals of the fire.

"Ouch! Yuck! How can you drink that hot, bitter concoction? I think I just burned my tongue!"

Leon pushed his hat back and scratched his head with a grin. "It grows on you."

"Yeah, well, that's the same thing you said about your baby griffin. He just seems to keep growing, but not on me."

Leon looked over at Ahab who was pruning himself, his beak edging suspiciously close to his hind end. There was no doubt he was growing and growing fast, but his hygiene fell far short of healthy decorum.

"You know you love him."

Kyra didn't respond as she brought over more water and doused the fire. He leaned back to savor one more cup, then scraped up another cup full off the bottom of the pot, grinds and all.

"Come on down to the water and bring your berry concoction."

"It's called Dimpleberry Paste, and I've noticed some missing every time I've left it out for you." She gave him a satisfied smirk.

"Fine, bring the Dimpleberry Paste. If this works, no one will likely mistake us for Bearskinners, for a while at least."

Taking their improvised coffee pot and mixing in a healthy dose of herb-infused Dimpleberry Paste, Leon then massaged the mixture into Kyra's curly mop of hair. He worked it in slowly, careful to saturate every strand. He also used a cloth to help wash all of her clan paint. Even though she preferred to re-apply the war paint every evening, he explained how it wouldn't do either of them any good to have her looking like a crazy Amazon where they were headed. The metaphor was lost on her, but she got the general drift of what he meant.

He couldn't deny that the clean, fresh scent of flowery herbs mixed well with the rich aromatic scent of the coffee. Kyra seemed to enjoy the sensation of having her scalp massaged as well. It took a lot of willpower for Leon to ignore the way the morning sun lit up the bare skin of her freshly washed face as she smiled up at him, with eyes closed. Despite the use of the war paint, her dark olive skin was flawless. Leon frowned when Grumpy moved in to take a sniff and remained close enough afterward to keep him focused on the task at hand.

When he was done, they traded places, and he knelt while she did the same for him. He could feel a tingling sensation in his scalp as she worked.

"Just so you know, I'm testing out my gift on your noggin. Hopefully, it works equally well on the rest of you."

Leon's eyes snapped open. "You mean you're not sure, and you're using it on me right now?!"

"Hahaha, relax, Leon! I'm just joking with you! I am using my gift, but I promise it doesn't work the way you are thinking. You will be fine. This isn't the first time I've used it on you either. I used it a few weeks ago when I doctored that blister on your foot. I can already tell it has helped, too. You're taller than you were when we first met!" Had he really grown that much? He decided to just leave her be and enjoy the scalp massage while it lasted.

Afterward, he didn't know how long to leave it in, so he advised they wait until later that evening to rinse once more.

# # #

When morning came the next day, and he finally saw his handy work in sunlight, he was thrilled with the results. Kyra's rich blonde locks were darkened up to a lighter honey auburn hue. She acknowledged the same for him when she pulled his hat off and studied his curly mess of hair.

They then revisited their overlook hill in an attempt to see whether their caravan was still camped in town. When they saw the town square empty, Leon suggested they pack up, fill their canteens, and head out.

As they approached the large wooden gate Leon couldn't help chuckling at himself. He could pass himself off as a ringmaster for a traveling circus back home. He led the Thunderbird by the reins with an owl perched on his shoulder and Merle at his side. Ahab rode up above their gear on the Thunderbird, wrapped in a cloth to hopefully prevent the type of unwelcome attention a tame griffin cub might incur.

They were followed by a wide-eyed beauty riding an enormous bear. He had no idea what type of reception they might expect, but he did have an explanation in mind, if needed.

"Hold it right there, young warrior!" a grizzled voice hailed him down from up on the wall above.

"State your business in Gambler's Gap."

Here goes nothing!

"Good afternoon, sir! We are simply merchants returning from a trade excursion along the Fae border. We carry supplies to trade to the Otterkin merchants in Hollinger."

A moment later, the side door to the main gate popped open, and a fat old man in chain-linked armor came hobbling out to eye them all closely.

"No one deals with the Ageless folk, boy." His eyes belied his words as he studied their unique clothing and the cargo lashed to the tops of the creatures they led. He took an exceptionally long look at Leon's hat.

Leon looked the man in the eye. "Well, I did."

The man studied him a long moment. "Perhaps you did at that. You take responsibility for them creatures? Never heard of a Cave Bear acting civil before. If he hurts someone, it's on your head!"

"I take responsibility. We just need passage through, and we will be on our way."

The man eyed them suspiciously a little longer, then whistled back behind him. The main gate creaked open. Before they could proceed, he held out an open hand. "That'll be two silver."

Leon had no idea how much two silver was worth, so he handed the man one of the gold coins he found in the Fae camp.

The man's eyes bulged when he realized what he had been given. His voice softened, and he leaned in conspiratorially, "Word of advice? Don't go throwing gold around like that in these parts! And take the longer southern trail to Hollinger." He touched his forefinger to his nose and winked, "Just had a rabble of slavers come through who might not think twice about adding a pair like you to their merchandise, if you know what I mean?"

Leon nodded, and the man gave him a wink in return before stepping aside and allowing them to enter Gambler's Gap.

There were a few cold stares at first, but people soon returned to their daily activities. Leon suspected those folks saw all sorts of strange sights from time to time, living in a border town as they did.

Though Kyra remained in enraptured awe at the sights and sounds around them, Leon was careful not to stop to talk except to ask directions on the quickest route to Hollinger. Once he verified the directions with two more random people, he took a beeline toward the other side of Gambler's Gap, right through the middle of town.

There was no wall on the other side of the Gap. The town just sort of petered out into open fields supporting miles and miles of farmland. When the road split, Leon took the northern route against the friendly advice of the gate guard. They couldn't afford to lose the caravan, and he didn't know precisely how much of a headstart the slavers had on him. Though, as an added precaution, he did have Merle sniff around to confirm they were on the right track.

# # #

As they continued their pursuit the drudgery of the day wore away. Farms became sparse as the terrain turned rocky. Twice Leon spotted large herds of curly horned sheep which fled when they saw his strange entourage, but they passed no other travelers.

The road grew even tougher as evening descended. They followed a twisted path, cutting switchbacks up and around large granite uplifts. The winds added a challenge of their own, making it hard for Merle to anticipate what lay beyond each dip and corner. Therefore, it shouldn't have come as a surprise when Leon was surprised, but it did.

He came around a rocky edge in the trail and saw the edge of a wagon before catching himself and diving back for cover. He wordlessly hustled everyone back, further off the trail, into the rocky uplift, then whispered to Kyra.

"They're right there! Don't know if they saw me. We need to get out of sight, fast!"

She took a look around and pointed to a ledge at least twenty feet up a steep but manageable hillside, then started climbing. It wasn't ideal but Leon could tell it looked like it might house a ridge, perhaps wide enough to provide some protection out of sight.

Grumpy followed right behind Kyra, making surprisingly little noise as he hoisted his bulk up the steep incline of loose rocks. Leon's creatures followed with quick nudge from his gift. The only creature to struggle was the Thunderbird.

He just couldn't seem to gain any traction with only two long legs. However, in a moment of inspiration Leon touched the bird, sending a calm picture of it using its beak to find purchase each time it repositioned its legs.

It still managed to slip a time or two, but it made it up onto the rocky ledge with the rest of them.

There was a natural cleft that might serve as a sort of shelter back against the cliff wall and once Leon had everyone calm and settled, he crawled forward on his belly to lay beside Kyra as she kept watch over the road leading round the bend. The whole ordeal had taken less than two minutes, but Leon's heart beat out of control with the adrenaline of coming so close to capture.

They waited there silent and still as the shadows continued growing longer around them.

Their voices came first. Deep hateful noises. Then three muscled up meatheads came stomping round the bend.

"You happy, Jitters? We checked it out. Nothing back down here at all!"

"Shut it, Kumba! I'm telling you I saw something!"

The other member of the party made a lewd comment at the expense of Jitters, and he and Kumba had a big laugh.

Jitters held up a hand. "You guys don't smell nothing strange?" The other two busted out laughing again.

"You're making it too easy on us, Jitters! Come on man, you've been squirrelly ever since we bagged us that Fae mob."

"I think he's just afraid someone will steal that saucy redhead from him before the boss gives in to his plea for first pick!"

Kumba had crossed the line. Jitters cocked an arm back and swung. The three of them went down in a tussle.

Meanwhile, Leon caught the message between the lines. He thought of Haddie out there, defenseless, in a camp full of monsters like that and his blood boiled. Thoughts of retribution sent a slippery surge of electrical current out from his chest. Then he pictured how easily he could take the loudmouth down one on one. His rage turned to hate. He hated everything about those men and what they represented. His hate gave birth to something new.

The pain he thought he had lost when he first took up the Blade was once again coursing through his veins. Its very presence fanned the flame of anger still growing in his belly. An untethered strength started exerting its power from deep within his chest, changing his body. He clamped his mouth shut and gritted his teeth against the burning and tearing before all thoughts of restraint slipped away like loosened shackles from his mind.

Then just before he gave himself to the storm, a firm hand curled around his neck. Warm breath from soft lips tickled his ear as words clawed at the door to the lucid corner of his mind. It gave him just enough of a pause to halt if not subdue the mounting rage that boiled beneath his skin.

"...back to me, Leon. Don't give in, don't lose control!" The soft sounds of her pleas broke through his rage and settled his mind. He slid a hand up to where she still clung to his neck and gave her a pat to indicate he was himself again.

A few minutes later and the fight below subsided. There were threats and shoves, but the three men tromped back around the corner and disappeared.

Leon's head still spun as he breathlessly whispered, "How come that happened? I thought this Blade was supposed to kill that part of me. To protect me from...from what I am capable of becoming!"

"It does and it doesn't."

"What does that mean?"

"It heals us of the control the sickness exerts over us, but it doesn't completely remove the taint. That, unfortunately, is still there, lingering in our bodies. It's incredibly powerful, and even a Bladed person can become addicted to its influence once more. Only, with the suppression the Blade provides, they are never as powerful as Unbladed individuals."

"So, what good is the Blade?"

Kyra looked at him, stricken. "Leon, taking the Blade gives us a choice that no one else can claim. We aren't subject to the twisted nature of the Unbladed, but that doesn't mean we can't choose to put ourselves back under that control from time to time. Often to our own detriment..."

Leon worked to calm himself while she continued to explain the merits of the Blade, still just inches from his face. She was beautiful and smart and way too good for the likes of him, but he was past thinking things through so deeply.

He reached up, lightly touching her cheek.

When she stopped talking, he leaned in and met her lips. It was a soft, gentle kiss, full of a tender thank you and more besides. She pulled back after a moment.

"I'm sorry, Kyra, I just…" he smiled, "I finally found a way to surprise you, didn't I?"

She leaned in and kissed him back.

When they broke apart again, she smiled, too. For the first time since meeting his beautiful traveling companion, Leon saw a full smile light up her face. Sitting so close, he could see tiny slivers of green dancing in those smoky blue eyes. He could smell the unique blend of fragrances in her hair. It was a radiant moment he knew he would never forget. Then it was gone. She placed a finger up between them. "Now, no more of that until we break my brothers free!"

He grinned back. "Are you trying to give me extra inspiration?"

"You already have inspiration." She winked at him, "I'm trying to keep you safe. If we manage to buy them out, and they later start to think we were canoodling all this time alone in the wilderness, things could get ugly!"

"Well, I'm sure not going to say anything!"

Kyra laughed. "Leon, you don't have to say anything, that's one of the things I like most about you though. If I kissed you every time I felt like it, you would be wearing it all over your face the first moment you met them." With that said, she scooted back and unpacked gear to feed the animals and set up camp.

It didn't matter that they opted not to leave the shelter of their alcove for another day. Leon could only sit there and grin as he replayed the first part of the last line she gave him through his head, over and over again.

Chapter 24

A few more wary days of travel led them into tall pine forest territory. Coniferous giants soared above both sides of the road, casting dark shadows beneath tall, tightly knit boughs of foliage. These new pines didn't have the rounded profile of the forests Leon had grown up around, they were skinny relative to their height, with long thick needles. They also weren't the size of giant redwoods, like the trees deeper within the Wild Forest, though they were still impressively large from his perspective.

The forest itself wasn't an empty woodland though, much the opposite. The roads were wide and well-traveled. Homes and small villages soon made more frequent appearances along their path, so much so that Leon made Ahab ride up under the blanket atop the Thunderbird more frequently around dawn and evening hours.

The main road was at times paved in gray slate rock, with lonely taverns and mercantile pit stops interspersed along their path. Their nightly game of cat and mouse with the slavers came to an end when Leon decided there were enough folks around that it would be safer to travel during the day while maintaining their distance in the evenings.

Small streams and gurgling brooks crisscrossed the main road, beneath wide but delicately crafted wood bridges. These small crossings were picturesque and peaceful, but more importantly, they allowed Leon and Kyra to keep their water bags well stocked and their clothes clean.

Leon found a trader who gave him a bulging bag of silver for the extra Fae clothing he managed to procure from the abandoned Fae camp. He had been reluctant to throw around any of his gold for fear that local word might reach the ears of the wrong sort of people, but the silver went a long way toward food and feed for everyone.

Most folks gave them a wide berth when they saw all the exotic animals traveling in their group. Not that all the strange looks bothered Leon. He was just happy to finally be in an area that seemed somewhat more civilized. He even saw children playing outside on forest paths, from time to time.

They did pass three large troupes of men marching off the way they had come, all in orderly tight formations. The troops looked well-disciplined and deadly as they stomped forward in a double-time cadence. Officers marched right along with the men. The only way one could tell the two apart was by their equipment. The soldiers wore light, chain-linked armor and carried heavy packs on their backs while the officers wore full breastplate coverings but carried no packs.

The majority of all the soldiers they saw marched with spear and shield, though a few of them carried crudely crafted crossbow contraptions. However, all of them were armed with intricately decorated bladed hilts hanging at the hip from cured leather sheaths. Leon could tell the blades they carried were well-crafted, though none of them appeared to possess any smaller, less flashy bone-handled hilts, like the one on the Blade at his side.

Though the men marched by peacefully, in orderly discipline, without a word said, they gave Leon slippery looks and made the hair on his neck stand on end when their eyes eventually settled on Kyra. Each time he saw them come, he was twice as happy to see them go.

On the seventh morning of their trek along the northern road, Leon came upon a scene so odd he didn't know whether to laugh and slow things to a crawl as they passed or to steer his crew into the woods to avoid what lay ahead altogether. Still, hadn't he just passed a quaint cluster of houses a mile or two back? He opted to take his chances moving forward.

A rich baritone voice belted out a greeting, "Hello! Hello, my fine young friends! Welcome to Wysman Slim's Traveling Emporium! Some folks may simply have what you need, others may only attempt to sell what they think you want. Wysman Slim provides that rare and unique blend of what you never expect and can't live without! Take a break from your travels! Step on over to my tents and give yourselves the chance to witness a stunning vision of exotic wares from distant lands!"

As the man continued to give them his silver-tongued sales pitch, Leon gave himself a mental palm to the face for not scurrying into the woods when he had the chance. He looked back at Kyra, hopeful they might avoid the charlatan's cheap gadgets and crummy supplies but saw it was far too late to salvage the day. Her normally fierce glare for anyone not him was already clouded over in faint lines of curiosity.

Wysman Slim had two carts displaying a hodgepodge assortment of colorful wares along the side of the wood, in a nice, shaded stretch of road. While strange masks, beaded hoops, small, elegant cages, different colored bottles of liquids, and a hundred other unique tchotchkes rested in random sequence along the edge of each cart, the intrepid entrepreneur himself stood before the covered opening to a large and gaudy tent, nestled between the covered carts.

The only thing Leon suspected was unexpected about the shyster was his name. Wysman Slim was a big, tall man, with the rounded physique of an Otterkin's water pig. Oblivious to all the apparent warning signs Leon had noted, Kyra climbed down from Grumpy and led the way to what Leon was certain would result in lighter pockets by the end of the visit.

"Ahh, I have seen the daughters of tribal kings carried upon golden litters by Hootsi slaves, I have witnessed the flying horses of the southern islands pulling South Fang merchant wives in wind-striding carriages over azure waters, but never have I stood in the presence of such an exquisite beauty riding master over such beastly brawn! Allow me to congratulate you, my young maiden, for being the first woman this decade to steal away the heart of this honest old merchant!"

"Laying it on a little thick, aren't you?" Leon couldn't help himself. The guy's nose should have been turned perpetually brown some time ago.

"Oh, ho! What failure! I have caused offense! To none other than a capable, strapping young lad! Where is my head? This lady is obviously spoken for, and I have no doubt incensed your jealous heart by speaking aloud what was only resting on the hem of my mind. It is so very noble of you, my young friend, to strike a belligerent pose in the face of my indiscretion. Please allow me to make amends by giving you a ten percent discount to any item you find that speaks to your heart in return."

"That is so very kind of you, Wysman! Please don't feel bad, I'm sure Leon is just tired, it's been a long day. Tell me, is that a Sojourner's Merchant emblem there?" Kyra pointed to a small benign brand on the corner edge of the merchant's main tent.

When Wysman turned his head to follow her arm, she turned and gave Leon the kind of look that admonished him to hush up for his own good. Leon couldn't tell what it was she was up to, but her normally reserved expression held the look of a predator which had just found its prey.

Still, he frowned. There were no price tags on any of the items that he saw laying out on the carts, and something told him he had just been chastised by the slippery-tongued old merchant, though he couldn't pinpoint how.

Wysman wasted no time acknowledging his association with the emblem on the tent and congratulating Kyra's keen eye while holding the door flap open for them to enter.

Leon was close enough to smell the heady scent of some cloven spice and floral incense billowing out from within the tent's provisional opening. He turned and gave all the critters, including Grumpy, the invitation to come in, claws out if they heard anything concerning. He also pocketed a pouch of gold coin from his pile of loot on the Thunderbird's back. By the time he turned back around the slippery salesman had already dropped the rug over the entrance and Leon could still hear his overly enthusiastic voice reverberating through the canvas walls.

This guy is totally gonna fleece us like the tubby pair of wooly lambs we are!

# # #

Two hours later and the haggling finally reached a crescendo. Much to his surprise, Leon was enjoying every moment of the drama playing out between Kyra and Slim. He especially relished the wilted look on Slim's chubby face as every form of flattery was masterfully repelled or redirected by a wide-eyed, and intentionally naïve Kyra.

Indeed, it hadn't taken him long to reach two new epiphanies. The first was that though Kyra often seemed naïve and sheltered, she understood the true value of the things of her world to a degree and depth he would never come close to hedging. The second was that she would take pleasure in prying the last penny from a poor miser's fisted hand if it meant she got the better end of a deal. He had no doubt Wysman Slim would forever rue the day he invited such a shark to swim with him in his guppy pond.

Wysman wiped his bald head with a cloth to keep the sweat from dripping down into his eyes, "My darling Kyra, alas, as much as I covet your goodwill, I simply can't part with these items for what you propose, but I could never forgive myself if I allowed you to leave here without the satisfaction of knowing you have truly touched the cured tusker hides of Blue Jade Armor. You see, these exquisite pieces were meant to adorn and protect the wildling mounts of the Jaffer King in the far jungles south of Fayden. These straps are said to be practically indestructible and can be cinched to comfortably cover the torso on any large beast one might adorn from the aggression of men foolish enough to test their mettle against an impenetrable wall of tooth and fang."

"My poor Wysman! It breaks my heart to tell you this…" she leaned in close and whispered for effect, "you have been deceived!

"Look here, as you may recall and have no doubt forgotten by the myriad of facts that populate your wise and noble mind, Blue Jade Armor contains a gray sheen with soft creases on a smooth surface. There is no sheen here, only pale gray wrinkles on rough ridges. This armor is in decent quality, but it is not from the Jaffer King. It's not bad quality, I'll grant, at least as good as boiled leather.

And look there, that wavy track along the seam shows it was processed in a cold climate, not a warm jungle locale." She let loose a deep breath wrapped in pity, "Let me do you a favor and take it off your hands for the two gold I offered on first glance, if for no other reason than to save you the shame of knowing you harbor a farce within this impeccable collection of treasures you carry?"

Slim's eyes bulged in a flash of anger as he studied Kyra, but she merely looked back at him in feigned sympathy. Finally, he deflated, looking a bit green around the gills, and nodded. "So be it, I can see you have a rare eye and as my eyes are older and less apt to see these things as clearly as your youthful orbs, I will defer to your judgment in this matter my good woman. I must admit this is one of the rare items I procured indirectly. However, I swear I will hunt down the scoundrel merchant that sold me these trinkets, to the very ends of the earth if necessary! I will in turn redeem my honor from his purse. For my gratitude, I will part with this whole parcel you have selected for twelve gold." Here at last was the climax to all the theatrics.

"Six," Kyra fired back.

"Ten." Slim's eyes narrowed.

"Eight, and not a copper more."

"Done!"

"Done."

They each bowed to one another. Kyra didn't celebrate the fact she had just talked the vendor down by over two-thirds off his original price. She turned to Leon and meekly asked, "Well, you're the one with the money, Leon. Did you see anything you like?" causing Leon to perk up and take a closer look around.

I've got a whole chest full of gold, why not spend a little on a nice souvenir?

Slim perked up as well, like a dog catching a new scent on a breeze, his greedy eyes sensed his day might yet be redeemed by the young man he hadn't previously attempted to coerce.

"Easy, Slim! Give me a little room to breathe and I might just find something worth buying."

"Of course, young master! Though I can see your eye has already spotted an item worthy of your attention."

Leon frowned down at the richly-colored pile of tiny rocks, each painted with artful symbols. "What are those?"

A hint of a grin twitched beneath Slim's mustache. "Minotaur fertility beans, for barren goats."

"That's a thing?"

"Goats that can't have kids?"

"No, never mind." Leon shot him a look but couldn't tell if the man was serious. He opted to move along, either way.

He continued perusing racks of curious items with Slim providing constant commentary each time his eye paused too long in one place until a thought struck him.

Leon pushed up his hat and scratched his head. "Slim, I've got to admit you have a ton of interesting stuff in here, but I don't see anything I need, except for maybe this braided rope. Is there nothing else for sale here?"

The old merchant's shoulders dropped. "I can assure you, master Leon, no decent merchant would ever hold back an item from a potential sale. Everything has a price."

"Everything?"

"Everything!"

Leon continued, "In that case, I did see something interesting outside!"

Kyra gave Leon her signature arched brow. He bit back a smile of his own as he popped his knuckles.

"How about we go take a look at those wagons out front!"

An hour later, Wysman Slim counted out twelve new shiny gold coins from within the comfort of his tent. Outside, Leon finished hitching his new wagon to an irritably disgruntled and armor-girded Grumpy as Kyra buckled the last piece of gray armor across Merle's neck.

As she stepped back admiring the ferocious figure the big cog cut, she couldn't hold it in any longer. "This armor is going to work out great for these guys, and the wagon is perfect! Not sure what you're going to do with that rope, but we make a good team, don't we, Leon!"

Leon chuckled. "Remind me never to get into a negotiation with you. You are an absolutely ruthless woman!"

She beamed back at him. "I just know a good deal from a bad one. This covered wagon was really genius, though. Poor Ahab will be so much more comfortable riding back here, as opposed to under a blanket on your stinky Thunderbird."

"Aha! He *is* growing on you!"

Kyra pouted. "I didn't say that. I just don't like to see creatures suffer, no matter how dangerous they may grow to become!"

Leon conceded the point and asked something that had been nagging at him all afternoon, "How did you know that armor wasn't true cured tusker, whatever that is…?"

"Oh, it's cured tusker all right. Mr. Wysman doesn't know that, though. When I realized he wasn't a true member of the Sojourner's Merchant guild, I took a chance he wouldn't know how true tusker hides were cured, and I was right! Besides, I never actually lied, I just denied the facts he used to construct the lies he used on us."

"How did you know he wasn't a real merchant?"

"Simple, if he was a true Sojourner Merchant, he would have known all cured tusker hides come from the mountains, not the southern jungles. My parents did business with Sojourner Merchants my whole life, they are all hard men who brave dangerous lands. Flattery is not their strongest attribute, at least not on the ones I know. This guy must have inherited some Merchant's gear. He's probably never been out of these woods, though he does know how to spin a good story!"

Leon just shook his head and laughed, there was nothing more he could say.

# # #

Four days later, they arrived at the valley of the walls of Hollinger. The sky was clear, and the sun was warm. Not quite warm like the Texas heat Leon knew from back home, but warmer than he had grown accustomed to in Fayden.

As they drew to a stop in the midst of a growing line, he could see the wagons of the slaver caravan a few hundred feet ahead. The line through the city gates stretched out in many directions, funneling down to one point.

Streams of merchants loitered in small camps along the road, attempting to sell all manner of items and services as weary travelers stood their turn in line for entry into the city. To Leon's surprise, there were also robed men walking up and down the lines offering *blessed blades* to all who had money for their cause. Just out of curiosity he bought one. It was longer than his own, and the pommel was decorated with dozens of tiny shiny rocks, but the guard was off-center, the edge was chipped, and the tang bent a hair to the left. It was junk, and the robed men were selling the junk like hotcakes.

Leon reached down into his vest where his true Blade was hidden. There was no comparison between the two. However, rather than simply discard the blessed blade, and risking insult with the robed charlatans, he stowed it down in his pile of loot resting on the back of the Thunderbird. He would find a quiet place to discard it later.

Another surprise to Leon was that the people migrating into the North Fang's capital didn't seem to have a preference for any one or two modes of transportation. There were animals of all kinds and types being used to carry things. Creatures as small as an oversized badger carried a farmer's box of produce in leather saddlebag-looking packs, while a whole family was crammed up onto the back of some type of hairy rhino that possessed one extraordinarily long horn. Though the sights were far from boring, it quickly became evident that their wait into the city would be long and sweaty.

He decided to tie the Thunderbird off to Grumpy's wagon and climbed up behind Kyra for a better view of the diverse mob of travelers growing around them. Several of the men nearby were already eying Kyra with unabashed looks of appreciation. Gone was her fur poncho. She was instead wearing one of the airy tops they had procured from the forest merchants. He instinctively slid his arm around her waist and drew her in against his chest as he caught their eyes and glared back at each one individually. The men took the hint and found more interesting sights to study when their eyes met his cold golden orbs.

Kyra waited a full minute to lean back and whisper, "Leon, I was just thinking of something…"

"Hmm, what's that?"

"I wonder how many of my brothers can see us from here?"

He glanced up at the cages not too far out beyond their current position and his arm dropped like it had been touching a hot coal. After a long minute of anxiety, Kyra's raspy laugh made him smile as well. "It is way too hot to be stuck together like this up here on a furry bear rug. We keep it up, and we might start smelling like Grumpy!"

"Heaven forbid!"

He scooted back away from her until he caught a glimpse of a brightly colored wagon standing in line from a spur in the road further off to their left. He sat up and tried to catch a better look, but a drover herding a dozen of those large curly horned sheep blocked his view from the road between them. Their bleating caused Merle to perk up.

"You mind if I go check something out?"

"No," she shrugged, "I'll be here." She, too, was busy looking around at the collection of characters around them and didn't seem at all curious over where he might be heading off.

"You'll be okay?"

"Grumpy? What do you think? Will I be okay?" Grumpy turned to show his teeth. He gave Leon a halfhearted huff. A not so gentle reminder of who was technically better equipped to protect their lady friend.

"Yeah, well, I'm leaving everyone but Merle here with you. Just heading over there to take a closer look at that wagon." He pointed in the direction where he had last seen the painted wagon.

Once Leon finally extricated himself and Merle from around the frantic herd of bleating sheep, all of whom had become extremely irritated at the sight of Merle slinking along behind him, he found the cart he had first seen.

A heavyset red-bearded man in a bright blue vest stood atop the cart, giving the evil eye to anyone who shuffled by too closely. He wasn't much taller than Leon despite standing on the cart, a good foot and a half off the ground. A filthy pair of warthogs were harnessed up front and the back end of the wagon was stacked high with crated merchandise.

"Excuse me, sir? Sir? Could I talk with you for a moment?"

The little man looked from one side to the next before narrowing his eyes when it dawned on him that Leon had addressed him directly. "What do you want?" His voice was nasally and irritated.

"Are you Otterkin?" Leon didn't know if it was rude to assume such a thing one way or the other, but Gus had always made a point of highlighting how the word 'ass-u-me' could be broken up to demonstrate a derogative connotation for those who use it.

"You soft in the head, boy? That why you ask fool questions, yes? Off with you!" He flicked his reins, and the warthogs took three slow steps forward.

"Sorry sir, I didn't want to… never mind. Do you know anyone from the Haberkorn clan?"

He hocked a loogie at Leon's feet and took a seat on a crate behind him, stroking his beard.

In a much calmer voice, he answered, "Might be I know of the Haberkorns, what's it to you?"

Leon stepped up closer and lowered his voice, though no one seemed to be paying the two of them any mind. "A friend of mine, Sved Haberkorn, he told me to give this to the first Otterkin merchant I was to come across. He said the Haberkorn Clan will be in your debt if you get word back to them as quickly as possible on where I am staying." Leon saw the man's beady little eyes light up in a green shade of greed.

"Let's say I do know how to get word to the Haberkorns? Where will you be staying, young master?"

Leon blinked. He hadn't even considered where he and Kyra might be staying.

The little man pounced on his indecision. "I take it you are new to Hollinger, yes? Are you...well-funded or...in poor condition, might I ask?"

Leon knew better than to give too much away. Still, he didn't want the guy to recommend some pigsty, "We're bringing in trade goods that should fetch a decent price. Where would you recommend?"

A smile spread across his face. "The Wounded Duck would be my advice."

"The Wounded Duck?" Those words did not have kind of taste that cried out *classy establishment*.

The man quickly intervened, "On my word, it's as decent a place as any in all of Hollinger. And it's run by a much-respected Otterkin relative of mine." He touched his nose and winked. "Just tell him Fat Fickleburr sent you. My cousin will take care of you. Honest, son, he will." Leon wasn't sure he trusted the man, but he was fairly certain he could trust the man's greed for the Haberkorn's indebtedness. He held out the small talisman Sved had given him.

"If you can, tell them everyone entered Hollinger today, but to hurry."

"Yes, sir! You can count on me!" The man grinned at the scent of easy money. He took the talisman, and it disappeared into a pocket between one of his rolls.

# # #

The drone of a thousand hawkers ringing oppressively in their ears matched the suffocating closeness of the masses on the crowded street. For Leon, it was uncomfortable, but for Kyra, it proved downright disorienting, though she stayed seated in her saddle, above the fray. On the ground level, Leon was forced to use his gift on all their animals to keep Merle close to his side, and to keep

Ahab and the owl huddled together within the covering of the wagon. He even made the extra effort to help Kyra calm Grumpy as they entered through the gates.

Tall signs in decorative calligraphies hung proudly over expensive-looking businesses on either side of the main entrance. Each storefront sported sturdy brick facades. The business establishments closest to the city wall were the largest and most opulent. They stood aloof in painted rows, adorned with bright flowers and verdant hanging gardens. Old, but full of character and with a smidgen of authoritarian charisma.

He was, however, grateful for one distinct attribute of the crowds, the slaver caravan had a harder time navigating them than his little group. Otherwise, he might have lost them before they ever made it in through the gates. Fortunately, the guards merely passed them through for a small fee, and he was able to catch sight of the cages.

He fell in a close distance behind before the wagons made the first turn. Leon led the way, following in the void created behind a collection of boisterous slave guards who shouted obscenities in every conceivable direction, pushing and prodding at any poor soul caught flatfooted in the path of their progression.

They followed behind the last cage in the caravan. It held a colorful assortment of spotted monkeys, all howling and screeching at every person they passed. Despite the palpable energy spawned by a veritable sensory overload of new sights and sounds, Kyra rode with drooping shoulders, a look of quiet contempt in her eyes.

Leon could empathize. To be so close to the people they cared about while still completely helpless to do anything for them ate at him until his knuckles turned white and he yielded to the urge to push his hat up and give his head a scratch.

The slavers hung a right down a moderately less busy lane of traffic. The quality of the establishments gradually dwindled. The people moving about didn't appear to step with quite the purpose and pomp as those buzzing around the city gates.

When they eventually stepped up to cross over a wide, heavy stone bridge, Leon caught a whiff of Hollinger's equivalent to the other side of the tracks. The air simply had a more pungent scent than what he had noticed clinging to the masses of people at the city gates.

Gazing out over a muddy river, Leon caught glimpses of all manner of merchandise, both people and otherwise, housed in stationary cages and open-air warehouse platforms along the river's opposite shoreline. Medium-sized cargo boats, that looked to him like ancient Viking vessels, bobbed gently up down over brown water. The boats were tied off to weathered docks. Each dock extended a third of the way out into the river. Indeed, an endless tangle of swaying docks, bobbing boats, and moving cargo lined the port on the far side of the bridge for several blocks in either direction.

On closer inspection, as they descended into the seedier side of town, the dingy buildings running parallel to the river were a mottled blend of old and new construction. The older portion contained the ancient remains of much more refined yet crumbling stone edifices. The newer portions included a hodgepodge assortment of wood and brick patches, poor substitutes for the former's quality. If Leon hadn't seen the remains of those wind-swept walls and abandoned rotundas on his first day in Fayden, he might have overlooked the truth that broken arches and chipped marble columns hid in plain sight. The slave market was built upon the ruins of an ancient Bladed City!

The slavers came to a stop several hundred yards north of the bridge. Leon tried to be as nonchalant as possible while stepping around the wagons parked along the edge of the street. He continued on like he had someplace to be, leading the Thunderbird by its reins alongside Grumpy. He didn't dare look to the right or the left, not trusting himself to peer into the cages.

He couldn't help but flinch as filthy clusters of now loitering slavers gave Kyra catcalls and crude solicitations for their impending celebrations that evening. He just kept his eyes forward and marched past them all, praying that Reed and Haddie might be looking his way when he moved past their wagons. He could give them nothing, but perhaps being able to see a familiar face sliding by in such a bleak circumstance might just leverage a sliver of hope their direction. It wasn't much, but it would have to be enough, for now.

Once past, he continued for another two blocks, then turned left down a side street. He looked back at Kyra. When she met his questioning eyes a solitary tear slid from her own, and she nodded yes. She had seen her brothers. They were alive.

He picked up the pace, continuing straight through another block, then turned left again. He wanted to put some distance between them and that filthy bunch of degenerates, but he knew he needed to circle back toward the bridge before he drifted too far into the slums.

He hurried them all through an empty back alley, thankful the sun still hung high above. If he could make it back across the bridge quickly, they might have a chance at finding the Wounded Duck before night came to the city. Who knew what night might bring in a city that sold people like appliances? He hustled everyone forward a tad bit faster. Making a hasty beeline for the water's edge.

Three large men dressed in the unmistakable gear of the slavers stepped out into the alley, directly blocking their path. The one in the center had porkchop sideburns and a lazy eye. He strutted forward with a shiftless swagger.

"Woah there, boy! You'll get them animals all hot and sweaty. No need for that! Can't blame you, though, if I had a looker like that…" he whistled low over his shoulder at his companions, "well, I'd be in a hurry, too."

His friends laughed at his joke though the humor never touched their eyes. They spread out to either side of the leader, blocking any easy path around the group.

Leon took a deep breath before addressing Mr. Lazy-Eye. He expected a fight would be coming any second, but he would at least attempt a peaceful departure. "Yeah, well, you're right about it being hot out today. We are looking for a certain merchant we were told works down at these docs. His name is Fat Fickleburr. You wouldn't know him, would you?"

The man to the left of the leader called out, "Sure, get over here, and I'll introduce you." They all broke out laughing once more.

Leon heard a scraping sound over his should and took a chance to peek back at the disturbance. Three more men stepped out into the alley behind them. When he turned back to the leader, he only heard the distant drone of a crowded street. None of the three in front of him were laughing anymore. A half a block away, past the scum, he could see people moving about the docks, going on about their business, oblivious to his worsening plight.

Lazy-Eye grabbed his attention once more... "You two think you're the only ones to ever try following a slaver crew back to the docks? Fools!" He spat at Leon's feet and drew a long ugly sword. The kind of sword only useful to someone who had an everyday type of use for it. "What is it going to be? Want to do this the easy way…or the hard way?"

"You do realize she's riding a giant bear, don't you?" Leon couldn't help but wonder how Lazy-Eye thought things would play out in his favor, even with the three goons behind him.

The only response he received was a hand signal from the leader followed by the resulting sound of a heavy thwack. Grumpy jerked back instinctively and reared up causing Ahab to tumble down out of the back of the wagon.

Leon glassed the rooftops above. Two men were leaning over the roof to his left, one held a loaded crossbow trained on him, the other looked to be loading the one just emptied.

Lazy-Eye smirked back at him. "That's an interesting creature you have there, boy. He'll fetch a decent silver, no doubt. I haven't got all day, and those bolts have enough nasty gunk plastered on the spike to freeze a rhino in his tracks! Give in now, and we'll keep this business like before we throw you both in with the rest of the loot. Make us work for it, and I make no promises!"

Merle was already growling, and Leon could feel his chest beginning to tighten. He held up a hand like he needed time to consider the man's offer while his mind raced through alternatives. Unfortunately, no workable solution came to mind. Reaching down with his right hand, he absentmindedly grazed his fingers across the top of his bone-hilt Blade as he studied the men before him.

If we could only take care of those two crossbows above, we might have a chance!

A surging pulse reverberated up through his arm from where his fingertips rested against the Blade. The pulse ricocheted through his chest and outward, leaving him gasping for air.

Ahab, who had circled and had taken the position opposite Merle, at his side, sprang into action. He raced forward faster than Leon had ever seen the young griffin move, catching everyone off guard. As he leaped directly at the leader's face, his wings, which were always tucked up firmly against his body, kicked open and spread wide. They twitched, and he sailed up over the man's head just as Leon heard the sharp thwack of a crossbow being released.

The bolt sliced down through the air, but Ahab was already gone. Instead of striking the griffin, it slammed into the bald spot on the top of old Lazy-eye's head. His melon cracked like an egg, and he was dead before he hit the ground.

Merle and Grumpy needed no invitation. They barreled forward next, each taking down one of the two remaining men. Though Merle was no two-thousand-pound bear, his growth, like Ahab's, had been further accelerated by Kyra's attention over the past month. A three-hundred-pound hound in full battle armor, bearing down on you at chest height was not good odds.

Leon drew his Blade and pivoted back to face the three behind him. They hadn't even moved. He backed up a step. A frantic scream came streaking down from above. A man fell, hitting the dirt alley not two feet in front of him. The man bounced once and moved no more. Seconds later a second fell dead beside the first. Each time a body fell, Leon and the slavers jumped.

Leon whistled. Ahab came gliding over the heads of the remaining three slavers from above, softly touching down to take a position at his side. The men were shaking but they continued to stare, eyes wide in shock. Leon didn't take his eyes off them until his little group had just about cleared the alley. Then he ordered Ahab back up into the wagon as they all turned and hightailed it for the bridge.

Chapter 25

It took Leon and Kyra another two hours to find the Wounded Duck. When they did finally track it down, Leon was pleasantly surprised. It wasn't necessarily in a bad location, just a block off the main drag.

The streets were still brutally busy outside when they arrived. They visited the stables first. It came as no surprise that stable hands wanted nothing to do with Grumpy. Kyra snorted at their mistrust of the big bear. They gave them a stall large enough to house the bear and the wagon both.

"At least now we have a place where we can stash all our gear without worrying about anyone getting too close," Kyra said.

Leon could tell she was in a much-improved mood after exercising a tiny portion of the total vindication she hoped to levy on the slavers. He did not share her upbeat attitude. At any minute he fully expected some form of city police to barge in and take them both into custody. For crying out loud, their creatures still had the incriminating blood of five dead slavers on their paws! Still, there was nothing to be done about it; what was done was done.

Gus always did say there's no sense in crying over spilled diesel, just till it under and keep on plowing.

The atmosphere in the tavern below the Inn was cheerful and accommodating. A short chubby lady, who Leon assumed was likely another Otterkin relative to Fat Fickleburr, sang bawdy songs from a corner near the bar. The music livened up the place while a barkeep served a mixed clientele of Otterkin and normal size people. The ceilings were high, and the air was decently cool. There were tables set up around the main room, though the evening crowd had not yet begun to arrive.

Leon gestured for Kyra to follow, and together with Merle, they all took a seat at a table with their backs against the wall. It didn't take long for a short, bearded barkeep to visit them. He had a ready smile and an honest face, much the opposite of Fickleburr

"Anything I can get you two?"

307

Leon caught the whiff of freshly baked bread coming from somewhere back in the kitchens before he answered, "Food, drinks, and rooms?"

"I can take care of the food and drink. Your gonna have a hard time with the rooms though, this place is booked solid on account of the Kingdom negotiations. You may want to try the Prickly Thistle closer to the docks?"

Kingdom negotiations?

"I was told by a friend of the owner we might find a room here, his name was Fat Fickleburr."

The man's demeanor changed. "So, Fatty sent you?"

"Yes, sir. I hired him to take care of some business for me, and he suggested I might be able to stay here while we tried selling some of our merchant wares."

"I see, well, if that's the case, fatty better cut me in on whatever little deal he has going with you, yes? Maybe we can scrounge up a room after all. I'm the owner, by the way, Tendlewren Fickleburr, at you service!" Leon didn't know what to say to that, so he smiled and extended a hand for a quick shake of the man's forearm.

"Leon Waldman, and this is Kyra Stonebreaker." They shook hands as well.

"Any chance you also have a bath available?" Kyra piped up before the man could leave.

He stopped and looked them both over once more.

"Talk to my wife, Higlebuns, once she's done with her set, yes?"

Soon enough, Higlebuns finished her set. A little while later she came by and ushered them all to an upstairs room. "Sorry, but we really are booked. Just have the one room left for special occasions." She gave Kyra a frown, not knowing whether to inquire further.

"It'll be fine, thank you," was all Kyra said in return.

The room was large, but best of all, in one corner, an open doorway led to an honest to goodness bathroom! There was a pull lever over a metal tub which allowed the user to fill a hot bath. Kyra went first.

"Careful not to scrub your hair too much!" was all Leon managed to say before the door clanged shut.

He made himself comfortable and set his owl on a perch near an open window. The evening breeze from three stories up didn't quite carry the stench of the streets below, it served to cool the room instead.

A half-hour later it was his turn. The warm bath and soap were absolute bliss after weeks on the road. When he returned to their room a small candle still flickered, though Kyra lay asleep on her bedroll in the corner. Leon gingerly scooped her up. She was fully dressed and armed, ready for anything. He snorted as he imagined she probably wouldn't know what to do with a comfortable pair of pajamas. He carried her into the bed in the center of the room where he tucked her in under a threadbare sheet.

Then, he rolled out his own bedroll and laid it nearby but couldn't fall asleep. For the first time in weeks, he pulled out Ferschall's medallion and studied it in the flickering lamplight.

"What is that?" said Kyra. She rolled up on her side and reached out with an open hand.

Leon couldn't help himself, he handed it over. Then he told her his story and not just the story behind the medallion, but the whole story. By the time he finished, she was as wide awake as him.

"So, you are a descendant of the Remnant who left before first culling?" She was practically beaming with excitement. Leon was just glad she wasn't super upset he'd held out on her for so long.

"That's a little over my head. I just know people like me have been around in my world for several hundred years."

"This is incredible! I knew there was something different about you. I've never seen a hat quite like the one on your head! I just never suspected anything so...outlandish?"

"You mind explaining the first culling?"

Kyra went on to explain how Bladed had been driven from the seven tribes in the past. The first time it happened, the first culling.

occurred after the Bearskinners were driven from the kingdom at large. Once the Unbladed uprising prevailed against the warrior tribe, they turned their hatred inward.

A movement grew to root out the remnant of Bladed who still lived among them. Many of those still left fled to the wilderness beyond the mountains or south beyond the Jaffer's borders, as had the surviving Bearskinners.

But Kyra's clan told the story of a large number of Bladed who barricaded themselves in one of the last of the ancient cities. When the armies of the Unbladed finally stormed their defenses, they found empty streets and silent buildings. Nailed to a large tree in the center of the city was a letter that promised those Bladed would return from their new world when their brothers and sisters of the six remaining tribes no longer hunted them because of their Blades.

"That had to have been a Royal Tree! Which city? Do you know which city they abandoned?" Leon asked.

"Yes, but that city, Leon," she shook her head slowly, "has been off-limits to all remaining tribes for generations. It's home to the most fearsome of all other tribes."

"Where is it? Please, tell me?"

"It's called the Silent City of the Vindarri. I don't know where it is. I've only ever heard snippets of stories I thought were exaggerated tales...till tonight that is."

Now, it was Leon's turn to stare wide-eyed at Kyra. He knew roughly where the Silent City lay, and he knew just as well the dangers of the tribe who ruled there.

An urgent knock at their door made them both jump. Merle scrambled to his feet with a low growl.

Leon and Kyra stood together. Once he quieted Merle, they stepped to the door. Both drew their Blades. Kyra took a position off to the side. Then, Leon yanked the door open and ducked down into a fighting stance.

Fat Fickleburr squealed like a stuck pig before Leon grabbed him by his vest and yanked him into the room. Kyra slammed the door behind him.

"Sorry about that, Fickleburr. You kind of startled us."

"Startled you? Startled you! I'm here trying to follow through on this big favor for you in the middle of the night and this is the thanks I get? Your people are gonna owe me big, yes?" the little man sputtered through a petulant scowl, but it was obvious he gave them a far worse scare than they managed to give him.

"Again, I apologize. But you wouldn't be here in the middle of the night if you didn't have news, would you? You have word from the Haberkorn's already?"

"Something like that. I sent your message, and I've been asked to take you two to their Market Holdings as soon as possible We need to leave…now."

#

The Haberkorn Market Holdings weren't a single large warehouse. Instead, they were more like a gypsy flea market with many colorful booths and tented shops. The location was on the south side of the river, just across from the slaver's port. Not the best real estate, but assuming they could haul their hippo carts in and out of the river with merchandise, Leon could see the usefulness of the spot. All told, the Haberkorn's holdings meandered along that riverbank for quite a ways. They were surprisingly large and held impressive provisions, taking up over a full three city blocks.

Fickleburr led them there through a maze of side streets while riding one of his ugly warthogs. When he dropped them off with a pair of Haberkorn escorts, he insisted upon on the spot payment. One of the escorts paid the man a small sack of coins, then Fat Fickleburr turned his smelly warthog and left without even a goodbye.

"You couldn't have picked any other Otterkin merchant to give the Heir's Promise?" said the older of the two small men leading them further into their maze of tents and booths.

"Sorry, didn't see anyone else standing around when we arrived," Leon said.

The younger man waved him off. "Don't let Scrimbleden here give you a hard time, he and fatty haven't seen eye to eye for years.

Ever since Fatty beat him in the Otterkin river races, yes? Fatty was once a more than a decent swimmer, believe it or not!"

"I still say he found a way to cheat!" Scrimbleden remarked.

Their two escorts led them through a maze of small shops before halting their march at a brightly decorated canvased booth. "Here's your stop."

Leon could see light shining from inside, between the seams. He put up a hand to stop the retreating young man. "Quick question. Scrimbleden talked about the Heir's Promise, was he referring to the clan's talisman Sved gave me?"

The little man chuckled. "That's just like Sved! Sveddleton Haberkorn goes by Sved, but don't let him fool you. He's actually the sole heir to the whole of the Haberkorn Clan."

At Leon's blank look, the man continued, "Sved is one of the richest men in the alliance of the three Kingdoms!" Then he turned and scurried off down the alley.

Leon pulled back the tent flap to reveal the interior before entering. The tented structure was much larger on the inside than it looked from the exterior. It was well lit with plenty of room for them and all their animals, including the wagon. A large brazier of hot coals and skewered meat sat sizzling at the center of the room. It was surrounded by plush pillows for comfortable lounging. At the smell of the greasy chunks of meat, Ahab chirped, and Merle's tail started to wag.

A minute later, a rather plain-looking young woman popped in from a back entrance.

"Oh, hello. I've been told to ask if you need anything else, yes? Your friends should be here soon. Oh, and you can bring the animals in as well."

They both assured her they were fine, and she disappeared the way she had come.

An hour later, and several skewers fewer, the tent flap opened once more. Sved came charging in full of energy, looking handsomely dressed but still just as surly as ever. He was followed by Dimples! Dimples, however, had changed significantly. He was dressed in rich black fabric, trimmed with stained leather armor, clasped with silver buckles. He looked perhaps more dangerous than ever, but he wore a smile for once and Leon could see the hint of a dimple in his left cheek.

"Ha! Leon you made it! And not alone I see?" Sved turned to Kyra, "Pleasure to meet you, my name is Sveddleton Haberkorn, but you can call me Sved."

Hugs and introductions were made all around. Afterward, Dimples went straight to Ahab, clearly amazed at how much the cub had grown. The griffin remained by his side, allowing the enamored Hootsi to stroke his neck feathers as they sat to talk.

Sved wouldn't share a word of his adventures until Leon shared the full story of his trip with Kyra. They all shed a tear as Leon explained the solitary burial he had given their friends. Only after his story concluded did Sved tell of how he and Dimples had trod their way through the backcountry along their path to the marshlands of the Otterkin. It was a very lively tale and Dimples felt the need to interject in several places to downplay some of the more extreme hazards described.

As Sved concluded, he gave Dimples a nudge. "There's one more thing. Are you gonna tell them, or should I?"

Dimples, still grinning, didn't say a word. Instead, he reached up behind his back and laid a Blade down into the carpet between them all. There was laughter and congratulations all the way around.

At last, they came to the topic at hand. Leon and Kyra explained where the slaver band had stopped as well as their run-in with the slavers earlier that day.

Sved stroked his beard. "That would be the clan of the Crimson Hatchets, yes? I've had my people doing their research on all the roving bands since we arrived. The Hatchets are a nasty, dangerous lot. I wouldn't worry about them trying to retaliate, slavers are a twisted sort of folk, you most likely did them a favor by taking out those five - it will mean more silver per share for the rest of them after auction. The city guard won't be nosing around in slaver's port either.

"I'll try to negotiate a purchase in advance, but the Hatchets are one of those groups notoriously hardheaded about selling *merchandise* anywhere but the Auction block, so we may have to wait."

"When will the auction happen?" Kyra asked.

"Typically, a day or two after the caravan arrives. All auctions are private, yes? There are at least three per day this time of year, though most just sell unique beasts. Don't worry, we won't miss it now that we know the who and the where.

"There's another problem, though. I just had word that large armies have been gathering beyond the Northern High Pass, with scouts seen in the mountain ridges south of that pass already this year. There is talk that there could be war with an outside kingdom, yes? As such, the Northern Fang has called a war conference between all six kingdoms of Fayden."

"When?" Leon asked.

"This week, two days from now, yes? As members of the Alliance, the Otterkin coalition and the Southern Fang already have representatives in town. We heard the Vin arrived last week. The Hootsi should be here any time for the annual prisoner swap. But I hear there is an Ageless Tribe contingent coming for the first time in recent history!

Leon looked at Kyra. He raised an eyebrow, she nodded, and he spoke up, "Sved, it's true. War isn't just possible, it's probably already here. Kyra and her brothers are from beyond the Anderle mountains. An army of giants is likely already moving for some high mountain pass as we speak.

Sved's fuzzy cheeks grew pale. He turned to Kyra.

"How? No one leaves Fayden, neither in nor out. That pass is guarded year-round!"

Leon cringed. He pushed his cap up and scratched his head.

It's time I come clean with these guys and lay it all out there on the table.

He divulged everything. The heritage he and Kyra shared, the truth of how he was actually from the world of the Bladed remnant and, last of all, he pulled out the Medallion and laid it before them. He and Kyra explained what they had been able to piece together.

Sved took it all much calmer than Leon had expected, there wasn't even a hint of doubt, "So, that's why you were searching for the Royal Tree? It's your ticket home, yes?" like always, the little man cut right to the truth in the bluntest and directest manner possible.

Kyra flinched. She knew he had been searching for a Royal Tree, but she hadn't truly had time to ponder the implications for why he wanted to find such an ancient relic of Fayden. He made a mental note to have a longer conversation with her about it all later.

"Hold up a tick, I haven't made up my mind on exactly what I'm going to do when if and when I find a Royal. I just know I need to send word back to my grandfather." It was the best answer he could give them, but the words surprised him at how right they felt as they rolled off his tongue. The tension in the room eased back a fraction.

"Leon, on my honor, these truths will not leave this room." Dimples looked him in the eye as he spoke, "Still, the news of the invaders weighs heavy on my heart. I see no path for a coalition of Tribes to stand against those hordes of giants, should they take the pass.

"I know my people. They will never stoop to fight alongside the Northern Fang. Their honor will not allow it. The Vin too, due to the powers they possess, do not believe they can be beaten. They will scoff at the coming armies and will return to the Quiet Forest to await anyone foolish enough to set foot within their sacred glades." Dimples sure knew how to kill a moment.

"Still, I need to get the news out to the Otterkin counsel," Sved hollered out the back of the tent, getting up.

A minute later, the serving girl popped her head in through the flap.

"Ah, yes, there you are! Caddie, please, be so kind as to go wake up Madam Hazzel. Tell her I have urgent news and will be along directly to inform her of the details." The girl looked absolutely horrified at the prospect of waking her clan leader in the middle of the night, but to her credit, she dipped her head and turned to leave.

Sved called out again before she could disappear, and she whipped around, hopeful the order would be rescinded, "How could I be so forgetful Caddie, please make sure you get Ferschall up too, he'll want to hear all of this as well, yes?" The girl sputtered at the prospect of the added impropriety. She fled the room before Sved could pile on another request.

"Ferschall's here!? How come you didn't say so in the beginning? What about Shana? Is she here too?" Leon cried. Kyra perked up as well, taking a sudden interest in Sved's response.

"Sorry, Leon. Ferschall is here, but he arrived alone. He wasn't able to find anyone in the chaos the night the Vin attacked. You can ask him about it in the morning, yes? For now, why don't the two of you follow me, we have a few spare beds in the back where you can sleep. Your fur and feather entourage can stay here if you promise to keep them from bringing the place down on all of us." He gave the giant snoring bear a critical glare before turning back to Leon, "You look exhausted, and tomorrow may prove to be another very eventful day, no?"

Sved led them each to a room of their own. Merle and Ahab both refused to be left alone in the big room and followed behind Leon into the room Sved indicated was his. Opulent didn't begin to describe the furnishings, but it could have just as well been a barn's loft, and he wouldn't have cared, as worn out as he was in his current state. As soon as his head hit the pillow he was out.

# # #

The next day brought some much-needed peace and quiet, allowing everyone to sleep late.

Later that morning, an old man with a tangle of white hair burst into Leon's room with a shout. Merle and Ahab nearly attacked before Leon was able to awaken enough to call them both off, but the old man didn't seem to give his near brush with death much thought as even his whiskers trembled with joy at the sight of Leon.

Before Leon could even extricate himself from his sheets, the old man scooped him up out of bed, blankets and all. Wrapping him in a bear hug, he proclaimed, "Leon! I have found you and you have grown!" Then, "What have you done to your hair?"

He didn't give Leon a chance to respond. Straining to maintain the embrace, Ferschall dropped him back down onto the bed and appraised him with a curious look, "At least two seasons in two months, and more besides, yes? You are always full of surprises! Dress first, then come and break your fast with me, we have much to discuss!"

He turned once more and stopped as if actually noticing Leon's four-legged guards for the first time. "Your War Hound has matured into a fine-looking beast!" He cocked his head as he studied Ahab, then swung back around to stare at Leon, a sly expression on his face, "A young silver feathered griffin from the Southern Islands? You do know his kind have never been successfully tamed, don't you? Sure, merchants sometimes manage to hatch an egg here or there, and the cubs are often sold as a novelty of the rich, but no one ever keeps them once they learn to hunt!"

"I don't know about all that. He's pretty well-behaved, just needs lots of meat," Leon defended.

"Yes, and he'll need more as he grows. Just make sure he sticks with a four-legged diet and doesn't go experimenting with any two-legged variety, yes? His kind don't normally grow as big as their mountain cousins, but they make up for it in aggression and athleticism!"

"Listen, just because—'

"And yet here he is, yes? Sitting politely next to an alpha War Hound and hanging on your every word!" Ferschall shook a bent knuckled forefinger his direction and ginned his snaggle-toothed grin, before reiterating his prior observation, "Always full of surprises, Leon, always!"

Minutes later they were both seated in the big room where fresh fruit, smoked eggs, delicate meat cakes, and cool drinks stood ready nearby. The smells coming off the trays were exotic and sumptuous. Leon licked his chops when his belly rumbled. It was like every meal at the Haberkorn Market was discount night at the Golden Corral!

They tore into their meal with silent relish for several minutes before Leon came up for air and asked the obvious question, "Ferschall, what happened that night on the Murk River?"

Ferschall finished chewing and wiped his hands on his pants before he gave an answer, "It was a Vindarri attack. They killed all in their path, but did not seem to care for the Otterkin, only Ben and his men."

"Did they get Ben?"

Ferschall shrugged, "Hard to say. I was a bit busy at the time, yes? But I don't think so. Not that first night at least. They hadn't returned before dawn, and I took off north on the eastern trail. Sadly, I could not wait, I had a higher duty to attend.

"I had a few small run-ins with bandits, but still managed to make it here a little over a month ago. My story is rather plain and boring when compared to yours though. Sved shared a little of what happened to you last night, but I would hear the story from you, yes?" Ferschall wriggled his eyebrows with enthusiasm.

Leon shared the full story of his journey through the Wild Forest and of his meeting and subsequent travels with Kyra. After a little more time, he also showed him the medallion from Gus. Ferschall's eyes went wide when he studied the map on the front side of the medallion. He squinted as he tried to cipher the small writing on the backside. Leon had hoped the knowledgeable old man might understand the writing, but Ferschall couldn't make heads or tails of it either. He did make a copy of some of the writing for further study.

However, it wasn't until Leon proudly showed his old friend the bag of pottery he had hauled with him across the better part of two kingdoms that Ferschall actually yelled loud enough to wake Kyra. He was still celebrating in his typical overtly loud and obnoxious manner when she came stepping out into the big room.

Ferschall dramatically sank to one knee when he met her. He quickly jumped up and drew her into a hug when she told him there wasn't any such need. Then he excused himself from their breakfast, proclaiming he was off to bring back a reward suitable for a job. "So, extraordinarily well done."

A few hours later, Kyra and Leon were sitting down once again to have lunch with Dimples when Sved came busting into the main tent.

"Quick, we have to go. Word of the possibility for war has reached slaver's port. Most auctions have submitted notice that they will proceed immediately. I've got us a bidder's box at the appropriate time slot for the spring caravan of the Crimson Hatchets! We don't have long!"

As much as his animals had become a safety blanket for him, Leon knew he would have to leave them all behind to attend the auction.

"Don't worry, Leon, Caddie will take good care of all your creatures! CADDIE!"

"I'm right behind you, Sved!" Caddie still carried a touch of agitation in her tone after his insensitive demands the night before.

"Oh, right you are! I have a new task for you Caddie, please take care of all my friend's animals while we are gone...I'm pretty sure they all eat meat, so give them lots to eat and you should be fine, yes?" Sved turned to Leon before Caddie could protest. "There, problem solved. Let's go!"

Leon looked at Caddie. She was momentarily apoplectic, sputtering to find the words to refute Sved's latest request, all to no avail. The little man was already scrambling through the front door, barking orders with his signature sarcasm to whoever awaited them outside.

Leon touched the pommel on his Blade and sent out silent instructions for all their creatures to remain put and behave themselves for the young woman. He sent a picture of juicy piles of meat coming their way if they treated her right. Then he, too, grabbed a slice of bread and a hunk of mystery meat and followed the others out the door.

# # #

The crowds at slaver's port spilled over. Every slimy-looking character in Hollinger appeared to be out and about that afternoon. Sved and a cadre of Otterkin guards, despite their size, were surprisingly skilled at plowing a path through the masses.

Yet, just as their group turned into a large open-air warehouse off the dockside road, Leon caught a glimpse of long wavy dark hair. He paused to take a closer look and the head swiveled just enough to see a face. It was only a sliver, but the profile was suspiciously familiar. Then it hit him.

Shana? She's here!

"SHANA! SHANA!" he called, but there was no way she could hear him over the buzzing of the crowd.

Kyra tugged at his sleeve and shouted to him, "What's going on? Come on, we have to go!"

He shook his head. "It's Shana, she's here. I have to try and help her!"

Kyra, was torn. He could see it in her eyes. "Kyra, go, I'll be right back. Save some spots. I'll find you in the booth." She gave an uncertain nod and slipped away to follow Sved before she was completely left behind.

Leon took off racing after his friend. He was taller than most people between them, and he could just see her dark locks bobbing between booths and around merchants. She walked with two other hooded companions. When she turned a corner, he raced to catch up, accidentally knocking a man into a meat cart in the process. There were shouts and angry taunts from behind, but he paid them no mind.

When he turned off on the same corner, he saw her entering a small booth a good forty yards ahead. He yelled her name again.

Just before she disappeared into the booth, she turned to look at him. He saw a flash of recognition, then a simmering look of loathing flashed within her eyes.

"Get out of here!" She motioned him off with a flippant wave of her hand, like shooing away a stray dog.

He just stood there watching her as she turned and ducked down through the entrance. At first, he was too stunned to think straight, then he caught the familiar stench of his old friends fear and anger as they reared their ugly heads and caused his pulse to quicken.

The only reason she could be acting like that is if she's in some horrible trouble!

Against his better judgment, he marched right up to the dark entrance, cracking his knuckles, and straightening his hat as he drew even with the door. He drew his Blade and parted the flap before allowing himself time to reconsider.

What he saw inside was not what he expected. Shana and Cooper were lounging together on a cushioned floor. Cooper had been whispering something and Shana was folded over, holding her side, laughing. Cooper's arm hung in a familiar embrace around her shoulders.

Nearby, two long-haired Vin were pushing back their hoods and flopping down into chairs, next to a third of their ilk. They appeared to be preparing to play some type of card game. All three men stopped what they were doing as soon as they noticed him. Everyone froze.

"Leon, you shouldn't have come here," was all Cooper managed to say before the Vin on the side of the table closest to him moved. Out of the direct sunlight in the confines of the tent structure, Leon knew better than to let the man get close enough to touch him.

He flipped his Blade around the way Sved had taught him. With a flick of his wrist, the Blade sailed gracefully through the air.

Its landing, however, was somewhat anticlimactic considering what he had in mind when he sent it flying. The hilt smashed into the man's head. Leon cringed. It definitely wasn't the heart-shot he had envisioned, but it scored a knock-out when the man was so startled, he stumbled back and hit his noggin once more on the corner of the card table. Leon felt only partially vindicated, but it was a start.

Without waiting to watch the body hit the floor he scooped up a bench lying near the door and siphoning some of his bear-skinner heritage, swung it over his head at the other two. They fell back under its weight, and Leon lunged forward to snatch his Blade from the ground.

"Quick, Coop, Shana, get out of here! Wait for me outside!"

They didn't move. In fact, when he glanced at them, they were just staring up at him, looks of surprise and bewildered alarm were etched across their faces. He didn't have time to ask questions. The two downed Vin came screeching up from under the bench. Eyes red, hair white, hands extended out, fully ready to inflict pain with their deadly touch.

Through clenched teeth, one of his two opponents spoke, "You would dare attack an emissary of the Vindarri Council?"

"You wanna dance, Goldilocks, or are you waiting on an invitation?"

Leon was still congratulating himself on a decent one-liner when the first one lunged at him from across the room. His momentary distraction nearly ended the fight before it even started. Still, he managed to move in time, pivoting in the sharp manner his time with Kyra had taught him as he sliced upward.

Three fingers fell to the floor. The Vin screamed again, this time in agony, and doubled over to cradle his hand. Leon reared back and kicked him in the face, like punting a football. The Vin went up before he went down. Then he hit the ground flat on his back, frozen in that stiff way a boxer is apt to clinch up when he's been knocked out cold.

The remaining Vin tried to use the distraction to leap in close and touch his arm. Leon rolled back and away. He came up in a fighting stance, Blade held loosely out in front.

Come on, Leon, you've got to start remembering to use the one-liners after the fighting part is over. Now focus!

They circled each other slowly. The Vin pulled a wicked-looking sword from over his back. It was much longer than Leon's Blade. He made a show of spinning it around in a large figure eight loops. Leon ignored the theatrics and watched the man's overall demeanor for the shift before the lunge, just like Kyra had taught him.

When the man's sword came up, Leon was already moving. He side-stepped, before taking a quick step into the Vin's guard. Using his taller height and greater reach, he blocked and parried an overhand blow with his Blade before it ever gained any downward momentum. Then, before the Vin could reach out with his free hand, Leon let loose with a left-handed upper cut that may or may not have been slightly strengthened by his Bear-skinner heritage. It was hard to tell. Either way, the man crumbled like he had a glass jaw and didn't get up.

Leon shook his hand out afterward. It had gone completely numb in the split second it connected with the Vin's face. He turned to Coop and Shana once more, ready to bask in their gratitude and adoration. What he found instead was stony silence. Shana looked about ready to punch him herself.

"Leon, you idiot! Those three are Vin royalty! We've been negotiating with them ever since they found us at the Murk River. They were going to send us home!" Shana shook she was so angry.

Found them? The Vin murdered a few dozen people that night!

"I'm sorry, guys. I just thought…"

Leon was cut off by Shana, "You thought what? That you would waltz in here and be the big hero? Save your high school crush?" Leon sputtered but she didn't stop. "Oh, you think I didn't know? Wanna know something funny? You might have had a chance with me, Leon, for a hot second, back when I was confused and desperate," she sneered up at him, "but you were never man enough to take it. You could have followed me into the river, but you panicked, didn't you? You froze! You left me behind!"

"Shana, no. I didn't—"

"I SAW YOU!" Shouting now, tears were streaming down her cheeks. "I saw you standing on that ledge! Too afraid to take the plunge. Too afraid to help us! Then I saw you turn away." She took a few deep breaths to steady herself, she was clearly losing control. When she finally got it together, she continued in a quiet voice, "I'm with Coop now Leon. We have a chance. Or at least we did. If there's even a remote possibility still left to us, we're leaving this Godforsaken world, so LEAVE US THE HELL ALONE!"

Shana's words struck him with more stopping power than a Vin's touch, but slowly, he rose up from under them. He had been wrestling with those very fears for weeks and hearing them voiced like that by every person he worried he had wronged, helped him at last to see the truth of the matter.

"Shana, I'm sorry I couldn't follow you that night. It ate at me, still does, but I couldn't leave Reed and Sved behind. I didn't leave you, Shana. We each had a choice to make. You made yours, same as me."

"Liar!" she screamed. Though stricken with guilt and shame, Leon couldn't help but notice there was something intangibly off about her voice, her movements.

He looked at Cooper for support. Cooper wouldn't quite meet his eye, but he spoke up anyway. "Just go, Leon. You're on your own now. Ben will figure something out. We have to make this right. You need to leave before he and the others return with Slade."

"Yeah, I'm leaving and, Shana…I'm sorry." Not wanting to stick around for another scathing retort, he pushed his way through the front flap, soon joining the foul-smelling streets once more.

Leon could still hear Shana's scornful remarks as he stumbled back through the crowds, but he wasn't hurt by her words, just saddened. His heart ached for the loss of his childhood friend but his mind was already moving past her, thinking of the others he needed to find, others that needed him now instead.

When at last he climbed the steps into to the slaver's auction for the Crimson Hatchets, a pair of guards nearly threw him out. He nearly punched the one that grabbed him first. It wasn't until one of Sved's men came to his rescue and explained he was part of the Haberkorn party that he was allowed inside.

Leon tried not to draw attention to himself as he took his seat next to Kyra but she took one look at his face and wrapped her arms around him. Her embrace smothered him in the scent of flowers and spice, it pushed back on the stench of the streets and the slaver's den, if only for bit. Nonetheless, a bit of a reprieve turned out to be more than enough for Leon to pull himself together.

After a long hug, Kyra finally pulled back. "Leon, what happened? Sved sent people back looking for you, but we heard nothing for so long. I was preparing to leave too when word came you were back! Did you find Shana? Why is there blood on your vest?" Nimble fingers prodded him as she spoke, quickening in their search for wounds when he didn't respond right away.

"I'm fine, Kyra. I did find her. But there was something off about the whole thing...then I nearly killed three members of Vindarri royalty. She didn't want to come afterward. It's just us now, me and Reed I mean."

Her eyes went wide, but she didn't ask any more questions. Her fingers found their way into his hands and held on tight.

"What's happening here?" Leon asked, coming up out of his mind and taking a look around.

"Sved and his men just won the bidding for my brothers and Haddie! They also managed to buy your friend Rezz. They are bidding now for Reed."

"Good. I'm ready to get out of here."

Kyra frowned, hesitating only for a second before continuing, "It's not that simple. The slavers lumped Reed in with the rest of the Fae. They are selling them all in one large unit."

He shrugged dismissively. "Can't Sved afford that, though? I'll throw in all the gold I found on the way here. It'd almost be worth it, even without Reed in the mix, if for no other reason than to see those smug faces deflate when they realize who bought their freedom, though we'd have to set them free soon enough. Slavery's intolerable, no matter what a person's done."

"I agree, and I think under normal circumstances, yes, that would work. But these aren't normal circumstances." She pointed across the room to another large box full of men and women lounging about in forest-colored outfits Leon knew well. They were matching Sved and his men, bid for bid. He pushed up his hat and scratched his head.

"More Fae?"

"Yeah, I'm told they were already in town. The slavers must have tipped them off to the fact their people were being sold. Sved heard they are willing to leverage half their kingdom to get them back, and the slavers have been instructed by the town's council of elders to give them any amount of credit they rack up!"

"It's got to be because of the Fae queen's son! He was there that night. He must be in the mix with Reed!"

A few minutes later the voices controlling the haggling of the auction went silent. A person who Leon assumed was some sort of Auctioneer broke the stillness, "DEAL!" and a gong-like bell was rung.

Sved hung his head and sank into his chair, cradling his face in his hands.

When he looked up at Leon his eyes red and puffy, "I am so sorry, my friend. I just don't have the means to go higher. Reed's fate rests in the hands of the Fae."

Son of a biscuit!

Chapter 26

Kyra's brothers were delivered to the Haberkorn Market Holdings the next morning. Once informed of their good fortune, all three Stonebreaker brothers encircled their sister in a hug. Tears were shed in astonishment over the fact that Kyra and her new friends had managed to do for them what they never thought possible.

After their initial emotions calmed, the brothers all wore smiles. Cheerful humor took the place of tearful sentiment as they gently teased Kyra for her hair color and then poked fun at how much Grumpy's girth had grown in their absence. After that, they hugged everyone, including Leon.

They were overjoyed to learn he shared their tribal heritage. To Sved and the Haberkorn clan, they pledged their loyalty despite Sved's protest that Leon and Kyra had already paid back the gold they cost. Their rambunctious reunion was a celebratory moment that lifted everyone's spirits, even Leon's, for a short while.

Haddie and Rezz were delivered a few hours later. If Rezz was surprised to see Leon, Dimples, and Sved again, he hid it well. He had been badly hurt in the fight with the Fae, but as he relayed, when the slavers threw him in with Reed, it was Reed's gift that had healed him enough to recover.

Haddie's reunion was different. Her skin was red and blotchy from over-exposure to the sun and her slim figure was skinnier than Leon could recall, but she didn't look to be physically injured.

As soon as she saw Sved, Leon, and Dimples, she broke into tears and fell to pieces. Madam Hazzel, Sved's mother, made her first appearance then. She was an older woman, with smiling eyes and benevolent wrinkles that reminded Leon in a distant way of his grandmother. She cradled Haddie in her arms and told everyone to be patient and give her space. She explained how a woman sometimes could use a little time to herself. She and Haddie wept tears of joy and sorrow together, as Madam Hazzel led her out of the room and straight for the baths.

The look on Sved's face when he finally returned from checking in on Haddie was timid relief. "She's sleeping now. Madam Hazzel says her dignity is intact. Not that they cared, no? They just felt a pretty girl like her would fetch a better price without...well, let's just say it's been a trying time all around, yes?"

"Will she be okay?" Leon asked.

"She will, though she only asks for Reed. We didn't have the heart to tell her what happened just yet."

"Speaking of Reed. Sved I've been going through my things. The chest I pulled from the prince's tent the day after they were taken contained more than just the gold, I used to pay you back for the Stonebreakers. There are some weird items in there, stuff that looks expensive. You think it could be worth a trade?"

Sved perked up. "It can't hurt to try! Show me."

A half-hour later, Haberkorn runners were sent to find the Fae delegation and inform them of the prospect for the trade Leon hoped to make.

Ferschall had never returned. When Leon worried, Sved assured him that was his way. He would be around when he decided to turn up and not a minute sooner.

While the whole group visited and snacked in the main room together, waiting to hear word from the Fae, the oldest of Kyra's three brothers, Fane, approached Leon and asked if they could talk. He was a very big man and the most subdued of the three brothers. The two younger brothers, Chocum and Daz, were young men, just a little older than Leon himself. Fane was at least ten years older.

His initial exuberance and joy over their release had run its course and as the day wore on, he began asking questions that brought him up to speed on the depth and condition of Fayden's kingdom defenses. His mind was already contemplating the ramifications of an impending invasion. In short, he was now the head of the Stonebreaker family, and it was clear he took the job seriously.

Leon half expected him to pull his Blade and clean his fingernails in intimidation as they settled down into some comfortable seats next to each other, across the room from everyone else. He saw Kyra throwing nervous glances his direction and tried to ignore whatever hints those looks were attempting to convey, puzzling on them would just make him more nervous.

Too bad he doesn't have a shotgun he can polish while he asks me "a few man-to-man questions."

To his surprise, Fane started the conversation completely differently than expected. "Leon, before we begin, I just want to say I don't know how to properly thank you for what you did for Kyra, and us by extension. My brothers and I could have shouldered a life of slavery, or worse if things turned out that way, but the thought of our little sister being alone out there nearly broke us...I'm just glad you were there for her when she needed someone."

"You're welcome." Leon leaned in and winked at him. "But I have to admit that the only reason I'm here now is because of her. Without her, I would likely be dead or worse."

Fane leaned back and smiled. "She's a very competent young woman."

Leon agreed, and Fane continued, "I imagine you and Kyra have become quite close in the time you have known one another?"

"Yes, sir, we have...but not like close-close..."

When Leon didn't add anything, Fane continued, "As our father is gone, it is now my duty to look after her. It would be a weight off my shoulders if I knew your intentions with her?"

"Intentions?" The conversation was taking a hard turn down a road he wasn't ready to travel.

"Yes, intentions."

"Uhh, well, I like Kyra, a lot, but I'm not sure what—"

"Do I need to spell it out for you or are you going to ask for her hand?"

Leon sputtered, "Hand?"

Fane was beginning to lose patience. His voice rose as he asked as directly as possible, "Do you want to marry Kyra or not?"

Leon's mouth was lost trying to keep pace with his mind. He just sat there moving his lips, like a fish out of water, but he couldn't find an answer in time.

Fane glared at him for another moment or two, then leaped to his feet and stalked off across the room.

Leon looked around the room. Everyone had stopped their talking. They were all staring at him. Kyra's glare stopped him in his tracks. She jumped to her feet and her stool clattered to the floor as she stormed out of the room. Daz broke free from talking with Dimples and followed after her.

Dimples sauntered over and squatted down next to him. "That was very poorly done, Leon. You have dishonored the heart of a young woman. That is the most dangerous offense a man can make. You better find a way to give her honor back or she will loath you forever." He gave Leon a solid pat and a smile like he had just solved his problem and shared one of life's greatest secrets all in one fell swoop.

Infernal Hootsi!

# # #

Leon was still trying to make sense of everything that had happened with Fane when one of the runners returned.

"Sved, the Fae haven't agreed to anything yet, but you've got their attention. They want to hear more. They will wait to see what we have to offer. However, their talks with the Alliance have deteriorated due to the stunt the slavers pulled. They plan to leave by dawn's light either way."

"How do they want this to go down?" said Sved.

"They won't send anyone. Said they won't put any more Ageless lives in jeopardy. They want the griffin tamer to meet them. Alone. He is to bring a small sample of what he has to offer. Their leader will judge if it is worthy of a trade."

Sved cast a look at Leon. "No, they need to do better than that!"

"We can't risk them walking out on this, Sved. I've got a chance to convince them to trade for Reed. I have to take it. It's my risk, my decision. I'm going."

Sved didn't like it, but he agreed it was an opportunity they might not have again.

As evening settled in outside, Leon changed out of his Fae clothing and into some swarthy outfit Sved's people were able to supply on short notice. He didn't want to risk angering Reed's captors by showing up dressed in the clothes of their dead kinsmen.

He wouldn't be taking his larger animal companions on this excursion either. He was leaving Ahab and Merle in Dimple's care. He chuckled to himself at the unforgettable expression on Sved's face when he asked him to watch after the Thunderbird. He could have left it to Dimples, but he opted for Sved instead, mostly just for the amusement of seeing that sour look on the little man's face.

The one creature he did plan to bring along was the owl. Leon thought the Fae might respect him more for taming and valuing an animal they held in high regard. Any edge he could get, he would take.

Under Kyra's care and guidance, the little owl had grown well beyond Leon's expectations. In his estimation, it was closer to the size of a hawk than the miniaturized hunter that had been described to him. Its talons were long, silver, and wickedly curved. Sved's tailor had added an extra layer of leather onto his shoulders, where the bird liked to perch, and it rested there like a parrot on his shoulder. He had also provided Leon with thick leather gauntlets and fingerless gloves, so he could handle those talons without slicing himself, if necessary. Looking at the bird now, Leon could easily how useful such gloves might become in the near future.

The owl's body had finally filled out to match its long wings. Mottled lines of black and spots of gray and purple overlapped a dark blue base plumage. Its eyes were dark orbs floating in gold, circled in rings of black and framed in small white feathers, the only white on the whole bird. Leon could now see the sleek form of the true hunter it was always meant to be. He remembered Olwena had called it a Forest Bandit at some point during their flight from the

331

Fae. The owl did have a bit of a bandit's look to it now that he examined him closely.

"How about I call you Westley, after another famous bandit from a place called Hollywood?" Leon chuckled as the owl cooed in response.

"Not the most fearsome of names, but it fits you all the same!"

He fed Westley a small sliver of rabbit from Sved's kitchens and set it on his shoulder. Then he turned and stopped, catching sight of himself in the mirror which rested in the corner of his room. He barely recognized the man staring back in the flickering lamplight. He was tall, much taller than he remembered, and his body had finally started filling out his lanky frame. His clothing style was similar to Ferschall's, back on the first night they met, but much newer and better fitting.

It was trim but loose. The inner fabrics were soft against his skin and cool to the touch, while the thick leather exterior on the chest, shoulders, and arms provided an armor of sorts. He preferred leggings to the long tunic Ferschall wore, and he had grown to appreciate the knee-high boots of the Fae. Both were provided in charcoal and tan colors that matched the rest of him.

He frowned at Westley, still resting on his shoulder. "I look like a wannabe pirate in a trucker's hat!" Westley just watched him with wide owlish eyes.

"Tough crowd."

Caddie had at least done him the service of washing his old tan hat, twice she claimed. The black CW stitching had faded to a dull gray, but the cap was in impressively good shape considering its use. As he stared at the image of his grandfather's brand, a dull ache caused him to clench his fists at the thought of all he had lost, but despite the hurt, his head remained clear and focused. He opened his fists, forcing blood back into white knuckles, and reached down at his side, rubbing his fingertips over the bone-handled hilt of his Blade.

There was a gentle knock at his door.

When he pulled back the flap, he saw Kyra standing there alone. She looked as beautiful and wild as ever. But her cheeks were lined in tear stains where she had been crying. She wouldn't meet his eye at first. "Well, you going to invite me in, or just stand there?"

Was that a small smile? A smile is good!

"I don't know…are you going to hurt me?"

"I'll hurt you more if you don't!"

"Good enough!" He moved aside, and she slipped through.

She was quiet, and he was afraid to start things off on the wrong foot. He walked over and grabbed another sliver of meat for Westley. He noticed Kyra studying the bird as he fed him.

"His name is Westley."

"What? Whose name?"

"The owl. I finally named him. He's been going dangerous places with us this whole time. Thought he at least deserved a name." He decided not to attempt explaining how the name actually came from a movie he'd watched as a child.

"Westley…" She tested it, "odd, but I think it fits him. I like it." She fidgeted over Westley for a moment while he waited for her to speak.

At last, she built up the nerve to attack the tension between them. "Leon, I've been thinking about what my brother did…I know you probably have different customs where you come from…what I mean is…I'm sorry…"

He held up a hand to stop her. He'd had time to think things through, too, and he knew, without a doubt, what he needed to tell her.

"No, Kyra, you don't need to apologize for Fane. He just surprised me is all. I should have answered him from my heart as soon as I knew what he was asking." He took her hands in his, then dropped to a knee and continued, "We do have a custom where I come from, though. When a man wants to marry a woman he loves, he takes a knee like this. Next, he looks her in the eye like this." Leon looked into Kyra's gray-blue eyes and saw a flicker of hope glimmering back at him. "He asks her a question with as much courage as he can muster."

Kyra was breathless. She whispered back. "What question?"

"Will you marry me? Will you be my wife? Kyra, I don't have a home to offer you, and I sure don't know what the future holds, but I've come to realize I care more for you than anything else in this life. If there's a future for me, I want it to be with you."

She made a high-pitched sound and pulled him up into her arms. Leon noticed for the first time that he no longer stood eye to eye with Kyra. Reaching into a pocket at her side, she withdrew a small clothe and pressed it into his hands. It was dyed purple and decorated with symbols sewn in golden thread. When his fingers closed around the cloth, she looked up into his eyes and answered him with one word, "Yes!"

Those first moments after their engagement were the most exhilarating moments of Leon's life. Their celebration was quiet and brief, but no less special than had he taken a knee and won a bride on centerfield at Cowboy's stadium. Before leaving Leon's room to announce their decision to the others, Kyra explained the purpose of the cloth. "I've stitched a symbol using a strand of my hair from an event in my life every year since I became old enough to wed. It's a tradition that once we are promised you will hold this for me until the day we are married. On that day you surprise me by giving it back with a symbol of your own there in the center."

"You'll have to teach me to sew." Leon grinned.

"I have a lot of things to teach you, Leon, but we can add sewing to the list as well."

Kyra's brothers graciously accepted his apology for any insult he may have caused to their family honor, though they did rib him that it took a visit from their sister to set him straight! Even then, he could see joy in their eyes at the prospect of a small slice of happiness for their baby sister.

Not one person commented on their age or their limited acquaintance, and though there were pressing matters at hand, everyone was eager to heap congratulations on the young couple.

At the lighthearted acceptance everyone gave them, it dawned on Leon that life could be preciously short in Fayden. Joy was to be taken where and when it could be found.

It wasn't until Leon was marching forward, alone, toward the elaborate building housing the Ageless Fae delegation, that the events of the past few hours were fully able to sink in on him. He had lost a childhood friend, but he was gaining a lifetime companion.

I'm going to be married!

But not just to anyone, he was going to be married to the hottest, toughest, most wonderful woman he had ever met!

He had to give himself a mental kick in the pants as he climbed the building's stairway entrance.

You only get to marry Kyra if you survive the next hour of negotiations, Romeo. Get your game face on and stop drooling on yourself.

Chapter 27

Two women escorted Leon into his meeting. The building that housed the Fae didn't seem large from outside. The rooms had to extend out underground. The passages they traveled felt like a maze. He would likely need their help finding the way out and that made him nervous.

His escorts were beautiful and unsettling. They moved with fluid grace and soft gestures, but he saw them for the predators they were and kept a healthy distance as he followed.

Small sconces lit the halls, but the lights were few and far between. He did his best to keep his eyes open for familiar landmarks, constantly surveying his surroundings for danger as they led him down dark corridors.

Every so often, mad laughter of some unmistakably Fae individual broke the silence. The cackling would echo through walls and around corners. He didn't know if it was intentional or not, but it creeped him out just the same. In fact, the whole ambiance rekindled painful reminders from the night of the Wild Hunt. Each wicked laugh added to the goosebumps climbing up his arms.

At last, the women came to a large leather doorway. They stopped, stepped to opposite sides of the hall, and without a word, simultaneously reached out and pulled back leather flaps to open an entry before him. They gave him coy smiles as he took a cautious step forward.

The room was large. At some point, it was likely a banquet hall. Yet all its former glory was stripped bare, save for a small party in its center. A cluster of people sat in a semi-circle, lounging on large pillows. A few of them were playing some type of reed-pipe instruments that played rhythmic, if not melodious, chords. Leon headed their direction.

As he drew close, he couldn't help but notice a dark look from a youthful face staring him down. The man's smile was plastered on while his eyes were etched in insolent disdain. His arms were folded behind his head and his legs were crossed out in front of him. A beautiful servant stooped down behind him to refill a cup resting on a short table at his side.

All the people around him were laughing and joking. Some were kissing. They all appeared intoxicated. Not him though. He didn't seem to notice anything going on around him. He just continued to stare. Even when Leon stopped ten feet shy of the party, no one appeared to take notice of his presence except the angry young man.

A commanding feminine voice spoke up from the opposite side of the room, "This celebration ended hours ago! Everyone out. I have business to discuss."

The response was an explosion of pillows and bodies as cavorting couples scrambled to their feet and scurried for exits. The young man didn't twitch. He stayed where he was, eyes still locked on Leon.

When the room was clear the woman who had spoken walked out into the torchlight. She looked to be older than the Fae he had so far met, maybe in her late twenties. While every Fae person Leon had seen in Fayden seemed to dress in one shade of green or another, she was dressed in black, from the top of her head to the bottom of her boots. Everything about her screamed dangerous, though outwardly, she looked to be the incarnation of sensual charm.

"You too, Dirk. I want to speak with this young man before I make my decision, and I don't need you here, distracting us both with your pathetic attempts to sway my thoughts." It didn't take much for Leon to figure out which direction Dirk would be trying to sway the woman.

Dirk lifted his chin to the woman, and a scour cut through his fake smile. His words were venom served cold. "Or I could simply order you to do as I command…Auntie Shay."

She snorted. "You forget your place, little big man! I'm in charge here and despite the humiliation of your capture, I alone deigned to free you. I wonder now, should I send you back?"

He rolled his eyes. "Don't be so dramatic!"

She squinted down at him and drew a long sword from a sheath at her back, it chimed like a bell when it was free, "You dare speak to me this way? In front of a foreigner? I'm not one of your playthings to fawn at your commands or shirk at your indignation." She paused to take a few practice swings. Each movement was lithe and efficient. "I know a thousand ways to end you while leaving none the wiser...but I'm not a monster." She stopped swinging and stepped in close behind him, laying the flat of the blade against his ear. "No, Dirk, I'll just carve one or two of your more important pieces off and send you to the healer in the morning! Now...GET...OUT!"

Dirk's dark features turned pale. He scrambled to his feet, knocking his cup over in the process. Humiliated, he stormed out of the room.

The woman studied Leon until he was gone and just the two of them were left. She tilted her head and smiled at him.

"Good start. Had you laughed, I would have laid you open from chin to trousers, treasure be damned."

Leon swallowed.

This lady don't play around!

She shouted a command to the far wall. A table and two chairs were carried in and set down before them. Two cups of some strong-smelling drink were brought out, as well as a bowl of fresh fruit.

"My name is Shay Softfoot, and you, I assume, are Leon?" He nodded, and she smiled back at him like they were already friends. "Right. Care for some refreshments, Leon?" Sheathing her sword, she plopped down at the table. Then without waiting for him to join her, she grabbed a large purple fruit from the bowl and took a bite. A tangy, spicy smell filled the air around them.

Leon cautiously sat next to her. He didn't reach for any food or drink.

"Nice-sized bandit bird. Make sure he doesn't shit on my floor." Juice ran down her chin, but she didn't seem to mind. She took another bite and swallowed. "So, what is this treasure you claim you have recovered for us?"

"Where is Reed?"

"Reed? Oh, you mean one of the Bladed Fae we got as a bonus from the slavers?"

"Yes." She knew exactly who he was there for, she was just toying with him.

"He's safe, for now."

"Can I see him?"

She leered at him. "You show me the stone, and I'll show you your friend." She leaned forward expectantly, finally deciding to wipe her chin.

Leon looked her in the eye and reached into his vest. He pulled out one of the amber stones, wrapped in a cloth, and set it on the table. He hadn't wanted it coming loose and touching his skin when he reached in to hand it over.

She leaned forward to get a better look, unfolding the fine linen wrap with a surgeon's touch. Once the stone came free, it rolled out onto the table, its amber light seemed brighter than normal. Her expression panned, but she recovered quickly, attempting to hide her surprise.

"Tsk-tsk, Leon, you are full of surprises! Want to tell me how you came across this trinket?"

"I found it, same as fifteen others like it."

She leaned back in her chair and whistled under her breath. "Don't play with me boy, I was curious before, now I'm starting to get annoyed. I have a lot to do tonight but I certainly don't have time to haggle over this. No outsider could have taken fifteen of these and lived to tell the tale!"

Leon's curiosity got the better of him. "What is it?"

"No, no, let's stick with my first question. How did you get it?"

"I'm not lying! I found them in one of the convergence tents after I managed to escape both the Wild Hunt and the slavers. I think it belonged to some prince who was in attendance. I heard them announce him, but I never saw him!"

Shay leaned forward. Her features shifted as her eyes took on a purple glow. Her ears grew dark and pointy as their tips curved back. "Care to bet your life on that Leon?" Her voice was still silky smooth, just a smidge huskier.

"What do you mean? I'm telling you the truth!"

"Then take my hand. My power is unique, but it doesn't work on Bladed people unless they let down the barrier it provides. Give me your hand and allow me to search your memory from that night. I will only search that night. You can push me out if I stray, but I need to confirm what you say."

"You can do that?"

She reached forward,. "Come on, this won't hurt, much."

He thought her soft laughter was perhaps the most normal thing about her as he extended his arm and put his hand in hers. What happened next jolted him. His vision went dark, and Shay's voice was in his head.

Leon, I need you to think about the night of the Wild Hunt.

Then he was there, or rather, they were there. He could feel her presence with him, though he could only see what he experienced that night.

He cried out in his mind, "*Not this! Go to the next day! The next morning.*"

The scene flashed forward. He was in the process of arranging Olwena next to the griffin in their communal grave.

She picked up the pace, skipping over details in fast forward until he stepped into the large tent. The whole scene played out once more, exactly how he remembered. After he opened the chest and found the curious treasures, the connection was severed.

His vision swam, and he doubled over coughing. Westley screeched and jostled for better purchase on his shoulder. Shay cursed and sprang to her feet. She screamed for her guards, then ordered them to find Dirk and bring him to her.

# # #

Leon could barely think straight for sometime after Shay released him. All the horrible memories from that night and following morning were amplified. They bubbled up to the top of his mind where they remained present, circulating over and over again. It was like she managed to dig up all the hurt and pain and leave it exposed, right where it was most hurtful.

Shay didn't seem to notice his distress as her anger continued to boil over for a time.

Once she regained her composure, she turned to him again. "Thank you, Leon. That was very helpful to me. It has clarified a great many questions I've carried for a good long while."

She sat down next to him once more. A knowing smile was plastered on her face.

"I'll make you a deal. I trade in secrets. I'll give you your friend and the two other Bladed Fae we received today in exchange for a small secret from you."

"What about the chest?"

"I'll obviously be taking that as well."

"What secret?"

"Tell me about your mother?

"My mother? I-I don't remember."

"Nonsense, I know her tribe just from looking in your head. The maternal bloodline leaves more of a mark on a person's mind than anyone suspects. Now tell me her name!"

"No, I mean, I literally don't remember. I can't recall anything prior to the age of six. I have no recollection of her."

"Fascinating!" She tapped her nails on the table, "She's Fae, you know that, don't you?"

"No, I don't know that. What makes you think that?"

"I just know, when you play around in people's heads as often as me, you tend to recognize these things. Like I said, her bloodline left a strong stamp on the configuration of your mind. Had she not been Fae, my job just now would have been much more challenging. I want to know more though," she then snapped her fingers, "I'll sweeten this for you Leon. Let me poke around up there," she pointed to his head. "back to the point where your memories stop. If they stop for me as well, no harm done. Either way, I'll give you your people when it's over."

Leon's head was still spinning from her first foray through his mind as he did his best to fully consider what she offered. "You will let them go either way?"

"Yes, I give you my word as regent to the queen!"

"Then let them go now, and you have a deal."

She laughed. "I would have asked the same! Done."

She gave an order, and a moment later, three men were marched past them, one of them was Reed. He was gagged but his eyes bulged when he spotted Leon.

Leon sent a silent pulse of instruction using his Blade, and Westley took off. The owl swooped across the room, landing on Reed's shoulder, causing him to flinch in pain. He wasn't wearing any extra leather on his shoulder.

It hissed at the guards around them, and they left him alone. They were all led away but Leon maintained a tiny connection with Westley. He could somehow tell when the bird left the building and cleared the street to where Sved and his men waited. He sighed with relief when he realized his mission was accomplished.

Shay finished her second fruit snack and licked her fingers. "Have you had enough of a break? Come on, I really do have a lot to do, but this is just too interesting to pass up."

Leon gritted his teeth and reached forward.

Immediately, she plunged in, taking him back to his earliest memories. Back to the day when he met Gus, back to where he first opened his eyes in a forest and took off running. Shay pushed and the vision went back still further to the darkness that was with him even before his eyes opened.

Pressure mounted in his mind. It grew painful. His head felt like it might explode at any moment. It was unbearable. He strained against it, begging for a release that wouldn't come, yet he didn't push her out. He had waited too long for answers. He held tight to that single thought and suffered through the pain.

Then, there was a pop! Fuzzy visions flowed backward at hyper-speed. Shay slowed them down, then played them forward. Until she found a place just before the darkness descended. She stopped and played things forward in real-time.

Leon could see daylight, but it was cold out. He was hauled along through a snow-covered forest by a woman with braided black hair.

A very large, muscular man ran at their side. He was draped in heavy furs. In his hands, he carried a longbow, and in his belt, he wore a Blade. His curly blond beard was frosted over, but he opened his mouth wide and shouted encouragement at the woman. Their pace increased.

Leon could see more than a dozen dark-headed men, dressed in Fae clothing, pursuing them through the trees behind.

A rock struck the woman's pack on her back, and she stumbled. The man scooped her up without breaking stride and raced on, encouraging Leon to race on, ahead of them both until he called a halt.

"Airrene, I'll hold them off. Get the portal open!"

The woman stepped around Leon and tore a Blade from the sheath at her hip. The was something familiar about what she was doing. When his child's eyes looked up, he saw why. A tree towered above them all. The woman cut her hand to wet the bark, then carved a portal into a Royal Tree!

The man continued his fight in the background. Leon's young head turned back to the man while the woman worked. He saw him drop his bow when he was swarmed by several other men, all at once. There was no way he could stand against them. Yet the big man prevailed. When the struggle ended, dead and dying men lay heaped in piles around him.

He turned back and yelled something at the woman. At that precise moment, a rock struck him in the temple. The woman screamed and pushed Leon behind her.

Leon's small head peeked around the woman's side. Another tall woman in white fur with hair as black as night came stalking

344

out of the woods to stop in front of the big man who lay unconscious in the snow. Leon heard the woman, Airrene, pleading with the new woman, calling her by name.

The woman just laughed. She drew a sword and plunged it into the man's chest in one fluid motion. Leon's young voice broke as he screamed, "Father!"

Airrene turned to him. Her beautiful face was stricken with terror and grief. She reached out with a goved hand, holding an amber-colored glowing rock, and touched his forehead. He clenched up, unable to move. The rock's touch did something to his mind, but as he fell, and before her hand left his head, she spoke to him, "Run little Waldman, run!" Behind her, Leon could see a sword rising.

He was still frozen from her touch, but the momentum of her push carried him back into a dark void, and it all went black once more.

Shay fell out of her chair and wretched. Tears came streaming down her face. She had disintegrated into a complete wreck.

Leon, though numbed by the tragedy, didn't feel the same pain as before. In fact, his mind felt whole for the first time in his life. Yes, he had seen his parents' deaths, but he had also seen their sacrifice. He had seen the love they had for each other and for him. Despite the grief those recaptured memories brought to bear, he considered himself gifted with a tiny glimpse of the family he might have had with them.

Then another realization dawned on him as subtle as a sack of bricks. He had always secretly wished to know what it was like to be raised in a normal family, with normal parents, who loved him in a way that blood loves blood, but the love his memory revealed in that long past snippet of time differed so very little from the love and security Gus provided that his heart burst with appreciation for both his adopted family and his birth parents. He hadn't been denied a taste of something everyone else consumed, something especially reserved for those whose parents shared their blood, he had been given a double portion.

His new memories also helped him understand and appreciate why Gus gave him the last name of Waldman instead of Silberman. Waldman was the only word he had been repeating when they found him.

All these years, I thought Gus was reluctant to give me his last name because I wasn't his blood, but it was just the old man's way of allowing me to retain a sliver of whatever I had when he found me!

The revelation brought a balanced sense of wholesomeness to him, he would never again question his father's love!

As Shay lay crying on the floor before him, Leon did his best to swallow down the acrid taste of pity forming in his throat. Despite his newly found sense of belonging, he also felt the need for justice. He stood to his feet and drew his Blade. He squatted down next to Shay and held the Blade to her neck. "The woman who killed my parents, who is she?"

Shay ignored his threat, answering through gasps of agony, practically oblivious to the Blade's proximity. "My sister!"

He watched her sobs a moment longer. The pity was gone, but he needed more information.

"Don't test my patience, lady. I'm well beyond half-measures here! My mother, Airrene. Was she someone you knew as well?" There was cold danger lurking in the tone he used to frame the question.

Shay looked up at him. Her tear-streaked eyes were back to a more natural shade of green. "Airrene was my sister too, Leon. My oldest sister. She was the rightful queen of the Fae!"

Guards came running into the room, silently drawing their swords and surrounding Leon, but Shay waved them off and stood on shaky legs. Her voice steeled and a commanding presence took the place of a grieving sister when she addressed them, "You return empty-handed?"

The lead guard narrowed his eyes at Leon as he answered his sovereign, "Yes, my lady. We just learned your nephew and over a dozen of his people have left the compound. Shall we attempt to pursue?"

"No! Continue your departure preparations as planned but assemble my personal guard. Tell them we will be moving out very soon. Now, leave us." she said.

The guard immediately left the room. Shay turned back to Leon. She was still breathing hard, but color gradually returned to her face. She placed a hand on Leon's shoulder.

"I swear to you, we will find retribution for your parents, for my sister. But that outcome requires we walk a slippery rope between tall trees. First things first, take me to those stones."

Chapter 28

Leon left the Fae compound with Shay and twenty of her guard. When Sved saw him walking together with Shay, he was startled to say the least. Leon told him that as part of the agreement they made for Reed's release Shay and her people would accompany them all back to where the stones were being held. He would just have to wait to relay the whole story.

Word reached Haberkorn Market ahead of their return. As they slipped into the maze of tents, it was like everyone knew the negotiations to recover the remainder of Haddie's party had been a success. The Otterkin all appeared eager for a reason to celebrate. There was celebration and dancing in the streets. Smells of delicious foods and exotic spices encircled their party on all sides.

Leon left Shay's side to catch up with Reed. "How are you, bud?"

Reed gave him a tired smile. "Happy to be free? I hear Haddie made it to safety as well."

"She should be around soon."

Reed just nodded with pursed lips.

Leon didn't know what else to say to his friend. He didn't want to push Reed, and he didn't want to leave him alone either. Reed seemed to be holding up pretty well considering all that had happened, but slavery wasn't something a modern-day American mind could easily grasp, and Reed had suffered greatly under its weight.

"How about you take your bird back?" Reed motioned to his shoulder where Westley sat.

"That's your owl, Reed. He's all grown up! He's actually a really smart bird."

"Even more reason for you to take him back. Rezz told me what happened to Olwena the night the slavers caught us. I won't be able to care for him and not think of her. Please, just take him." Leon saw a fragile hurt in Reed's eyes that hadn't been there before. He held out his arm and Westley hopped off his shoulder perch.

When they reached the center market, Haddie came barreling through the maze of tents to find Reed. Reed dutifully embraced her, but Leon could tell there was something forced in the way his arms held the small woman. Leon sighed. There wasn't anything he could do to help the two of them, they would have to figure things out themselves.

Kyra wasn't far behind Haddie. Her appearance was a bit more subtle, although her relief was just as palpable. He could tell by the way she wrapped him so tightly in her arms just how worried she had been over his visit to the Fae. He had to cry uncle when her hug nearly cracked a rib.

The whole group filed into the big tent, and to his relief, Leon saw that Ferschall was back. The initial reception of the guests was cordial, but Leon could tell Shay was nervous. She kept glancing toward the exit and made more than one comment on their need to finish their business. But Madam Hazzle would have none of it. She made an appearance and gave a proclamation, "Any royalty to arrive at Haberkorn Market must be treated to the fullest of Haberkorn hospitality, yes? Please, enjoy dinner!"

She then proceeded to clap her hands. The candlelight somehow dimmed, lyrical music filled the void of silence in the background, and the resulting stream of waiters bringing in trays of food and drink quickly produced the most decadent feast Leon could ever imagine, considering his vision of a decadent feast prior to that point involved a prolonged relationship between an outdoor smoker and a brisket.

If Shay ran low on patience, she didn't show it. Though a few of her guards participated in the meal, his aunt mirrored his earlier reluctance for food or drink. Instead, she plastered on a smile and made small talk with his eclectic collection of friends. Though those friends were all a bit cold toward the leader of a people who had been so cruel so recently, no one was outright disrespectful.

Finally, Shay raised her hands. "On behalf of the Fae court, I thank you for this feast, it is second to none. However, I really must insist Leon and I conclude our business." She tilted her head to

Madame Hazzle. "With your permission, might we find a quiet place to complete our transaction?" The old woman smiled back at Shay and acknowledged her request with a dip of her head.

Leon brought Kyra, Reed, and Sved along with him. It took Reed a moment to unlatch himself from Haddie's hip, but he managed to follow along. Rezz refused Leon's offer to join them and Dimples was nowhere to be seen as he had opted to leave with the animals, to another room, before anyone arrived. Leon knew he wasn't much for celebrations.

Shay seemed distraught when his three friends followed them into a small room with a large table, further back down a hall from the main area.

# # #

"Shay, I didn't get a chance to properly introduce you all earlier. Sved is one of my closest friends, and I trust him completely. Reed comes from the same world as me…" There were gasps from his friends that he had conveyed this truth to Shay, and there were gasps from Shay over the fact she sat next to another one of the remnant. Leon quickly continued before questions came, "And this is Kyra. Kyra is my fiancé, and my trust in her goes without question." Shay's brow lifted at the revelation that the beautiful girl before her was, in fact, Leon's fiancé.

"Everyone, this is my aunt, Shay Softfoot, Royal Princess of the Fae throne." The gasps from before were replaced by stunned silence.

Reed asked first, "Leon, you want to bring us up to speed here?"

Shay interrupted, "Leon can fill you all in later, but I've stayed here long enough, I need to see the remaining stones and get back to my people. We leave with the sun."

Leon lifted the box from a pack at his side and placed it on the table. When he opened the lid, Shay gawked.

"Now tell me, Shay, what's the mystery here?"

"It's one thing knowing these were here, it's another thing to see them sitting before me. These aren't mere stones, Leon. These are the highest form of imbued stones. They can only be used by those of us with Fae blood." Her eyes were as large as one of Ferschall's plates.

"You mean those of the Fae tribe?"

"No, I mean only a child of the Fae, no matter the tribe, can use one of these stones." Leon could see the question in her eyes.

"So, I can use them as well?"

Shay picked up the book and thumbed through the pages, "I don't know."

"What do you mean you don't know?"

"I've never seen a Bladed person attempt to use a Fae stone, much less one of these. I'm not sure you can."

"What do they do?"

Shay glanced up. "For a natural Fae? An imbued stone generally reduces or reverses the process of aging, depending on the strength of the power in the stone."

"You capture that power in the stones you throw, when using your powers, don't you?"

She nodded and continued turning pages like she was intentionally looking for something. Her answer came when she paused, "But these are different. These stones are all amber-colored. An amber sheen is a sign of the strongest imbued attribute.

"It means those stones were used on Fae and not just any Fae, they were used on Bladed Fae." She paused to look at each of them in the eye, "We don't have many laws where I come from but using a stone on another member of the Fae Kingdom is strictly forbidden, even for the few who are Bladed within our forest, killing any Fae citizen in this manner isn't allowed. Such an act is always met with a swift and immediate response. Death. There is no tolerance."

"Yeah, well, that didn't stop them when they were trying to kill Reed, Olwena, and the rest of us with stones like these during the wild hunt."

She nodded. "That would have been the only exception to the rule. You all trespassed into Fae territory and Reed is not of the Fae kingdom. I understand Olwena turned traitor and forfeit her protections. It would have been justified.

"Long ago, all Fae outside the kingdom, especially those that were Bladed, were hunted without mercy, precisely for the attributes these stones provide. While other stones fade away if not used in a few months and the effects from other creatures or people are only small, temporary enhancements, these stones never fade, and the attributes received from touching such a stone are not only able to reverse aging and add years of youthful vigor to a life, but they also grant permanent physical enhancements like strength or beauty or any number of other perks."

"Why carry them around then? Why didn't Dirk simply touch them all and absorb their power."

She shivered at the idea "Doesn't work that way. Touching more than one stone with less than a year to acclimate to the enhanced power you receive between each dosage is dangerous. The body can't handle such focused power. It was what killed many Fae during the times of the original Wild Hunt.

"Even worse, if you touch too many enhanced stones, over time the powers begin to bend the mind, similar to what happens to day-changing rogues who experience sun sickness. It isn't pretty. People who abuse the stones stay young well beyond their time, but not one of them has ever lived a life of sanity beyond a normal lifespan - it is the fate of the Ageless, both a gift and a curse."

"So, the Wild Hunt was started back when Fae hunted their own kind, yes?" Sved said.

Shay nodded.

"Dirk came to the convergence when the queen heard there was a Fae who could potentially fail the test for entry into the kingdom?" Leon added.

"I believe that's right. My sister, Queen Constance, was never the strongest or smartest of any of the three of us growing up. Yet she has matured into a fearsome dictator who has ruled the Fae kingdom with an iron fist. Despite our natural proclivity to despise authority, she has cast down two open rebellions and survived multiple assassination attempts on her life. I never even considered a possibility like this, but I feel I now know how she has managed to stay above the fray all these years.

"Ah! Here it is, on this page here!" Shay interrupted her train of thought while pointing down at a page in the Fae book which she had been casually flipping through, "This is the queen's journal. It looks to contain a consolidation of her research regarding how to most efficiently capture Fae Stones, but that's not what I was searching for." She traced a finger across a few lines, "None of you read Faye Skrill, do you?"

Everyone shook their head.

"It talks about some forest ruins north of the Northern Pass. It mentions a tree of power that steals the souls of those who enter. And just below that, here, it talks of how she found and touched her first Fae Stone. She was at least smart enough to leave out any mention of what became of my sister." She looked up, and her eyes met Leon's.

"Leon, I believe Airrene touched you with a Fae stone, and then sent you through the tree, perhaps to disguise and protect you."

"When was the last time you saw her?"

"Airrene? She went missing over twenty years ago, while our father was still king."

Shay's explanations helped clarify so much for Leon. It finally made sense that his body started changing earlier than most skin-changers his age. He was at least two years older than he looked when Gus found him!

Could it also be why I was always so scrawny growing up?

Shay continued, "She had this crazy notion to search out the lost cities of the Bladed ancients, even crossed the mountains in search of clues. She wanted to prove all tribes were factions of one people in a bygone era."

"So, back to the queen. She's been touching Fae stones imbued by the deaths of Fae people? How? You said this is outlawed, and that there aren't any Fae left elsewhere in Fayden," Reed asked.

"Yes, I don't think she could have pulled this off in our kingdom, but perhaps…perhaps there are more like Reed out in the world somewhere?" She paused to think. "We have a pact with the Vindarri. Very few know of this, but the queen takes Dirk and a few personal attendants to visit the Vin once a year. I've always stayed behind to oversee things in her absence. Now, it makes me wonder…"

"Why did Dirk have all of this on him?"

A lightbulb came on in Shay's eyes, "I just remembered something! This is the end of the summer season. The queen always makes a trip to the Vin this time of year. Only, with word of foreign armies and mountain spies this year, she was forced to send out a small contingent of diplomats to parley within the Quiet Forest in her place. I ignored it like I do every year. Most Vin I've ever met are self-righteous twits, I could never see the benefit in relations with them.

"Dirk was tasked to accompany the excursion. The queen must have sent word to Dirk of the presence of Reed before he made it home. I bet he split off from his party in an attempt to capture another amber stone! In his arrogance, he carried her most precious secrets off to be recovered by you, Leon." Shay laughed darkly. "The young fool could have never guessed that things would play out the way they did!"

# # #

Madam Hazzel and Ferschall burst into the room. Leon had not once seen the old matriarch ruffled in the least, until now. Her voice quivered when she spoke, "The Fang Guard is searching our Market. They claim to be seeking a Fae traitor in possession of an extremely powerful artifact of Fae Royalty. I have word the accusation is backed by both the Fae and the Vin delegations! Sved, tell me you haven't gotten us mixed up in this, no?"

"It isn't how it looks. We have to get Shay to safety," Leon responded.

The woman ignored him and continued to look at Sved. Ferschall waited quietly at her side.

The little man gave a nod of agreement. "There is more here than we have time to pour over, but Leon is right, it isn't how it looks. It's time we left anyway mother. The true invasion is coming. Any hope for a unification of the Fayden Kingdom has dissolved. There is nothing more we can do here, yes?"

"And what of them?"

Sved shrugged. "We bring them along?"

"Even her?"

Sved turned to address Shay, "Do you request the protection of the Otterkin Kingdom, and do you promise to, in no way, seek to undermine our authority or rule of law?"

"Yes." She didn't skip a beat.

Everyone stood up as Sved responded, "That's settled then, we flee Hollinger on the Brindle, yes?"

Kyra nudged Leon. "So, we're going to run from the wolves into the arms of the northern invaders?"

Sved chuckled at her. "Kyra, you've never been to visit the Otterkin have you?"

"No, why?"

"There's a reason why Fayden's smallest tribe in stature has never once been conquered, yes?" He proudly glanced at the faces around the room and sighed at all the owlish expressions looking back at him "Our kingdom is a network of islands in a land of swamps, continuously fed by hot springs and snow melts. Even in winter, our waters never freeze. And while they have never gone dry, us Otterkin are all very good swimmers! Even giants can drown in the byways of our swamps."

Kyra's shoulders relaxed. "Good! I'll get the others." She gave Leon a soft kiss on the cheek and hurried from the room.

Shay, too, left to inform her guard of their change in plans.

Leon pulled out Gus' medallion. Only Ferschall and Reed were left with him. He looked to Reed. "There's something else I need to tell you. I saw Shana and Cooper the day you were sold at slaver's port. They were staying with Ben and his remaining men. I think they were there to free Slade."

"Well, where are they now?"

"That's the problem. Ben is now allied with the Vin! I nearly killed at least one of their escorts trying to free them and even cut the fingers off another, then Shana flat out told me to get lost. They claim the Vin know of a way to get them home, I'm guessing they know the location of one of the remaining two Royal Trees."

As Reed studied the medallion, Ferschall inserted himself into the conversation. "Leon, I promised you a reward for what you did in bringing me my pottery, yes?"

"No worries, Ferschall. We can settle up later."

The old man chuckled but continued, "I think I know where."

Leon had to do a double-take. The old man wasn't making sense. "You know where what?"

"I think I know precisely where one of the last two Royal Trees reside! It took me a few days of research, but I thought that writing on the back of your medallion looked familiar. I have been able to decipher the messages! They are directions, yes? This is from the first age of Fayden. Back in a time of prosperity, when the seven tribes were ruled by Bladed leaders. Each emerald gem represents the location of an ancient stronghold," he flipped the medallion over, "each message corresponds to the general locality of one Royal Tree within the stronghold."

"Ferschall, that's great news, but I think I already know where one of the two last Royals reside. One is in the Silent City, and that's practically impossible to visit from what I've been told."

Ferschall shook his head like he was about to give some bad news, he pointed at one of the green emeralds in the center of the medallion. "The Silent City killed their Royal Tree ages ago after the first culling departed."

"How do you know that?" Leon asked.

Ferschall's excitement waned. "Because my father was of the Vindarri Tribe. Trust me when I say, nothing green thrives within the Silent City, but…" Ferschall's finger moved up to the topmost emerald on the map, "this is nearest to the Northern High Pass, where I suspect one of the remaining two Royals is located."

"It certainly matches up with what Shay was able to confirm from her book!" Leon said.

The others leaned in to follow Ferschall's finger.

Sved walked back into the room after a talk with his mother. When they filled him in on Ferschall's newfound discoveries and showed him the location on the medallion, he whistled, "Am I wrong or is that nestled up in the forested ruins just east of the Northern High Pass?"

Leon frowned as he realized something. "Ferschall, if that's the case then I think that's the tree I originally used to travel out of Fayden. How do you know it isn't withered like the Royal Portal was when we arrived?"

"Was there a fourth Royal in your world, near where you lived, that had withered and died after you arrived as a child?"

"No, actually, you're right! Gus and Ethan both believed no one had used a Royal Portal for hundreds of years. Gus would have surely known if there was another Royal that had withered in recent years!"

"So, you see, the tree may still be available for one to use, yes?"

"Then how come the Royal we used when we arrived died?"

"Ah, now, that is an interesting question!" Ferschall scratched his chin as he considered the implications, and Leon could tell there was a question forming on the tip of his tongue.

Reed cut in, "Still, guys, there's an army of giants about to attack that pass. Why would the Vin be helping Ben and his men to get all the way up there unless Ben shared our story with them as well, and they were working with the Fae all along?"

"Another good assumption, and I don't think it bodes well for your world or mine. We need to get to the Otterkin Kingdom first, then we must decide our next steps, yes?"

Haddie popped her head in the room. "Guys, we have to go!"

Reed clenched Leon's arm and brought him in for a half hug and a back thump before they too left the shelter of the Haberkorns. "By the way, Haddie filled me in on your trek behind the slavers. Thanks for what you did to free us."

"Are you kidding me? Have you met my fiancé? Believe me when I say any effort on my end was well worth the trouble buddy!"

# # #

Leon caught his first glimpse of the Fang Guard as he and his companions piled themselves and their gear onto floating barges tied off along Haberkorn Market shores. Haberkorn merchants had led the Guard on a merry chase through their patchwork maze of tents, but the officers had at least seen through the misdirection. They arrived to intercept his party just as the Otterkin were cutting the mooring lines to the barges.

Thick leather breastplates and scimitar swords appeared to be standard issue for all city guard warriors. Several stopped in their tracks and hunched over, changing form from the shadows near the edge of the market's tents.

When they straightened once more, ethereal howls broke loose from toothy maws. Then the lupine skin-changers charged the fleeing barge boats. Leon did notice one Fanged officer attempting to calm the situation and stop the impending violence, but he was utterly ignored.

A vain effort was also made by several of Sved's men to broker peace before the fighting ensued, but their pleas were disregarded entirely by the wolves. When one of the Otterkin was cut down where he stood, the remaining men fled back to the water's edge. Following their attempts to avert hostility, Otterkin men plunged into the river all around them.

Shay gave an order, and her people faced their attackers together. She and her Fae changed shape as well. Their eyes glowed purple and mocking laughter broke the spell of fear generated by the chorus of howls. Glowing stones were flung into the mob of charging warriors. A few went down. Some simply dove for cover. The majority made it to the shore without missing a beat.

Almost all of the barges were tied within relatively close proximity to the shore when the wolves attacked. Their lupine bodies leaped from the shoreline to the barges. Each of them came down swinging heavy scimitars at any target close enough to slash. A few of their savvier individuals grabbed anchor lines and flung them like grappling hooks, further pinning the barges in place. Kyra and Leon stood with her brothers and Grumpy on one barge. Dimples, Rezz, Merle, Ahab, and the Thunderbird stood on another.

The Fae were spread out over three more. Madam Hazzel, Haddie, Reed, and the two other Bladed Fae rescued with Reed were at the front of the line. They had boarded first and managed to disengage their lines and drift out far enough away that no wolves or grapples could reach their barge. No one else had time to do the same.

Leon gave a request through his Blade to Westley. The owl took flight before the first wolf made it onto his deck. He also sent a directive for Merle and Ahab to defend Dimples and Rezz.

Then the wolves came calling on his barge and his focus was pulled back to his immediate surroundings. He and Stonebreaker siblings met saber with Blade. The first wolf to come down attempted a quick slash at Kyra. She had already gracefully stepped back out of reach. Simultaneously, Fane darted in to stab his Blade through the wolfman's sword arm. Chocum went in low and cut his hamstring on a leg.

Daz simply stepped forward and kicked him square in the chest. Though the wolf-changer stood nearly seven feet tall and could move with lightning-fast precision, everything happened at once and the wolf had no room to dodge the big man's foot. He stumbled back and fell into the dark waters below. Leon only saw small ripples and a few bubbles break the surface above where the man sank. Small flickers of movement from below the surface told him Otterkin were providing some form of cover from below.

Then two more men leaped onto their boat. One well-timed swat from Grumpy took care of the first. The second one made a mistake when he tried to fight through the three Bearskinner brothers and forgot about Leon and Kyra. The two of them cut him down from behind and once again, a wolf was tossed from their boat into the water.

The fighting became hot and heavy from there on out. As soon as one wolf would make it onto the boat, another two were leaping in from behind. However, boarding room was limited and as the Stonebreakers all tapped into their Bladed gifts, the playing field remained level.

Kyra's strength surprised more than one wolf. Chocum could move with such superhuman agility he was able to dodge and contort himself out of every tight situation that came his way. Daz had a unique ability to roar. He could stop any wolf directly before him, dead in its tracks. Fane, however, was art in action. The man possessed a unique combination of speed and an uncanny ability to find weakness, which allowed him to go toe-to-toe, at least for short spurts, with a fully changed wolf.

Leon marveled at their prowess but, at the same time, did his best to remember his training. He would dart in and out of exposed openings when his attackers were distracted. His Blade was somehow always there to save Kyra from a powerful back-handed slash or a lunging stab from a newly arrived wolf and, thankfully, hers was there on more than one occasion to do the same for him.

The group worked well together and fell into a rhythm. Daz would roar to distract the incoming guards, while others worked to hack and push them back off the barge. Grumpy pretty much did his own thing, mauling anyone that came within his reach like some giant grizzly waiting on a fat trout to come jumping upriver, right into his angry paws.

Things were going better than expected until one wolf managed to grab hold of Daz as he fell backward into the Brindle. Kyra's brother didn't have time to react. He was pulled overboard and disappeared before even Chocum could nab his flailing arm.

There was a brief break in the fighting at about that time and everyone held their breath watching the ripples in the water until they heard sputtering laughter from the other side of the boat. Daz flopped up onto the deck smiling like a madman.

"Those wolves are fools to jump at us out here on the water! It's murky as can be down there, but I think there's an army of little furry Otter-men surrounding us, all armed with three-headed spears!"

It was true. Leon noticed with mixed feelings of relief and trepidation that not one wolf that went down had yet managed to re-enter the fight.

Everyone had a moment to catch their breath just in time for a larger wave of wolves to arrive.

"Incoming!" Leon heard Chocum yell. It definitely sounded like the brothers were enjoying the fight.

Leon remembered the anchor lines which held their barge in place. "Cover me while I cut these lines," he said. Then considering the other barges, "Everyone, cut your lines!" he shouted above the sounds of battle. He saw several individuals on other barges working frantically like him to sever the mooring lines and extract the improvised grappling hooks before the next batch of wolves arrived.

As he worked, he looked up and down the edge of the market, searching for any sign of the giant hippos he had met on the Murk Water river. They were nowhere to be seen. However, what he did see brought a smile to his face. Bound and gagged wolves were being spewed up onto shore about a hundred yards downriver. Their location was partially blocked from view, so their brethren on the shore would be hard-pressed to find them anytime soon.

Then the fighting picked up again and Kyra and her brothers fell back into their roles of harassment and attack, freeing him to finish freeing their bonds. Only one wolf managed to make it past their guard. He leaped onto their barge with two others. Leon looked up to see a wolf leering down at him at the last possible moment. Observing the bloodlust on that snarling face was enough to freeze him in his tracks. Just as the wolf lifted his sword to deliver the killing blow, Westley came diving in, attacking the wolf's eyes with his talons. The howl of pain was immediately silenced by Fane. No one came close to interrupting his work afterward.

A few more rounds of heavy fighting and the last line dropped free. Moments later, there was a large disturbance at the edge of their barge, just below the surface of the water. The slack grew tight on the ropes hanging from the front of the boat. The barge jerked forward, and everyone stumbled back into Grumpy at the sudden movement. Soon, Leon's barge was also too far from the shore for any wolves to board.

The fight, however, was still going strong. He looked back at the others. Shay was a one-woman wrecking crew with her long, delicate sword. She managed to injure or maim just about every wolf that landed on her barge. Her immediate guard split time helping her to clear the deck and slinging rocks at the steady stream of new arrivals. Dimples, Rezz, and Merle were also working well together while Ahab circled from above, diving down to knock wolves off their trajectories and into the Brindle as they leaped towards his floating barge.

The remaining two barges, full of the rest of Shay's guard, were not fairing so well. Leon could see that two of the largest of the wolves to have arrived had managed to find purchase amongst the Fae warriors and the results were devastating. More and more wolves leaped onto those barges, boarding, and cutting through the Fae like furry buccaneers from some lupine pirate ship until the few surviving guards simply bailed off into the water.

The small victory for the wolves, however, was short-lived. Those two barges mysteriously and abruptly sank. Then, the wolf guards who were on them were individually yanked beneath the surface as they attempted to swim for shore. Meanwhile, the few surviving Fae guards popped up beside the other barges and were quickly helped aboard.

Soon all the remaining barges were moving forward. The barges continued to pick up speed while a larger contingent of enraged guards kept pace at a safe distance from the shoreline. Yet the guards lost the race to the barges when the presence of buildings, interspersed along the water's edge, blocked their path.

An Otterkin man breached next to Leon's barge, nimbly landing on the barge deck. The man wore waterproof pants but was covered in a short auburn coat of fur. He shook himself like a dog and the water splashed everyone. His hands and feet were webbed, and his frame was sleek. The fur looked dry after only the one shake. He made an odd noise from the back of his throat.

A moment later his skin changed back to that of a little man and Leon realized it was laughter he had been hearing. He also realized he knew the man.

"Sved! What happened back there? Are your people going to be able to pull these barges for very long?"

"Ha, no. Wish we could have got going more quickly, but we had to round up transportation."

"What are you talking about?"

"We keep a herd of freshwater womb-fish close at hand here at the river's edge. They are powerful swimmers and will get us to our border in only three or four days."

"Womb-fish?"

"Sure, watch this." Sved slapped the water, and a sleek teal fin broke the surface, followed by a leaping green dolphin. As he continued to watch, several more dolphins broke the surface out in front, they took in air and re-submerged to continue pulling them forward.

"Man, that is amazing!"

"Good, now you all help me restack these boxes along the edges of the barge, yes? The Brindle narrows at the edge of the city and if there's a wall patrol nearby, the wolves may seek to cut us down with crossbows." Leon could see other Otterkin helping the remaining barges to shift similar piles of boxes and gear to provide the same measure of cover.

"What about the northern bank?"

"There's no bridge ahead. And the guard will all be coming from the southern portion of the city, yes? I doubt even the wolves have the speed to circle slaver's bay in time to catch us at the Narrows."

Leon and the crew quickly re-stacked their boxes to protect the southern side of the barge, then they hunkered down to wait while the dolphins pulled them toward the Narrows.

#

While the barges were still moving at a steady pace toward the edge of the city, ripples of water came closing in from behind. Before anyone could shout an alarm more Otterkin warriors surfaced holding up long hollow sticks as if they were hoisting treasured trophies. Shouts of celebration broke out among the ranks of their original Otterkin escorts.

"What's going on, Sved?" Leon asked.

"The city guard may have crossbows and arrows, but now we can fight them on an equal playing ground, yes? These men snuck back into our storage tents while you all were fighting off that pack of Guards. They brought back poison blow darts!"

The barge shifted and Leon could see the City wall ahead. Madame Hazzel in the lead barge spoke up, "Everyone who can swim, into the water. Now! Those who can't, take cover!"

Splashes could be heard all around them, and even Haddie and Madam Hazzel dove down.

Leon pulled off his shirt as he prepared to follow the Otterkin into the Brindle. He glanced over at Kyra and her brothers. They were in some sort of argument. Fane threw his hands in the air. "Leon, talk some sense into her, will you?"

"I don't need you to tell me what to do Fane, and neither does he. I'm a good shot with a bow, and so is Leon. There's no way we are going to leave Grumpy up here all on his own, are we?"

Leon, who was quickly trying to pull his shirt back on over his head, felt four sets of eyes on him. He opted to freeze where he was, afraid to pull his shirt down and see the steam coming from Kyra's ears.

I'm definitely going to pay for this later!

She threw her hands in the air and grumbled, "You are all free to go! But I'm staying!"

Minutes later Kyra, Leon, and all three of her brothers crouched down behind the cargo boxes while their barge slid quietly by the towering south wall. The Fae on the barges around them crouched together, their leather slings resting ready at their sides.

The barges had almost all made it through the narrows without a hitch, and still, there was no sign of the city guard. Leon breathed a sigh of relief. As if on cue, an arrow buried itself in the back of one of Shay's guards. The man screamed as he splashed back into the Brindle. A second later, a glowing stone struck the head of another one of her guards.

"From the north! They're shooting from the north!" Shay shouted.

Leon pivoted around, firing into the shadows with a bow he had been given back before the left Haberkorn Markets. It wasn't as powerful as Rezz's bow, but it got the job done. While he and Kyra continued to fire at vague shapes keeping pace with them along the shoreline, Kyra's brothers resituated crates once more to provide better cover for them all.

However, the effort seemed pointless. They weren't the target. All the aggression seemed to be aimed at taking down Shay's barge. Two of her Guards jumped between her and incoming arrows before Shay finally dove down into the safety of the River.

Three ghost-white Vin soared through the air to land on her barge.

Son of a biscuit! Forgot about the ups on those creepy white guys!

They immediately tore open crates. Leon tried to target them, but the enemy fire had shifted to the surrounding barges, and he was forced to dive down and take cover.

Meanwhile, the Vin wasted no time looting their treasures from Shay's gear. One of them pulled up the queen's journal and leaped off the barge. A second Vin lifted the box of Amber Stones and crouched down to make his escape when a dozen hollow reeds rose out of the water and turned him into a floppy pale pin cushion. Before the third Vin could respond, they did the same to him. Then, closer to the north shore, Leon heard the compressed puffs of dozens of oversized spitballs. Any of the surviving aggressors quickly retreated out of reach and discontinued slinging their arrows and stones.

Everything was quiet for a time, then Ben's voice spoke up, "Leon. Looks like you made it, boy. I didn't peg you as a survivor, but it's good to know I can still be surprised."

"Ben! You told me you were one of the good guys, what happened?"

"Oh, come on now, Leon! Grow up! There is no good or bad here. There's only survival or failure. Cooper told me you had some secret metal object. How about we make a deal? Pull the barges over, and I'll give you Shana in return for the scrap metal and the rest of those glowing rocks."

Kyra squeezed Leon's arm in encouragement, perhaps she thought he needed it. But Leon had given up being so easily ensnared. "If Shana's out there with you Ben, you tell her she made her choice when she dove off that ledge. I didn't leave her. You tell her I'll always be her friend, but I heard her loud and clear at the slaver's port, and I'm not interested in rehashing that conversation."

Ben lost patience and cursed before continuing, "I'm done fooling around, boy. This is your last chance, throw me the stones and the metal object!"

"Come and take it!" Leon yelled at the top of his lungs, with just a bit of his bear heritage tinging his voice with raw power and emotion.

There was a long silence afterward. Then Ben's mocking voice struck one final time, "You're a fool Leon and a traitor to your kind! You are going to be stuck here in some mythic level invasion while we head back for reinforcements. Don't worry, though, I'll make your old man pay for all the trouble you've caused me.. with interest!"

Leon screamed in blind rage and lurched forward ready to swim ashore and rip the man to pieces. The only thing that held him back was three pairs of brawny arms. Still, he fought against their combined strength, finding reserves he didn't know he had. He dragged them all toward the edge of the barge. It wasn't until soft but strong hands gripped his face and pulled his head around, allowing him a glimpse into the pale blue eyes of the most beautiful woman he knew that the fight in him finally slipped away.

Kyra drew him close and whispered in his ear, "Don't give in to his lies, Leon! Can't you see he's just trying to provoke you? He hasn't won, not yet!"

Chapter 29

Ben and his men disappeared after their partial failure at the Narrows. Leon was thankful for a brief window of peace and quiet. It gave him a chance to spend hours just talking with Kyra and, for the first day at least, it gave her brothers a chance to get to know him better. That first morning on the Brindle, their interest spiked all the more when he and Kyra explained how he was sort of from the Remnant. Though the revelation caused his stock with them to soar initially, it somehow dwindled back to normal over time.

They pestered him endlessly, nudging him to relay stories of his world, then they took turns solemnly shaking their heads in disproval or flat out laughing at how backward so many of his responses seemed to them. Kyra took a twisted sense of pleasure in allowing Leon to squirm under her brothers' inquisitions, but the smiles he received after suffering through those trials on her behalf were somehow always worth the hassle.

Like Gus used to say, sometimes you've just got to grit through the rough ride up to enjoy the pretty view down!

Before the first day ended, Leon convinced Kyra to hop barges with him and they were both able to spend time with all his companions over the next couple of days.

Kyra didn't take to Haddie quite as quickly as Shana had the first night they met, but Leon noticed their friendship developing more naturally, budding slowly as they spent more time around one another. Haddie had certainly lost some of the spunk she possessed when Leon and her first met. Strangely though, it seemed to make her an even better match for Reed.

Though Reed was still fighting his own struggles, her sometimes quiet moods did wonders to draw him out of his head as he attempted to distract her from the types of dark thoughts they both shared. Leon suspected it also helped her to truly get to know his quiet friend on a deeper level, especially since Reed had finally become moderately proficient in common Fayden. Their relationship was growing at a slower but richer pace than before.

Reed's new friends were interesting as well. Through snippets of conversation between them and Reed, Leon put together that those men had been shackled next to him and Rezz in the slavers' cages. Though they had been out for his blood on the night of the wild hunt, their shared circumstances, paired with the constant cruelty of the slavers, served to forge a bond between them all that went deeper than casual friendship. Somewhere along the journey, those men elected to take up the Blade when Reed made them the offer.

Initially, they feared reprisals when they learned they would be traveling to the Otterkin Kingdom, but Haddie and Sved forgave them the moment the men apologized for what they had done to them and their companions. There was an unspoken understanding between all of them that the deeds of that night would never be brought up between any of them again.

Surprisingly, the one person Kyra really seemed to enjoy talking to most, apart from Leon, was Dimples. It turned out that the stoic Hootsi was a bit of a shepherd himself.

In addition to the Anastashe cats, his clan raised goats, similar to Ferschall's, in their arid homeland. Leon found that Kyra was able to draw out details from his past that Dimples had never before discussed. He had simply never felt comfortable asking the types of questions about the Hootsi way of life that Kyra asked, mostly due to a lingering sense of shame over having been loosely associated with the men who slaughtered Dimples' men.

However, once Dimples warmed to Kyra's questions, Leon was able to join the conversation as well. The three of them exchanged many stories on ranching and animal husbandry, and Leon found himself warming more and more to the man's quiet confidence. Dimples, for his part, still held Leon's gift with animals in the highest esteem. He hadn't yet learned any of his Bladed gifts, but his adoration for powerful animals made him hope he might someday find he had access to something along those same lines.

Shay and her people remained cordial while maintaining a standoffish presence. Gone though were their cavalier attitudes and mocking laughter. Leon suspected they were well aware of the insult their kingdom had leveled against the Haberkorn heir.

Rezz was quiet. His eyes never left the northern shoreline, even a day after the attack was over his silent vigil continued. When Leon finally asked him why he was so uptight, he responded, "My people are hunters, Leon. They would never give up a fight so easily. Something is off, and I want to be ready when they spring the trap." The Vin Ranger's words sent a shiver down Leon's back and sobered him from the relaxation he had so easily embraced.

Soon though, Leon was distracted from his thoughts of pale-faced phantoms when Ferschall took a moment to pull him aside for a few questions of his own.

"Leon, when you all came through the Royal Tree, and the tree died, you had to have done something wrong, yes? What specific method did Ben use to open the portal?"

Leon considered the question carefully, then walked Ferschall through every step of the events of his last night back on the ranch.

"Hmm, yes. I suspected something like that, but you've shared more than I ever hoped to learn as well." He smiled his gap-toothed smile. "The method of carving the door into the exposed wood has been lost to us Bladed here in Fayden for generations, yes? You just confirmed the process for one of the most hotly debated techniques in recent history! One cut the outline of the portal out in one long cut, and then push the door inward! For centuries, many of our kind have suspected just such a process, but no one dared risk a Royal to prove a theory."

Ferschall returned to the original topic. "So, Ben received the direction from his father, yes? But he used a knife not a Blade to hack away the bark in small strips? No wonder the great tree died when the portal closed."

"Well, don't hold back. How come it died?"

"Wetting the wood with blood is tradition, but it is not necessary when one has a Blade. In order to restore a Royal after a portal is used, the bark must first be stripped in one solid sheet, yes? Then once the path is no longer needed, the sheet must be placed back over the portal. Only when these proper steps are followed, will the power that connects our worlds reseal and restore the bark, allowing for future use. With the portal damaged beyond repair on your end, it quickly consumed the power within the Royal on ours. That must have been how the ancient tree on our end dried up and died so quickly!"

Leon nodded. It made sense in weird kind of way. But then his memory with Shay came to mind.

"Ferschall, when I was pushed through the portal as a child, the last thing I saw was the Fae queen preparing to cut my mother down. How could that tree not have died if she struck my mother down? The queen isn't Bladed."

Ferschall sighed. "It is all guesswork now, but perhaps there was someone there with the queen, yes? Someone who knew how to seal a Royal?" He looked on Leon in compassion and spoke softly, "Or perhaps your mother was spared for a time?"

"You think there's a chance she's still alive?"

"No...I'm sorry, Leon, but the queen would not be who she is if she passed on such an opportunity. I think perhaps the more likely answer is that we have a traitor within the Bladed Society itself."

Leon's emotions were starting to fray at the ends just discussing the subject, so he changed the topic.

"So, what do you think Ben is going to do now? He only has two trees left on our end."

"I think Ben has figured out his mistake. While researching the script on your medallion, I learned that two of the Elders of the Bladed Society living in Hollinger had disappeared yesterday. After last night, I am concerned Ben may have those men."

Leon agreed, it sounded just like something Ben and his men would do. He just couldn't sort out why. Why was Ben so stinking secretive? Why wouldn't the man just ask for help?

Ferschall went back to reading some old scrolls and Leon was left alone with his thoughts for a while.

The Brindle was a big river, both wide and long. Though its depths were murky and slower moving within Hollinger, it had a north fork just west of town that carried more than two thirds of its reserves around the northern perimeter of the city, providing a natural fortification of sorts for the hodgepodge of ruins within slaver's port.

Along their journey, Leon noticed the Dolphin's progress slowed considerably once the barges pushed past the fork. The current continued to strengthen the further up-river they traveled. According to Sved, the waters grew deeper when they narrowed.

The night before they arrived at their destination the Otterkin men all bailed off the boats. Squads of little men spent the evening hours adding their webbed feet to the effort of moving upriver, helping to accelerate the slow trudge of the dolphins. Their efforts provided considerable influence and helped to push things along far faster than otherwise.

The Brindle grew a tad shallower and a lot wider by the time morning broke. Water was still moving but without the surging currents from the night before.

Three days after their battle in Hollinger, the barges crossed an arbitrary border into the Otterkin Kingdom.

# # #

As dawn broke on the Otterkin Kingdom, Leon's first impression of Sved's homeland was that if giant Cyprus-type trees and miles of bearded moss were major commodities, he could totally see how the little man's family had become filthy rich! Otherwise, he was at a complete loss.

Everywhere he looked, he saw clustered hamlets of dry land between towering rows of brown bark, surrounded by knobby stumps, poking up from crystal clear water. It was like looking into a Cajun swamp above the water and a deep mountain stream below. In fact, Leon and his companions quickly discovered they could peer over the sides and see clear down to the bottom.

Countless colored rocks along the bottom's surface sparkled back up at them in the glistening light of the rising sun.

Occasionally, young Dolphins could be seen dancing through the barge's shadow in the waters beneath them.

When he noted the seeming incongruity of habitats he observed, Sved explained that the clarity was because the waters were always flowing. The colored rocks were the remnants of some ancient glacier, carried down from the Anderle mountains that stood peaking above even the tallest of trees, while the warmth of the spring waters provided a year-round atmosphere that allowed southern trees to thrive in the northern climate, even over harsh winters.

When they officially crossed over into Otterkin waters, Madam Hazzel gave a formal speech to everyone in their party. "I hereby welcome all travelers under Haberkorn hospitality to the Otterkin Kingdom. You will be our honored guests while you remain!"

The sentiment was appreciated, but Leon thought the announcement was more for the faces he saw peeking between the wooded islands than for her guests on the barges. In any event, it took another half day's journey to the northwest before Sved informed them they were actually on "Haberkorn lands."

He was clearly proud to brag about his clan. "Our clan's home encompasses a tenth of the whole of the Otterkin Kingdom. It includes the northern boundaries of the realm."

"So, who's actually in charge of the *kingdom*?" Leon couldn't help but wonder if there was some otter king who might take issue with the Haberkorn's violent escape from the Northern Fanged Kingdom.

"No one...and everyone, yes? There are fifteen clans total within the kingdom, each with equal representation and voice on the council of elders. Madame Hazzel is our council's representative."

Just then the barges slipped past another set of islands to reveal a monstrous fortress Leon had not been expecting. It too was positioned on an Island. But where Leon had been anticipating some type of cozy hobbit hole-looking abode, he was blown away when he observed an actual full-sized castle!

"Welcome to Haberkorn Hall, Leon! What do you think?"

"I think I've been underestimating you at every turn since the day we met Sved! You never cease to amaze buddy!"

"Ha! Otters rule Leon, and don't you forget it!"

As the barges were being unloaded and the Leon and his companions were stepping off onto dry land, a large group of serious-looking red-headed men came streaming out of the castle gates, they were all armed to the teeth. Madame Hazzel went to intercept them and two of the little men grabbed her without warning, binding her wrists and tying them to a wooden stave above her shoulders.

Sved shouted and his men all moved to intercede for their matriarch. Yet still more guards came pouring out of the castle. Leon looked around and saw wicked-looking blow darts emerging from the water surrounding the barges.

"Sved, don't do anything rash!" Madam Hazzel cautioned her son as if speaking to a child learning a school lesson. "We will get this all sorted out soon enough!"

Soon, Leon and the rest of his companions were trussed up just like Madame Hazzel and frog-marched through the castle gate. Leon had to send a message through the Blade just to keep Grumpy and Merle from completely losing it when the little men attempted to herd them all to a holding cell apart from the rest of the group. He had seen the damage that a dozen poison darts could deliver, and he couldn't risk allowing his animal companions to forfeit their lives to fight a losing battle against the tiny aggressors.

"Sved, any idea what's going on?" Leon asked.

"Not yet, no."

Inside the inner courtyard, over a dozen immaculately decorated tables were set up. Sitting at the head of each table was a very severe-looking little person.

Sved spoke up to all of them when he saw the layout. You all try not to say a word, yes? Leave this to us."

A solemn white-bearded old man got up from his place at the head of one of two middle tables and rang a bell three times to quiet the crowds once everyone was seated once again. Then he pronounced in a sad, gravelly voice, "Two days ago, we received a writ from the Fang Kingdom's capital by way of Nesting Doves. The message has been confirmed twice over, yes?

"The Haberkorn clan attacked Fang guards who were peacefully attempting to apprehend known fugitives of the Vindarri and Ageless Tribes. Unless those fugitives are returned immediately to Hollinger, the Fang Kingdom will levee a tariff on all merchant trade coming from the Otterkin Kingdom, yes? Haberkorn Market Holdings are already forfeit and will be liquidated to recompense the aggrieved. What say you Madam Hazzel?"

Madame Hazzel stood up to her full height and glared back at the little old man penitently sagging in anguish before her, "I say you're still diving after shiny rocks in waters too fast and too deep for your flaccid flippers Hagglesneed Boarbuttons, you pompous twit! I'll wager this whole mix up has your slippery little paws written all over it, yes? Now, someone untie me, or has the council sunk so low as to pronounce judgment before hearing reason!"

Her outburst kicked off a tirade of angry little voices all speaking at the same time but, eventually, her bindings were cut, and questions were directed her way.

Leon felt the proceedings might have been over within the hour if someone wasn't always interrupting someone else. By the time evening descended, the council had still only managed to create a verbal maze of rabbit trails.

In fact, just as Leon dozed off a guard kicked him and ordered him up. "Where are we going?"

"You lot will be held in the dungeons until a Fang delegation arrives to take you back to Hollinger to suffer for your crimes," the little man confessed in a soldier's cadence.

Leon looked around. "Where's Sved and Haddie?"

"On house arrest with the rest of the Haberkorn clan for their part in the disruption of profits. Move it already!" He poked Leon in the back with a long, pointy stick.

Shortly after entering the underground prison, Leon felt Merle's presence. If nothing else, Leon drew comfort from the fact that his animals would be waiting nearby when they were locked away. Everyone was confused and angry, but no real answers were given.

#

Late that night, Leon was nudged from sleep by Fane. "Wake up, there's a light ahead. Someone's coming."

Sure enough, a small candle drew closer and closer until a robed figure lifted a hood and a bundle of wavy red hair spilled out behind a sad smile. Haddie deftly worked the keys, releasing the dozen or so cells that held Leon and all of his companions, including the animals.

"I'm so sorry, everyone. Follow me. Sved and I are going to get you out of here," Haddie whispered.

Reed stopped her. "Are you sure you want to do this? Aren't you and your family on trial, too?"

A coy smile split her cheek. "Oh, Reed, you have so much to learn about Otterkin politics. We may be small, but we aren't dense. Despite what Hagglesneed Boarbuttons may want to believe, Madam Hazzel carries more water on the council than he could ever hope to wield, yes? When she warned of conspiracies and an impending invasion, others listened. Over half the guards from the other clans have slipped away already this evening. The castle will be back under Haberkorn control within the week, but Madam Hazzel doesn't want to set you that far back in your mission. You're leaving tonight!"

"Wait, you got all of that done during that complete meltdown in the courtyard earlier?" Reed sputtered.

"No, silly. The argument was just for effect. The real negotiations were done behind the scenes, yes? You didn't notice all the notes behind passed back and forth that whole time?" Haddie looked genuinely worried for her boyfriend.

Kyra thumped Reed. "I think this is where you say thank you and keep moving."

377

A little way deeper down into the dungeon Haddie slowed her march. "Oh, here we are!" She led them into a dead-end corner cell at the very back of the dungeon corridor.

"Thanks," Reed mumbled.

Haddie winked at him, then fumbled around with the bricks on the back wall of the cell until a gear popped and the wall folded inward, revealing a well-lit corridor leading down a short flight of stairs. Sved was at the bottom of those stairs lighting a sconce.

Sved hissed up at them all. "Took you long enough. Well, what are you all waiting for, a written invitation?" He mumbled as he turned and moved down and out of sight.

Leon reached out and gave Kyra's hand a squeeze and the whole group clamored down the stairs and through the secret passageway that Sved had lit before them. The passage was surprisingly large. Even Grumpy and his bulk could fit between the sconces with room to spare.

Sved led them around several twists and turns, followed by a long straight walk. Leon had no idea where they were going, and he would certainly be lost if he was suddenly abandoned. But the little man stopped when he came to a pool of water at a dead end.

"Okay, everyone. I've got waterproof bags over here." He motioned over to a pile of sleek-looking bags. "Put anything you don't want wet in there, then climb down into the pool and dive down and forward. You'll feel it open up above once you pass the rock ceiling. From there, you can swim to the surface.

"The bulk of your packs have already been moved to the small boats resting up top. We are standing beneath Glacier Springs Swamp on the north side of an island a good ways north of the castle. From here, I can take you to the plains of the Northern Pass. I believe that's where you need to go, anyway." He gave Ferschall a nod, and Ferschall returned his nod with a bow.

Leon looked back at his animals and motioned for Sved to come near, "My friend, there's only one way I feel I can ever repay you."

Sved's eyes grew large, and a greedy little smile split his beard when Leon laid his hand on the case carrying the gold on the back of the Thunderbird.

"Ah ha!" Sved exclaimed. "I knew you wouldn't forget about your good buddy Sved!" He rubbed his hands together in glee and said, "Give it over, Leon. I'll take good care of it for you. May even make a little interest off it before you return!"

Leon reached forward, grabbing the reins instead and dumping them in Sved's hands. "As you wish, good buddy! I hereby leave this mighty stinky Thunderbird in your care and deed her to you for the rest of her life!"

Sved went pale. "What? You can't do that to me! What about the gold?"

"Oh yeah. Well, I'm leaving that in Haddie's care. But I think you're definitely getting the better end of the deal, don't you?"

Leon was still laughing when he packed Westley into an airtight bag and gave his other animals instructions on how to follow him down and up to the surface. All but the Thunderbird, at least.

Chapter 30

The next morning, when Sved dropped Leon and his companions off on the dry land of the north most tip of the Otterkin kingdom, all they could see before them were wide-open, straw-colored rolling hills. Way off to the northwest, hazy mountains rose, just peeking up over swaying grass. Closer still, immediately to the west of them, towering white-capped peaks dominated the skyline.

"I believe that tall crest just to the right there is where we are heading." Ferschall pointed to one of the small blips on the horizon, way off in the distance. Then he shouldered his pack, including a condensed repackaging of his odd collection of pottery, and trudged forward.

Leon took one last look back at Sved. "I hope to see you again, my friend."

"Yeah, well, I still owe you for *the gift* you deeded me, so you had better show up sooner than later and reclaim her or I'm apt to take up cooking, yes? When I do, my first order of business is sure to be a culinary deep dive on how to roast a pair of giant drumsticks!" His feigned anger faded. "Take care of yourself and those with you, my friend!"

Leon reached out and gripped the little man by the wrist. "I will, but drumsticks aside, you steer clear of any giants who come sniffing around. I know Haddie really wanted to come but tell her I'll do my best to send Reed back in one piece."

"You'd better or she'll be leaving you and me both in pieces. And don't you worry about us, we'll know how to deal with overgrown meatheads around these parts. Been doing it for years!" With that said, Sved turned and pushed off from shore. Leon watched his little friend scurry back to the front of his boat where he gave out a terse series of orders to the men manning the oars.

He turned as well. With Kyra and his companions at his side and all their animals close at hand, he marched out onto the field, once more following the lead of Ferschall.

The hills were endless. Up one and down another. On and on they marched. They weren't necessarily moving with speed, but it was a steady, hurried pace. They kept at it until early afternoon when everyone agreed to stop and take a rest.

Leon was just sitting down next to Kyra when a *boom* like thunder split the air from somewhere far to the west. Everyone instinctively dove to the ground, driving themselves into the side of the hill where they rested.

That sounded like someone just set off a bomb!

After several long moments spent waiting for something else to happen, Ferschall climbed to his feet and scrambled up for a better view. He called the others up after him.

"I suspect the armies from beyond the western range have just broken through the Northern High Pass that separates Fayden from the rest of the world. If the sealed wall of the ancients is gone, we must hurry!"

Leon asked the only sensible question that came to mind, "How far is the wall from where we are standing?"

Though from the proximity and strength of the blast, they must have been close, Leon hadn't seen a hint of the infamous wall at any point during their travels so far that day.

Ferschall shrugged. "A half day west, maybe more, maybe less. Let's go."

Once again, the whole group took off. Their pace grew a bit more urgent. Then, before they had even cleared the next hill, Shay asked them all to stop. "Do you feel that?"

The others blinked until Rezz nodded back at her. "I feel it, too!"

A few seconds later, and everyone felt it, as well as heard it. The sound quickly intensified. The earth itself shook, and an intensifying sound of pounding feet came heading their direction.

"Impossible!" was all Ferschall managed to choke out.

There was nowhere to go and nowhere to hide, so they all once more ran to the top of the nearest hill and looked west, prepared to face the new threat now bearing down upon them.

Leon immediately noticed the heavy cloud of dust expanding outward as it approached. Eventually, those responsible for the dark cloud burst through the haze and into his field of vision over the top of a plateau, less than a quarter-mile away.

The earth-rattling pounding of feet wasn't from some supernaturally fast mob of marauding giants. Instead, the thundering emanated from the hoofed vibration of thousands of head of massive stampeding bovines!

Just like every other creature Leon had encountered in Fayden, these cattle stood at least a full head taller at the withers than any of the men in his party. Like American bison, they all carried the majority of their bulk in their shoulders. The largest specimens in the herd were covered in thick red fur with a pure black strip down the back, while the smaller cows amongst them were colored a solid chestnut brown.

All of them sported deadly sharp forward-facing horns, curved up like Spanish Fighting bulls. The herd gradually turned north, easing away from their position while still thundering up and down the grassy hills.

Ferschall did not appear to share Leon's relief. "That Aurochs herd must have been startled when the wall fell. I hadn't heard the fall herds were grazing this far west this year."

"Is that a problem?" Leon didn't see why Ferschall appeared so down about some stampeding cattle. Granted, they were huge and scary looking, but it looked like they were going to miss him and his friends by a mile.

"This could set us back to the point where I don't know if we can continue. By the time we make our way around the herd, giants could be swarming these hills!"

Leon still didn't see the problem. "Lighten up, Ferschall. Those cattle will be seven counties away before we make it to the next hill!"

"Leon, you sometimes use words that make no sense, but you're wrong about the 'cattle' being gone any time soon." He pointed further west. Leon could see the same dust plume growing way off in the distance. It continued far longer than a mile or two in length.

"Just how big a herd are we talking about here?"

"I once knew of an Aurochs hunter who was separated from his companions on a long hunt. He found a small herd bedded down in a cold winter storm, between himself and his home. It took him three days and two fingers lost to the cold to skirt around the main body of the herd. These hilly plains extend to the north and east further than the area of all six kingdoms of Fayden combined. They are a no man's land, and the size of the herds that wander here can be enormous. They have to be. The creatures that hunt them are dangerous as well."

Leon shrugged. "Fine, then we go through them?"

Ferschall and all the rest of the Fayden natives simply laughed. Shay decided to answer, "Those horns aren't for decoration, Leon. Even the smallest of the bulls amongst them would trample half our party to pieces and put up a good fight against that bear!" Even Kyra couldn't stifle a laugh at his expense.

Leon curled his upper lip and stood a little taller. "This may not make sense to any of you, but I'm a Texan, and not just any Texan, I cut my teeth on rough stock, both on the ranch and in the circuit. I may have been a calf roper on most days, but that doesn't mean I never cinched up on a two-thousand-pound freight train of nasty for a full eight seconds! If it's got horns on it, I can rope it, and if it's got hide on it, I can ride it! I've seen plenty in this world that has given me reason to pause, but cattle are what I know, and I'm not about to start backing down to no high-headed arm jerkers!"

When Leon finished defending his Texan heritage, he could feel his chest poking out just a little bit further than normal. Unfortunately, his impassioned speech didn't have the effect he had been shooting for. Kyra gave him the eyebrow and Reed just rolled his eyes before turning back to watch the endless herd of cattle now slowing to a walk as it continued its eastern trek. The rest of them gave him looks like he might be just a bit unhinged as they attempted to make sense of all the mixed English phrasing he had included in his impassioned defense.

Kyra eventually relented and gave his arm a sympathetic pat. She was the only one apart from Reed who had any idea what he meant when he talked about roping and riding, as he had educated her on such things during their time together. "Why don't you just show us what you can do, love?"

# # #

Leon practiced throwing a loop over Merle several times to get a feel for the braided rope he had bought from Slim. Wysman Slim had claimed it had been made of the impenetrable hide of some Rock Goat from the eastern coasts. Leon had been skeptical at best when said goat's hide was presented to him in the sliced-up form of a rope, but it did feel sturdy, and it definitely resembled the same thickness of one of his old reata ropes from home. It wasn't the stiff synthetic type of roping lariat Leon was used to using, but it was a tight rope that folded well and held a loop. It would have to do either way.

Thirty minutes later, and he mounted Grumpy with sixty feet of rope tied off to a hole punched through the top of the bear's saddle. A Honda Knot for a lasso finished out the other end of the rope. He sent a message to Grumpy through his Blade and they eased their way forward toward the now calm but apprehensive herd of cattle.

Gradually closing in on the grazing beef, Leon could see that a good number of them stood taller than Grumpy, and though the bear likely had most of them beat in sheer bulk, it was a close call on some of the larger bulls. One bull in particular took immediate exception to their presence. Walking out in front of the herd to meet them, he pawed at the ground and slung snot bubbles in every direction, challenging them with a not-so-subtle warning to turn back.

Leon eased Grumpy forward at an angle, aiming just to the left of where the bull stood. When they had just about closed the distance, the bull bellowed and made a bluff charge. It was what he had been hoping for. He spun the rope around and tossed a wide loop. It swallowed the head and luckily fell just right over both horns. It wasn't his cleanest catch, but he flicked the slack away and prayed it would do for what he had planned.

As expected, the bull put up quite a fight against the rope when it tightened around his neck. Leon sent Grumpy the opposite direction, but at an angle to keep from getting his leg pinched when the slack tightened.

He slowly fought the bull as it left the comfort of the herd. By some miracle, the rope and the saddle held. Nearby cows bellowed in alarm but mostly just watched the foreign struggle playing out before them.

Eventually, when Leon and his entourage were far enough from the herd, he attempted to send a message through his Blade to calm the bull. Only, it didn't quite work like he expected. The bull just continued to fight against the rope as he had all along, completely ignoring Leon's request.

Leon gave Grumpy directives to keep the tension tight and hopped off the bear's back. He approached the bull, talking to it softly, using his Blade, still attempting to calm the beast and win its trust. Only, instead of growing more docile at his approach, it grew more aggressive.

Leon suddenly became a target. The bull gave up on fighting the taught line and charged right for him. It moved fast. Too fast for Leon to consider a way out of the predicament. Then someone pushed him aside, causing him to tumble down just before the bull could trample him.

When Leon got up and dusted off his hat, his jaw about hit the ground! Standing there, talking calmly, and patting the nose of the biggest bull Leon had ever seen, was Dimples. He looked back and shrugged at Leon, "I am sorry to ruin your *ro-de-o*, Leon, but you looked like you needed help."

Son of a biscuit!

It took them all a bit of head-scratching to finally realize that Dimples had finally discovered one of his gifts. It also became blatantly obvious that Leon had grossly overestimated one of his own. Kyra was the one who sorted things out in the end. "Dimples must be gifted at developing an immediate bond with plant-eaters, while Leon is gifted at doing the same for predators!"

Once Leon came to terms with the fact that he would never be the horse whisperer he had always dreamed of becoming, he modified his plan, and he and Dimples went to work. In less than two hours, using Leon's roping skills to separate the surlier individuals from the herd and Dimple's gift to subdue and calm them, they managed to domesticate fifteen large bulls. Then Dimples used his gift to make certain each bull would be a willing mount for one of their companions. Shay's guard had been significantly decimated, but several of the guards remained.

Leon stood by, amazed at how deftly Dimples took to exercising his gift until Ferschall quietly took him aside to explain. "I think Dimples always knew he had a gift for animals, yes? Even you, Leon, are likely going to be better on some level at working with those bulls than any of the rest of us. I've watched Dimples attempting to exercise that gift on all of your pets for days. It didn't mean he wasn't honing his skill at using his gift, just that he wasn't applying it appropriately. Now though? Now we see what he was truly meant to accomplish!"

That night, under Dimple's guidance, they rode their cattle straight through the lumbering herd of Aurochs without causing the herd to bat an eye. Dimples had been simply amazing. He even convinced one to allow Merle and Ahab to ride on its back. He had them all form a ring around Grumpy, escorting him through without causing too much alarm to the herd at large. It was a special moment, one Leon certainly wished Gus could have been there to witness.

# # #

Leon awoke with a funny feeling early that morning. It was still dark but something in the air just wasn't right. He fumbled for his Blade and his vision sharpened. As he concentrated to pinpoint what woke him, he closed his eyes and extended his senses, testing the air. All at once, his sense of smell improved dramatically. It took him a moment to come to terms with the sensory overload, and then a bit longer to identify the scent wafting in on the west wind.

It was fear. Somehow, he was smelling fear, but not just fear. Fear mixed with sweat and exhaustion. He looked down and saw his hand still clinging to the hilt of his Blade.

Perhaps another newfound gift?

The thought excited him until he realized what the gift was telling him!

Someone…no, several someones were about to run right through their camp. He sprung to his feet, facing into the west wind that brought the scent into his face. Across the camp, he saw Daz standing much like him, looking out into the darkness beyond.

"You smell something off?"

Daz flashed a smile and tilted his head. "You are full of surprises, my friend." Then louder, "Everyone, wake up! We have company coming soon!"

The first of the shape-changing wolfmen to clear the rise found himself eye to eye with a giant bear. He skidded to a stop. A dozen fiercely sharp Aurochs horns had him surrounded in the blink of an eye. The people riding the beasts were just as intimidating. He fell to his knees and transitioned more fully into his human form. They gave him some time to compose himself, then Ferschall spoke, "Would you like to explain why you've been running yourself half to death?" Leon suspected he knew the answer, but they needed the details.

"Giants!" the man panted. "Giants have breached the wall! One moment…it was standing strong…the next, it was blown to pieces and crumbled to the ground!"

"You were attacked?"

The man shook his head emphatically. "Not that anyone could see. A huge army was camped miles away, but they weren't attacking. The wall was just blown apart! Then they came!" He looked back over his shoulder. "They are still coming. If you value your lives, flee. But have mercy and allow me to escape as well!"

Ferschall shook his head and there was just enough moorlight for the man to see him gesture, "We are heading that way, yes? You are welcome to join us, or you can continue in the direction you choose, but that is up to you."

The man's eyes bulged, but he accepted the decision, "Let me go. You all have to be fools to go that way. Brave fools, but there were many at the wall who stayed to defend what remained. They were brave, too, but it didn't slow the tide of enemies now pouring into our lands." Without another word, he shouldered his way through their ranks, changed back into his wolf form, and took off once more into the night.

Dimples wheeled their mounts and behind Ferschall's lead they all took off once again. They passed many more deserters before dawn. All of them fleeing the giants' army. They didn't bother to stop any of them again.

Morning brought them much closer to their destination than Leon would have expected had they not been riding swift-footed cattle throughout the night. So far, he had seen no sign of the giants who were allegedly pursuing the fleeing guards. But that didn't mean they weren't near. Everyone kept an eye peeled each time they topped a hill.

By midmorning, the terrain changed. They were at the foot of the mountain range and the once gentle hills turned steep, gaining altitude. Dimples sent the cattle back to the herd with their thanks, and the companions soon found a natural game trail leading up into the highland forests.

Trees that looked like pines appeared more frequently as they hiked up out of the grassy plains. Leon had a funny feeling he had seen those trees before. Until it dawned on him just where he had seen them. He gave Shay a questioning look. She nodded back and patted the bark of a nearby sapling, "Yes, I recognize them, too. This is no coincidence. We are getting close."

As the group approached a bend in the switchback trail they followed, Leon heard an awful screeching noise from just up ahead.

Some animal was clearly angry and in pain. When they rounded the bend, the hairs on his neck stood on end.

There in broad daylight, next to the still bodies of two men, stood a fully changed Hootsi woman. She was chained to a tree by her neck. He took a step forward, and she lunged at him, but her chains stopped her short. There was just enough slack for her to entirely block their path up the remainder of the switchback.

The looks on the faces of his companions told Leon they were all as horrified as him at what they were witnessing.

Reed gasped. "A rogue!"

Shay clucked her tongue, "We need to put her down quick, it will be a mercy." One of her guards pulled out a leather slingshot and loaded a stone.

"She's right." Rezz said, "No good can come of appeasing a Day Walker."

Leon jumped between the rogue and the Fae. "Wait a moment. Let me try something?" All eyes turned to him.

Even Kyra tensed up, though she still gave him an encouraging nod.

He turned to face the Hootsi once more. As he stepped forward, the woman growled and backed down into a crouch. He continued to walk forward until he was just beyond the reach of her chain. A firm hand gripped his shoulder and Dimples stepped gingerly to his side. Neither of them made any sudden moves. Leon spoke calmly to Dimples. "You have any experience with this?"

"Some. The light of the sun addles their twisted minds. The times I've seen it happen before never ended well. But I've never had a Blade before either."

"Any advice?"

"Don't look her in the eye and don't turn your back, even if she calms. She is a day changer now. She cannot be trusted ever again."

The Hootsi continued growling low the whole time they talked. Leon squatted down on his heels and dug out some jerky Sved had given them for the journey. He gently tossed it a foot or two within her reach.

The woman's nose quivered at the scent of meat. She shifted over, and Leon got his first good look at one of the men lying beside her. It was Cooper!

The shock threw him off balance. He landed on his butt and crab-walked backward when the Hootsi sprang at them again. Dimples held his ground and sang softly to her from where he stood.

Leon turned back to Reed, "It's Shana! They did this to Shana! And that's Cooper, I think he's dead. We can't leave her like this Reed, we have to try to save her!"

The rest of the morning was spent feeding Shana jerky and attempting to coax her back into her human form. Everyone had an idea they tried, but nothing they did seemed to have any true effect. Their attempts lasted through the noon hour and by early afternoon Ferschall split time scouting their back trail and brainstorming ways to calm the rogue with the rest of them.

Shay empathized with Leon over the loss of his friend, but in her eyes, Shana was already gone. She saw what stood before them as an impediment meant to slow them down from reaching whatever lay beyond. Kyra gave Leon her full support, though Leon could tell she carried some uneasy tension in the way she would randomly glance over at Shana's crouching form.

Everyone was restless. However, Leon's biggest ally in delaying the inevitable surprised him. He didn't know whether it was Dimples' uncompromising sense of Hootsi honor or a certain nostalgic empathy for another outcast of his own kind that drew the man to his cause, but he was thankful for the support.

I know she's in there somewhere. If only I can find a way to get through to her, there has to be a cure! I can't give up on her!

Late in the afternoon, Ferschall came sprinting back up the trail. "There is a group coming up the same pass we followed! I'm sorry, Leon, we need to get moving."

"Giants?" Leon asked.

"Too far to see anything clearly, I just saw movement and caught a glimmer in the sunlight."

While everyone but Leon turned to study the trail behind them, Dimples drew his Blade and stepped forward. Right into the boundary of Shana's chain. Leon saw what he was about to do and rushed to stop him, but Shana was faster. She pounced on the man knocking him to the ground with her unnatural strength and speed. He held her off by the chain at her neck, keeping her fangs from finding purchase on his face. Her claws sliced right through his leathers, opening bloody seams down his arms and torso.

Still, he held her. With his free arm, he plunged his Blade into her side.

Leon screamed for him to stop, but the deed was done. Shana immediately shriveled in on herself. Her fight weakened. Still, Reed held the Blade in place. He didn't remove it until she changed back into her human form. Her light gray fur subsided, claws retracted, and her beautiful features reappeared.

Reed rushed to her side. He used his gift to heal her side and seal the wound. Then he administered aid to Dimples as well.

Dimples bowed to Leon. "I am sorry I hurt the girl. Sometimes the only way to heal though is to endure a little hurt. I swear to care for her until she recovers."

When he was done, they broke her chain's shackle from the nearby tree. After they bound her wrists and feet, Dimples scooped her up into his arms and carried her up the trail. No one said a word as they followed.

Cooper was long gone. He, too, had been shackled to the tree.

Leon flipped the other man over but didn't recognize the face. Neither did anyone else nearby. However, when Leon shifted his coat and saw what rested by his side, he froze, the man had been Bladed.

"I think they killed this guy!" Leon frowned.

"It doesn't look like he went down without a fight though." Reed pointed out several puncture wounds in Cooper's chest, all the size of a Blade. Just up the trail were the warm ashes of a campfire.

Ferschall walked over and peered down. "I knew him, or knew of him. He was an elder in Hollinger's Bladed Society. Whatever happened, we have to get going, yes? We can't stay here." Ferschall got everyone going once more, but before he started back up the trail, he gave Leon a sad look that seemed to confirm both of their fears. Ben was up to something dangerous.

They continued on that way for another hour until they came to some old ruins. Worn and crumbled stone once supporting beautiful buildings and elegant homes sparked an all too familiar memory for Leon. The dilapidated debris was remarkably similar to the ruins from Ferschall's home, back in Hootsi territory.

Ferschall scouted out a safe place to hole up until morning and promised to do a more thorough job of scouting the area to find the Royal Tree, as well as those who had left Shana in her current form. Reluctantly, Dimples acknowledged he was best suited to help Ferschall and left Shana's side for the first time since lifting her that afternoon.

"I'm coming, too," Leon said, "I can bring Westley, Merle, and Ahab to help. The eyes from the air should help things go quickly."

He could tell Kyra didn't like leaving his side. But a smaller party was less likely to be seen and, with Reed staying behind to continue helping Shana with his gift of mending, Leon was confident his ability to work with his animals would give the scouting party an edge.

Chapter 31

Leon and the others spent the better part of the evening tracking their quarry over inhospitable terrain. Soon though with the help of Leon's animals, they managed to flank a large camp of people from downwind.

Evening had settled in when he and his companions got their first look down into the camp. The hike up the hill that evening was a hard steep climb, and the bare cliff face gave no protection from the chilly north wind. Leon had to will himself against allowing his teeth to chatter in the frosty mountain air.

Rounding the cliff, the forest ruins tapered out, funneling up into a point. At the terminal end of that forest, stood an incredibly large Royal Tree. Beyond it were the cluttered remains of another ancient ruin followed by another steep drop-off. The tree itself was just like Leon remembered from the childhood memories he and Shay had so recently recanted.

The camp had been positioned between the edges of the forest and the Royal. It was illuminated by a large fire. The only person he was able to identify was Ben and only then because he could the big man's self-assured strut from a quarter-mile hike up a mountain. Ben appeared to be busy giving orders and hurrying people along.

Leon and the others crept down closer, and things grew easier to distinguish. Leon could tell there was a trio of prisoners sitting near the fire. Their arms were bound to staves above their shoulders and they were lying down, flat on their stomachs. As the guard watching over them moved up and down their ranks, Leon could see a long strip of golden-white hair reflecting off the flames.

"He's got Vin guards with him down there," Leon whispered to Ferschall.

"Hmm, yes, true. Dimples, you think you can get close enough to catch a snippet of what they are planning?" Ferschall asked.

The Hootsi's only reply was a sharp nod. His black outfit and stealthy skills allowed him to completely vanish from their side without a sound.

Leon felt wetness strike his cheek. He looked up when another tiny little icy sliver hit his arm. It was rain. A steady dribble of misting rain was just beginning to fall.

Better cold rain than snow or sleet.

"Ben wasn't simply here to re-enter our world, was he?" Ferschall asked.

"The only thing he ever told me was he planned to take back the land he thought was his birthright. I've been thinking about that though. I think it's more than that, I think that for people like him it's becoming really hard to hide their identities in our world. With the technical advancements and large populations, it's a miracle people don't know about skin-changers already. If they ever do find out, it could be bad, real bad. I think Ben is looking to carve out a place where he can flee in case things go bad on earth. I don't think he plans to stay here, not now at least. I just can't puzzle together why he's so secretive about it. There has to be something more, you know?"

Ferschall grunted. "Not surprising, people like Ben bluster about justice and causes, but in the end, they are usually only motivated by fear. You see, I've been busy these last few weeks, yes? I've made inquiries and have learned that Ben has used his newfound connections within the Vin to begin stockpiling odd materials, almost like he is planning something big. He has stash houses all around Hollinger.

"The Bladed Society may be fewer in number these days, and we are less tolerated year by year, but there's still quite an extensive network of us out there."

"Wait! You're part of that Bladed Society? Why are you just telling me this now?"

"Because I think Ben is planning something and bigger than both of us, yes? I have no doubt he has weapons that make him very dangerous, but there are other dangers beyond our borders worse than giants. Now that our borders are exposed, and our kingdoms are falling into disarray, I fear he will be making a move to grab power.

"Only, he doesn't know just how dangerous our land is going to become. None of the Unbladed these days really understand such dangers, yes?"

"What kind of dangers?"

"Old foes and savage monsters will find their way here when they learn of our vulnerability. We can't allow him to destabilize the independent kingdoms of Fayden for his own purposes or the empire itself may fall, no?

"Leon, I'm sorry to tell you this, but we may need to sever their connection to your world before you ever have a chance to send word home. Is that something you feel you are able to do if needed?" Ferschall turned and looked him in the eye.

Without flinching or hesitation, Leon responded, "I'll do what needs doing."

Ferschall gave him a warm smile in return, "As will I, my friend," then he thumped him on the back. "Good man."

Before long, Dimples returned, silent as a thought. But before he could relay what he had witnessed, another commotion took place below.

Leon's stomach dropped when he saw most of the rest of his party being marched out into the firelight. The ones who could still walk were helping those who couldn't. He released a breath he didn't know he held when he saw Kyra still standing upright. Her arms were bound, and she had a slight limp, but she seemed to be walking on her own.

Chocum was now the only brother with her. He carried Shana over his shoulders. Shay was carried by one of her men. Reed and the rest of the Fae, including Grumpy, were nowhere to be seen. The remnant of their group was surrounded by several Fae soldiers, all armed with swords and slings.

Dimples broke the silence. "Those in the camp are waiting on more people. A lot more people."

# # #

Leon and Merle followed Ferschall and Dimples halfway down the steep cliff, closer to the camp. Ahab and Westley continued to circle high above, well out of sight. Once they were close enough to make out individual faces in the fire, Leon saw more movement from the south side of the camp.

To his surprise, Slade Jung came strutting out of the forest, looking as big and mean as ever in his human form. Following him were two similar-sized men, a Vin with an eye patch and a Fae warrior, as well as two others who Leon didn't know. These normal-sized men were followed by a dozen massive bodies that stood at least half again as tall as Slade.

Ben's celebratory greeting could be heard from all the way to where Leon sat. The leader jumped to his feet and walked forward to clasp forearms and embrace his subordinate.

"You did it, Slade! Took the wall down and forged a treaty all in one move! Genius, brother, pure genius!"

Yet not all of the giants following Slade stopped behind the big man. One walked over and stomped on the head of one of the three original prisoners lying prone on the ground.

Ben stopped gushing over Slade, long enough to start yelling at the towering meathead. The Vin soldiers standing behind Ben appeared to be caught off guard. They jumped up and drew their bows, aiming at the giants behind Slade. Yet before a single arrow could be released, a barrage of purple stones struck them from behind. The Vin with the eye patch standing next to Slade didn't lift a finger to help his tribesmen.

Ferschall gripped Leon's arm, "Deceit within deceit! Patience Leon but be ready. We must find the right moment!"

The ambush was over quickly. Ben broke away from Slade and his men, belatedly yelling at the Fae to stop the attack. He stepped over a dead Vin as he approached the obvious leader of the giants.

The rain fell in a solid mist, but Leon could still clearly make out the scene around the fire. Cold cruel eyes looked down on Ben from a pale blue-skinned face, painted over in black splotches, appraising his every move as he drew near. The giant and his men all wore their blue-gray hair long and loose in heavy knots. The giant's chests and legs were enveloped in thick furs. Even still, muscles bulged where fur failed to cover.

Ben ignored the obvious danger oozing from every pore of the leader standing before him. He spread his arms wide and looked up at the expressionless behemoth as he spoke in an authoritative voice. He was talking in the Fayden tongue and his grasp of the language sounded almost native! Leon caught Slade making a motion to the giant from behind Ben's back. Then, as if swatting a fly, the giant swung a club that looked to Leon to be the size of a drive shaft from a hay tractor, caving in Ben's chest with one mighty swing.

Everyone in the clearing below stopped what they were doing. Ben's knees hit the ground a second later, and he crumbled, face first, spitting blood the whole way down. The giant, at last, thundered out a retort, using a few words from a guttural language Leon had never heard. One of the men behind Slade answered the giant in the same language.

Leon heard deep rumbling laughter from the remaining giants, most of which had spread throughout the clearing.

The traitor, Slade, stepped up and motioned for Ben's remaining two men to stand down. Then called out to the remaining Fae, "Let's talk things over. Drop your weapons!"

Ferschall decided to act in the moment, "Now! The Fae won't take orders from non-Fae! We attack now! I'll go left, Dimples right, Leon, you and your animals hit them straight on!" and with that, they were racing down the mountainside.

As Leon dodged boulders and hurdled bushes with Merle at his side and Ahab and Westley swooping down from above, he could see glowing Fae stones bouncing off the hardened skin of impossibly large men. Rain clouded his eyes, and he squinted through the moisture, pushing himself recklessly faster.

Any of the remaining Fae who dared attack the giants with swords were immediately cut down by large clubs before they could move close enough within range to land a single blow. The one-eyed Vin and the Fae with Slade trained their ranged weapons on the remaining Fae and joined in the massacre. They saw Leon and his friends well before any of them were noticed by the giants.

Even sprinting at full tilt, he didn't fail to miss seeing Slade slink back into the shadows of the trees before the up-close fighting could really kick off. A few seconds later, he saw what looked to be some type of messaging flare shoot up above the tree line, from the woods where Slade had vanished.

He's calling back up!

He did his best to ignore the flare messages. There was nothing Leon could do about Slade. When he saw a number of the giants move toward the rest of the defenseless prisoners, his Blade pulsed, permeating him to his core with an unyielding feeling of true purpose and power. Something snapped together in his mind, bringing new clarity. There before him was a true enemy.

The giants weren't of Fayden heritage. They seemed off in some intangible way, twisted beyond the inherent disease that afflicted his people. The power in his Blade surged as he closed in proximity to their tainted presence.

For him, there was no longer any hesitation, no uncertainty in his path. He wasn't racing toward vengeance. He didn't nurse a need to make anyone pay. He simply saw the necessity to protect those he cared about from the pure malice before him. It was him or them, and the lives of his friends and loved ones hung in the balance.

He gripped his Blade tight against the palm of his hand. Strangely, its warm presence was the only thing that made sense to him anymore. He sent a pulse through his gift to his animal friends.

Defend the prisoners, attack the giants!

As he came bounding across the clearing and over the burning pyre at the center of camp, he announced his presence with a roar of defiance that rattled the ground under his churning feet. Even the giants paused to take a second look. Then, just as the leader closest to him lifted an arm to batter him down as he had Ben, Westley's talons raked down across those hateful eyes.

Leon wasted no time. He was so tied into his animal companion he had been expecting Westley to intervene just when he did. As such, he had never stopped moving forward. His leaped up at the last moment and buried his Blade to the hilt, straight up and under the giant's chin.

Before the first behemoth fell to the ground, Leon spun himself into the guard of the next two. They hadn't yet noticed their chief lay dead. Instead, they were busy staring up with concern as an adolescent griffin, the size of a full-grown jaguar came screeching down out of the night's sky.

Before they could even raise their clubs to batter him away, Leon's Blade was there. He sliced tendons and severed arteries. Skin that had been as hard and unyielding as stone under the attacks of the Fae soldiers moments before held no challenge for the edge of the Blade in his hands. Large bodies fell, shaking the earth all around him.

Two more broke away from the main group still battling the Fae and charged to their aid. They had seen the ruse he used with his winged friends and kept their heads down, eyes focused on him. Yet they failed to account for one other ace up his sleeve. Merle.

Leon's old ranch dog had been growing for months. His sizable mass either came from exposure to the new world or due to Kyra's gift or both, but for whatever reason, Merle would push the scales closer to the size of a full-grown male lion. He plowed into one of the two charging man-mountains, gripping a club arm within his vice-like jaws and whipping his head from side to side. They tumbled down together.

That left just one for Leon to deal with all on his own. The giant slowed as he drew close. He too carried an oversized club brimming with spikes on the end. He was angry but cautious Leon could tell he wouldn't be underestimating the ferocious little man before him. He circled to the right, but Leon couldn't allow anyone to come between him and those sitting defenseless behind him, so he attacked him head-on.

His first move was a feint and a pivot he had learned from his time with Kyra. The giant didn't bite. Still, Leon managed to catch the shaft of the club with his Blade before a backhanded strike could build momentum. It was a monumental struggle to hold off the giant's unyielding strength. In the end, he simply couldn't match the power. Even with both hands supporting his Blade, the giant forced him back down onto a knee using just one arm, then he backhanded him with the other.

Leon stumbled back several more steps, landing in amongst the still bound prisoners. He couldn't see any of his friends from where he fell, but Kyra's voice came to him from behind, "Leon, don't try to overpower them, use the Blade's strength, let it do the work." She washed away any doubt that was slowly creeping into his mind as he struggled back into a crouch.

He wiped away the trail of blood trickling down his nose and smiled without taking his eyes off the now laughing giant. "I love you, no matter what happens. You know that, right?" He didn't wait for an answer, didn't need one.

Then he charged back into the fight. He could vaguely hear her shouting his name and returning his love from behind, but his focus was honed on what was out in front.

The giant took a step back and held his club up, like a major league slugger getting ready to punish a walk-off homer. Leon stutter-stepped to the left and dove into a feet-first slide to the right, on the backside of the giant. The whoosh of the spiked ball passed just inches above his head. Then, before he slid entirely past, he turned his Blade and severed the Achilles tendons on both enormous feet. The giant fell to his knees screaming in agony and Leon wasted no time in jumping to his feet and putting an end to the big fellow's agony.

When Leon turned to confront his next opponent, he was face to face with seven more. While he had been fighting the others, they had apparently mopped the floor with the remaining Fae. There were no smug looks of disdain. No laughter. They backed him up until his back was to the cliff below. Then, one of them stabbed him in the leg with a long, wicked looking spear, while the next closest drew his club back for the *coup de grace*.

The pain in his leg was sharp but he ignored it as best he could. With nowhere to go and no time to block the final swing, he did the only thing he could do, he forced his grimace into a smile and raised his Blade in a silent taunt. He wouldn't go down cowering to the monsters before him, and he sure wasn't gonna waste a good one-liner on them either.

Then, a blur of motion took on the form of a man, dropping down from above. Ferschall kicked the spear back out of Leon's leg as he barreled in amongst them, causing Leon to stumble to the side. The old man caught the giants club with his Blade, and Leon was free to roll out of the circle.

Yet the strength of the blow crumbled the double-handed block Ferschall used to defend himself. The spiked ball on the end of the club was only partially deflected by the Blade. It still sank deep into his belly with a wet *thunk*. It was quickly torn free. Another giant backhanded Ferschall and the old man tumbled backward, stumbling off the cliff and into the dark chasm below.

"Ferschall!" Leon screamed out his name, but the sacrifice had already been paid. Ferschall was gone.

Leon didn't have time to think, he continued stumbling back out of the path of two more descending clubs, racing to create more space. Ahab dove through the ranks of those pursuing him, distracting them enough to give him some much-needed room to breathe. Then he took a sidestep and a hop when someone bumped his shoulder from behind.

Dimples caught him before he fell. The man gave Leon a bloody grin that spoke volumes. Something told Leon the Hootsi would no longer need to seek justice against Ben's two remaining men. Someone had managed to slice him from the outer corner of his eye to the bottom of his cheek, but he was still standing, more than Leon assumed could be said for Gunther or Griggs.

There was no need for words. Their battle was only half-done, and they hadn't killed enough giants to free their friends. Together they faced the inevitable, stubbornly refusing to admit defeat, even as it bore down on them with cold indifference in the eyes of the brutes before them.

# # #

Their standoff was a tense moment that dissolved all too unexpectedly.

Ahab came screeching down like a missile once more, heading directly for the giant fighting Merle, further back from the main group. Only, instead of veering off this time like he had before, the griffin struck the giant square in the face, simultaneously raking his back claws into the giant's eyes, and clawing deep furrows into its neck with his talons. His wings folded up over the head and shoulders. The big fellow fell to his knees, keening in agony, arms still locked in his struggle with Merle.

Then Ahab broke free, spinning nimbly from his face, just before a wild swing from the club of one of his comrades could connect. Instead of dispatching the griffin, the club ended the agony of the lacerated giant.

At that moment, an arrow connected with one of Ahab's wings. The griffin fell hard but managed to scamper into the safety of the trees before being caught. Leon spun around to see who had fired the arrow and felt cold malice creep back into his heart when he saw the Vin Ranger with the eye patch, walking back out into the firelight alongside Slade.

Merle followed Ahab off into the woods and out of reach. Two of the giants holding spears took off after them. Leon knew they would lose their pursuers in the wooded terrain and circle back soon enough. He steadied his resolve on those left before him. By that time, the Vin had an arrow trained on Leon, just waiting on Slade to give him the word.

No one expected the two giants to come bursting back out of the woods almost as soon as they had entered. Behind them was one angry, bloody, mountain of a bear. Riding above him, right into the middle of camp, was Daz Stonebreaker, and following behind was Rezz, slinging arrows mid-stride.

Forgetting Leon and Dimples for the moment, Slade, the Vin, and all the giants turned to face the new threat. Daz leaped from the saddle as Grumpy caught the first of the two fleeing giants from behind. He let loose one of his gifted roars, which momentarily stunned the group of opponents clustered before them.

Dimples wasted no time scrambling up the back of the nearest opponent and burying his Blade into its meaty neck as the big fella still struggled to regain coordination.

Rezz shouted some taunt at the pirate-eyed Vin, and arrows were soon flying between the former tribesman. They both dodged, zigging and zagging, and diving into the woods before disappearing.

Slade had already vanished again by the time Leon remembered to keep eyes on him.

That man's as slippery as a greased pig!

Over the din of the fighting, Leon heard someone calling his name, "Leon, the tree! Stop them from coming through the tree," Dimples yelled.

Knowing his leg was busted, and he would be a liability, Leon turned and stumbled back toward the tree. The odds had evened up a bit, and he had no choice but to trust that his friends and animal companions could hold their own.

He didn't pause to embrace Kyra. Both she and her brother were bound hand and foot with the crude chains of the Fae and there was only one way to buy them all the time they needed to free them, assuming Daz, Dimples, and Rezz came out on top. He simply continued to sluff forward on his good leg until he made it to the base of the Royal's trunk. The swirling dark opening was somehow still open.

It was obvious Ben had done his homework if the solid chunk of bark on the ground beside him was any indication. He could smell the tangy wild scent of pine sap flowing out from the corners where it had been stripped. Perhaps doing it the right way added time to the portal's existence?

The hairs on his arms stood on end in such close proximity to the power of the portal. Leon halfway expected more men sharing Ben's insanity to come marching through that darkness, right over the top of him, at any moment.

With Dimples taking out his two remaining witnesses for him, Slade would definitely take control, and with him in charge, there could be no telling what scheme he would try to enact. Regardless of how it played out afterward, Leon had no doubt he and all his friends would be instant collateral damage.

Only, he had no idea how to end the connection. He could try to stick the bark back up where it belonged, sealing the portal, but then those on the other side could simply create a new path. The tree was massive. Bigger even than the one through which they had arrived. He was still sorting through his options when a haughty voice from behind broke his concentration.

"Drop the Blade and turn around, you fool. You're in my way, and I want to look you in the eyes when I end you for the trouble you've caused."

Leon knew that voice. It was as slippery as it was arrogant. Though he'd only formally spoken to the man once, there was no way he could forget the disdain in his cousin Dirk's Fae accent. The man likely had no idea they were cousins and wouldn't care if he did. But Leon had one last possible ace up his sleeve with nothing left to lose.

He hobbled around to face the son of the woman who ironically ended the lives of both his parents in the exact same spot where they now stood. The tip of Dirk's sword pressed tightly against his neck, almost like he wanted some type of reaction from Leon so he might savor every ounce of fear and pain he could cause.

"You kill me, and you won't be getting any more pretty rocks anytime soon. Let me live, and I'll tell you where they are?" Buying time, he reached down with his free hand.

Dirk smirked back at him and put more pressure against his skin, causing blood to well up under the point of his sword. "That's one secret you can take to your grave. Slade and I have a deal. I help him get established here, and he lets me hunt Fae there."

"What about your men?"

Dirk smiled an evil smile. "Those fools weren't my men, they were my mother's pawns. Between Slade's GUN POW-DER here and my ability to increase power through the Fae in the world of the Remnant, we will reclaim the balance of power in both worlds."

Dirk, it seemed, viewed Slade's gunpowder as some type of magic. He also happened to be a hopeless narcissist who couldn't help himself from gloating.

This guy has obviously never been to the movies.

"So, that's your master plan, huh? Yeah, well, good luck with that. Slade had a deal with Ben, too. You saw how that worked out."

Dirk ignored him and scoffed. "Any last words? I kind of want to hear you beg, though it won't do you any good in the end."

As carefully as he could, using Kyra's promise cloth to protect his fingers, Leon reached into the one pocket that held several round items. He lifted his hand slow and easy, so as not to incite the young man holding cold steel to his neck, and gently placed a glowing stone on the flat edge of Dirk's sword. The man's eyes grew wide, reflecting the amber light pulsing off the stone. "I bet Slade didn't mention there are no more Fae left in our world? Reed was one of the last, if not the very last."

Dirk shifted to study his eyes and read the truth behind Leon's words. Then his focus returned to the stone. Leon saw a hungry look start to form where only disdain had been present moments before. He didn't notice the extra bulk resting within the fabric still wrapped around Leon's hand.

While Dirk was still pondering the stone on his sword and the revelation Leon had just leveled, Leon took the opportunity to toss four more of its companions into his face. Dirk only had time to flinch before the first amber stone struck him.

Each stone lost its color as it bounced off the bridge of his nose and fell to the ground. At first, Leon felt a chill of doubt like he had been wrong about the stones all along and now he might die from some foolish assumptions. But when Dirk continued to remain still and unblinking, even after Leon took a step to the side, he knew something significant had happened to his estranged cousin.

Leon limped around behind him, noticing the glowing amber and purple lines working their way through veins and capillaries as they crisscrossed his face and crawled down the back of his neck. The tainted coloring flowed out into his arms, down to the tips of his fingers. When Leon came to a stop directly behind him and the man still hadn't moved, Leon whispered in his ear, more for himself than for his cousin. He was doubtful Dirk could still hear him.

"For what it's worth, you were never my enemy, cousin. I forgive you for what you've tried to do to me, but I can't allow you to do what you have planned for others. Hope you end up in a better place…but I doubt you'll be back to tell me about it anytime soon."

He then reached around and snatched up the last stone, still balanced on the edge of Dirk's sword, before he gave the frozen body of his cousin a gentle shove forward. He tumbled into the void and was immediately sucked into its inky blackness. Leon didn't spare him a second thought.

Only two giants were still on their feet in the battle back near the center of camp. Win or lose, Leon suspected more giants in the valley below would be coming to check on them all sooner than later. He and all his friends were living on borrowed time. But he could only control what was in front of him. He had to make certain the tree was out of commission before Ben's backup came to call.

He glanced back and glanced at Kyra while he puzzled over the problem of the open path to his world. She seemed torn between watching over him and her brother, her head was on a constant swivel between him and the battle on the other side of the camp.

Chocum did his best to comfort and encourage those around him. The selfless noble gestures and smiles of the tough savage-looking young man brought back memories from his childhood. He thought of the stories Gus used to share. His Blade pulsed at the same moment as more of those memories surfaced in his mind and Leon remembered a particular story Gus had told him years ago, the pertinent part involved the way in which Native Americans used to clear trees from wooded forest areas.

That thought then melded in with his memory of Ethan's Blade when it effortlessly sliced into the Royal back at home. Together, they gave him a rough idea for something a little out there.

Why not? It's worth a shot!

He took his Blade and drove it in at the base of the tree, just below the open portal. It sank in like a hot knife through butter. Leon stepped forward, easily slicing a line in the bark parallel to the ground. He slowly worked his way around the tree's trunk, never allowing the Blade to skip a patch. Twice, his injured leg gave out, and he fell, but he never removed the Blade.

The whole time, he worked he prepared himself for the inevitable, waiting for a mass of men to come pouring through the void. Only they never came. Once he made it all the way around and sliced through the last inch of bark, the void disappeared like it was never there. In its place was a charred spot of yellow wood, stripped bare of bark.

He closed his eyes and released a deep breath. It carried equal parts anguish and relief. His leg threatened to give out again, and he leaned forward to brace himself against the tree. Heedless of the charred wood, he lowered his head to rest against its marred surface. It was rough against his skin when he whispered an apology for his broken promise to his grandfather.

Chapter 32

Leon turned his back to the tree and sank to a knee on his good leg. He stretched his injured leg out before him. It throbbed. The exhaustion of the fight had finally caught up with him.

Dimples and Daz teamed up to take out the last giant. Grumpy was down, not moving. Merle moved with a limp, nursing a wound on a front leg. Ahab was nowhere in sight. Only Westley continued to swoop in and out of the fight around the giant's head like some angry feathered hornet.

He had just about decided to risk the pain of hobbling over to Kyra when the soft rustling of footsteps on the forest floor alerted him of someone's approach.

"You look like you could use a hand," Reed said quietly as he came gingerly stepping up from Leon's left, holding his right arm as if it was wounded.

Leon grimaced. "I could say the same for you."

"Too bad I can't heal myself. I can help you, though. Hold still a minute." Reed crouched down and placed his good arm over Leon's wound.

The sharp pain followed by the relief that came flooding in behind helped to clear his head. Though he might still nurse a limp for the next day or so, the gouge in his thigh was reduced to little more than a nasty bone bruise. He let out a deep sigh of relief and gave his thanks.

"Ferschall's gone, Reed." Leon choked back tears. "He took a blow intended for me. It was over before I could even think to help!"

Reed didn't say anything for a while, then he sighed. "Don't go blaming yourself. I did that for a while after me and Haddie were captured. It didn't do me any good then, and it won't do you any good now. Ferschall was a good friend to all of us, and he cared about you most of all. Still, I think he would have done the same for any of us."

"Yeah, but still hurts. Where's Fane and your friends?" Leon tried to change the subject.

Reed's mouth puckered. "They didn't make it either. One of Shay's guards slipped away while we were waiting on you all. He must have been with that Prince's faction the whole time. Anyhow, it wasn't long before the attack came. Shay went down fighting like a madwoman from what I saw, so I doubt she's to blame. But Fane, Liesel, and Hume were all struck in the head with imbued stones. They were gone before the fight even started."

Leon turned to look at Kyra once more. She was too far away to hear their conversation, but she must have seen the horror in his eyes. She turned to watch Daz as he checked his downed opponents.

It wasn't until that moment he noticed the tear streaks on her cheeks. How much more pain and loss would she have to endure? He struggled to his feet to go and comfort her.

Reed grabbed his arm before he could move. "There's more. I managed to get away with only a glancing blow to my shoulder, and though it slowed me down, they didn't seem too interested in pursuing me at the time. The long walk here gave me a chance to snag a good view of the valley below. There are torches from campfires for miles...and there were torches moving up the path this way, too, from way down at the bottom of the trail."

"That must have been why Slade set off that flare. How long?"

"Two, maybe three hours?" Reed shrugged. "I'm guessing they move pretty fast."

Leon's awareness of his surroundings came more clearly into focus. What he noticed landing on his arm wasn't water, not anymore at least. He looked up into the dark sky and saw thousands of small fluffy snowflakes drifting down from above.

"We've got to free everyone and get out of here."

Reed looked around. "Where? We're up against the side of a mountain that, a few hours ago, looked to be impossibly steep the further up you go. We could climb up higher, but they'd just flush us out in the morning."

"I don't know, but let's find the keys and free everyone."

One thing at a time, Leon. Just focus on what you can do, not what lies beyond!

Reed helped him up but stayed back near the tree as Leon limped to the center of the camp where everyone else was gathered. He checked on Merle, relieved the big happy mutt was only nursing a nasty flesh wound. He sent the hound back to Reed.

Grumpy, on the other hand, would not be getting up. He had gone toe to toe with a handful of giants and took one too many blows from those mighty clubs. But he didn't go down alone . There were three big blue corpses lying nearby.

Ahab came trotting out of the woods a few minutes later, practically prancing at the praise he received from both Leon and Rezz, despite the arrow injury to his wing. Rezz explained how the griffin had helped to distract the one-eyed Vin long enough for him to score a hit with his bow. Apparently, he and the Vin Ranger he called the captain had been working to settle an old score.

"I definitely wounded him, but I know better than to chase a wounded predator into cover. I just wish we had the time to flush him out. That man is evil and dangerous!" Rezz was more unsettled over the appearance of his Captain than he seemed to be over the dozen giant corpses scattered around them. It made Leon realize just how lucky he was that Grumpy and the gang came to his rescue when they did.

The griffin cub, too, had saved more than one of their companion's lives that night. Leon sent him back to Reed to get patched up.

Finally, Westley lighted down on his shoulder and nestled up against his neck, a toasty warm fuzzball of feathers, oblivious to the snow drifting down on them all. His calm presence lessened the ache of loss as he helped Daz check the bodies to make certain there were no further surprises.

Leon heard a moan coming from near where he slew his first giant. He unsheathed his Blade and crept forward to investigate.

When he drew closer, he saw a hand twitch. It was a man-sized hand and when he made it to the body, he saw it belonged to Ben.

Gently, he rolled the grizzled warrior over. Blood was still running fresh on Ben's chin. The giant's spiked club had pretty much gutted the soldier. His stomach was a mess. Leon at once forgot about his hatred for the man. He yelled for Reed to come help.

A weak voice spoke up, "No need for hysterics, boy. Can't you see when a man is dying?"

"Weren't you the one who said we leave no one behind, even me?"

Ben smiled, coughed and winced, and more blood ran down his chin. Leon went to mop it up with his sleeve, but Ben stopped him,. "You have a good memory, Leon. You'll need it if you can ever hope to beat Slade."

Leon couldn't help but remark, "I thought I just did?"

Ben shook his head. "Unless a man's down, he's not beat. Thought I taught you that lesson already."

"Who is he really? He wasn't just one of your soldiers, was he?"

"One of mine? No. I recruited him, but now…starting to think it was…the other way around. He was CIA. Said he needed to work with his own kind. Been with me four years…I never saw it coming. I had plans, to transition from our world to this one, gradually. Slade has plans…I think…to plant a foot in both."

Leon still felt simmering anger towards the dying man, but something about seeing his enemy suffering like that melted his cold resolve, just a tad. He propped up Ben's head up and told him to hold on while Reed made his way over.

"I'm sorry, boy, I wanted to carve out a fallout spot here in Fayden, a safe spot. Didn't start out…intending to hurt civilians. Slade though. He's a killer."

Leon had always felt a begrudging respect for the man deep down. He had wanted to beat him senseless on more than one occasion, but Ben was an idealist in the worst possible way, and Leon could identify with that on some level.

He pulled his Blade out and held it over him, hilt first. "You may not have ever wanted this, but if you're dying, Ben, what have you got to lose?

"Besides, a soldier-guy I know once told me that if things go south, a man should have a weapon in his hands, even an *old guy* like you." Ben smiled faintly with recognition of his words to Leon back on the Hootsi border bridge,. "You know the story behind the Blade? What you have to believe when you take it?"

Ben nodded.

With wide eyes, the dying man reached up and gently grasped the bone handle. His arm fell back to his chest almost as soon as his fingers closed around the hilt. Leon knew what to expect, but he still gasped in awe when he saw the bone-hilt handle of a second Blade still clutched in his hand.

Ben's eyes widened even further for several seconds, and he took a deep breath that rattled in his chest. Then he let it out and smiled up at Leon. His eyes held the first genuine look of appreciation Leon had ever seen on the cunning man's face.

When Leon shifted, Ben's eyes didn't follow. They remained open, gazing off into the snowy darkness beyond.

Leon felt a cold lump in the pit of his belly. For some reason, deep down, he had believed everything would work out for Ben when he grasped that bone-hilt handle. When they didn't, the last vestige of Leon's innocence flickered and died. Leon yelled again for Reed.

He moved into position to begin giving chest compressions. Over and over, he pumped. Ben's last smile never faltered as Leon worked to save what was already gone.

Rezz pulled him off when Reed made it to his side. Reed did what he could for Ben while giving Leon quiet encouragement.

At last, Reed drew himself up off Ben's chest. He placed a scrap of cloth over his eyes. "He's gone."

# # #

Rezz tended to Ben's body, while Leon held Kyra in his arms. She was a strong woman, but the loss of her brother and her bear was tearing her apart. At first, he fought to find the right words to give her comfort, but soon he stopped fighting and just held her tight.

If there was one thing Leon was thankful for, it was that she and the rest of his group hadn't been bound with manacles. The Fae simply hadn't had time to do more than tie everyone up and march them into camp before the attack occurred. Dimples easily freed them with his Blade while Leon and the others were working on Ben.

Still holding Kyra, Leon took a look around. Clearing the area would be impossible. There were too many bodies to bury them all, and no one even considered touching the giants. Surprisingly, Dimples didn't mind the request from Leon to help bury Ben. He claimed burying Ben was at least repaying him an equal measure of the charity he gave his fallen warriors, the day of their massacre.

Hootsi honor never ceases to amaze.

Kyra's remaining brothers, Daz and Chocum were nearby. They reverently stripped the tusker armor and saddle off Grumpy and stacked them gently around him.

Leon could only look on in muted pain as Dimples and Rezz piled rocks over their one-time nemesis. It was ironic that he felt such pain at the loss of a man who had inflicted such tragedy on them all, but forgiveness is an odd acquaintance.

While they worked, Shay's one remaining bodyguard found the body of the Vin who held the keys to all the shackles. He worked to free the three hooded prisoners still bound.

Minutes later, Leon caught the tangy scent of a very familiar cologne. A scratchy old voice spoke his name and Leon froze. He clenched his eyes shut where he stood but he couldn't hold back the tears of joy welling up from within.

Without moving, he spoke to Kyra, who he still cradled in his arms. "You don't have to do this with me now, but I think...I think my grandfather, Gus, is here."

She drew back, wiping her eyes. "No," she smiled a sad but beautiful smile, "I want to meet the one who raised the man I am to marry."

They turned together to face Gus. The old man was smaller than he remembered, and his hair had traded out more pepper for salt, but for only the second time in his life, Leon saw tear tracks in Gus' face. He stumbled forward and, at long last, gave his adopted father a hug.

Then he had the surreal experience of introducing Gus to Kyra. Gus couldn't make a sound when he learned she was to be Leon's wife. Despite the language barrier, he gave her a tender hug and a whiskery kiss on her brow.

"Gus, how did you get here?"

"Ben brought us over. I guess he knew you all were headed this way. Maybe we were a little added insurance for him?

"The rest of his men were mobilizing from all over the country. He had them planning to come barreling through that portal at any moment. But listen, we can sort things out later. Is Reed here? One of those big fellas kicked Ethan. He's been bleeding pretty bad. I don't think he has much time left to say goodbye."

"Of course!" Leon called out. "Reed, get over here, fast as you can! It's your uncle! He's here, and he's hurt."

Much to Gus' stunned bewilderment, Reed was able to mend Ethan's injuries, and restore him to a restful sleep. He was also able to mend Shay from a wound where an imbued stone had glanced off her back shoulder and from a head wound from when she fell from the stone's blow and bounced her noggin off a rock. Lucky for her, her leather armor protected her skin from the power of the stone. She was restored to consciousness soon thereafter.

Once all the introductions were over, and Gus had been brought up to speed on Shana's condition, the whole group moved further up into the dense jumble of ruins, just north of the Royal Tree. They rummaged through the remains of the supplies from Ben's camp and, for some reason, Leon was relieved to see Ferschall's condensed pack of pottery had somehow made it into camp with the rest of the loot the Fae had hauled in after their attack on his friends. He immediately lashed his smaller pack to

Ferschall's, making a promise to himself that he wouldn't leave without it.

Dimples and Rezz moved downhill to scout out the torches advancing from the valley below. Kyra fought through her grief and volunteered to help Shay administer some private care to Shana. Leon found himself alone with Gus for the first time.

"You've grown, boy!"

"Yes, sir, I guess I have."

"I don't just mean you finally sprouted some muscle and gained a couple inches on me. I've been watching you. You've grown in other ways, too."

Leon gave a noncommittal grunt of acknowledgment.

"What I mean to say is, I'm proud of you, son." Gus scratched at his long whiskers. "And I'm fairly sure there ain't no way I would have recognized you when I first seen you if you hadn't been wearing them company letters on that beat-up cap!" They both chuckled at the old joke.

"Now, give me as much of the full story as you feel willing to share."

Minutes later, Leon's attempts to bring Gus up to speed weren't sticking too well. Despite the more fantastic details that dealt with herding giant rats on hippos or rustling up Aurochs from the back of a bear, Leon doubted much of his account really made much sense to the old rancher. He could tell the conversation wasn't going anywhere by the fact that Gus started doing what he always did when he grew uncomfortable, changing the subject to small talk about inconsequential things.

When Leon didn't rise to the bait of a prolonged conversation about the sorry state of beef prices during his absence on the ranch, Gus laid an arm across his shoulder and whispered conspiratorially, "You still have that medallion I gave you?"

"Actually, I do." Leon had completely forgotten about the old medallion. He pulled it out and handed it over.

Gus held it up against the light of the smaller campfire they were burning between two crumbling pillars. Leon had a much better understanding of the symbols on the metal than when he first arrived, but he still felt he had missed something.

"You know this is a map, right?" asked Gus.

Leon nodded his response.

"Good, and I'm guessing you didn't come through that tree over there when you first showed up?

"No, sir."

"Any ideas on where that one corresponds?" He jiggled the medallion and pointed in the direction of the massive Royal.

"Yeah. We're here," Leon pointed the topmost gem on the Medallion, "just north of that big empty pass between the mountains."

"Hmm, thought maybe that was the case." He flipped the gem over, "You haven't learned to read the ancient script, too, have you?"

"No, but Ferschall, our friend who died, managed to cipher out some of it in the last week or two."

Gus returned his attention to the script in his hands, "Hmmm, I'm sorry about your friend son. He's gone through, and you're still here.

"Did you know that the small circle there, just above this northmost gem here, serves as more than just a hole to slip a chain through?"

"Uhh, no? What are you saying?"

"Well, I guess I'm saying I know how to read this old language on the back of this here lump of metal. I guess I'm saying that maybe we shouldn't all be sitting around like we're waiting on a hearse to come pick us up...I guess I'm saying..."

Leon cut him off, "Are you saying there's another way out of here?"

"Oh, well, yessir. I guess I'm saying that, too!"

"Well, why didn't you just say so?"

"I was gittin' there," Gus mumbled.

"Hey, everyone, gather 'round, quick!" Leon spoke to the others in the common Fayden tongue.

"Okay, Gus, what are we looking for?"

"I don't know exactly...but the writing on the back of the medallion here says something about there being a 'path of last resorts in the first breath of the king's shadow.'"

Leon translated, and everyone puzzled over the quote on their own until Shay finally spoke up, "It's a riddle. It has to be."

Reed nodded. "And the king could be a reference to the Royal Tree?"

"The sound's right, but what's the first breath of the king's shadow?" Leon mused.

Everyone spent a few more minutes contemplating the rest of the puzzle.

Rezz and Dimples sprinted into camp and broke their collective concentration. "Reinforcements are moving in. We maybe have another thirty minutes, at most, before a much larger band of giants arrives."

Everyone threw out suggestions at that point. Though none of them made much sense to Leon. It wasn't until Daz spoke up from the back of the group that he was provided a renewed glimmer of hope.

"Could the first breath of the king's shadow be referring to an actual shadow? If so, could it be saying it's where the tree's shadow ends up on the cliff face in dawn's first light?"

Everyone turned to stare at the rock face along the west side of the camp. Leon, Ferschall, and Dimples had been perched up on that rock wall only hours prior. Leon used his Blade's sight to study the ledge.

"Was anyone here at dawn?" Gus looked around the group as Leon conveyed the message.

"We weren't, but my guess, based on what we saw earlier, is that the sun rises there." Reed pointed out into the empty night. Everyone turned, and those with the Bladed gift of sight could see a tall hill, rising directly where Reed pointed.

"Good enough. Then that means the entrance could be two-thirds of the way up that rock face. Grab what gear we can take.

We're all heading up there together." Leon shouldered his gear. Dimples shouldered a bag of torches and scooped up Shana, who was still very much out of it.

Twenty minutes later, and the group was still searching. Pockmarks and shallow depressions dotted the ledge. Their presence made the task that much harder for everyone as Leon and his companions struggled to recognize any sign of an escape passage. Already, there had been a half-dozen false alarms.

Westley shifted around for a better look at something below from his vantage point on Leon's shoulder. In turn, Leon followed the owl's gaze and spotted the first flicker of torches marching up the trail, just beyond the clearing.

"I think I found something!" Kyra called.

They all raced to where she crouched, a little higher up than anyone else had bothered to look.

"It's maybe nothing, but these edges to this crevice look like something was used to carve them."

"She's right," Reed said as he searched up and down the rock ledges framing a rather ordinary, nondescript-looking impression. The carved stone looked to be resting in a track of some sort.

Kyra's brothers prodded and pulled until the big slab came loose and tumbled down the hill, alerting everyone in the valley below of exactly where they stood.

Dimples took a torch and crawled down into the opening. His legs soon disappeared from view and everyone held their breath while they waited for word as to whether it was another dead end.

"You all had better hurry up! We don't have long!" Shay exclaimed from a little lower on the slope.

She and her one loyal guard scrambled up to join them.

"Keeps going, opens up further down, I think. This has to be it!" Dimple's voice sounded muffled as it echoed up from much deeper down in the hole.

"You heard the man. Let's get going, they're almost here." Leon waited while everyone filed in past him. Only twelve of his companions were left, counting an incoherent Shana, presently cradled in Gus' arms. He gave Leon a wink as he gently laid her on a blanket and pulled her in behind him, down into the darkened recess below. Merle and Ahab followed. It was a tight squeeze, but both of them managed to fit.

Before ducking his head to enter the cavern, Leon took one last look down the hill. He used his gift to see more clearly through the falling snow. The view from up on that ledge would have been quite beautiful if he hadn't been fretting for his life moments before. A small dusting of snow was only now beginning to stick to the tops of the ruins near the fire below.

More and more giants thundered into the camp. They spread out to comb the area, nudging their dead and bellowing in rage. A few made a beeline toward the ledge where he stood. He wasn't worried. They would be far too large to follow where he was headed.

Just before he turned to dive in behind his friends, he caught a glimpse of three smaller figures standing together down below. The tallest man's back was to him, but Leon had seen them enough that night to easily identify at least two of them.

Slade stood by the now smoldering fire, calmly conversing with the one-eyed Vin, whose arm was bandaged. Next to them was one of the men who had arrived with Slade. Then the big man knelt down and gently pulled up a few small bundles from within his pack. He turned and made his way toward the ridge where Leon stood.

Son of a biscuit! I hope that isn't what I think it is!

Leon turned and dove into the mountain behind the others.

Chapter 33

The initial descent took longer than Leon would have guessed. He ducked and shimmied to accommodate the low ceilings while the passage extended down at a sharp angle, several hundred feet into the mountainside.

Leon, who was never a fan of tight spaces, didn't feel capable of taking a full breath until the tunnel opened up, squeezing his companions and him out into a large, natural cavern.

While sliding into that cavern, Leon heard a muffled shout from back up toward the tunnel's entrance. It sounded like, "Fire in … hole!"

He yelled for everyone to run before jumping up and taking his own advice from his spot near the back of the pack. They all followed Dimples' torch deeper into the large cavern.

Just as his whole crew was about two-thirds of the way across, the ground shook and a blast of fire and rocks came spewing out of the tunnel's mouth. The percussion knocked half the group to the ground and left the other half with a ringing sensation in their ears for a few moments afterward.

Any chance they had of waiting out the giants and reusing the passage for their escape was gone. The tunnel completely collapsed.

It took another half-hour for the smoke to clear. They didn't lack for light, though. Not only did Dimples have the original torch, but he had scavenged a half-dozen more of the torches off the bodies of the giants before leaving the clearing. Those torches, like large candle flames, were made of solid, green chunks of wood, doused in some dark black resin material. Daz, who had witnessed the giants many times in the past, swore each torch would take a few hours to burn.

Leon was just grateful Dimples thought ahead before they left the camp. Though his gift of night-vision seemed to super-enhance his ability to discern contrast in whatever limited light was present, he didn't care to wager whether it would illuminate complete darkness. The canvas sack that held those torches quickly became the greatest treasure in the group's possession.

Thankfully, once the smoke and dust subsided, the Stonebreaker brothers stumbled into a stream, and since there appeared to be some type of worn path along its banks, the group decided to follow the flow of the water. For hours upon hours, Leon and his companions pursued the stream. The path along its banks angled them down and around the contours of the cavern system, threading a twisting, winding road through a swiss cheese network of bedrock.

The musty smell of the cave came and went as small breezes crisscrossed several narrow openings around them. The stream itself continued to grow in width and depth as they trudged along its banks, deeper and deeper through the core of the mountain.

Leon dropped back to check on his fiancé when he thought she could use a break from his aunt. She was still deep in conversation with Shay, as she had been for the last several hours.

"You doing okay?"

"Yeah. Better, at least. Your aunt and I have been talking…about a lot of things." Her eyes darted tentatively over to Shay. "I think you should just tell him."

Shay nodded, her face full of resolve. "Leon, I want my sister to pay for her crimes just as much as you. However, to do so, one must bring forth a reliable witness, verified by three or more practitioners, skilled in the type of mind art I practice. They must see the act committed first-hand as I have seen through your memory.

"I've considered this from a hundred different angles and can only draw one conclusion. To my knowledge, not only are you the only person capable of testimony that would put an end to her reign, you are the only one qualified to truly replace her on the throne."

Leon chuckled until he noticed her expression was still stone-cold serious. He stammered, "First of all, I'm not even Fae. Do you really think they would allow me to sit on their throne? Second, they may technically allow your practitioners to validate my memory, but what makes you think your queen won't cheat the system, after all she's done? And last, but not least, we're stuck in a cave a long, long way from your forest!"

Shay gave him an indulgent grin in return. "Exactly, Leon. I don't think there's anything we can do about my sister, the queen, and even should we escape this cave, I never want to return to the Wild Forest while she rules. Instead, I'd like to swear my oath to another...if you would have it."

Leon sputtered, and Kyra cut him off, "Give her a chance to finish, Leon."

"Just because the Fae have only ever been ruled by Fae does not mean we have any rule excluding one such as you from sitting our throne. Perhaps we all perish in this hole, perhaps not. It doesn't matter, though. What matters is that I do my part to restore what was stolen."

Leon was speechless, he didn't know what to say to that, but Shay wasn't finished.

"I'd also like to take up a Blade. Kyra's been telling me about all the ways it has changed her and those around her, and before something happens that makes it impossible for me to make the choice, I'd like to at least see if it can do the same for me."

Leon could see Shay had been struggling with sharing this for some time. It was obvious she saw the gesture of an oath to him as a way to restore some semblance of justice to her murdered sister, but he was no king. He sure didn't want his friends treating him any different either. "

"Shay, I'll for sure give you my Blade, and I am honored you want to give me an oath, but honestly, you're my aunt, and you are way more qualified to rule than me...you don't need to give me any type of pledge to try and make up for what was done in the past. My mother may have been a princess, but I'm just a rancher. I wouldn't know the first thing about how to rule over anyone. '

"Precisely! That's exactly why I need to do this, Leon. I'm not looking for someone to rule over me, I'm looking for someone with a right to challenge the current queen should the opportunity ever arise. Until then, just think of me as an advisor who's going to be invested in seeing you learn to lead."

Kyra interrupted before Leon could respond, "Leon, Shay isn't giving you something, she's asking for something from you. You may not ever lead the Fae, but like it or not, you *are* a leader. Leading isn't about telling people what to do, it's showing them how to do it. As your soon-to-be wife, I advise that you consider her offer."

"Hey, everyone, hold it up there. Let's take a break."

After thinking things through while everyone else took a seat to relax, Leon turned to Shay, "Okay, I'll take you up on your offer, but I'm not promising to step in as a king of any kind, just so you know that going into this…?"

She nodded.

"I assume Kyra has shared the details on how and why you take the Blade?"

She nodded again.

He extended his Blade out to her, hilt first.

When Shay gripped the hilt and pulled on the Blade, she gasped when she saw Leon still holding the original in his hand. The residual shock took her out of commission for a little while afterward, though not for as long as Leon would have suspected.

When she recovered enough to speak, she sank to a knee and with a solemn voice, gave her oath, "By this Blade, I, Shay Softfoot, swear loyalty and truth to the rightful ruler of the Fae, Leon Waldman, for as long as I live."

Leon felt an itch from the Blade in his hands. A response bubbled up in his mind, and he stepped forward to place a hand on her shoulder.

"I, Leon Waldman, accept your oath. I promise, in return, to honor that loyalty and truth with character and wisdom." He knew as soon as he spoke the words that things had changed between them. Not that the change was bad, but a weight of responsibility that hadn't been there before suddenly settled upon his shoulders. Yet it blended surprisingly well with the small measure of joy and comradery he also found to be present.

Moments later, her last loyal guard, Nort Dawner, asked he be allowed to take the Blade and make the oath as well. By the time they were ready to move out again, the only person in the party who didn't have a Blade was Shana, though she was still delirious as she moved in and out of consciousness, never truly coming to terms with her surroundings. She continued to sleep most of their journey away. Still, though, everyone agreed delirium was a slight improvement over unresponsiveness.

Leon couldn't help but notice Dimples took exceptionally good care of her as they continued along. The Hootsi likely wouldn't have even allowed Gus to help spell him from time to time if Gus hadn't been forced to convey how he was, in fact, her blood relative.

"Are you sure you don't want someone else to help carry the girl?" asked Chocum.

"No, thank you, my friend. Honor dictates I care for her myself."

"Why is that?" Leon asked. He kind of figured Dimples felt guilty over stabbing her earlier.

"Because she is who I originally came to save."

"What do you mean?" Leon pressed.

"I mean, she is the reason my clan and I pursued Ben and his men, to rescue her."

"Didn't you know she was with us? That she wasn't actually being abducted against her will?" said Leon.

"It didn't matter. She was a woman being taken from Hootsi lands. Our customs mandated we intervene."

"You know that's kind of messed up, right?"

"I know a great many things we all do are kind of messed up, Leon. But I also know if I let this woman slip away for good this time, the sacrifice of my men's lives will lose a little more meaning. The senselessness of their deaths under my leadership already haunts me enough. So, you see, I am not as selfless as our friend Ferschall. I'm giving her all I've got for the sake of my own honor's redemption."

Leon didn't know how to respond to what Dimples shared and it must have shown. Gus quietly asked for Leon to bring him up to speed on the conversation.

"You're over-thinking things, young man," Gus responded to Dimples. "Reed told me a bit of what happened to you and your people. That's a heavy plow for any man to shoulder. But are you sure you ought to be wallowing in all that poison?"

Leon dutifully relayed his words.

"Poison? What poison?" Dimples asked.

"The poison of putting yourself in chains that aren't yours to carry. That Blade you've got there is awfully useful for lots of things beyond just saving us from the distortions of the disease that has ravaged our people, but the bonds it's best at cutting are those we never see." Gus used a stern word, but his voice was gentle.

When Leon finished conveying his words, Dimples frowned. "What do you mean?"

Gus spoke to Dimples, but his eyes moved to Leon, "I've had months to sit on my haunches with nothing but this Blade. In that time, I did a lot of thinking, and not all of it was good. I did my fair share of whimpering over past mistakes, crying over spilled milk, and so on, but not long before Ben came to bring us here, I came to understand one small truth."

"Yeah? What's that?" Leon asked.

"There are some things you can't control and other things you only think you can. When bad things happen, I mean, really bad things, things that cut a man to his core, it's better for that man to consider what he ought to do in response, and to do what he can, rather than chew on why it all came crashing down around him."

He paused for Leon to finish translating for him and switched his focus back on Dimples.

"You just keep taking care of little Shana, son, even if you aren't sure you're doing it for the right reasons just yet. She'll wake up sometime soon, and when she does, you make sure you're there to give her your Blade. She'll be okay, you'll see.

"But when we come up out of this hole, you leave behind all that guilt you been carting around. That goes for the rest of you too. I don't know the whole story on what all has happened to some of you," he glanced at Leon, "and maybe I just as soon not know all the details. But you folks are all young, with lots of life to live. When you bungle things up, which you will, or things get bungled up by some other knucklehead down the line, you just remember how you got that Blade at your side, how it straightened you out when you were warped. Knowing who you are, and what you aren't, will put your head back in the game."

Dimples straightened to stand tall as he slid Shana from his back and cradled her in his arms. With mute tears rolling down his cheeks, he gave Gus a small bow.

"I think we see a light up ahead!" Reed exclaimed. He and Ethan had been walking out in front of the rest of the party for most of trip. They had just reached a quarter-turn in the path.

"I see it, too!" Daz called back a moment later, as he was next to make it to the turn.

As Leon came around the bend, he saw the light as well.

Who could have ever thought such a small sliver of brightness could ever be so beautiful!

It couldn't have come any sooner. The last of Dimples' torches wouldn't have held out much longer. Thankfully, the light continued to grow as they marched forward.

# # #

When at last Leon and Kyra stumbled out into the searing light of day, the sun was shining down directly overhead.

The mountain air was sweet and cool with the added flavor of the promise of freedom from the cave. Leon took a minute to allow his eyes to adjust before he followed the banks of the stream out to the edge of a waterfall. The roar of the rushing water cascading down the mountainside muted all other sounds, and the sight below left him speechless. From the tip of that ledge, he gazed out in wonder at a majestic valley of woods, meadows, lakes, and streams.

On all sides, the valley was framed by tall mountain peaks. Those peaks reflected sunlight off snowcapped ridges and added to the brightness of the clear skies above. The cliff where Leon and his companions stood, abruptly ended, on a near-vertical angle, dropping several hundred feet into a blanket of tall, sturdy evergreens. Amongst those trees, on a small rise, off to the right, Leon could just make out crumbling remains of yet another ancient city peeking up through the canopy.

Dimples, still holding Shana in his arms, pointed further down into the valley. "Look, are those Aurochs moving through those clearings way out there?"

Sure enough, there were some sort of large beefy creatures grazing on chest-high grasses within large, verdant fields. The snow Leon saw falling on the east side of the mountains hadn't yet found its way into the sheltered floor of the valley below.

Ahab and Westley took to the air to explore their new habitat. Merle took a seat at Leon's side. He wasn't even looking at the view below, and, if Leon didn't know better, he would say the War Hound pouted while his friends rode the wind to the forest below, dodging and diving, like two tiny treetop fliers, as they moved out of sight for the time being.

Gus finally found his voice. "If I had known it woulda been this pretty, I'd have cut me a hole in one of them trees years ago, just to have popped in for a glimpse of paradise, if for no other reason at all."

"Well, I admit, it's pretty up here, on a vista that grants us an unencumbered view for miles around, but the question is...what's it going to be like down there?" Ethan replied.

Leon grinned at the two older men's banter,. "You're both right, you know? Looking out onto this world for the first time can steal your breath away with beauty, but if you know what you're looking at it can also give you an anxious twitch, all in one glance.

"We must have come almost straight through that mountain back there with less of a drop in elevation than I suspected. Let's take an inventory of what we've got before we try and find our way down. I've got a ton of pottery, some jerky, some water, and a rope. How about you guys?"

Leon repeated himself in common Fayden for the benefit of the others in their group and soon people were rummaging through their things and calling out the various tools, equipment, and weapons they were carrying.

As Leon rifled through his packs, he opened up Ferschall's pottery bag for the first time. Inside were stacks of plates, wrapped individually, in leather bundles. Despite his best efforts to care for that pottery, even the ones on top looked cracked or broken. As he rearranged a couple of the rare exceptions that were still whole, a small watertight bundle of leather slid free from under one of the plates. It fell to the ground at his feet.

Picking up the bundle, Leon opened the sealed flap and looked inside. Lying within was a letter, stamped with wax. Resting next to it was a signet ring. There was a symbol of a Blade carved into the face of the ring. It matched the seal on the wax. He pulled out the letter and handed it over to Kyra. "Can you read what this says?"

"Yeah, it says it's to you."

Leon felt fascinated as he asked her to open it and read the letter. After a quick read, Kyra looked back at him with a sad look in her eyes.

"Well, what does it say?"

"The first page looks to be some sort of reference letter. It describes you, who you are, what you look like, and something about how you are from the remnant. It's hard to make out in some places because the leather holding it wasn't as waterproof as it looks.

"Then on this second sheet, Ferschall says you are to take this letter to the Chief Elder in Hollinger if anything should happen to him. It looks like some water got on this one as well. Only the damage is worse. I can't make out what it says there in the middle, but it's something about how the binding between the plates is key? I'm sorry, I can't make out the rest."

Leon frowned. He might never know why Ferschall valued his pottery so highly, but now he knew it had something to do with the colorful grout that held them together.

At least I don't feel so bad about breaking so much of his pottery.

He decided he would keep the letters, at least until he could read them himself.

Reed stepped up to his side, he reached into his pack and pulled out a small branch. He held it out for Leon to see. "This may not work out at all, but then again, it could be useful, too…to some of you at least. I won't be using it again."

Leon took a closer look at the branch Reed held in his hand. Its bark was silver, and the end that had been cut was wrapped in wet linen."

"A cutting? From the Royal?"

Reed continued in Fayden, "I took it after you left. The tree didn't seem to be dying as fast as the one we entered through. I just thought that maybe if I was able to regrow the tree, you might someday be able to get a message through to Gus and Ethan." He smiled. "I guess it's kind of a moot point now, though."

Leon didn't know what to say. Everyone else, himself included, had been fighting the feeling that they weren't going to make it off that mountainside in the last moments of the fight while Reed had somehow managed to think ahead, preparing for their eventual escape. "Reed, even if we never use that tree, I want you to plant it when we get wherever we are going. I want you to make it grow. That way, when it's nice and tall, it'll be a symbol. Every time one of us looks at it, it's going to remind us to never give in, never give up!"

Leon turned back to the valley. It was large and wild and full of risk. He reached down and touched the hilt on the handle of the Blade at his side. A gentle pulse tingled in his arm and a warmth lingered in his fingers.

Others in the group continued to call out items they had on their person, which they thought might be useful on the next leg of their journey, but Leon stopped paying attention. He closed his eyes and took a deep breath, savoring the mountain air once more. When he opened them, Kyra was at his side. Her blue-gray eyes sparkled in the sun, and her smile was full of promise.

"You ready?" she asked.

"Yes," Leon answered. He grabbed her hand to give it a squeeze as he turned back to the group. Everyone was done with their gear, and they were all waiting, looking to him for some reason. He smiled back at them with genuine confidence. "Tomorrow isn't promised, but we've got a chance down there. It's going to be a long winter. Let's go find a warm place to weather the cold."

About the Author

DN Woodward, or Danny as his friends know him, is a native Texan who still resides in the central Texas area. He has undergraduate and graduate degrees in Ecology and Aquatic Resources, though he can't remember the last time he was able to apply all that biological knowledge to anything deeper than his tomato garden.

Instead, he's had a career primarily focused on helping oil companies clean up environmental messes with heavy equipment. When he isn't selling cleanup services, he enjoys raising cattle. Yep, he has a hobby business on the weekends where he hopes to someday raise a show steer so fat and meaty that one of his three kids will waltz away with a giant blue ribbon at the Houston Livestock Show (his wife still laughs at him for this, but a man can dream).

Writing was initially another hobby in a long string of hobbies which he started a few years back, but during the pandemic it somehow morphed into a habit he can't seem to kick.

If you're interested in learning more about Leon and his future adventures, or you just want to reach out and connect with Danny, visit his website at www.dnwoodward.com.

Many Thanks!

Made in the USA
Las Vegas, NV
24 September 2021